Suddenly, the bearskin was shoved aside, allowing a tall figure to enter the lodge. Honor could see very little in the low light cast by the small fire, but she was immediately struck with the masculine strength of this man. He spoke in the Indian dialect, bowing his head formally, as though asking permission to enter. Honor kept her head bowed, not wanting this new Indian warrior to become interested in her.

"You have a name?"

The voice was deep, authoritative and sent a strange quiver through her. She dared to raise her eyes to cast a furtive glance at the stranger. Shadowed in the flickering light she could not tell if he was smiling or not, but as he moved forward a little, she gasped at seeing eyes of silvery-blue staring back at her.

He was white!

Honor Bound

a novel by

Theresa Conway

FAWCETT GOLD MEDAL • NEW YORK

With Thanks to
Arlene Friedman, Barbara Dicks, and Belle Blanchard

HONOR BOUND

Published by Fawcett Gold Medal Books, a unit of CBS Publications, the Consumer Publishing Division of CBS Inc.

ISBN: 0-449-14340-6

Printed in the United States of America

First Fawcett Gold Medal printing: July 1980

10 9 8 7 6 5 4 3 2 1

1

The Trail

1857

One

"Miss O'Brien, it is time to get up! Mr. Houlihan and your brother are awaiting you downstairs."

Honor groaned, determined not to allow anyone or anything to awaken her from the lovely dream she had been having. She was dreaming that she was back in Charleston and John Graham was kissing her outstretched hand and asking her for the next dance at the county cotillion. John was certainly a handsome man, but never did he seem so handsome as in her dreams of the home she was not likely to see again.

"Miss Honor, please wake up."

Honor opened one eye tentatively, focusing slowly on the round visage of the English girl who had been installed as her maid while she and her brother took advantage of the hospitality of Edward and Patricia Houlihan during their stay in St. Louis. The Houlihans had been good friends with her own parents, and when they had found out that Reid and Honor O'Brien were passing through St. Louis on their way to Independence, Missouri, in order to join the first available wagon train, they insisted the brother and sister stay with them.

The maid was smiling anxiously, her plump hands rolled like a large white sausage beneath her wad of apron.

"Oh, Martha, must I get up now? It has been ages since I've enjoyed the comfort of a real featherbed. How can Reid expect me to get up so early?"

Even as she said the last words, she realized their incongruity in the face of the long journey they had already undertaken from Charleston to St. Louis, nearly 800 miles—sometimes by stagecoach, sometimes by ferry or buckboard. They hadn't had enough money to travel by train.

Honor frowned, remembering with a brief flare of anger how they would have had enough to travel by ship from Charleston to Monterey, as her father would have wished, if Reid hadn't lost almost all of the money her father had left them in his foolhardy business ventures. He had been the prime target for a pair of scoundrels who had quickly sheared him of all but a pittance of his fortune.

Of course, how could she truly blame Reid? He was still young and inexperienced. If only their father had lived a

7

little longer—long enough to see her safely on board a fleet schooner bound around Cape Horn for the rich land of California—and the arms of her fiancé, Don Esteban Sevillas.

Honor sighed unconsciously, her eyes closing as she tried to conjure up a picture of the young man she had met so many years ago on the occasion of their formal betrothal. She had only been twelve and he a much more mature twenty-year-old who had hardly had time to converse with her as her father and mother had kept him steadily busy with social engagements and functions which she had been too young to attend. It had seemed an incongruous pairing then. She wondered idly why Don Diego Sevillas, Esteban's father, had ever consented to it.

Reid had exclaimed angrily more times than once that it was obvious to any numbskull why the Sevillas wanted to be tied to a settled American family. Times were hard in California for the original descendants of the first explorers. After the Mexican-American war and the annexation of California, the Americans had come from everywhere, greedy to gobble up gold and silver and anything else they could. When the gold had dwindled, some of the more astute forty-niners had begun demanding land, compelling the original owners to sell out at ridiculous prices. The only way the Sevillas had been able to save their rancho was to prove themselves loyal to the Americans—and what easier way than to have the eldest son and heir betroth himself to an American girl? Reid assured her that the Sevillas had been shrewd enough to take advantage of a casual acquaintance between Señora Sevillas and their mother in order to save their beloved lands.

Of course, it was clear to Honor that Reid did not care for the match, and if he had had the ability to do so, he would have seen the marriage contract annulled, but legally his hands were tied. And now that he had no money of his own, he had grudgingly admitted that he would go with her as far as Santa Fe, where he would break with the wagon train and go searching for gold in the New Mexico territory, where, rumor had it, there was a gold vein as thick as that found in Sutter's Mill.

"Miss Honor?"

The maid's query brought Honor out of her daydreams and she stifled a huge yawn of well-being. "You know, Martha, I almost wish we could stay here in St. Louis longer than just three or four days, but, of course, my brother is in a frenzy to get to Independence. We have such a long way to go," she sighed, her chin in her hand. She tried to envision the tedious sameness of day after day in a wagon train through a land she had no conception of. It was impossible and she shook her head, causing the honey-colored braids to swish across her silken-clad shoulders.

She climbed out of bed and allowed Martha to help her into a dressing gown so that she could brush her hair and ready a tub bath for her. Ruefully, Honor suspected the luxury of a bath would be unheard of on the trail. She might as well take advantage of her host's hospitality.

The copper tub was filled quickly and she washed and rinsed herself energetically, remembering that her brother and host were awaiting her downstairs. They most likely would have gone ahead with their own breakfast and were sitting with coffee, conversing about the future.

"Bring me the lavender muslin, if you please, Martha," she called out as she patted herself dry with a fluffy, sun-dried towel. "I vow it already seems summer here in St. Louis although it's barely May," she added, more to herself.

Martha, who had overheard the remark, nodded. "It's the humidity, miss. We have it terrible here next to the river."

Honor stepped into the muslin frock after first putting on her chemise of fine linen and stockings of pure silk. Her hair had already been parted in the center and smoothed on either side to a demure coil at the nape of her neck.

Her large green eyes gazed back at her from the polished mirror and she saw with some consternation that her normally pale ivory skin had taken on a sunburn after their journey and her cheeks were glowing like ripe peaches. She ran her tongue over the fullness of her dry lips.

"My complexion is ruined," she sighed in despair, noting the scattering of faint freckles across the bridge of her nose. "All the time and effort I spent in Charleston making sure I wouldn't have those horrible freckles—and now just look at them!"

Martha smiled. "You are still beautiful, miss, and the sun puts health in your cheeks."

The fine-drawn mouth grimaced. "I look twelve years old again! Esteban will wonder if I have grown up at all in the last six years." She gazed fretfully at the perfectly formed peaks of her breasts, then shrugged.

After a sprinkle of perfume, she left the room to be tidied up by Martha and made her way along the waxed, shining banister to the hall downstairs. She arrived in the dining room just as the two men were being poured another cup of steaming coffee, served in the French custom with plenty of sweet, thick cream.

Much of St. Louis, Honor had observed, still retained a French atmosphere. The streets were shaded by locust trees and one could look down from long galleries and wave to passersby below, as the galleries themselves fronted both top and bottom stories of every house. She had noted upon their arrival that every sort of person could be found in this river city. Hunters and trappers in fringed buckskins, Indians in blankets with painted faces, and tough-looking soldiers from Jefferson Barracks who mingled with giggling women in white caps and sabots. The city was like a gem set out before the frontier wilderness.

"Ah, my dear Honor, you look fresh and lovely this muggy morning," Edward Houlihan said gallantly, standing up to bow to her.

"Thank you, Mr. Houlihan," she replied, feeling the blush stain her cheeks. She noted that her brother stood also, but seemed preoccupied.

"Reid?"

He looked at her then and grinned boyishly. "Sorry, sis, but I was just thinking about the two hundred fifty miles we've got to cover tomorrow to get to Independence. Mr. Houlihan has kindly arranged passage for us on a public stagecoach that should get us there in less than two weeks. I'm sure hoping it lives up to its promise, as I can imagine that most of the supplies for the wagons have already been sold."

Honor could sense his frustration at being constrained to remain in St. Louis for her comfort. If he hadn't had her tagging along, he would have gone straight on to Independence.

"I'm sorry to be a burden to you, Reid," she said quickly, "but if you had put me on a ship bound for Monterey, you wouldn't have had to put up with me!"

Her barb was sure and she was immediately sorry for her waspish tongue—but he made her feel so—so useless! Reid grew red-faced and kept himself from continuing the quarrel with an effort.

They all three sat down, Edward sensing the constraint between his two young guests. He smoothed it over with a small talk while Honor ate her breakfast glumly, already wishing that she had not goaded Reid with her thoughtless words. She must learn to control her Irish temper, she thought morosely, or she would find herself in more trouble during the long, tedious days on the tail.

Two

Brice Devlin pushed the blanket off himself and stood up on the hard-packed earthen floor to stretch hugely. Turning, he pulled the cover from the young woman still snoring gently in the bed and slapped the rounded curve of buttock.

The woman started and turned swiftly, glaring up at being awakened in such a manner. She rubbed her dark eyes and pushed at the heavy mat of black hair that had fallen forward against her cheek.

"Get up, Lola, you lazy wench!" he laughed, pouncing on top of her as she attempted to roll back over and return to sleep. "I'm hungry, squaw, and I'll eat you if you don't move fast enough!"

The Indian woman's lips curved wickedly. "You eat Lola then," she whispered huskily, catching him in her arms and trying to press his flesh against hers.

She was a big, broad-boned woman, but the white man caught her hands and pressed them away from him with the ease of toughened muscles long used to being relied on to save his own life. Lola licked at the flat, hard chest, nearly as brown as her own from constant exposure to the sun. She looked up into the very blue eyes with the touch of silver in them that had many times been the only thing to betray the fact that he was, in fact, white and not an Indian.

"Lola loves you, Brice," she murmured, and then bit hard into the skin above his left nipple.

"Damn! A funny way you have of showing it, woman," he yelled, pulling her head back with ungentle fingers entwined in her thick hair. "Now get up before I kick you out of bed!"

Lola rolled her eyes, pursed her mouth, then sighed and heaved herself out from under him. She pulled a buckskin shift over her nakedness and walked into the next room, which served as a kitchen, in order to light the stove.

Brice listened to her soft, unhurried movements as he lay back on the bed, his arms folded beneath his head. He enjoyed his brief interludes with the squaw, even though they were all too few. He seldom stopped in San Antonio these days except for fresh supplies. Trading as he did with the Indian tribes, he normally had no need to come back to the civilization of white men, but he had made the journey in order to buy packhorses and other provisions he couldn't get from the Comanches.

It amused him to see the looks on the faces of those he dealt with. They all considered him the lowest of the low, worse than a half-breed since he was a white man who traded with the savages. A nomad, so to speak, a renegade who moved among the Indians as an equal.

Brice laughed to himself. Oh yes, they might hate him, these haughty Spanish dons and grim-faced Americans, but they were more than eager to sell him anything he wished when he produced silver or fine furs. He could fairly hear their palms rubbing together with glee. Then it didn't matter where he got those things he traded with. Money was money and it could buy anything in this land.

He thought for a moment about that, recalling with a stab of fury that day, over ten years ago, when, at the tender age of eighteen, his father had cast him out of their fine Savannah home—tossed him out because of an affair of honor, he had called it. Brice remembered the affair only as a boyish prank when he had been full of whiskey and his friends' dares and had crept into Annabelle Reeves' house through the second-story gallery and into her bedroom. Nothing had happened, for the girl's screams had awakened everyone within five miles, but his father, steadfast and steeped in the "old traditions of the South," had deemed him unworthy to live in the same house after that day.

It had been so stupid and wasteful, he thought now, the quarrel, the accusations, the heated words between them that couldn't be taken back. The small incident had blown up into something that had bewildered both father and son. He had been sent to a cousin's home in New Orleans where he had learned infinitely worse things than he and his friends in Savannah could have ever dreamed up.

From New Orleans, he had moved on to the Texas territory at the idealistic age of twenty-one, hoping to join the Texas Rangers, but his fame had preceded him through an old friend who had joined his escapades in New Orleans, and the Rangers did not want him. So he had drifted like many others in the great territory of Texas, until he had chanced

12

upon an old codger—a half-breed—who was selling whiskey and blankets to the Indians in exchange for valuable furs and gold nuggets. Brice had joined up with him, almost as a matter of course, and Sam Peckins had taught him a thing or two about Indians, about Mexicans, about his own people on the frontier. Old Sam had been a teacher of sorts and he had taught Brice, above all, how to survive.

Sam had died two years ago and Brice had quite naturally taken his place as trader to the Indians, a mediator between savage and civilization. He had never betrayed his country nor his Indian friends by selling information to either, and for this reason, because he would not cooperate with the government in revealing Indians' locations and hunting grounds, the people had labeled him a renegade.

He had learned during his travels that his father had died, leaving him, ironically, all the wealth that he no longer needed or wanted. It had been too damn late, he thought. He had lived among the Comanche, with other frontiersmen who respected him for his skills, and he had no use for the trappings of that old way of life. He was blood brother to Katala, who would soon inherit his father's place as chief of the largest of the Comanche bands in western Texas. He had an Indian wife, Tutalo, in the village. It would have been ridiculous—and impossible—for him to return to Savannah and the idle ways of the rich.

He was welcomed and feted on his arrival in the Comanche village. His strength and courage were well known and only Katala could boast of equaling them. He remembered the summer of his coming to the Comanche, how he had gone through their rites of manhood and been accepted completely into their society, how he had painted his face with the bright reds and yellows and gone with the warriors to hunt down the hated Apache, their sworn enemy. The lance and bow were no strangers to him and his buffalo shield, carefully kept by Tutalo, boasted many Apache scalps.

How could he ever have returned to that peaceful, dreamlike existence in a faraway place called Savannah? The money had been placed in a New York bank at his request, one last defiance against the South of his youth, and there it would stay for as long as he wished. Brice laughed bitterly to himself—it could stay there forever.

The smell of cooking reached his nostrils and he sat up, shaking the past from his mind. God, it was so good to have an honest woman like Lola in his bed. She had never been coy with him—had come to him of her own free will as a virgin three years ago. She had been sweet and gentle and patient.

She appeared now in the doorway, her eyes sliding over his nakedness. He had taught her that bold stare, he thought, had taught her all the ways of love, even the dark and wicked ways that most white women couldn't even dream of. But Lola had learned everything and gave totally of herself. She had never been embarrassed or outraged at Brice's baser desires, but had pleasured him with every part of her body that she could.

"Breakfast ready," she said shortly.

He sprang from the bed, lithe as a panther, splendid in his nakedness, like an animal with sleek, taut muscles and sinews that moved like honey beneath his sunbrowned skin. The silver-blue eyes that looked out from beneath long, dark lashes were keen and bright as an eagle's, Lola thought. If she had known of such things, she might have thought that his eyebrows were shaped so perfectly that it almost seemed as though their owner must have them plucked. The long, night-dark hair that curled against his neck made him look like a savage.

Lola did not think of each of these things separately—the hollowed cheeks, the square-cut jawline, the firm, hard mouth, the long, brown hands with such slender fingers. She only knew that, as she looked upon this man, she knew him to be the handsomest of all others she had ever seen, even the princely Spanish dons that strode haughtily by her in the streets—and that she loved him with her entire being.

"Are you going to stand in the doorway all morning, Lola?" he laughed, springing toward her to wrap his arms about her broad hips. "Or will you get my breakfast on the table?"

"It is ready," she smiled.

They sat down together at the wooden trestle table and talked quietly while they ate.

"You will be leaving soon?" Lola asked, already knowing the answer.

He nodded. "Soon."

She clasped his hand longingly. "Lola asks you to stay," she pleaded softly, as though this would be their last meeting.

He looked at her sternly. "You know I have business with the Comanche, Lola. Appina is expecting me." Appina was

14

Katala's father and Brice's friend. It would never do to insult the great chief by keeping him waiting.

Lola fought back the tears of weakness. "Of course, I know you must go," she admitted solemnly.

He softened a little at her downcast face. "But that will not be for two or three more days, little one. We still have time for each other." His brown hand raised her chin forcefully.

She blinked through her tears and smiled shakily. "Yes, Brice."

He gave her an answering smile and continued with breakfast, talking of little things which he knew might interest her. She was born a Comanche and, although she now lived in a city of white men, her heart was still with her blood brethren. They talked of the successful raids that had been led by Katala as a measure of his manhood, signifying his readiness to take over his father's place.

"There are more and more wagon trains traveling through Comanche territory," Brice mused to himself. "Even though the gold strikes in California have dwindled to a paltry few, people with crazy ideas in their heads still throw away everything they've worked for and join up the first chance they get. Most of them take the overland route through Utah, but now that gold has been discovered in the Southwest, the Santa Fe Trail is becoming popular again." His fork clattered angrily against his plate. "The fools don't know what's waiting for them in that country."

"Apache," Lola commented knowingly, a disgusted twist to her mouth.

"Apache, yes, but also hot desert and scorching sun. Why any man would be stupid enough to leave a good dirt farm in Illinois or Kentucky and run to a land like that—" He stopped suddenly, feeling almost ashamed at his emotion. What concern was it of his if those damned fools got themselves killed? Gold! Old Sam used to say that men got the fever for gold and couldn't shake it no matter how hard they'd try. It was like a sickness with some. It ate into their veins until they were ready to sell everything they'd worked for for years just to have the dubious joy of sitting on a mountain of dirt and shoveling through it for an ounce or two of dust. It hadn't made sense to old Sam, who'd had his own way of making gold.

Brice chuckled at fond recollections, then his face grew more somber. Gold—money! Back again to the almighty dollar, he thought wryly. Well, not for him. Give him a warm

15

woman, plenty to eat and drink and the freedom to do what he wished, and he felt sure he would be happy for the rest of his days.

Three

Independence, Missouri, was a crowded, dusty town of makeshift lean-tos filled with people awaiting the formation of new wagon trains to take them on their four-month journey to California. Honor O'Brien looked around at the flurry of activity and felt more than a little apprehension at doing any dealing with the people here. She was obliged, of course, to put all her faith in her brother's ability to be dealt with honestly when he went to buy a wagon and team for the trail plus all their supplies—and, remembering how the two swindlers had left them nearly bankrupt in Charleston, she felt even more concern.

The ten days on the road in the stagecoach had been wearying for both of them and they had looked forward to reaching Independence with hopeful hearts. But now that they were here, Honor felt an overwhelming urge to be gone. She didn't like the scores of jobbers who trailed up and down the streets, selling things at the top of their voices and eyeing her with shifty, hungry eyes.

They found a hotel presently that looked fairly respectable and Reid had to leave his sister in the lobby as there were no rooms available.

"I'll only be gone as long as I have to," he said, somewhat dubiously. "I've got to make all the arrangements and I don't want to be worrying about you." He gave her a brotherly pat on the shoulder. "Now you stay put until I get back."

Honor, hating to be left to do nothing, watched him saunter out with mixed feelings. She wished desperately to stay with him for her own protection, and yet she didn't like the idea of rubbing elbows with some of those disreputable types they'd seen from the stage. She was somewhat relieved when an elderly lady came to sit next to her on the settee.

"Good morning, my dear," the woman said kindly, extending a lavender-mittened hand.

"Good morning," Honor replied, glad to have company in this strange new place.

16

"I suppose you're here to join one of the wagon trains?" she inquired, straightening her mittens and then brushing a wisp of snow-white hair behind the brim of her bonnet.

"Yes," Honor agreed. "My brother has only just left to inquire about suitable arrangements."

"Your brother? But, my dear, haven't you any parents to join you in the rigors of the trip—just you and your brother?"

She nodded, gazing at the older woman's bright blue eyes, which reminded her, unaccountably, of a bird of prey. She drew a little away, not knowing why she did so, as the woman patted her hand lightly.

"Well, I'm sure you two will be fine. Still, it's a shame to think of a pretty young thing like yourself being exposed to all sorts of—things—out there on the trail. Ah, the pretty young women I've seen pass through here in these last weeks," she went on almost to herself. "Do you know that there is a two-week waiting list just to cross the Missouri River by ferry?"

Honor shook her head. "My brother only just went out to—"

"Oh yes, of course. I can imagine his chagrin when he finds out he must wait so long to get started, but at least that will give you some time to enjoy the comforts of our little town."

Honor looked around doubtfully. "I hardly think I will enjoy the wait."

The older woman laughed with understanding. "I know you must think us terribly primitive, my dear. Judging from your Southern accent, I would guess you're from Virginia—the Carolinas?"

"South Carolina," Honor affirmed, suddenly becoming a little nervous in the woman's company. She looked pointedly at the door, hoping for her brother's appearance, then realized that in all probability he would not be returning for some time.

If the woman noticed her sudden discomfiture, she paid it no heed, but continued talking lightly. "I daresay you'll need some clothes for the heat, my dear. That frock you have on will cause you no end of torment, although I do admit it is of unusually fine material. You should look into finding a seamstress to make you up a few things before you leave."

"I—I'm sure I will," Honor hesitated.

"Oh, but my dear, I haven't even introduced myself. I'm

17

Pearl Holliday. And it just so happens that my sister, Lavinia, is renowned for her sewing talents. Really, my dear, if you would only allow me to introduce you to her?"

"No, I thank you for the kind offer, Mrs. Holliday, but my brother instructed me to——"

"Oh, posh, my dear, I simply can't believe he would mind if you walked me upstairs to my room and talked for a moment or two with my sister. Ummm—did you have any baggage with you? You could leave it upstairs if you like since it might get stolen in this crowded lobby." She sniffed with disdain.

"N-no, we left our luggage at the stagecoach office until we found some living quarters," Honor quickly interposed, wondering at the nervous feeling that had come over her.

"Well, that's probably better," the woman agreed lightly. "At any rate, I'm afraid you've forgotten to introduce yourself, my dear." She waited expectantly and Honor felt it would be unforgivably rude if she didn't rectify her error.

"Honor O'Brien, ma'am."

"Honor? What a—different name!" she exclaimed in delight as though at some private amusement. "Wherever did you acquire such a name, my dear?"

"It is a family name, but——"

"Oh yes, I expect your father was one of those wonderful Southern gentlemen who make the South so much more homey than any other place in the world. Am I right?" She was smiling cheerily now, nearly beaming at the younger girl, and Honor felt some of her distrust melting a little.

"Yes, my father was truly a gentleman," she said, feeling a sense of warmth from just speaking about him. "He and my mother were two of the most gentle people I have ever known. We lived in Charleston and our house was constantly besieged by guests for the simple reason that our hospitality was the talk of the city."

"And your parents—they are dead now?" the woman asked sympathetically, capturing Honor's hand once more and patting it softly.

Honor nodded, swallowing a lump at the remembrance. "Yes, only Reid—that's my brother—and I are left and he is determined to go to the goldfields in the New Mexico territory and try his luck."

"And you? Certainly you cannot tell me you are going to stay in that dreadful desert!" The woman looked shocked.

18

Honor shook her head. "I am betrothed to someone in California."

"Ah, how romantic," Pearl sighed, but her eyes were not soft as they watched the girl by her side. "My dear, I really insist that you come upstairs with me. I know a cup of tea will do you a world of good and your brother will be gone for hours. I'm sure he would be happy to know that you are enjoying a bit of rest and good company after the tedium of your journey."

Honor felt rather inclined to agree with the lady at this point. She hadn't realized how sore her muscles were from the jolting ride and the idea of a hot cup of tea sounded like heaven at this moment.

"Perhaps it would be a nice respite from this busy lobby," she agreed. "I am tired and you've been so kind, how can I refuse you?"

Pearl Holliday seemed to beam at her. "That's a sensible girl. You'll see how much more able you are to cope with all of this—after you've had a little rest and some genteel conversation, Lavinia will be anxious to get your sizes. I'll make sure she has some things ready before your departure date."

"I do appreciate your kindness, Mrs. Holliday. I suppose I was lucky you sat down beside me," Honor laughed, standing up to shake out her skirts.

Pearl said nothing, but a telltale gleam in her eye might have warned Honor if she had happened to look up.

As they walked toward the stairs, Pearl took Honor's arm in motherly fashion and inquired conversationally, "You do look terribly young to be suddenly uprooted from your native soil, my dear. How old are you?"

"Just eighteen," Honor admitted. "And you are right—I already miss my friends—although I'm sure I shall make now ones, once I am joined with my fiancé," she hastily amended.

Pearl nodded, chuckling. "It wouldn't be hard for you to make friends, my dear, you've just got to know what pleases them."

"Pardon?"

"Oh, nothing, just thinking out loud. Ah, here we are now." She tapped on the door softly. "Lavinia, it's your sister, Pearl, with a customer for you."

It took some moments until the door was opened slightly, permitting a much younger woman to peer out shortsightedly. "Pearl? Oh yes, come in."

The door was opened and Pearl hurriedly ushered her young charge inside. Honor looked around curiously, noting a man's buckskin shirt lying carelessly on an unmade bed. Pearl noted the direction of her gaze and hurried to explain.

"Lavinia is quite good with animal skins too, Honor. You'd be surprised at how nimble her fingers are."

Lavinia laughed almost raucously, producing a scowl from her "sister."

"Come, you are tired, my dear. Have a seat here and let me get you that tea."

Honor sat on a horsehide chair and looked idly out the window. Outside, people milled about, jostling each other, sometimes falling in the street, other times starting small fights here and there. There were very few women outside, and she was grateful for having found Pearl and Lavinia Holliday to take care of her until Reid came back for her.

"Now then," and her attention was diverted to Pearl's smiling face. "Here's your tea, my dear. Drink up."

Honor took it gratefully, noting that the cup was badly chipped. It looked as though these two ladies had fallen on some hard times too. She could surely sympathize with them as she sipped of the contents. The tea, itself, must have been sitting on the shelf for some time, for it tasted a bit moldy, but she continued to sip, afraid of upsetting her two hostesses.

She looked up to see both women watching her with a strangely intent gaze and she smiled back at them, feeling her mouth droop stupidly at the corners. The reaction puzzled her and she made an effort to pull the corners up, to no avail. She laughed and the sound seemed silly.

"What's the matter, my dear?" Pearl asked her kindly, taking the cup from her hands.

"Nothing, nothing. I guess I'm more tired than I thought," Honor mumbled in a strangely slurred voice.

Her eyes seemed to be blurring a little, as she looked up at the two kindly women once more. Lavinia, she realized, was really much younger than Pearl. Their mother must have had a great space between her babies. She flushed at the unladylike thought and tried to fold her hands on her lap. Pearl was saying something and she mustn't be discourteous to her benefactress.

"Well, Vinny, what do you think of my little find?"

Lavinia laughed, that raucous laugh again. "I think she's a

rare one, Pearl, but you've certainly kept your touch, old lady."

"I should hope so. It wasn't easy running that house in St. Louis for twenty years, till the bastards nearly tarred and feathered me. But I'll set me up a nice cozy bordello in the goldfields or my name isn't Mother Pearl." She laughed too and then both women turned their attention toward Honor, who was leaning back in the chair.

"My goodness, Honor, you really are tired, my dear," Pearl chided, coming to stand beside her. "I think what you need is a nice long nap in bed, my dear."

"No, no, I really couldn't—must get downstairs—my brother—" Her disjointed phrases frightened the girl and she struggled against the numbness that had descended over her limbs. What was happening to her? She looked up into the blue eyes of Pearl Holliday and saw them boring into her like those of a merciless eagle. Why had she ever thought the woman was kindly-looking?

"Don't fight it, Honor. Just relax," she was saying now in a confident voice.

"But—this—is—so—stupid of me," Honor got out with difficulty, feeling the room beginning to sway gently around her. Pearl seemed to be coming nearer and then moving farther away.

"Call Randy in now, Vinny," Pearl was ordering, although her voice came as a blurred whisper to the drugged girl.

From the corner of her vision, she saw a big man emerge from behind a screen. He wore no shirt and Honor thought he must be coming back for the fringed buckskin on the bed. Then, oddly, he seemed to be coming toward her. A spark of fear grew somewhere in her brain, but was quickly snuffed out as the drugged tea washed over it.

She was being lifted from the chair, put on the bed and, good heavens, her clothes were being stripped off. She watched with lassitude as her jacket, her bodice and skirt, even her stockings were taken from her. Only her linen chemise remained and Randy's hand had closed hungrily about the thin stuff until Pearl said something sharp to him and he retreated.

Even as the big man retreated, so too the two women's forms blurred and became mixed together, and then a thick blackness completely engulfed her.

Four

Honor lived the next three days in a hazy dream, her body curiously apart from the world of reality. All she could remember was waking up a little to be given some hot tea to drink and then falling back into the void.

She would come out of her daze for little snatches of reality here and there. She knew she had been moved from the hotel room, for she could hear flies buzzing around her during the day and felt the chill breeze off the river sometimes at night. She tried to think where she might be, and would seize at a distant memory of the lean-tos that had been set up by people waiting to join wagon trains. That must be it—Reid had managed to get them one and they were waiting their turn to take the ferry across the Missouri River into Kansas.

One day, she heard the distinct clank of a covered wagon over a dirt road, and then the lightning crack of a whip over straining animals. A ripping oath would tease her ears or perhaps a barking dog or whinnying horse. Then she would sink once again.

On the fourth day, she came awake in the middle of the afternoon and was surprised to see a canvas top over her head. She must have been terribly ill, she thought hazily. She had taken sick in the hotel, right in front of that dear Mrs. Holliday and her sister. Other memories pushed into her brain, but she was too tired to think about them.

Reid must have found her and had been able to get an early ferry across the river to enable them to join the first wagon train out. They were on their way! She wanted to talk to Reid about a few things. She felt so silly, becoming ill before leaving, and now she had no idea what supplies he had brought along, what arrangements they had made with the wagonmaster.

"Reid!" Her voice was still thin, but Pearl Holliday heard it from the seat at the front of the wagon.

"She's awake again," she said to Randy, who was driving the wagon. "I suppose I'd better give her some tea again."

"Aw, Ma, she's been out long enough. We're three days out from Independence. There's no way she's gonna be able to get back to her brother."

22

"Hush up, Randy. I haven't come this far to see my dreams ended because of some girl. Now keep your eyes in front of you!"

And once more, Honor was given the soothing tea before she had time to wonder about Pearl being in the wagon with her.

"I'll start lessening the doses on you, magpie, once we get close to our first stop," Pearl said, more to herself than to the sleeping girl.

"Where am I?" Honor's voice was nearly hysterical. She had awakened from her lengthy dreams completely and found herself in the company of Pearl Holliday, her "sister," Lavinia, the strange man they called Randy and two other young women who looked as bewildered as she. "Where is my brother?" she demanded.

Pearl attempted to lay a soothing arm on the distraught girl, but Honor pulled away suspiciously. "Firstly, my dear, you are in Council Grove, Kansas, on the banks of the Neosho River, the first stop for the wagon train, ten days out of Independence."

"Ten days! But where—where is Reid? Which wagon is he in?"

"My dear Honor, your brother is most likely still back in Missouri awaiting his turn to cross on the ferry. I told you there was a two-week waiting list."

"But how is it that I am here if—"

"Oh, we'd been in Independence twelve days when I chanced upon you, my dear," Pearl continued gently.

"I don't—understand," Honor went on, raising a trembling hand to her forehead. "I know there must be some perfectly logical explanation for this, but I'm afraid I can't see it." She turned to the woman. "Why am I here with you and Reid is still back in Independence? I can't seem to remember . . ."

Lavinia laughed, jarring her nerves. "Dearie, you've been recruited to Mother Pearl's little caravan of free love. You and those two sitting next to you."

Honor glanced at the other two girls. They were no help and she turned beseeching eyes on Pearl. "What is she talking about?"

Pearl lowered her eyes. "Well, my dear, Vinny wasn't quite right. This is definitely not going to be free. I daresay the men will be willing to pay a good deal of their hard-won gold for a chance at your three. I've still got a good eye, if I do say so myself."

She tittered. "I suppose it's time to make myself clearer to you poor dears," she went on. "I was once the proprietor of a grand establishment in St. Louis which served men of only the highest order. For twenty good years I reigned over the brothels along the riverfront, but, unfortunately, one of my clients was about to be embroiled in a bit of a scandal with one of my ladies and he 'contrived' to have me thrown out of town before I could open my mouth against him. The bastard nearly killed my poor Eliza. He had all my girls rounded up and thrown into jail, but Vinny and I escaped through the kind service of the guard, who had enjoyed our services through the years—bless him."

"What are you talking about? What has all this to do with me?" Honor asked in mounting horror.

"Since I have been threatened with loss of my life should I attempt to regain my position of renown east of the Missouri River, I have decided to forge ahead to the golden land of opportunity! In California, you three girls—and you too, Vinny—will be the start of Mother Pearl's greatest achievement. A new house where—"

"Stop!" Honor held out her hands as though to ward off the beaming face of her benefactress. "You—you can't be serious! I'm not some poor, destitute girl without name of family! You can't possibly believe that my brother will not find me. He—"

"He has no idea where you are, my dear. Oh, he may search frantically around Independence for a few days, but he will have to give up the search and join his wagon train if he wishes to see the goldfields before they are totally overrun by other young opportunists."

"Then—then he will find me when we reach the New Mexico territory!"

Pearl shook her head sadly. "I'm afraid you weren't listening, Honor. We are already ten days ahead of him—probably more by the time he leaves Independence. We will have already passed through Santa Fe before he reaches it."

"But he will inquire about me!"

"I doubt it. For what reason? How could he know that you would have been on the wagon train ahead of him—probably one of several ahead of him? No, my dear, I believe I've covered every possible means of escape." Again that look as though she truly sympathized with her.

24

"But there is no one to stop me from telling the other people on this wagon train about what you've done!"

"Honor, everyone on this train knows my business already. None of the men would believe you. They'd sooner tumble you themselves than listen to some foolish story about being kidnapped from your brother, tsk, tsk! As for the women, I'd not try to win their sympathy, my dear. They hate us already, knowing their men have been giving our two wagons the eye since we left the Missouri."

"Oh, how—how could you?" Honor wailed, shaken to her depths at the dastardly deed this woman had perpetrated on her and the other two young girls. "Why did you take me?"

"I'm sorry, my dear, you just happened to be sitting in the lobby of my hotel and—well, things just went on from there. I'm not one to look a gift horse in the mouth, so to speak. Now I suggest you just settle down to the idea. Someday, when you're lying in piles of gold up to your lovely bosom, you'll thank Mother Pearl." She laughed thoughtfully. "Don't worry about losing your chastity on the trail, my sweets. I'll let no one touch you until we're at the goldfields."

Reduced to tears of self-pity, Honor wept into her hands, hearing Pearl and Lavinia quit the three girls in order to prepare dinner.

A cool hand on her arm made Honor whirl about, only to meet the frightened brown eyes of a girl around her own age.

"Do you think she's mad?" the girl wondered, trembling at the thought.

"I—I don't think so. She seems too—calculating," Honor answered her. "I'm Honor O'Brien," she continued, desperately needing a friend.

"Barbie Hampton, and this is Lee Ann Colter."

The other girl smiled nervously, her eyes as big and frightened as Barbie's. "What are we going to do?"

Honor was at a loss. Nothing in her upbringing had prepared her for such a situation. She had no one to turn to now. The other two girls were as lost as she. God, if only she could convince someone in the wagon train to help. But if what Pearl had said was true . . .

"We've got to think of a plan," she said slowly. "At least we know that we won't be—molested as long as we're on the wagon train." There was little conviction in her tone. She felt as though she couldn't trust Pearl as far as her arm could reach. If giving them over to anyone would benefit her own plans, or make her any kind of money, she would certainly forget about her promise.

"Perhaps we could steal a gun somehow. I noticed that big bear, the one called Randy, carries a pistol in his belt. If we could steal it . . ."

"I wouldn't get close enough to him to touch his belt," Barbie scoffed at Lee Ann's timid suggestion. "Besides, you know what would happen if we tried and failed. If Pearl wasn't around, you'd get a fitting punishment from that pig! And if she was around, we'd probably be fed drugged tea for the rest of our lives!"

"We've got to make someone believe us in the wagon train," Honor said.

"You heard the old witch, Honor. She won't let us get near anyone else, and besides, they probably think we're whores just like Vinny," Barbie replied.

It was clear to Honor that Barbie was not completely naive and she wondered, suddenly, if the other two girls were virgins too. She couldn't ask them such a delicate question, but Barbie sensed the curiosity in her furtive glance.

"It's still there," she laughed, as though remembering a time when it had almost been torn asunder. "I've managed to keep the men at arm's length, although I'd be the first to admit I like their company. Lee Ann? I don't even think we need to ask her. She looks like a frightened little lamb."

"You don't look like much else yourself!" Lee Ann retorted, miffed.

"Well, shoot, there's three of us and——"

"Four of them!" Lee Ann put in quickly. "They've got a Negro driver for the other wagon, the one where our two ladies of the evening sleep. Randy sleeps beneath us, because I've heard him snoring more than once."

"What can we do?" Honor said helplessly.

"Like you said, we've got to think of a plan first." Barbie's brow puckered in thought. "Maybe we could escape once we get to Santa Fe. It might be easier then. I mean at least we'd be in a town, among civilized people, not out in the godforsaken desert."

Five

Honor found out quickly enough that Pearl hadn't been lying about the other pioneers' reaction to them. The women literally shunned them if they tried to make any friendly overtures and the men were even worse. They seemed to peel off their clothes with their eyes and Honor had caught one grizzled old man licking his lower lip as though wondering what her flesh might taste like. She shivered, thinking of being forced to lie in bed with such a man. What exactly they would do in the bed was still far from clear. It was the one thing the three of them never discussed in their fervent conversations and plans. Perhaps it was because none of them truly thought they would be forced to do such a thing against their wills.

At least Randy, for all his hungry looks, seemed to be amply assuaged by Vinny's lithe, young form, and for this, Honor was exceedingly grateful.

The days seemed to go by routinely now and Honor found herself doing the same things over and over each day. Washing over the barrel of rainwater, getting dressed in the plain yellow muslin gown, helping Vinny prepare the table since Barbie held a better skill at cooking than the other two. Packing things in the wagon, enduring the ten to fifteen miles they covered each day until it came time for supper and then to bed. It was a wearying routine.

Day by day, they covered more miles—each day taking them farther away from Reid, from safety. The names of the places where they stopped, a colorful collage of landscapes—Diamond Spring, Cottonwood Creek, Turkey Creek, Little Arkansas River, Cow Creek—until they finally left the tall prairie grass behind and emerged onto the semiarid Great Plains. Each morning the loud bellow from the wagonmaster, "Catch up!" and the day would start over again.

Approaching the Arkansas River, the train had entered a belt of sand hills fancifully corrugated by the plains wind to form odd shapes. It had broken up the usual routine when the three girls had played guessing games to see what they thought the various shapes resembled. Unfortunately, the game had been ended when Lee Ann tearfully cried out that

27

one of the shapes reminded her of her Ohio farm on the banks of the mighty Ohio River.

Just beyond the sand hills they emerged at the Great Bend of the majestic Arkansas River, some 270 miles from Independence. They were now in buffalo country and Randy, along with others of the men led by the train scouts, proceeded to haul down buffalo meat for the cooking pots. Juicy roasts of hump ribs offered a succulent change from the usual fare of salted beef or pork.

Of course, Honor had heard the warnings whispered along the wagon train. They were crossing through Comanche and Pawnee Indian territory and the scouts were kept on twenty-four-hour watch every day in case of attack. The thought of real Indians attacking the train caused a shiver of fear down her spine and bothered her more than any talk of bordellos.

The caravan was moving west now, along the north bank of the Arkansas River. There were sandstone carvings and pinnacles standing high above the land, and Honor learned that one such pinnacle was called Pawnee Rock, a further reminder of the danger that lurked beyond the safety of the camp at night.

They also had to cross many small streams that coursed southward to join the Arkansas and these river crossings oftentimes proved difficult for the heavy wagons. Many would stick in mud or rocks and it would take several men the entire afternoon to dislodge them. More than once, Honor and the other two girls were obliged to quit the haven of the wagon to endure the stares and whisperings of the women while the wagon was pulled from a mudbog.

"You shouldn't be traveling in the same train with good Christian folk," one woman hissed maliciously at the three young girls on one such crossing. "Going to California just to add to the evil that's already there!"

Honor had valiantly kept back the tears of humiliation and was obliged to lend an arm for Lee Ann to lean on for moral support. They both cast glances toward Pearl and Vinny, who were standing a few feet away. The insults, though, seemed to roll off them like water off a duck's back.

"You don't understand," Honor began brokenly, turning toward the group of women. "We didn't come on this train willingly. Pearl—"

"No use denying it, you hussy!" sneered another woman. "Just don't expect any of *our* men to come sniffing around your wagon!"

It was no use. The women weren't about to believe them. Perhaps, if they had been ugly or older, Honor thought cynically.

She plodded after Lee Ann and Barbie as the wagon was pulled up through the stream. She realized that Pearl's plan had been worked out to perfection.

That evening as camp was made, Honor stood wearily by the cookfire, watching the beans while Barbie started coffee. The liquid was strong and hot, but Honor gulped it down with the rest of them as she remembered longingly the icy lemonade her mother used to make so long ago. She shook off the threat of tears and stirred the beans furiously.

"I'll do that," Vinny snapped, taking the spoon from her. She had been angry since one of her trunks had slipped out of the wagon into the water and ruined her gowns. They were displayed around the two wagons now as she tried to dry them out before repacking them. "Go get some salt pork from the wagon barrel."

Honor hurried to do as she was told, but, to her dismay, Randy was lounging against the back of the wagon, watching her progress with hungry eyes.

"Excuse me," Honor murmured, seeking to push past him.

He grinned casually and put a hand across to the other side of the wagon so that he had put his arm between her and the barrel. "You never talk to me, gal," he accused softly. "You afraid of me, huh?"

Honor took a deep breath and looked around covertly for Pearl. When she did not see her, she looked back at the big man in front of her, eyes narrowed. "If I never talk to you, it's because I have no wish to. If you remember, I did not come on this wagon train of my own free will. I hold you responsible just as much as Pearl and Vinny."

His brows went up and the bright eyes regarded her reproachfully. "Aw, now, you shouldn't blame me for what my ma did. I don't have nothing to do with that. I'm just coming along for the ride. When I get to California, I'm gonna split with those two and head for the hills. I could take you with me if you want."

She almost laughed and barely kept herself from smiling sarcastically. "Why in heaven's name would I want that?"

He eyed her more closely. "Because I think you'd rather have one man getting on top of you every night than a whole passel."

She blanched at the implication. "Not," she ground out

slowly, "if that one man was you. Now get out of my way, before I call your mother!"

His face went red and for a moment his hands tightened as though he would have liked to throttle her, but then he shrugged. "All right, gal, you do as you want. Just don't look for me to make the offer again."

Honor breathed a sigh of relief when he moved away and she hurried to get out the meat and return it to Vinny to put in the beans.

"I saw our brutish friend talking with you in back of the wagon," Barbie whispered later after the three were in bed. "Was he bothering you?"

Honor laughed softly. "He wanted to know if I'd run away with him once we arrived in California." Her laugh ended rather forlornly.

"He asked me the same," Barbie confided.

"Me, too," Lee Ann said, raising herself on one elbow.

"You mean we all turned him down?" Honor asked, suddenly seeing the humor to the situation. "Poor Randy!"

The other two looked at each other and began laughing. Soon all three were nearly hysterical with mirth until a sharp pounding from below the wagon silenced them instantly.

"Shut up!" came Randy's voice grouchily. "Can't a man get some sleep!"

The next day, Honor was sitting up in the driver's seat with the old Negro servant who had been with Pearl since her days in St. Louis, when one of the scouts rode past the wagon, going down the line to give the latest news. He rode beside Honor for a few minutes, taking his hat off to wipe his forehead.

"We'll be going past the Caches pretty soon," he informed her.

"The Caches?"

"They're mossy pits on the riverbank which we have to be careful of. You could have a wheel sink in one in less than five minutes. Keep your oxen behind the wagon in front of you. Don't veer off to the left. We'll be coming to the Cimarron Crossing of the Arkansas River. You'll need all your strength and your wagons will have to be in good shape."

"Is it dangerous?" Honor asked worriedly.

He looked up at her and noticed that his eyes had the same look in them as did most of the other men's on the train. "Honey, if you fall in, I'll come and rescue you person-

30

ally. I'm still looking forward to the end of the trail when I can come calling." He laughed insultingly.

Honor stiffened, but the Negro put a hand out as though to silence her, then thanked the scout for the information. When Honor was able to collect herself, she turned on the Negro impatiently.

"Tobias, why did you do that? That man insulted me! I have more pride than to take something like that in silence!"

"Miss Honor, you has better learn the diff'ence 'tween an insult an' a compliment in dis profession," he returned quietly.

Honor was effectively silenced. She rode in silence the rest of the way, pulling the brim of her bonnet lower over her forehead as they drove into the setting sun. By the end of the day they had reached the Cimarron Crossing, nearly 400 miles from Independence, Missouri.

As she looked over the half-mile-wide stretch of river, she was reminded of the great Mississippi River that they had crossed from Illinois into St. Louis. But then, they had been on a ferry and she had felt relatively safe from the treacherous current that flowed beneath the logs. This time, they would be crossing in the wagons. She shivered with apprehenion.

Six

The line of wagons had turned abruptly south in order to forge the river at the Cimarron Crossing. Double teaming was necessary and there were twelve oxen in harness to take the first wagon across the river. It would take nearly all of the day to get the fifteen wagons across and Honor was in the next to the last wagon, along with Barbie, Lee Ann and Randy.

It was nearing evening and the wind had started blowing up by the time the extra six oxen were harnessed onto Honor's wagon. Randy was going to drive and the three girls huddled together behind him as they started into the swift-running water.

Honor already knew the river concealed treacherous quicksand pits since they had lost one wagon and barely salvaged another by means of ropes. The stranded family was immediately taken in by another couple and Honor wondered hopelessly if such courtesy would be extended to them in such an event. Behind their wagon, Tobias was guiding the oxen up to the riverbank in preparation for crossing as soon as they should reach the opposite side.

Randy was confidently guiding the oxen through the brawny strength of his arms while the girls watched. A sudden shout from the opposite bank caused Randy to take his eyes off the oxen to see two barrels from the half-submerged wagon in the quicksand coming downstream toward him. Cursing he laid the whip on the team, but the barrels were coming too quickly and the first one struck one of the animals, spooking him.

Frightened, Honor watched as the scared animal bellowed and rammed into the ox in front of it, causing the whole group to spook. Their frantic efforts to get out of the water caused the wagon to teeter ominously.

Clutching each other, the three girls were thrown into the back of the wagon. With a forlorn cry, Lee Ann was tumbled out the back of the wagon into the churning water. The current took her swiftly and she was tumbling head over heels downstream as the crowd on the other side ran down the bank, some of the men grabbing rope to toss out to her. But Lee Ann was beyond rational thought as she screamed, was ducked under to swallow a mouthful of water and was carried farther away.

Honor screamed at Randy to swim after the girl and the man looked at her as though she were insane. Frantically, she called to the opposite shore for more rope, but there was nothing they could do. They were still a quarter of a mile away and the last thing Honor saw was Lee Ann's bright red hair bobbing above the water once more before it disappeared around the bend of the river. She wept into her hands, Randy's curses hardly touching her conscience as he tried to get the oxen to pull together again.

It seemed an hour before they finally scrambled onto the opposite bank. Honor was ready to run down the shoreline in order to search for Lee Ann.

"Maybe she was pulled to the shore. She may be hurt, in need of help. We can't leave her!" she wailed, pushing against Randy frantically as she sought to escape his arms.

"Goddammit, gal, she'd be dead by now!" he said gruffly. "She's drowned for sure."

Beside herself, Honor refused to be comforted, even by

Barbie, and she spent the long night with her own thoughts, staring at the wall of canvas, wishing with pent-up desperation that she could be anywhere but here in this godforsaken land.

The next morning, she was awakened to the sound of "Catch up!"—a sound she would grow to hate, she thought gloomily.

Finally, when she had moped part of the day away, Barbie caught her by the shoulders and shook her hard. "Stop this stupid sniveling, Honor," she said briskly. "God, don't you think I'm sorry Lee Ann is gone? She was our friend and I cared for her as much as you did. But you can't let it get you down. My God, before this journey is over you might see me die too! Or someone else! You've got to pull yourself together or you'll go mad!"

"How can you be so—so hard, when Lee Ann is dead!" Honor shot back angrily, trying to free herself.

"Maybe she's better off being drowned than being killed by Indians or starving to death or dying from thirst," Barbie continued, and at Honor's blank stare, "Yes, all of those things could still happen to us! I know something about this land we're going through. I've listened to the scouts and I've taken geography in school in Philadelphia. You didn't know anything about Lee Ann, Honor. She was an orphan, traveling with a married couple who were distant cousins and couldn't care less about her. She was almost glad when she was thrown in with you and me. At least we cared about her! Just remember, at least you gave her that much!"

Honor was crying again. "B-but she was so young and it made no sense—how she was killed."

Barbie shrugged. "Nothing makes sense in this world sometimes, Honor. You're going to have to look out for yourself. The past is gone. Lee Ann is gone."

Honor wished she could see it from Barbie's point of view. But it all seemed so cold. Instead, she picked up on something the other girl had said earlier—anything to keep her mind from thinking too much about her friend's death.

"You—you're from Philadelphia, Barbie?" she asked haltingly, making an effort to stop crying.

"Yes," the other responded shortly.

"Tell me."

Barbie shrugged. "Nothing to tell really. I was the only daughter of a fairly well-to-do family. My father was in the

33

banking business. Unfortunately," and she hesitated for a moment before plunging on, "he decided he could use some of that money that was passing through his hands for his own gains."

"He embezzled money from the bank?"

She nodded, then looked fierce. "Yes. My father was way ahead of his time. He gave my mother more freedom than any other woman had then. He saw to it that I had lessons that would equal any boy's education. He wanted to use the money for a girls' school—not one of those mindless finishing schools, but a real educational facility so that women would have a chance to improve their minds. It was a great dream."

"What happened?"

Barbie sighed and closed her eyes. "He was caught, thrown in jail. My mother nearly went crazy from the separation. When he was killed in jail by one of the guards in an escape attempt, she—" Barbie stopped and her eyes were bleak.

Honor guessed what her mother had been driven to do and she felt a compassion for the other girl at what she had been witness to. "How did you wind up in Independence?" she asked softly, wanting to bring the girl out of her sadness.

"I came west by myself," she said with sudden pride. "My father taught me to be independent and I was going to be what he had hoped. Except," and she was able to smile ruefully. "I didn't bargain on Mother Pearl and her friends."

"Nor I." Honor shook her head. She related, briefly, her background and why she had been on her way to California.

"Well, at least you won't be destitute once you arrive," Barbie said hopefully. "You might get a letter off to your fiancé and he—"

"He wouldn't want me after I was in the goldfields," Honor cut in quickly. "To him, it would be the highest form of dishonor. I—I couldn't burden him with that."

"But he needn't know." Barbie persisted. "Don't talk nonsense, Honor. It's a way out and that's the only thing that's important."

Honor shrugged. "I'll have to see," she replied noncommittally. At least she felt better after her conversation with Barbie. She could honestly say that there was someone else whose luck seemed to be worse than her own. And Lee Ann would have to remain a fond memory.

The two girls looked out the flap of the wagon canvas at the back and could see the trail the wagon train had already gone over. Behind them Tobias wiped his forehead and grinned.

"Sho' is hot out here, misses. You'd bes' stay inside if'm you don' wan' to get yo' noses burn'."

He was right. It was blazing hot suddenly after the coolness of the river and Honor was impatient to hear the scout's report at camp that night.

They found out that they were crossing the Cimarron Desert, a barren, flat plain of sand, fifty miles wide, where the only things that lived were the lizards that scurried everywhere. It would take them three or four days to cross the desert, which was why the wagonmaster had had them fill all available vessels with water.

"At least we won't have to worry about Indians," Randy said, repeating the gossip he had heard that day. "Pawnee and Comanche won't ride out here, but," and he grew serious, "they like to wait at the end of the flats for a surprise attack."

"How much farther is it until we reach Santa Fe?" Honor asked.

Randy shrugged. "Three hundred miles, maybe more."

She sat back dejectedly. Three hundred miles or more! It seemed like forever. They had already been traveling over a month and still they had so far to go. She wished—ah, but there was no use in wishing. Barbie had told her to be practical. She would have to learn.

The Cimarron River showed like a small silver ribbon in the distance as the caravan moved toward it from the flats. The oxen, mules and horses, even the dogs, smelling the water, strained toward it. Some of the beasts nearly went crazy as they hurried to get to the cooling liquid. Honor herself felt her mouth salivating, for they had taken the last water that morning and she had not been able to wash for the last two days. It would be heaven to be able to take a bath.

The wagons were formed into the circle of defense and then, led by scouts, each family was able to take their animals and lead them to the river. They were also allowed to fill all their water barrels and jugs although they would be following the Cimarron River for the next eighty-five miles and would have little need of large supplies of stored water.

When it was their turn to go, Barbie suggested they take a quick dip in the river, but their scout instantly dissuaded them from doing so. Indian sign had been sighted along the trail ahead and it was most likely that they might have some trouble in the next couple of days.

"I'm sure those redskins would get an eyeful if you gals decided to wash up now," said one of the scouts, grinning at them lecherously.

"Well, at least that might keep them busy until you were able to get a shot at them," Barbie returned sassily, turning her nose up.

"By God, honey, if you'd like I'll give you a taste of what you'll be getting in California," the scout replied, putting his rifle down for a moment and starting to walk toward her.

"Don't you touch her—or you'll be the one who I'll be takin' a shot at," Randy spoke up, coming up to them. He turned to the two girls. "Ma says to get back to the wagons, pronto!"

Honor and Barbie were only too glad to do so. In the distance, they heard a gunshot and wondered if someone had sighted Indians. They waited nervously with Pearl and Vinny until a whoop was let out and one of the scouts came through leading a wild pony upon whose back was draped the body of a single Indian.

"What happened out there?" the wagonmaster asked sternly.

"Didn't mean to shoot, Sam, but this damned redskin came out of nowhere. Scared the bejesus out of me," the scout got out quickly. "I nailed him clean with the first shot."

"Goddammit, Mel, you'd just better hope he didn't have his friends too close. They get word their buddy was killed and we've all got our necks in the noose!" The wagonmaster turned away disgustedly.

"What'll I do with the body?" The scout was beginning to look more apprehensive than proud of himself as he waited for further orders.

"Bury it outside the camp," was the gruff reply.

Honor shivered, eyeing the dead body briefly. She could see the long black hair hanging down the side of the horse, streaks of red still dripping from it. The pony itself was shying nervously, its nostrils dilated at the smell of fresh blood.

"Well, you've seen your first Indian," Pearl said, watching the two girls from her place on a stool. "What do you think?"

Honor shook her head. "I hope I don't see any more."

Pearl laughed heartily. "I'll add my vote to that—leastways

not any live ones. The dead ones I can handle." She laughed again.

Vinny simpered. "I've heard those savages make wonderful bed partners," she said, casting a sly look over to where Randy was watering his horse from a wide-mouthed jug. "They say those Injuns can do it three, four, maybe even five times a night."

Randy grinned. "You want it five times a night, gal, I can give it to you," he said with bravado, putting down the jug.

She laughed. "Honey, you're all used up after number one," she accused, taunting him.

"Dammit, gal, don't go riling me or you'll see just how savage I can be!"

"Hold on, you two!" intervened Pearl, holding out her hands. "For heaven's sake, let's not air our difficulties in front of our two innocents here." She inclined her head toward Barbie and Honor, whose faces had pinkened at the conversation.

"Ah, hell, they're dying to know what it's like!" Vinny exclaimed crossly.

"Yeh, Ma, I'd be glad to break 'em in for you," Randy added, forgetting his argument with Vinny.

"I said to shut up," Pearl warned. "Honor, Barbie, you two get some sleep." She gave them a commanding look. "Now do as I say," she added.

Seven

"Lord, it's hot in here!" Barbie murmured to Honor fitfully, fanning her face with a towel inside of the wagon. She crawled over to the canvas flap and tied it back, peering out with weary eyes.

"You get yo' nose inside!" Tobias called out behind her in a stern voice.

"Oh, Tobias, we can't see a blessed thing out there," Honor answered, going over beside Barbie. "Why must we sit in this wagon, melting to death? God, I didn't realize how humid it could be. It's worst than the desert almost."

"I know you're uncomfortable, my dears," came Pearl's voice from the other wagon, "but we must do as the wagonmaster told us. His scouts have seen more Indian signs and it's better that you stay safe inside here while we wait our turn to cross the river."

Honor would have continued to grumble, but realized it was no use and only made her feel worse. She sighed and helped Barbie to close the flap once more. They were last in line to cross the river. It seemed that hours of waiting and fidgeting stretched ahead and Honor laid her head against her arm, pushing her moist hair from her face.

Randy was outside, standing by the lead ox now, awaiting his turn in the now broiling sun. Anything seemed better, though, than the stifling atmosphere of the interior of the wagon.

Barbie was loath to talk because of the heat and after a few moments, Honor went forward to the driver's seat and scanned the horizon hopefully, but dropped back upon seeing only the third wagon cross the small river that was a tributary of the Cimarron which they had been following for nearly forty miles already.

She could see clearly the sparkling river and the trees, sparse in number, that lined one bank. A few small hills reared up craggily from the sandy soil of the small depression they were in. The sky was a pitiless blue without even a bare wisp of cloud to signal any relief. High above, the white orb of the sun shone indifferently on the small group of travelers and seemed to have scorched the sides of the mountains beyond.

Honor turned away from the sight and wished they were far away from here, back in St. Louis or farther ahead in California. The first stage of their journey had not been like this. The crossings had been somewhat difficult, but the intense heat had not been ready to burn skin already pinkened from exposure.

When she crawled back inside the wagon, Honor sat down dejectedly among the barrels and crates, waiting listlessly for the wagon to move. She sat with her chin in her hand, thinking about nothing, watching the canvas opposite where a lone spider crawled. Barbie sat a few feet from her, likewise enthralled.

They both started when their wagon suddenly went forward and went to the front to look out, only to see Randy walking slowly beside the oxen as their wagon followed the next one in line to the river. Honor looked somberly once again at the landscape, her eyes panning the rock formations idly. She stilled for a brief instant. Had she seen something moving farther up in the rocks? She strained forward, almost positive that she had seen a flash of something, as though the sun had glinted for a moment on metal. She continued watching for any further signs, but it was as though she imagined it.

"Did you see anything?" she asked Barbie warily.

The other shook her head. "Did you?"

"I'm not sure. I thought—but it was probably this heat or the sun."

In front of them and on either side was the small river with the low foothills stretching away from it, ascending slowly to meet the mountains some forty miles away. Beyond the mountains lay the town of San Miguel, perched on the silvery Pecos River. But that still lay two hundred miles away and it was torture to think about it now.

It seemed to Honor that for the most infinitesimal moment, everything around them was completely quiet. A stillness had settled over everything—a waiting stillness that she couldn't comprehend. Even the squeaking of the ox harness was only the faintest of noises. She could barely hear the spider's legs scratching against the wagon canvas.

Suddenly and incredibly, there was a rustling noise nearby, seeming almost to lift the hair off her forehead, and then she was staring at Randy as he dropped quickly to the ground, as though someone had chopped off his legs at the knee and left him to fall like a felled tree. She kept on staring, watching the bright yellow feathers of the arrow, still quivering a few inches from his neck where a pool of red had already smeared the collar of his shirt. He was making horrible gurgling noises and she could only stare at him, frozen in disbelief.

And then there were more of the curious rustling noises, seeming to fall all around her now, and yellow feathers were sticking out of the oxen's hides, causing some to drop in their tracks. Ahead, she could see wagons being circled by yelling savages on horseback until the Indians jumped off their ponies to crawl over the canvases, their upraised arms wielding tomahawks and knives with incredible ease. Screams and yells mingled with the dying groans and bellows of wounded animals.

"Barbie!"

Something inside Honor snapped and she jumped to her feet, catching Barbie's hand. My God! My God, they were being attacked! Honor twisted her neck around to look back with dilated eyes into Barbie's wide brown ones. All around them they could hear snorting ponies and screaming savages.

"Look!" Barbie pointed a trembling finger as, behind them, Indians, their long black hair braided with bright feathers and ribbons, streamed over the white canvas of Pearl's wagon, chopping their way through the ribs to where Vinny and Pearl must be cowering in fear. Tobias was already dead, slumped over in the seat.

"We've got to get out of here!" Honor cried out.

"Yes, yes, but where, Honor? We—we can't outrun them," Barbie almost wailed. She was bent over as though in pain.

The cries and screams were dreadful now, causing a wall of noise around her, and Honor wished she could put her hands over her ears and shut out everything. They must try to get away!

Quickly, she jumped down from the seat and stifled a scream as an arrow stuck abruptly in the wood where she had just been standing. The smell of burning wood was drifting slowly in the windless air toward her and with horror, she realized the Indians were setting some of the wagons on fire. Beside her, Barbie stood trembling, trying to pull herself together.

"What can we do?" the latter asked uncertainly.

As if in answer, there came the sounds of rifles firing and Honor realized that some of the men were firing back, taking aim at the swarming Indians. Other rifle reports answered them, but they were all too few and Honor realized that the Indians had planned the attack well. They had waited until the train had become separated, attacking with speed and surprise, catching the white man standing impatiently beside his teams.

One of the scouts rode by quickly on his horse, his face set in a grim mask, "Comanche!" he shouted to the two girls. "They're repaying us for the redskin I killed. Damn them! Get to cover!"

"Give us some help!" Barbie called after him, but he had already thundered away, his rifle firing as he rode.

For a moment, the two girls clung to each other. Then they bent low and crawled beneath the wagon, their fingers digging at the dirt in their frantic efforts to escape unseen. Honor peered out and could see Pearl and Vinny being dragged by the hair from their wagon. She turned away quickly as their captors pounced upon them, intent on rape.

Sweat poured from Honor's face and the ground seemed to

40

dance away from her, further and further away until she knew she was going to faint. Behind her, Barbie gasped and swallowed sand as she let her head fall heavily.

They lay there for a long time, the noise and the fury of the Indian attack beating on their ears. Finally, the sounds of rifle fire ceased altogether and Honor raised her head to look fearfully out from beneath the wagon. She could see the Indians rummaging through wagons they had not already set on fire.

A small, huddled group of white girls stood cowering beneath the shadow of a river birch, watched over by a tall, angry-looking Indian who kept them at bay with two long, braided lariats which he swung at them like whips. Honor could count perhaps fifteen women among them and struggled to make out Pearl or Vinny.

"Oh, my God!" Barbie whispered, tugging on Honor's arm.

Honor looked where she pointed and quickly closed her eyes as an Indian neatly took the scalp from Randy's skull, but she could not stop her ears from hearing the horrible "pop!" the scalp made as it was lifted up. Beside her, Barbie was forcing herself not to retch.

The two girls pressed themselves into the earth, but some of the Indians were coming closer, apparently to ransack their wagon. Suddenly, an Indian had dropped to his knees and was looking in on the two in surprise. He reached to pull Honor out by her arm, but with as much strength as she could manage, Honor pulled her arm away from his grasp and pushed Barbie to the other side of the wagon.

"We've got to get out from under here," she yelled.

They stood up on the other side of the wagon and began running toward the stream, crossing it with heavy splashing. Beyond the stream was a clump of small trees which grew below a ridge. If they made it, they could climb the ridge and hide. Would it be possible to reach its cover in time?

Barbie was pulling viciously at Honor's arm and the two half-crawled, half-ran along the ground until they reached the rocky formation. They fell down, scraping their knees and palms against the stones.

Behind them, they heard the pounding of hooves in the dirt, splashing across the water, riding toward them furiously as though to run them down. The trees were too sparse to provide any real cover and they turned toward the ridge.

A pony suddenly reared up in front of them and they were separated. Barbie fell to the ground, trying to keep from being kicked by the horse. Honor clutched her skirts and ran. She looked back once to see the black eyes of an Indian staring at her intently. His face was banded in bright red paint. In his upraised arm, she could see his tomahawk as though he were about to fling it forward to cleave her skull in half. She ducked wildly as the hatchet missed her, falling with a bright ring against the rocks in front of her. Without thinking, she scrambled toward it and felt the smooth shaft in her palm.

"I'll kill you!" she screamed, not caring that he couldn't understand her. "I'll kill you, you heathen savage!"

She clutched the tomahawk tightly in her hand and backed toward the rocks, her eyes sweeping over the two Indians still on thir ponies watching her with a kind of incredulous surprise. They seemed to wait endlessly, just sitting and watching her as she continued to the ledge behind her. She could see the attack was over.

She was climbing upward now, breathing fast, still watching them, her eyes flashing in her pale face, knowing that she wouldn't hesitate to use the hatchet on the first one who came toward her. She had climbed to the low, flat ledge and was perhaps twenty feet above them when a sound close by caught her ear. A sudden gust of wind blew by her and something heavy had fallen on her, rolling her over and over in the sand.

Her startled eyes stared into the dark, menacing eyes of an Indian. His hand closed tight as death on her wrist, wrenching the tomahawk from her, hurting her arm dreadfully. He waved it over his head with a loud cry and she thought he was going to bury it in her skull, but instead, he threw it down the hill from whence she had just come, as though to insult the Indian who was its owner.

Her attacker wore no shirt, only buckskin breeches and an orange breechclout, and she could find nothing to hold on to to try to pull him off her and over the side. In any case, her strength would not have matched his and, in hopeless fury, she balled her hand into a fist and struck him hard on the cheek. He reeled for a moment at the unexpected blow and she was able to roll out from beneath him, her knees brushing against his hip so that she felt the bulk of his hunting knife.

Quicker than thought, she reached down and pulled the deadly knife from its sheath as she rolled away. Like a cat, she was on her feet, her anger and hatred buoying her up, giving her a strength she had never known. The Indian, after the first moment of surprise, had jumped to his feet too and was eyeing her warily now as he circled around her.

Honor was careful not to let him back her toward the hill side of the ledge, for she would be sure to lose her footing and go crashing down to the others who waited below. She kept her eyes on his face, watching instinctively for any change of expression which would signal his moment to spring at her.

God, it would be better to have him kill her like this, she thought despairingly, than to be put to the torture or herded off to God knew where. As the Indian continued to watch her, moving lightly on the balls of his moccasined feet, she felt the throb in her wrist grow to a worse ache until the knife felt as heavy as lead in her hand. How long, she wondered, before his comrades climb up behind me and finish me off for good? But she didn't hear anyone else coming toward her, nor did she see the Indian's eyes flicker upward as though watching for help.

Her breath seemed to sear painfully through her lungs now in the unbearable heat and she could feel, with a part of her, the heat on her head, burning the part in her hair which divided the two braids, which had fallen loose from their pins and were swinging heavily down her back now.

"God! Why don't you do something?" she screamed in desperation at the Indian, who still moved silently from side to side.

The moment finally came, and came swiftly, as Honor felt a drop of sweat roll down from her forehead over her eyelid. She blinked in a reflex response and immediately the Indian sprang, knocking her on her back. Blindly, she struck out with the knife and felt it slide smoothly into something solid. Something warm splashed on her breasts and a few drops wet her face. She opened her eyes and saw the knife sticking in the upper part of his arm, her palm still curled around it. She shuddered in revulsion, but would have pulled it out and struck again, if something hard hadn't come down on her arm and loosened her hold. His fingers squeezed until she cried out in pain, and then she lay panting on the ground beneath him, staring up at him with hate-filled eyes.

He stood up and barked something out to the Indians below. The two scrambled off their horses and hurried up to the ledge. Honor was pulled roughly to her feet and half-dragged back down the incline, the loose rubble pulling both her shoes off and hurting the soles of her feet dreadfully. She noticed

43

dazedly that a group of Indians was watching her warily and that the dead enemy had been heaped into a large pile. She looked frantically for Barbie and located her huddled with the group of women prisoners.

The Indian who had been wounded by her knife thrust was standing in front of her, his dark eyes filled with pain and a grim vigilance. He nodded to one of the others, who pulled out the knife. He wiped it on his leggings and put it back in the sheath at his hip, ignoring the slow trickle of blood that continued to run down his arm and drip slowly to the ground from his fingers.

"I wish I had killed you!" Honor snapped out fiercely, but could say nothing else as he cuffed her smartly on the cheek, her head jerking sideways.

Tears came to her eyes as she saw him nod to one of the braves, who came behind her, pulling her arms cruelly back and tying them with a stout cord that bit into the skin of her wrists. Honor tried to kick at him with her feet, but her action only brought amused guffaws from the others and she merely succeeded in bruising her toes against his hard shins.

The Indian who had tied her hands went back to his pony, and for a moment Honor was free. She ran with a sudden spurt of speed toward the flats. She hardly felt the stones digging into her feet, but she could hear the loud whooping cries of the Indians and the hooves of their ponies. She kept running despite the certainty that at any moment, she would feel cold metal between her shoulder blades.

A pony galloped up alongside her and reared up, preventing her for the moment from going forward. She saw the bloodshot eyes and felt the foam from its flaring nostrils spraying her shoulders. She turned to go the other way and nearly fell between its flying hooves, but was suddenly jerked roughly by her hair, which had fallen free of its pins in a cascading shower.

She was jolted backward, then dropped to the ground on her bound wrists. A stab of agony shot through her wrists that nearly took her breath away and she lay, dazed, struggling to get back to her feet before the pony would trample her to death.

She succeeded in getting to her knees and looked up to see the Indian that she had wounded spring off the pony and come toward her. She waited helplessly for him, knowing she had no more strength with which to fight him. He caught her beneath the arms and hauled her to her feet, the white mask of his face leering crazily at her through the mist of pain that was centered first in her hands, then in her feet, then in her arms. She whimpered softly, against her will, then clenched her teeth.

He pushed her along toward his pony and she stumbled along the ground, her head whirling now with pain and dizziness. To her surprise, she felt his hands at her waist, swinging her onto the broad back of the pony. He leaped up behind her quickly and clasped the reins in his hands, imprisoning her between his arms. She felt his left arm against hers, the blood soaking her sleeve.

He shouted something to the others and each took one of the captives and started their ponies forward. Honor was jolted on the pony's back, helpless to hold herself straight with her wrists tied behind her. She would have fallen off the pony if the Indian had not kept his body so tight against hers. She shied away from his paint-streaked chest and leaned forward, her forehead touching the sweaty mane of the pony.

The sun continued to beat down on the wreck of the wagon train and the bodies of the dead as the vultures circled wearily above, drawing closer to the carrion. Nothing else moved among the wagons.

She must have blacked out against the horse's neck, for the next thing Honor knew it was nightfall and the Indians were slowing their hurried pace. She could hear voices speaking unintelligible words mingled with the voices of the women, crying and weeping with alarm.

A rough hand was thrust into her tangled hair and pulled her back sharply against a hard chest. Honor would have squirmed to get free, but was too tired to care what he did. He seemed content just to hold her body against his, his good arm clamped firmly across her belly while his wounded arm held the reins.

They approached the place where they would camp through a screen of pines. Honor's eyes were beginning to clear again and she scanned the luridly painted faces in the light of a hastily built fire. She bit her lip and attempted to escape the arm of the Indian, but he merely grunted and pulled her closer against him as though afraid she would jump from the pony and run through the thicket of bushes at the far end of the camp.

Honor felt her captor slide quickly to the ground, and then pull her down beside him by one arm so that she staggered

45

against him when her feet touched the ground, causing the pain to flare up once more in her bruised soles. He pulled her toward the fire and she hung back, loath to be set up before the eyes of all the others. His grip was painful and he brought her up sharply, touching her breast and then his own while speaking to the others. His words were swift and the others nodded in agreement. Then he led her away to where a blanket had been spread on the ground. Honor realized that he must have been telling the others that she was his property.

He pushed her to the ground, where she sprawled awkwardly, because of her bound hands. She was able to push herself up to a sitting position and saw that her skirt had been sadly torn and that a large rent from thigh to hem was open now, exposing her leg, covered only by the stuff of her chemise.

The Indian squatted down beside her and drew his knife. She gasped as he brought it close to her and then used it to cut away her chemise from her thigh. For a moment, his hand ran smoothly along the pale flesh all the way up to her hip. She tried to wrench free of his touch and he laughed shortly, then took away his hand and began tearing the cotton into strips. She watched him dully, wondering where Barbie was, as he got up and went to the campfire and returned with a box in his hands as well as a strip of meat and a bowl of some liquid.

He squatted down again and snapped the cord at her wrists with his knife. She cried out as the blood began circulating through her numbed hands again and she rubbed them slowly together until the tingling stopped. He pressed the meat and the bowl into her hands.

For a moment, Honor blinked uncomprehendingly at it, then she looked up and saw his eyes on her. He nodded and she realized that he had brought her supper. She was starving and, without preamble, began to tear the meat with her fingers into smaller pieces. She sipped the contents of the bowl sparingly, feeling the liquid cool and minty in her mouth.

Meanwhile, he had gone back for his own food and sat, cross-legged, opposite her, tearing at the dripping meat with sharp teeth and drinking thirstily from the bowl he had brought for himself. When they were both finished, he took the bowls and laid them next to his blanket.

"Katala!" he said suddenly, pointing to his chest.

Honor shook her head, not understanding. He gazed back at her impatiently and tapped once more on his chest.

"Katala!" He touched his forehead, then drew his finger down his chest to his knees. "Katala!"

She understood then that that must be his name. Well, she'd be branded before she'd tell her name to a savage, she thought angrily.

His finger pointed to her and she shook her head haughtily. His face came closer and he laid a hand on top of her head. She started to shake it again, but quickly, he struck her a light slap on the side of her face. Once more he pointed and she pressed her lips together obstinately, glaring at him with fiery eyes. He seemed amused by her resistance.

He brought his knife out and pressed the point to the edge of her collar at her throat. She sat still, her hands on her knees, and continued to stare at him with hatred. With a slight hiss, he drew the knife down, ripping the buttons from her bodice until the dress came away a little, just to the beginning of her breasts. Quickly, she brought her hand up to clutch at the material.

"You savage!" She spat at him and let go of her dress to claw at his face.

He ducked from her curved fingers and pushed one fist into her stomach so that she fell backward and lay prone on the blanket as he slipped on top of her.

"Get off me! I'll kill you! I'll kill you!" she cried helplessly, but her wild thrashing was slowed as the knife was pressed to the division between her breasts, causing a tiny trickle of blood to well up from the pinpoint in her flesh.

When she still refused to do as he wished, he let out an exclamation of disgust and threw the knife to the side. His hands grabbed at her bodice and would have ripped it to shreds in his sudden fury, but Honor caught at his hands and nodded quickly. She did not want to invite rape, and angering this savage further would probably lead to just that.

She gritted her teeth. "Honor," she said sullenly, glancing away from him.

"Honor," he repeated and his eyes seemed to glow even more threateningly from behind the white mask. He smiled then, as though well pleased at her submission, and Honor felt her anger rekindled.

But, to her surprise, he slipped off her and helped her back to a sitting position. He brought out a small canteen filled with water and shoved it into her hands, then pointed first to the box-shaped clay vessel which he opened to reveal a powdery substance, and then to his wounded arm. Honor understood that he wanted her to tend his wound, and she would have recoiled, but he let his eyes drop deliberately to her torn bodice and she nodded.

She touched his arm gingerly and poured a little of the water over it in order to clean it. He laughed again and pointed to the substance in the box and then to the water. She mixed some of the water with the powder to make a watery paste, then applied it to the wound. He did not show any pain as he watched her.

He pointed to the strips he had torn from her chemise and she bound his arm tightly, tying the bandage securely. She looked up at him and tried to divine the expression in his dark eyes, but he was contemplating her work on his arm with a satisfied look.

Guardedly, she glanced over in the direction of the other captives and saw them still tied, their heads nodding forward while the Indians sat around the fire, talking and smoking aromatic-smelling pipes. She looked back at Katala and shivered, wondering why he had not tied her up with the others.

The Indian warrior pointed to the canteen and Honor took it in order to wash her bleeding feet. With what paste was left, she smeared her feet and bound them tightly with cloth. She looked down at her handiwork with grim amusement. Well, if it meant having some protection for her feet, she was willing to wear anything, no matter how ridiculous. For a moment, she looked up at the Indian and almost smiled.

But then the memory of the hideous massacre reared ugly in her mind and she felt tears gathering in her eyes. It wasn't that the Indians had killed anyone close to her, she thought honestly, but Pearl and Vinny and Randy were all she had left to take care of her. Except for Barbie . . . She glanced over at the captives once again and looked for the brunette tresses and brown eyes of her friend. But it was impossible to make her out from any of the other dirty, tired prisoners. She would try to make contact with her tomorrow, she resolved.

The warrior touched her shoulder and she turned her face away, afraid he might read the fear in her eyes. His fingers caught her chin and turned her face back as he said something in a low voice. She didn't understand what he said, but thought vaguely that he was trying to comfort her. She watched him as he got up to go back to the others. She did not think of escape now. She was too tired and too filled with despair.

She sat on the blanket, clutching her knees within the circle of her arms, and watched the warriors as they continued to smoke and talk both with words and wide gestures, each one obviously reciting his acts of bravery during the attack on the wagon train. Honor saw one of them take out a long piece of rawhide with hair dangling from it. In horror, she realized it must be the scalps he had taken. Her eyes sharpened and her hand went to her mouth as she recognized the bright red strands of hair that hung from the end. Lee Ann! She bit back the cry of bitterness that threatened to escape.

She turned her eyes away, sickened, and tried not to listen to their excited voices. Wearily, she lay down on the blanket. Pillowing her head on her arm, she quickly fell into a troubled and uncomfortable sleep.

Eight

Someone was talking to her, speaking some insane gibberish and shaking her roughly, pulling the warmth of a blanket from her shoulders. Honor opened one eye and found herself staring into the black eyes of the Indian called Katala. Memory came back in a swift tide of anger and misery and she started to roll away from him.

But he would not be ignored and his hand came down swiftly to strip the blanket completely off her, leaving her shivering in the cool, misty dawn. She whirled on him.

"What are you doing now, you crazy savage?" she said, rising quickly to her feet when he came toward her. "Can't you leave me alone?"

He gestured to a screen of bushes toward the outer fringe of the camp and then back to her. Honor flushed at the suggestion, but quickly left him to attend to herself behind the bushes.

When she returned, she could see that the camp had already been broken and the Indians were ready to leave, tying the captives on spare ponies or seating them in front of themselves. Katala cantered over on his pony and caught her arm,

49

easily lifting her in front of him. He signaled the others and they urged their horses swiftly through the pines and out onto the broad plain, where Honor could just see the pinkish-orange of the sun beginning to peek over the horizon.

She wished desperately for a bath, noting the sad state of her frock, which was torn from waistband to hem on one side and from neck to breast at the bodice. It would afford her little protection from flies and mosquitoes, and gazing down at the firm, pale flesh of her thigh, she could see a red bump where some crawling thing had bitten her in the night. She shuddered, wondering how many such insects were lying sleeping in her hair. It tumbled in tangles, many of which were knotted with stray pieces of grass and pine needles. She wondered if these Indians—had someone called them Comanche?—ever bathed and wished there was some way to communicate with Katala. She sniffed experimentally, smelling the odors of bear grease and something else which must be the paint on his face and chest.

Katala rode silently behind her, his arms held tight, bringing her close up against his chest so that she would not try to jump off the pony. She looked down nervously at his brown arm, so dark against the whiteness of her camisole, where it lay beneath her breasts. His fingers curled casually at the side of her left breast while his other arm held the reins firmly as they trailed over her bare thigh.

They rode this way for hours until the sun was quite high in the sky and Honor began to feel as though her throat were made of sandpaper. Her head lolled back on the Indian's shoulder and her face was sunburned from the long day's exposure. Her eyeballs stung behind her eyelids when she closed them and she wondered how the Indians kept on so stoically with no words among them.

Finally, as the afternoon grew longer, the Indians came to a shaded hillside where a small stream ran between large boulders of rock. They stopped to water their ponies and give their captives a rest.

Honor was dragged with the rest of the girls toward the stream, and by means of a sign language, the young women understood they could bathe if they wished. Honor looked at the others and met Barbie's brown eyes.

"Do you think we should?" Barbie asked. "I mean, with those savages watching us?"

Honor sighed wearily. "It hardly matters, I suppose. If they want to rape us, they could have done so before now, and if

50

they mean to do it later, there's nothing to stop them." She looked at the others. "Besides, I've got to wash the—smell from me." She looked down at the blood on her sleeve. It had stiffened and darkened under the sun's rays.

Honor stripped off her gown and stepped into the water until it reached her waist, leaving her chemise on despite her own brave words. Barbie followed her in and the others, after making sure all was safe, did the same.

"I guess good Christian women don't mind talking with us fallen women when the circumstances demand it," Barbie whispered half-jokingly as she and Honor scrubbed at their scalps.

"I don't think they're making any distinctions now," Honor whispered back. "We're all prisoners of the Indians now. I guess that makes us sisters."

"I suppose so," Barbie agreed. Then her voice grew serious. "Did you see what happened to Pearl and Vinny?"

Honor shook her head.

Barbie shuddered. "I really disliked those two, but I have to admit their fate was terrible even for them. I guess the warriors thought them too old—at least Pearl was—but Vinny. Can these savages pick out the women of easy virtue, do you think?"

Her question was half-serious, half-hesitantly curious.

"I don't know if they even know of such things," Honor said. "I wish I could understand their language. I feel so—so defenseless sometimes."

"I know what you mean," Barbie agreed, shivering, "I can't understand that Indian who I ride with when he talks with me—and when he doesn't talk to me, he just stares until I feel naked all over."

"Don't think about it," Honor said firmly. She walked back to the place where she had laid her dress and took it into the stream to rinse out the dust and blood and pine needles.

Barbie stayed close behind and when they were finished, they laid the garments out to dry on a flat shelf of rock and sat down to comb their fingers through their wet hair.

"Your Indian seems to like you," Barbie commented after a moment.

"Good heavens, Barbie, he's not *my* Indian," Honor returned, struggling with a knotted tangle at the back of her hair.

"Well, I mean the one you ride with. I saw you last night when you rode into the camp—the way he let the others know that you were his." She blushed uncomfortably. "I would almost feel better if one of them would do that with me. As it is, I hardly know if I'm considered communal property, or what."

"Don't think I'm anything special to him," Honor said. "Whatever the others decide to do with the rest of us, I'll get the same treatment." She sighed impatiently and finally freed the tangle so that her fingers could comb through her hair smoothly.

The other women had finished bathing and most washed their dresses, although some chose to slip them back on immediately, gazing fearfully to where the Indians had appeared again and were seated close to where the ponies were tethered. Honor did not glance toward them, but laid back to let the sun finish drying her hair. Beside her, Barbie also dozed a little.

They both awakened at the same time, a sense of unease alerting them. Two Indians stood in front of them and Honor recognized one as Katala, despite the absence of war paint on his lean brown face. He gazed first at her hair, dry now and curling in soft honey-colored waves down her back, then at her breasts, the upper slopes of which were revealed by her dry chemise. His eyes traveled lower, seeming to penetrate the muslin of her undergarment.

Self-consciously, Honor pulled the two halves of her chemise together to cover the leg that was exposed. She looked up to see his eyes once again on her breasts and her skin paled beneath the sunburn. After a moment, he reached down for her dress and handed it to her, signing that she should dress quickly.

Barbie, who was also hurrying into her gown, glanced briefly at her. "Maybe—maybe they don't intend to hurt us at all," she whispered. She received a cuff on the chin and understood that she was to keep silent.

Honor struggled into the ripped frock and found her hand taken by Katala so that she was led back to his horse and once again seated astride it. He leaped up in back of her and urged his horse forward.

The Indian band rode more swiftly now, as though they knew that home was not far away. Honor felt the hard ridge of the pony's spine on her backside and knew she would be bruised by morning.

They had climbed to a small plateau and, in the distance, Honor could see campfires lighting the darkening skies. She straightened up to peer into the twilight and heard Katala behind her, saying something to one of the other braves, who immediately kicked his pony forward ahead of the others and rode into the village.

The others slowed their mounts and Honor glanced uneasily over to catch Barbie's eyes in mutual anxiety. They remained just outside the village, which was partially sheltered behind a windbreak of evergreens so that Honor could only see the tops of the tallest teepees. She began to fidget impatiently and felt her hair pulled sharply from behind.

At the same moment, Katala kneed his horse forward at a walk with the others following. Honor kept her attention ahead until they passed the windbreak and could see the entire village, which was surprisingly large.

She could see, in the center of the village, an immensely large teepee covered with various insignia and signs. Spreading outward from it, like the spokes of a giant wheel, avenues of wickiups in varying sizes stood, smoke coming from the vents at the tops.

Katala stopped at the first fringe of teepees and pushed Honor off his pony so that she fell awkwardly to the ground, losing her balance. He shouted an order to her and she knew he wanted her to stand up and walk beside him. She glared up at him and shook her head, so that he kicked at her with his foot. Slowly, she got up and felt him encircling her neck with his lariat. She blushed with shame at the degradation and wondered at this change of mood. Glancing guardedly around, she saw the others were being treated likewise.

The young women were made to walk next to the horses of their captors until they reached the main street of the village. Here, a reception party awaited them and Honor's eyes widened as she perceived an old, gray-haired woman coming toward them, a long pole in her hand from which waved countless scalps. She was walking sedately enough, her toothless gums emitting a loud singsong chant, and behind her, several more women were leaping and shouting, stamping their feet on the earth, and waving their arms toward the sky.

Honor wished desperately that she could turn and run away from this weird procession that was descending rapidly on her. She looked up toward Katala, but he rode upright, tall and proud, his gaze straight ahead as though the singing women hardly concerned him.

The women's singing grew louder and they threw themselves into the dust to bow to the warriors returning home, shrieking welcomes and praises. Honor unconsciously cringed closer to Katala's pony, seeking protection from these crazy, shouting women who had now begun to eye her with considerable interest.

With a few words, Katala turned the lariat that was wrapped around Honor's neck over to the woman carrying the pole, who accepted it graciously, then handed it to another matron who stood behind her. Each of the warriors did the same with their captives. With more shouting and singing, the captives were filed into the village, the ropes around their necks cutting into their skins as they were pulled toward the large teepee in the center. The warriors rode before them and, one by one, they dismounted in front of the teepee and disappeared behind the bearskin that covered the opening.

Honor, standing outside next to Barbie, guessed that this must be the chief's teepee, and wondered if the captives would be ushered inside also, or left to wait in the dark while their fate was probably being decided within. She was tired from the long day's ride and wished she could at least sit down, but a glance from the woman who held her rope told her that she would not be allowed such a commonplace luxury.

The old woman who held the scalp pole shouted to the others and the captives were made to stand in single file while she went down the row as though examining them for a sale. Her eyes lingered on a girl's red hair and she touched it experimentally with crusty fingers.

The old woman moved on and came to the girl who had the glow of the campfire in her hair and the spark of its light in her eyes. Tentatively, she let her finger trace the curve of one cheek. As she expected, the girl frowned.

"You old witch! I'd spit in your face if my mouth weren't so dry!"

Honor was silenced immediately as the old woman struck her a blow on her chin that jerked her face around. The commanding fingers pinched her cheeks to pry open her mouth as the rope was tightened around her neck.

Nevertheless, Honor kicked out at the old woman and caught her fairly on the shin so that she bent over, cursing angrily. Another swift blow and the rope was tightened once again so that Honor wondered if they meant to strangle her. Still, her eyes blazed in her sunburned face and she saw the old woman rub her shin and then straighten up to look once more at her.

54

Her fingers probed the rip in her bodice, feeling the size and texture of her breasts, causing Honor to struggle in helpless fury against the rope. The old woman laughed, pointing to her own flabby breasts, which hung down to her waist below her doeskin dress. Then she pointed to the teepee, laughed again and whispered conspiratorially, "Katala!"

The other women laughed and giggled and nodded their heads. Without more words, the old woman signaled to the others and Honor felt her gown being ripped from her body. She saw Barbie struggling valiantly as her dress was pulled off, as well as the others. The woman gazed curiously at the white chemises and petticoats of the white captives and then nodded her head.

Honor found herself naked except for the bandages on her feet. The Indian women stared, prodding and pressing in their curiosity, giggling among themselves as they examined hair and teeth. Honor endured their curiosity, only hoping they would take them somewhere where they could put on some clothing before the men came out again. She shivered in the deepening darkness.

As though by a prearranged signal the Indian women began separating the captives, each woman taking one of her choice to a teepee. The old woman, laughing a little to herself, caught Honor by the arm and shoved her toward a wickiup that stood not too far from the main teepee.

"Barbie!"

"Honor!"

The two friends looked forlornly at each other, but Barbie's captor pushed her hurriedly into a wickiup and Honor was led to hers.

Once inside the teepee, Honor was impressed at its size. It appeared, though, that the woman lived alone, for there was only one bed of skins in a corner. A small depression in the middle of the earthen floor had a few twigs and branches in it and she assumed it was the firepit to provide warmth for the interior of the lodge.

"I am Magda," the old woman spoke English slowly.

"You can speak English!" Honor moved toward her, then stopped at the cool look the woman bestowed on her.

"You are white woman, prisoner of Katala, son of our chief. You wait here for him—perhaps," she cackled softly.

"Wait for him? To do what? Am I to be—"

"No questions now, white one. You wait."

Magda threw a skin at her which Honor used to drape her

55

nakedness. "Katala have you already, white one?" she asked curiously.

Honor flushed. She shook her head vehemently.

"You not know man yet? Maybe Katala not want you then. He always take woman on trail—never wait. Maybe then you present for Magda. Magda's slave." The old woman seemed pleased at the idea and settled down to smoke contentedly.

Honor watched her warily. Slave? Slave to that strange old woman? "Why would Katala bring me to you as a slave? If he is the son of your chief, why wouldn't he keep me for his own household?"

"Magda not know that word."

"Household—his home. Does he have a wife?"

Magda smiled. "Lianna is mother of Katala's son. She very beautiful, more beautiful than white woman!" She spat into the fire. "Lianna not want white woman in her lodge."

"I'm glad," Honor said fervently. "I don't want to be Katala's woman."

"If he wants you—you will be!"

"But you just said—"

Magda laughed at the girl's confusion. Honor, frustrated by the woman's ambiguity, was silent. Suddenly, a great commotion ensued from outside the wickiup and she jumped to her feet, backing toward the shadows, afraid that Katala was coming for her. Magda did not glance at her, but continued to sit contentedly smoking as though the noise outside did not concern her.

Finally, Honor's curiosity got the best of her and she questioned the old woman tersely. "What is all that noise about?"

Magda continued smoking and Honor was made to wait interminably before she answered, "One of our people has returned to our village." She looked at the girl curiously. "He will come here to receive my welcome."

"He is your son?"

She shook her head. "He is husband to my daughter."

Honor couldn't imagine having the old woman as a mother. But perhaps Indians were different. Certainly her own mother would never have led a procession of dancing, shouting women down Main Street to greet the men of the town.

Suddenly, the bearskin was shoved aside, allowing a tall figure to enter the lodge. Honor looked up in alarm at the intruder, instinctively seeking the shadows of the lodge. She could see very little in the low light cast by the small fire, but she was immediately struck with the masculine strength of this man. She wondered if, perhaps, he was also the son of the chief of this village.

He spoke in the Indian dialect, bowing his head formally, as though asking permission to enter. Magda answered, nodded and signaled for him to sit across from her.

The man, sensing another's presence, raised a question, to which Magda, chuckling a little, answered quickly.

"White one, come out from shadow and present yourself to Devlin," she ordered, a thread of amusement in her words.

Reluctantly, Honor scooted forward on her knees, keeping the skin tight around her with both hands. She kept her head bowed, not wanting this new Indian warrior to become interested in her. Magda's reason for introducing her baffled her a little and she didn't want to be caught in some kind of trap. Why would she care if her son-in-law met her?

"You have a name?"

The voice was deep, authoritative and sent a strange quivering through her. She dared to raise her eyes to cast a furtive glance at the stranger and saw midnight-black hair curling softly against the collar of his buckskin shirt. His face was lean, shadowed in the flickering light, and she could not tell if he was smiling or not, but as he moved forward a little, she gasped at seeing eyes of silvery blue staring back at her. She realized in a flash of intuition that this man was not an Indian! He was white!

"Your name," the voice repeated from lips that had curled a little in an appraising smile.

"Honor—Honor O'Brien," she half-whispered, caught in that silver-blue gaze like a mesmerized rabbit.

Dark brows lifted like sardonic wings as he repeated her name. "Honor O'Brien—an Irishwoman by the sound of it," he laughed. Then he sobered as he assessed the loveliness of his mother-in-law's captive. Honey-gold hair fell in rippling waves down her back and shoulders, framing eyes as green as a cat's and just now narrowing at his effrontery. The oval of her face was tilted upward as her pointed chin stuck out in determination. Her mouth, full and blushed with pink, trembled a little at the corners despite her angry pose.

Brice Devlin had heard of the attack on the wagon train and knew the reason for it. Katala's cousin, Sito, had been killed by one of those foolish scouts who should have known better. Katala had vowed revenge and exacted it quickly. He

57

looked at the girl again. She was young, probably seventeen or eighteen. But he wasn't sure of her position in the village.

"She is your slave, my mother?" he asked Magda in the Indian language.

Magda shook her head. "She belongs to Katala, and yet, I may have whichever woman I wish for my slave, he has said. I would choose her."

Devlin's eyes narrowed. He was sure that Katala had already had his way with the girl on the trail. Perhaps she was no longer interesting to him. If he allowed Magda to keep her, he was sure the girl would not be treated unkindly. He glanced once more at her kneeling figure and knew a moment of intense attraction. He shook himself, thinking that it had been a long time since he had reacted toward a woman so strongly—no, childishly was a better word, he thought. For a moment, he was remembering Annabelle Reeves and his dumbstruck reaction to her beauty and untouchability. He pushed the thought from his mind. This girl was not untouchable. She had probably known men before.

"Go to sleep, white one." Magda's voice disturbed his thoughts and made him aware of the girl's position.

"It is time for me to greet my wife," he said in Comanche. "She has delivered the child?"

Magda shook her head worriedly. "She still holds him within her," she answered, "but perhaps she has only waited for you to return."

He nodded, then bowed once again and left the lodge without another glance at the white girl.

Honor watched him leave and would have liked to question Magda about the man, but kept silent. He was, after all, her son-in-law. The thought of such a man having a wife surprised her—and then she wondered why it should surprise her. Was it because he seemed so hard, so indifferent to her as he had looked at her? She shivered and curled onto the bed of animal skins that Magda had indicated. The noise outside soon dimmed in her ears and she was lulled into sleep.

Nine

Honor awoke with a start the next morning, prodded by a foot in her backside. She looked up to see Magda standing above her.

"Get up, lazy woman," she was saying good-humoredly. "You Magda's slave and will go to stream to fetch water."

Still befuddled by sleep, Honor struggled to get up. The animal skin slipped from her shoulders, reminding her that she was without any clothes. She looked at Magda questioningly. The old woman grunted and threw a shift of tanned doeskin at her which she hurriedly scrambled into.

"Where is the stream?"

Magda mumbled disgustedly and pushed her out the opening of the wickiup into the new morning. "That direction," she pointed, handing her a clay jug.

Confused at her freedom, Honor started walking in the direction Magda had told her, surprised that no one stopped her or asked her what she was doing. Then she realized that they knew she could not escape the village, not having the means to do so, nor the slightest idea which way to run. She sighed and balanced the jug on her shoulder, stepping carefully around other wickiups where Indian women were cooking outside in big iron pots with little interest in the white woman.

Furtively, she looked for Barbie's familiar face. Perhaps whoever she was living with had sent her to the stream also. The thought caused her to walk faster until she reached a small stream shaded by cottonwood trees. A few other women were there, filling jugs and other vessels, but she did not see any of the other white captives.

She lingered at the stream, hoping for sight of her friend until she heard a shirll voice behind her. She looked around to see an Indian woman signing for her to move to allow her access to the stream. She obeyed quickly, exchanging looks of mutual curiosity with the woman. The Indian, however, did not say a word, and so Honor sat for a few more minutes by the stream, hoping for sight of Barbie.

After a time, she became aware of another Indian woman staring at her and turned her head to see a girl of about her own age looking back at her, her belly stretched to the bursting point by her pregnancy. It seemed at any moment that the stuff of her shift would tear down the center. Honor smiled tentatively, but the girl quickly averted her eyes and whispered something to her companion, another young girl who was washing a small child in the stream.

Beside her, the Indian woman who had pushed her aside tapped her on the arm.

"You white woman—you Magda's slave." It was not a question.

Honor nodded uncertainly. It seemed that many of these people spoke her language, although some chose to remain silent. Perhaps the white man called Devlin had taught them English.

The woman laughed almost sarcastically. "You have Spirit of Good with you. You lucky one."

"Lucky!" And then, fearfully, Honor's mind formed a question that she almost dared not say out loud. Licking her suddenly dry lips, she asked, "Where are the others that were brought with me?"

The woman smirked again. "They lay upon their captor's buffalo hides and receive his manroot into their white bodies. Again and again, the warrior will have taken them last night until blood soils their thighs and they moan with their agony."

Her ferocity caused Honor to shiver. "How—how can this be when I have not been abused by the one who captured me? You are lying!"

"I not lie, white one. Katala fight for you in council, for you most valuable—a white woman of courage. Only the greatest of them may enter you." She laughed softly. "But Magda take you for slave. Too late for Katala." She chuckled again as she gathered her things and strode away.

Confused, Honor watched her go. Could she possibly have been telling the truth about the other captives? That would certainly explain why they were not given the freedom that Magda had given her. The thought of Barbie being forced to serve one of those—those savages—nearly nauseated her.

She got to her feet to go and turned too swiftly in the soft mud. With a cry, she fell down, twisting her ankle and spilling the water from the jug.

"You have hurt, white one?" The girl with the bulging stomach had come up beside her in order to help her up.

"I—I think I've twisted my ankle. It's nothing really." She

smiled at the girl, who was holding her arm. "Thank you for your help."

The girl veiled her eyes. "You stay with Magda?"

"Yes."

"Magda is my mother. Mother of Tutalo."

Honor looked at the girl in surprise. This, then, must be the wife of the white man she had met last night. Her eyes widened and brushed away from the stomach bulging with the fruit of their intimacy.

The Indian girl noticed her embarrassment and smiled. "It will be boy," she proclaimed softly. "Devlin has said."

"I—I think I'd best be getting back to your mother's lodge. She will wonder why I have been so long." Honor hurried on, wishing to get away from the girl in case the man called Devlin should come up. She waved shyly to Tutalo and her companion, then sped up the incline.

Back at the village, she noticed several ponies tethered near the lodge of the chief and wondered if Indians visited back and forth between villages as she and her mother used to visit between plantations. The idea seemed alien to this new, savage land she had encountered. She quickened her pace when she saw Magda outside her teepee, placing an iron pot over the outside cookfire.

"You take too long," was the old woman's grumble as she took the water jug away from the girl. "You watch food now."

Honor sat down, cross-legged, as she had seen the other Indian women do, and leaned over to stir the contents of the pot. It looked to be some kind of stew with pieces of meat mixed with peas, corn and turnips. After an hour of watching it boil steadily, she looked up to see the visitors coming out of the chief's lodge. Curious, she sat back on her haunches and watched.

Four warriors, painted with bright red and yellow bands on their faces and chests, were still conversing with the Indian whom she remembered as Katala and an older man who, she assumed, must be his father, the chief. The chief was dressed in tanned buckskin leggings and a bright pink shirt, sewn crudely with various insignia. She wondered for a moment where he got the shirt and then remembered the wagon train attack and no longer wondered. His hair was graying, long and kept back from his forehead with a stitched band of rawhide. He seemed in late middle age and she tried to

61

remember the name Magda had called him. Appina—that was it.

Her attention was once more on the four warriors as they indicated six of their ponies. A young boy was called who took the six ponies away. Appina shouted a command and an Indian woman appeared at the entrance to a nearby teepee, holding the hand of one of the white captives. Honor did not know her, but shuddered at the smudged eyes, the tangled hair and ripped shift which she must have hurriedly donned. The four warriors took turns examining the girl, then one of them nodded and she was set docilely on one of their remaining ponies. Another order from Appina and Honor watched as another white captive was brought out. Her breath escaped her in one huge rush. It was Barbie, her brunette hair hanging limply in her eyes, her body bent inward as though still aching from the night's abuse. Honor stood up in an involuntary action to go to her, but was stopped abruptly by Magda's crusty fingers on her arm.

"That girl is my friend," Honor protested.

"She is sold to Pawnee warriors for ponies," Magda said expressionlessly.

"No!"

Honor broke free from Magda's hold and rushed toward the hunting party, which had mounted their ponies with their two captives and was preparing to ride away.

"Barbie!"

The girl turned and saw Honor, and her face with its ringed eyes, looked haunted. "Honor," she wailed pitifully, "they're taking me away!"

"No, Barbie, no!" Honor cried. She would have thrown herself at the departing horses, but strong arms suddenly caught her to a hard chest.

She was pressed effectively against a man's body, struggling futilely as Barbie was taken away. Her cries tore at her throat. They couldn't have sold her only friend! They couldn't! She kicked backward at the legs of the man who held her, furious as his hands closed over her breasts.

"Let me go! Let me go! I must go after her!" she cried out.

"She has been sold to the Pawnee warriors, Honor O'Brien," came the deep, masculine voice that somehow managed to convey that odd sense of intimacy even at such a moment. "You can do nothing."

"She was my friend," she cried, tears rising to spill down her cheeks. "They couldn't do such a horrible thing!" She was crying in earnest now, not caring that Katala and his father, Appina, were watching her with disgust now.

"Quiet, Honor. It's no use. Go back to Magda." The arms loosened a little and she slipped away from him, turning on him furiously.

"Get away from me, you monster! How could you let them take a woman of your own race and treat her like—like a piece of merchandise! You're horrible, worse than any of them because you have known civilization!" She was breathing deeply, her green eyes flashing as they met the silver-blue ones without flinching.

His look was sardonic, insolent, as he watched her with an enigmatic smile. "You'd better go back to Magda's lodge, Honor, before someone decides *you'd* best be traded for a few ponies." His eyes slid appraisingly over her, missing nothing, causing a blush to suffuse her cheeks. "I wouldn't mind you warming my bed this winter."

"Oh!" Before she thought about the consequences, her hand shot up and slapped him hard on the cheek.

Immediately the offending hand was held in a viselike grip that made her gasp in pain. The look on his face was stormy, but there was a spark in those silver-blue eyes that was something else—anger, amusement, desire? He seemed to recover himself swiftly, though, and released her hand. With a mocking bow, he sauntered away from her.

Left standing alone in the open space, Honor was suddenly aware of the eyes that had been watching her. She caught Katala's look, smoldering with passion, and was sickened. The women were watching her with open curiosity as though she were some freak, or sick. Defiantly, she wiped the tears from her eyes and went back to Magda's lodge, stirring the stew with swift anger.

"White one acts without thought," Magda murmured, her fingers busily lighting a pipe in order to sit near Honor and smoke.

"That girl was my friend," she explained, and the thought once more brought tears to her eyes.

The old woman shrugged. "Pawnee warrior will treat her like Comanche," she said thoughtfully.

"You mean, she will be forced to—" Honor shivered, then turned to the old woman.

"Why have I been the only one to come as a slave to one of the women?"

Magda laughed. "Because Magda wanted you for slave.

Other women will wait for their warriors to finish with the white ones. It is the same thing." She eyed the girl knowingly. "You would not take friend's place?"

Honor blushed. "I—I am glad you let me stay with you, Magda," she said.

"Katala still look at you with eyes of lover," Magda pointed out. "If he wants you—he will find way to have you."

Honor quickly changed the subject, not feeling brave enough to challenge her claim. "I have met your daughter, Tutalo, at the stream this morning."

Magda nodded. "She is heavy with child." She frowned.

"You are worried about her?"

"Tutalo not strong, no flesh on her bones. Baby too big."

Honor looked sharply at the woman. "You don't think she will have trouble with the birthing, Magda, do you? Don't you people have any doctors?"

Magda shook her head. "The spirit will decide. Our shaman will help her."

"Shaman?"

"Medicine chief, very powerful man," Magda explained. Then she closed her eyes and leaned back against one of the lodge poles. "Enough talk."

Honor silently stirred the stew. From the sound of Magda's words, Tutalo would not have an easy birthing. The girl looked huge already and still the baby was not born. Honor remembered when the wife of one of the planters in Charleston had been pregnant and the physician had said she was too small to birth the baby. The woman had died.

"Your daughter's husband," Honor began uncertainly, feeling the blush on her face deepen. "He is white . . ."

Magda roused herself from her doze. "Yes, Devlin is white."

"How did he come to marry your daughter? How did he come to live among the Comanche? Is he—is he wanted by the law?"

Magda crooked an eyebrow at the girl. "White one talks too much. Devlin does not belong to you." Then she closed her eyes again.

Ten

Honor had been with the Comanche for almost a full month. She reckoned that it must be near the end of August, for the days were beginning to cool off a little bit, although the heat was still intense. She had learned many things among the Comanche, most of them from Magda, who had become her teacher in the ways of the Indians. The horror of the wagon train attack had receded into the back of Honor's mind and she had begun to look upon the Comanche as human beings like herself. Even the thought of Barbie's fate had been pushed resolutely away for the moment. She knew she would go mad thinking about her. She could only pray that she was being treated as well as she herself was.

The thought of escape, despite her peaceful surroundings, was still uppermost in her mind. And she constantly observed the ways of the Indians and asked Magda questions. She had even learned a little Comanche, though the language did not come readily to her. She had made no friends in the village, although she saw Tutalo at the stream often, usually with her companion, Lianna, the wife of Katala. Lianna was not adverse to speaking to the white girl, but as the wife of the future chief she was not sure if it would be proper, and so her reticence passed itself on to Tutalo, who had still not been delivered of the child.

Each day, when Honor went to the stream, she felt sure that Tutalo would not be there, but each day, she was and Honor marveled that her belly hadn't burst. Devlin—his first name was Brice, she had learned—had left on one of his little trips, trading and learning the news beyond the Indian village. He would be back today.

Honor had thought about Brice Devlin often during the month, wondering about his reason for being here in the village with an Indian girl for a wife. Had he been cast out of his home for some dire reason? Was he, indeed, a criminal, a fugitive from justice? What crime had he committed? She shivered at the thought of those steely blue eyes watching her over the barrel of a gun, or those long-fingered brown hands closing about her throat to strangle her. Could he truly be a murderer?

She had caught heself more than once thinking about him in quiet moments when she was stirring the dinner in the iron pot, or helping Magda sew animal skins together for new shifts. It must be because he is white like myself, she told herself. She would deliberately recall his coldness when Barbie had been sold to the Pawnee warriors and remind herself that he was not to be trusted at any rate. Although—and here was what intrigued her most—he had the ability to come and go as he pleased. He would be the perfect person to aid her in her attempt to escape—if she could somehow persuade him to help her.

She was seated Indian fashion in front of Magda's lodge sewing a garment when she heard the welcome party go out to see Devlin's arrival. He had several packhorses with him, heavily laden with articles which the avid eyes of the women hoped would be jewelry or trinkets for themselves.

Carefully, she continued sewing, stitching with deer bone and sinew the scraped skins that she had softened as smooth as butter with hours of work. She realized that she was glad she had worn a clean, whitened deerskin tunic with long fringes at sleeves and hem, cinched at the waist with a bright yellow sash that Magda had no longer wanted. Her hair was parted in the middle and braided into two thick honey-colored plaits and around her head was a band of stitched cloth which she used, Indian fashion, to keep the hair from her forehead. She hoped that she looked pretty and then wondered at the thought.

It was not long before she heard him walking toward her, on his way to greet his revered mother-in-law as she knew he would. Son-in-laws hardly ever spoke to the wife's mother unless it was to greet her formally after being away on a hunt or raiding party. The etiquette of the Comanche seemed strange to Honor, but she had long ago stopped questioning it.

Honor could see his dusty black boots in front of her now and, hesitantly, she raised her eyes, feeling suddenly shy as though she had just been introduced to a distant cousin in a crowded ballroom.

"Hello, Honor."

She met his silver-blue gaze with her own and smiled softly. "Hello, Brice." She blushed at using his first name, as no one else in the village seemed to do so.

Looking down at the exquisite girl at his feet, Brice Devlin felt something move him strongly. He had bent over a little as though to reach down for her and draw her up against him. God, he hadn't realized she had gotten under his skin so well. Quickly he pushed his thumbs into his belt.

"You are well?" she was asking shyly, her green eyes wide and soft in her sun-browned face. The sprinkling of freckles across the bridge of her nose made her seem vulnerable, even younger than she was.

He gritted his teeth against the unfamiliar feeling. "Yes," he answered shortly and passed her quickly to go into Magda's lodge and greet her.

Put out by his curt tone and lack of courtesy, Honor jabbed the bone into the deerskin and succeeded in cutting her finger. She was sucking it gingerly when Devlin came out of the lodge. As she looked up, she caught him regarding her with an enigmatic look. A plan slowly evolved in her mind. Perhaps she might persuade this arrogant man to help her escape, she thought, by playing on his masculine pride. Instinctively she sensed he was attracted to her.

Testing this new plan, she fluttered her lashes up at him and ruefully showed him the wounded finger. "You made me so angry that I jabbed the needle in my skin," she accused softly. She tried to remember how she used to flirt with the young men in Charleston, but it seemed so long ago. Besides, she wasn't sure this man would respond to the simpering gestures of her adolescence.

He smiled and the silver-blue eyes suddenly flamed a little as though he already knew her little game and was willing to play along. "I'm sorry, Honor. I didn't mean to make you angry," he returned, squatting down beside her.

He captured her hand in his and Honor felt the pulse leap to her throat. His slender brown fingers on her flesh sent a shudder through her and she valiantly attempted to keep the blush from staining her cheeks.

"I don't think it's serious," he said in a teasing voice, his hand still imprisoning her own. "No emergency care required."

The expression in his eyes was a kind of waiting and Honor was suddenly at a loss. He seemed to be expecting something from her. She was unsure exactly what she should do.

"It was—silly of me," she offered tentatively. "I suppose—I was glad to see you again and I had hoped for a warmer greeting."

The expression changed, the blue deepening his eyes and the mouth curving into a lazy grin. "I would be most happy to oblige you," he said in a low voice. "My warmest greetings could be conveyed more easily down by the stream—say an hour after sundown?" The challenge was clear in his tone.

Honor dared not look at him, for fear he would read her intentions in her face. Silently she nodded, hoping he would take her attitude for feminine embarrassment.

Laughing softly to himself, he released her hand and stood up. "I'll be expecting you, Honor."

She watched him go and felt her heart throbbing in her breast. Did he guess at her intentions, she wondered. What would he say when she asked him to help her escape? He must help her! He must! She would do anything to get away from this village!

She had been fidgeting in the lodge for fifteen minutes when Magda asked her sharply what was the matter.

"I'm not feeling well," Honor explained quickly. "I think I'd better go outside."

The old woman looked at her suspiciously. "You not look sick to Magda," she pointed out.

"I—I feel hot and I think my monthly cycle is close upon me," Honor improvised hurriedly. "May I go, Magda?"

The woman gazed at her thoughtfully and then her mouth split into a knowing smile. "You need man, white one—a man will quench the fire of fever in you."

Her words would normally have caused a sharp retort from Honor, but tonight she was desperate and she merely nodded. Finally, with an exclamation of disdain, Magda waved her out while she lit up her pipe in preparation for a long, thoughtful smoke. She was worried about Tutalo and really couldn't be bothered with the white girl's problems just now.

Gratefully Honor left the lodge and hurried toward the stream, hoping to encounter no one on the way. Luck was with her as she approached the stream and called out softly, "Brice, are you here?"

She walked along the bank hesitantly, wondering if, after all, he had decided not to come. She had walked upstream along a line of river birch when a warm hand caught hers and jerked her around quickly.

"So, you've come," he said shortly.

"Yes," she whispered, trembling nervously at his nearness and their solitude. She knew he must feel her trembling as he held her arm tightly now.

68

He pulled her along behind a screen of juniper bushes, pushing her down to the ground and then folding his long legs to sit beside her.

"I'm wondering exactly why you wanted to meet me—why you agreed," he began, leaning toward her, his voice as intimate as though he had caressed her.

Frantically she sought to clear her throat, which seemed as though it had been glued shut. "I—I wanted to come—to talk with you, Brice," she got out finally in a hushed voice. Perspiration seemed to pop out on her forehead and her palms were damp as she rubbed them against the material of her tunic.

"I'm waiting," he replied, and he was so close to her that his breath fanned her cheek.

"Brice, I—I came west on the wagon train because—because I was kidnapped by a woman named Pearl and her two accomplices," she began. "Pearl was a woman who ran—a—house of . . ." She stopped, sensing that he was losing his interest in her story. Then, determinedly, she went on. "Pearl was the owner of a brothel in St. Louis and was run out of the city. She wanted to set up a new house in California and had kidnapped me and two other girls . . ."

"Kidnapped?"

"Well, she—drugged me in her hotel room after my brother left me to . . ."

"Honor," he said, catching her arm to pull her even closer to him, "I'm not interested in what you're trying to tell me." His other arm was suddenly around her shoulders and his mouth was almost touching her own. "I'm interested in only one thing right now."

His mouth brushed hers softly at first, then harder until its force was causing her lips to smash up against her teeth. Honor tried to pull out of his arms, straining backward against his strength. He let her go, and she sat for a moment catching her breath, avoiding his eyes.

"What game are you playing, Honor?" he wondered, watching her attempt to regain her composure. His voice was deceptively silky and Honor took heart.

"Brice, you must know that I cannot stay here in this village much longer. I must get back to my own people. I'm a stranger here."

He considered her reasoning, cocking his head to one side as he regarded her thoughtfully. "And you had hoped to enlist my aid in making your escape?"

Fearfully she nodded, all deception gone as her eyes beseeched him in the gathering darkness. If he would not help her, she would never be able to get away on her own.

"That's asking a lot, Honor," he went on slowly, toying with her.

"I—I'd be willing to pay," she breathed.

His smile was positively wicked. "Give me a kiss, Honor, and I'll think about it."

She hesitated, but realized that if she did not comply, he would most likely get up and leave her. Grasping at the one straw left to her, she leaned toward him, closing her eyes and pursing her lips much as a child would do before kissing her parents good night.

Brice had to smile at the innocent gesture, but his arms went around her once more and gathered her against him, as his lips came down on hers with swift purpose. His kiss was deep, demanding. He would have no half-measure this time and he felt her resistance as his mouth opened her lips. She would have struggled out of his arms once more, but he held her fast, bending her backward toward the ground until she lay prone, his body resting on hers. The trembling in the flesh beneath his told him clearly that her nervousness was increasing. He released her mouth and nuzzled her ear.

"That was better, Honor," he murmured. "Now just exactly what was it you wanted me to do for you?"

His face was too close to hers and Honor found herself unable to think about escape. She desperately wished he would let her up, but he was resting on his elbows now as he watched her, bending down to plant small kisses on her face and ears.

"You have the freedom to come and go as you please," she began all at once. "You could leave on a journey and take me with you."

He looked in mocking surprise at her earnest expression. "That is your plan? That I leave the village with you riding one of my packhorses behind me?"

"Well—I know that you would have to think of an explanation—I mean Katala would—"

"Katala would never let me do it," he interrupted. His frown worried her. "Katala has been watching you this last month and his desire has grown day by day. He would never let you leave his sight."

"What do you mean? He has a wife and child. He cannot

70

think that I would wish to go to him," she protested vehemently.

He laughed tersely. "Honor, you're too much an innocent. If Katala wants to bed with you, he will find a way."

"Oh, you sound like Magda now," she accused, putting her hands on his chest to push him off. "Let me up—you're no help!"

He continued to lie atop her. "Don't be in such a hurry to leave me, Honor," he said lazily. "There *may* be a way to effect an escape . . ."

She stopped struggling to look up at him eagerly. "Then you will help me?"

For a moment, he wavered in the light of her complete innocence, but the feel of her body beneath him waved his stab of conscience aside. "I'll have to think about a way," he hedged. "But you said you would be willing to pay."

She nodded. "Of course, I have nothing now, but when you help to get me away, I will—"

His lips came down to silence her as his hands discovered the buckskin ties at the neck of her tunic. Deftly he untied them, pushing aside the material so that his hand could slip inside to caress one firm, young breast. Her body stiffened, but the feel of her soft, fragrant flesh made him oblivious to her outrage.

With quick determination, she caught his lower lip between her teeth and bit hard, drawing blood.

"Damn!" He took his mouth from hers and stared angrily down at her.

"How dare you!" she hissed, suddenly a raging wildcat. "You have no right to touch me as you did. Now, let me alone!"

"No right! Why, honey, I thought being alone here in the dark with you gave me every right. Why else did you come?" He was trying to keep his anger in check, but he would have had infinite pleasure in shaking her into submission.

"I came for—" She stopped and began to beat on his chest with her fists. "It doesn't matter. You're not going to help me now!"

He caught her hands in his and brought his face close to her own. "Listen, baby, you came down here because you wanted to be with me. You were willing to let me kiss you if you could use me for your own end. But when the situation got out of your control, you turn into an outraged virgin!

71

Don't tell me that Katala hasn't already enjoyed you on the trail!"

"That's a lie!" she cried out. "He never—"

"Don't bother," he interrupted ruthlessly. "Dammit, you've come here willing to pay the price for my help. Now you'll pay it with or without your consent!"

He brought her hands above her head and held them with one of his own while he tore at the tunic with his free hand. She was struggling silently beneath him, twisting her body to avoid his encroaching hand, but he finally succeeded in pushing the garment up to her neck, leaving her body naked to his gaze.

He whistled softly and, releasing her hands for a moment, he reached down and drew the tunic above her head and threw it to the side. She slapped him on the cheek and tried to rake the nails of her other hand across his face, but he caught them again, grinning ruefully.

"Any more of that, baby, and you'll find yourself getting repaid in kind," he warned.

"I don't care. You've proven you're a brute, more so than the savages you live with! Is that why you remain here instead of in your own civilization? Did they throw you out because you weren't fit to live with decent people!"

She saw his face tighten, the mouth hardening to a thin line. She could not see the color of his eyes in the darkness, but she quailed at the expression on his face. Had she gone too far? If he was a murderer, would he kill her now?

"Honey," he said in a hard voice, "you've just reminded me of things I don't like to remember. Now, you'll pay for your stupid upper-class snobbery with a little taste of lower-class brutality!"

He swept her body with ungentle hands, causing her to cringe at his boldness. No part of her body was safe from his exploration and she could only turn her head from side to side in protest at his actions. He grasped her breasts, cupped them in his palms as he circled the tips with his thumbs.

She shrank from his lips as they nibbled her neck, then went lower to her bosom, where they sucked at the flesh that he was offering with his hands. Tears slowly dripped down the sides of Honor's face as she endured his humiliation of her. Please, please, just let him finish and leave me alone, she thought desperately.

His hands were rough as they slid down her ribs to her hips, grasping them strongly as he pulled them toward himself. With a sudden shock, she realized that he was pressing his own nakedness against her flesh, even while his mouth captured her nipples and continued to torture them with his teeth and tongue.

"Please, stop," she sobbed in sheer panic. "Please don't do this to me!"

The pitiful words jarred him deeply, softening the sexual brutality that had engulfed him before. But he couldn't stop now. He wanted her too much to let her go. He was aching to feel the soft, warm flesh pressed in the most intimate caress. He opened her legs, slipping his hands between her thighs to caress her.

Honor jumped beneath him and thought she would die of shame as his fingers sought her most intimate places. Something subtle had happened, although she could not be sure she had felt anything beyond the barrier of her deep humiliation. Still, as his hands caressed and his mouth softly kissed her stiffened breasts she felt a softening somewhere, a warmth and lightness that responded to his touch.

"Don't," she whimpered breathlessly, bringing her hands down to clasp his own.

"Let me go, Honor," he whispered back.

She sobbed and released his hands, then felt them on her thighs, pushing them out. He bent his head to kiss her trembling belly, then dipped lower to help prepare her for his entrance.

"Brice, please," she whispered one last time, knowing already her plea was futile. "This should have been my fiancé," she ended to herself.

He heard her plea and wondered if, perhaps, she had been telling the truth. Perhaps Katala had not had her on the trail. He smiled to himself—he would know soon enough.

He knelt on the sandy soil and pulled her legs around his waist, feeling her warm wetness pressed against his own throbbing hardness. Gently, he leaned forward over her, propping his weight on his hands as he thrust into her.

Honor's breath caught in her throat. She had no idea what he was doing to her. Something hot and rigid was pushing between her legs, trying to get past a barrier within her that held it back. She wished she could see what he was doing, but his face was above hers and she closed her eyes as he leaned down to kiss her deeply. The kiss, his tongue twisting against her own, his chest pressed to her breasts, made a tingling in her belly that seemed to be answered by his thrusting.

73

Thoughts flew from her mind as she concentrated on these new sensations in her body.

A warm feeling of well-being washed over her, so that she wriggled her hips upward to meet him. A slight pressure, uncomfortable, was building somewhere within her and she wished it was gone so that she could enjoy this new delight, but it persisted until, finally, something burst inside and she would have cried out in bewildered pain had his lips not crushed hers so completely. She could feel him deep within her now and the panic threatened to come back. She struggled a little, but he kept her firmly clamped to the ground while he continued his strokes until the ache lessened considerably.

Her arms, which had been lying at her sides, came up now to encircle his neck and her thighs grasped him tightly around the waist. He was whispering words in her ear between kisses, sexual words, hot and intimate, that shocked her even as their utterance drove her wildly against him. He continued his movements, listening to the soft keening of her voice deep in her throat.

A new sensation was sending tingling fingers of wild abandonment through her entire body, as Honor felt his strokes coming faster and faster. He seemed to be in the grip of some deep emotion, as his eyes closed and he buried his face in her neck. Honor herself moaned deeply and felt herself being uplifted, her body flung to the sky as rockets burst inside of her.

Afterward, as their breathing returned to normal, she placed a tentative hand on his damp hair. The expression on his face was fulfillment mixed with a curious look of wonderment, as though he was not quite sure of the outcome of what had just happened between them, or as though he was fighting within himself as to whether to allow himself to trust her.

"Brice, I—"

"Hush, honey," he said softly, kissing her eyes and cheeks.

"Brice, was I—did I make you happy?" she asked tentatively, realizing that she hoped she had conveyed something of her own ecstasy to him.

He smiled indulgently, but his expression was suddenly tender. There was no need to say anything and he felt, suddenly, as though there had been a great weight lifted from him. Annabelle Reeves was gone forever. He felt a strange and alien need to protect this girl.

He slipped off her and clasped her hand to help her sit up. He was aware of her embarrassment at her own nudity and he handed her the tunic to cover herself. He knew that she cast covert glances at him through her lashes as he buttoned his trousers and shirt. Ah, there would be more time for experimentation with her, he thought with relish. She had been a virgin, had given him her priceless possession and he would cherish that gift. Gently, he pulled twigs from the thick braids that swung against her shoulders.

"Brice," she began uncertainly, her face turned up to his. "Brice, is it possible—could I be falling in love with you?" she wondered. She waited trustingly for his answer.

The word grated on his newfound peace and he realized that he could not honestly say that he had fallen in love with her. Because of his own mixed feelings, he did not want her to cling to him. Her love could wrap itself around him so tightly that he would feel trapped. He realized that he had been free too long for commitments. He looked at her warily.

"Honor, this—thing—between us. It just happened. We were together and I wanted you—and you wanted me. Let that be enough for now."

He helped her to her feet and brushed dirt from her dress. Clasping her hand, he walked with her back to the camp, keeping his thoughts on anything but her downcast face. A little way from Magda's lodge, he released her and she turned steadily toward him.

"I do love you, Brice," she whispered softly, then turned and walked quickly to the lodge, disappearing inside, leaving him to grit his teeth in perplexity.

Eleven

Honor saw little of Brice for the next three mornings afterward. She was hurt at what she thought was his deliberate avoidance of her. Things had looked different in the light of the next day and she found herself needing reassurance from him that what she had done had been the right thing. As there was no reassurance forthcoming, she found herself beginning to blame him for her seduction. And worse, she had been unable to exact a promise from him to help her escape.

She went about the routine of each day with hard purpose, trying to drive thoughts of Brice Devlin out of her mind. That she had given herself to him—a stranger—was bad enough to make her pound her fist with embarrassment, but that she had told him she loved him! She could imagine him smirking at the admission. Was it one of many that a silly lovestruck girl might have made? Her thoughts were torture to her, but they continued in her mind until she had worked up a righteous hatred of Brice Devlin and vowed that he would never touch her again!

Finally, one morning Lianna came running to the lodge, her face revealing her concern. "Magda! Tutalo has begun to deliver the baby!" she cried.

Honor rushed out with Magda, intent on helping Tutalo in any way she could. The fact that she had made love with her husband added to her guilt feelings and she wanted to make amends to the unknowing, wronged wife. Deep inside, she wanted to see Brice Devlin, too, despite her own protestations.

"You stay!" Magda commanded, pushing Honor back when she would have followed the old woman.

"But I might be able to help," she protested.

"You stay!" Magda repeated and hurried off after Lianna to the lodge of Tutalo.

Honor gnawed her lower lip and sat down to wait. She knew that Magda was worried about her daughter. The baby must be very large from the size of Tutalo's belly, and Tutalo herself was delicately thin. Even in Charleston, such a pregnancy would cause concern among the physicians. Honor could only pray that Tutalo would be delivered safely.

Restless, she fussed with the fringe on her sleeves, not knowing how long she would have to wait for news. It took hours sometimes, she knew, but she had never really been interested in such things before and she wondered now just how long it would be.

She sensed a presence behind her and whirled around quickly, half-hoping it was Brice. But to her disappointment, it was Katala and she veiled her expression quickly. He came toward her on light feet, his look predatory. She knew now that he understood and spoke English and she waited for him to speak.

"White one thinks of someone else?" he questioned softly.

She shook her head. "You startled me. I—I was nervous thinking of Tutalo and her baby. I want to go to help her, but—"

76

"White one not belong with woman of he who has pierced her." Katala spoke sharply now.

Honor turned white and gazed at him in fright. He knew that Brice and she had been at the stream. Had he been there, watching them? Her paleness changed to a red flush as she refused to answer him.

"Katala take white one now," he said, moving closer.

She backed away, her arms stretched out to ward him off. But he was the chief's son, she reminded herself, and even Magda had said that he could take her if he wished.

"Please do not take me away from Magda," she pleaded as his hands encircled her wrists.

He smiled crookedly. "Katala has talked with shaman. You bad medicine for Devlin. You belong with Katala!"

"No, I don't belong to anybody!" she cried out, feeling him draw her closer against his chest. His black eyes were looking down at her possessively.

"You will come with Katala!" he ordered again and began to drag her toward his own lodge.

Protesting, struggling to get free, Honor glanced at Tutalo's lodge and her eyes locked with silvery blue ones that were regarding her with an expression she couldn't divine. Her eyes sent out a mute appeal, but the answering look was one of almost brutal command. He was telling her to go with Katala, she thought. He didn't care that another man was going to do to her what he had done only three nights ago. She wanted to weep and strike out at him, but, with an extraordinary effort, she was able to control herself and follow Katala to his lodge. She thought she saw relief in Devlin's eyes.

Inside Katala's lodge, she looked around for sight of Lianna or the boy. She remembered that Lianna, of course, would be with Tutalo assisting her in the birth and the boy was probably outside somewhere playing. She was completely alone with this Indian who was watching her grimly as though determined to overcome any resistance she might put up.

"Magda will return," she said, licking dry lips. "She will wonder—"

"She will not wonder," he said.

"I—I cannot stay." she cried, wringing her hands now, hardly prepared to give herself to this man as he so obviously expected.

"You have fear of Katala?" His question was half-amused, half-serious.

"Yes—no!" She shook her head at her own indecision. "Yes," she admitted softly, then turned her eyes up swiftly as he came nearer.

"Do not be afraid, white one. I have not hurt you."

"But you—you," she blushed with embarrassment. "You will treat me without dignity."

He laughed. "Katala wants you in the way that any man would want such a woman for his own. I will not act cruelly toward you—I am only cruel to my enemies." He had moved close enough to touch her and his words sounded somehow like a threat.

"I am great warrior of the Comanche. When Appina dies, Katala will become next chief. There is honor in giving yourself to me, white one."

"What honor, when you will cast me aside soon enough so that another man of your village will come for me as you have come," she protested. "You talk of honor! My very name holds such promise, but already I have been dishonored by the man you call Devlin!" Her words were angry now and she stood up to gaze fiercely at him. "In my world, there is no honor without marriage!"

"Marriage?" He considered for a moment. "If you prove worthy, you may be wife to me, little one." He seemed pleased at the solution.

"But you are already married," she said.

"Comanche chief allowed many wives," he proclaimed.

"No!"

Her word hung between them for many minutes. They glared at each other, then Katala shrugged and regained his composure.

"Katala goes now to talk with Appina. You will stay here, white one." He left the lodge abruptly as though afraid to remain longer with her.

The whole experience had happened so quickly that Honor was not sure what was expected of her. She stepped outside and was flustered at seeing Devlin coming toward her.

"Why are you here?" she demanded angrily, feeling as though he had deserted her earlier.

She could feel his shrug. "I wanted to explain something to you, Honor. You must do as Katala says. He could have you tortured, branded and—"

"He knows that you—that you—seduced me at the stream," she said hurriedly, her eyes dancing away from his gaze. "Because of this, he thinks I am anyone's property."

78

She missed the fleeting look of regret hovering in his eyes. "Don't be a fool, Honor. Katala will protect you from the other men of the village . . ."

"I don't want Katala's protection," she snapped back angrily. "I only want to be gone from this place. When I think of what a silly fool I was with you—"

His expression hardened and he regarded her insolently. "I almost forgot, you did give yourself to me for a price, didn't you, Honor?" His words were cutting. "I seem to recall that in your 'civilization' as you called it, women that did such things were called whores."

"Oh! How can you? How can you dare to say such a thing when you know that I—" She stopped and collected her self-control. "Go away," she said steadily. "Why did you come?"

"Well, I'm left without a woman to keep me company tonight," he said, deliberately intimating her availability.

"Don't look to me," she returned haughtily.

He laughed. "God, what I wouldn't give to be able to throw you on your backside and show you what rape really is. You remind me of a girl I knew a long time ago in Savannah."

"Savannah? What a liar you are! You've never been east of this godforsaken country in your life!" she returned.

He was silent, as though regretting his previous divulgence.

"If you're really from Savannah, how did you get out here, mixed up with these savages?" she pressed him.

"Never mind, Honor. I think Katala will be back soon. I'd best leave you two alone."

"Don't you care what might be happening to Tutalo?" she asked him sarcastically, not willing to let him leave without a parting shot.

"Go inside," he said, ignoring her question, "before I forget that you're Katala's woman now."

She wanted to retort something suitably scathing, but could not think of anything quickly enough before he had slipped away. She sat down on the ground sulkily, waiting to hear news from Magda or Lianna.

The hours dragged slowly by and still she did not hear a baby's cry. The sun beat down as she stared at Tutalo's lodge, willing the baby to be born. Soon the sun had dipped below the horizon and twilight had settled on the village. She heard footsteps coming toward her and saw Katala watching her expectantly. He caught her hand and pulled her up to bring her into his lodge.

Honor trembled at his touch, then drew away to stand beside the bed of animal skins. Please, she thought, please leave me alone. Please go away.

But he was not going away. He was undressing quickly, signing for her to do the same. She would have protested, but she recalled Devlin's warning to do as Katala wished or a worse fate might await her. Reluctantly she drew the doeskin over her head and sat down to cover herself with skins.

Katala was beside her in a moment, pushing her down, positioning her without preamble. She bit her lip to keep back the cry as his turgid organ pushed through her flesh without tenderness. His hands, holding her arms above the elbow, dug deeper as his pleasure increased. His long hair brushed her breasts, but he did not caress them with his fingers and so there was no moistness within her to lighten the pain. Despite her resolutions, she could not stop the single cry that escaped her.

Outside, standing, smoking outside his own lodge, Brice Devlin heard her scream and his white teeth ground down hard on the cheroot.

Twelve

The next morning, Honor awoke to terrible cramps in her belly and she rolled fitfully from Katala's arm to stand up on shaky legs. Immediately a trickle of blood dripped on the ground and she knew that her monthly time was upon her. Gazing down at Katala's sleeping form, she was relieved when she saw Lianna enter the teepee.

"Lianna?" She was not sure how to tell the other girl.

Fortunately Lianna took in the situation at a glance and signaled Honor to dress in her shift and follow her. Honor was embarrassed, wondering what thoughts were going through the wife of the man she had just lain with. She hoped that Lianna did not hate her, but the expression on the woman's face told her nothing. She was led to a lodge that stood a little distance away from the others in the village and she looked at Lianna questioningly.

"Such things trouble men," she explained quickly. "Our women stay in this lodge when the sickness troubles us until we are well again." She passed a weary hand over her forehead and Honor could see the lines of strain around her eyes.

"Tutalo's birthing was not an easy one?" she inquired with sympathy.

Lianna gazed at her for a moment until Honor grew uneasy. Then the Indian woman shivered and shook her head. "The malechild died," she said flatly.

"Oh—I'm sorry," Honor murmured. "And Tutalo?"

"She still lives, but she is not good. She—she cries out that evil spirits have taken her baby. The shaman points to you as bad omen."

Honor stifled a gasp of surprise. "He blames me for the baby's death? But surely you cannot believe such a thing, Lianna?"

"Her baby died by the cord that brought him life in the womb. Tutalo has much grief. She believes what the shaman has said."

"But many babies must die like that. You cannot believe that my presence could cause such sadness."

"Many babies die, it is true, but you, white one, would have cause for Tutalo's baby to die. You would hate the seed of Devlin to grow in her body. Your eyes follow him with desire. Our shaman thinks you have cast spell on him." She glanced up with accusing eyes. "You cast spell on Katala."

"Oh, Lianna, I did not want to go with Katala, but I was afraid that if I did not, he would find another way to hurt me. I had no choice."

"I must go now, white one. You will stay here in this lodge and food will come to you. When your time is finished, I will bring you back to Katala. I must go now to Magda."

Magda! Honor shivered. When Lianna told her where Honor was, she would know that she had lied that night when she had met Brice at the stream. She would most certainly damn her for what had happened! And, as an elder of the tribe, Magda had much influence. Visions of being tortured to death came to her mind and she doubled over in panic.

She was a stranger, an outsider! The sound of tom-toms broke into her thoughts and she wondered, with alarm, what the commotion might mean. She did not find out until later in the evening, when Lianna returned with food as she had promised.

"That is our shaman making noise to scare away the evil spirits that seek to take Tutalo's life. Shaman calls for much noise. He hangs drum over Tutalo's head to drive away bad spirit."

When Honor expressed amazement at such primitive methods, Lianna shrugged. "You not know our ways, white one."

She laid out the meal and told her to eat, that she would be back in the morning. Honor ate listlessly, her nervousness making it impossible to enjoy the food.

The morning brought her no comfort as she looked out of the lodge to see the long funeral procession for the infant filing from the village, past her teepee, to the burial grounds beyond the stream. All of the women of the village and most of the children walked in the procession, all wailing and tearing at their hair with frenzied movements to show their grief.

Honor shrank back against the lodge as she saw Tutalo making her way in the file, the shrouded body of the infant held in her arms. The Indian looked with burning eyes at the white girl—eyes that burned with hatred as much as fever.

Tutalo loked ghastly and Honor thought that at any moment she would surely fall and never get up. How she had summoned the strength to walk to the burial grounds was a miracle. What had the shaman done to enable her to do this? Then, as Tutalo came nearer, she saw the shaman himself, his black eyes gazing at her with death in them. Honor shivered.

"Oh, Evil One, you who have killed Tutalo's only son," spoke the shaman in a croaking voice, in English for Honor's benefit. "Let the God of the Comanche bring down death to you. Let you never rest until vengeance has been done in the name of the son she bore." The others added their own incantations in the Indian dialect and Honor was forced back into the lodge, fearful that they would tear her to pieces.

The procession wound on and Honor closed her ears to the sounds of the women's fury and anguish. When some hours had passed, she ventured to look out again and once more, in the distance, she could hear the drums beginning again, the signal that Tutalo had returned to her lodge and was undergoing the medicine chief's "cure."

Restlessly, Honor waited in the lodge through four more days of worry and despair. Each day, Lianna would bring her food, but no more words passed between them and Honor knew that Lianna had decided to believe her shaman.

When the fifth day had passed, Lianna came to take her back to Katala's lodge and her expression was stony. Honor did not dare to question her, although she was anxious to hear whether or not Tutalo still lived.

"You wait for Katala." The words were short.

She did not have long to wait until Katala entered, signaling for Lianna to leave the lodge. After she had gone, Katala sat, cross-legged, in front of Honor, studying her soberly as though searching for some mystical sign that would tell him if she was demon or not.

"Tutalo has died."

"No!" The word broke from her lips before she could stop it and her hand flew to her throat as though imagining the knife he would use to slit it open.

"You hold sorrow for her death?" he asked curiously.

"I'm sorry she is dead—and her son also. I have no wish to see anyone die." Her mind flew back to the wagon train, to Lee Ann's drowning, the attack, Barbie's loss. She had witnessed too much already, she thought.

"You did not wish for her to die? You held no hatred for wife of man you carry desire for?" His words were filled with a jealous pride that struggled with his love for his blood brother.

"No, I did not want her to die. As for the man, Devlin, I feel nothing for him but resentment that he—used me as he did. I have no desire for him."

Her eyes widened as he drew closer and his hand closed lightly about her neck.

"You must tell the truth, white one. Already the council calls for your death. Many believe you are a demon, a witch sent to cause death among our people."

She shook her head, but stopped as his grip strengthened. "I am no witch, I had no desire to come to your village. It was you, Katala, who brought me here."

He started as she threw the subtle accusation at him. Then his frown deepened as he stood up, drawing her up with him. "Come, the council awaits you."

Trembling violently, she was shoved ahead of him toward the great lodge where his father, Appina, sat surrounded by others of his tribal council. The older man gazed steadily at his son, then at the white girl whose eyes mirrored her fear. He signaled for the council to begin.

Honor sat slightly forward of Katala as the council members talked. The words were angry at times, calming at others, and she had no idea if she was close to death or acquittal. She had despaired of seeing Brice Devlin there, the

83

only man who would know with a surety of her innocence of witchcraft. She supposed that he had not been allowed to sit at the council.

The hours dragged by and she began to slump until Katala's fingers jabbed her in the back, causing her to sit straight again. Erect, she eyed the members fearfully, seeing their eyes slide away from hers as she met their gaze.

Finally, Appina barked an order and Magda appeared at the entrance to the lodge. She looked first at Honor, then at Katala, and nodded, speaking slowly to the members. Appina issued an order and she brought out a buffalo horn filled with liquid.

Katala poked her in the back once more. "You will drink."

"Why must I drink?" she asked warily, as Magda drew closer with the horn.

"If you drink and nothing happens, you are no demon," he answered. "But if you refuse to drink, or if liquid spews from your mouth, you are witch." His eyes brooked no protests.

Wondering what Magda had put in the horn, Honor took it gingerly and sniffed. God knew—would there be poison in it that would kill her? She looked up at the old woman and could see nothing in the sharp eyes that watched her so closely. She was, though, the mother of the woman whom she was to have cast the spell on—and she knew now that she must have lain with her daughter's husband. She must hate her.

Carefully, she raised the bowl to her lips and sipped it experimentally. It was slightly bitter and with one quick breath she downed the contents, forcing herself not to gag.

The council members watched her as the minutes went by. A slight nausea made Honor fasten her eyes on the opposite side of the lodge. She could feel beads of perspiration breaking out on her face and a distinct burning deep in her throat. There was no doubt that Magda had added some sort of pepper to the brew. With all her willpower, she forced herself not to vomit the noxious stuff, realizing that her life depended on it.

Finally, after eyeing her keenly, Magda let out a derisive snort and left the lodge. Appina clapped his hands, drawing Honor's attention, then signaled for her to stand. She obeyed, feeling the dizziness reach up to engulf her. Behind her, she could sense that Katala had stood also and let herself sway slightly against him in order to remain on her feet.

"Do you wish to keep this white woman, my son?" Appina spoke in English.

Katala nodded. "She is no witch, my father. She has pleased me much and will produce many sons."

"Lianna?"

"Lianna bears no more children since my son. This white one will be second wife to Katala."

Honor was only half-listening, her mind whirling slowly in a widening vortex that threatened to burst through her skull. She knew, with a terrible certainty, that she was going to retch. But she closed her mouth stubbornly and refused to give in to her weakness.

With relief, she realized that Katala was ushering her out the bearskin flap, that she was in the cool of the night. It helped to revive her somewhat, enough to turn to Katala and ask humbly to go to the river to wash.

Pleased at her servile attitude, he allowed her to leave him with the promise that she would not be long. He went back to his father's lodge, leaving Honor to run as fast as she could to the stream's edge and promptly throw up the contents of the buffalo horn behind a willow tree where the dirt was damp enough to cover the evidence of her "witchcraft."

She was still shaking from the ordeal and plunged her face into the cool waters of the stream, rinsing her mouth out and patting water on her hot forehead. She wished that she could stay here in this secluded place all night—and the thought made her think of Brice Devlin. Determined to put him out of her mind, she concentrated on the words Appina and his son had spoken tonight and they registered now with infinite bitterness. She did not want to be the wife of an Indian chief, nor did she have any wish to bear his children. She shuddered, remembering Tutalo's fate as an Indian mother.

Honor sighed deeply and thought of Don Esteban, wondering if he knew yet of her disappearance, if the news of the wagon train's fate had reached him yet. Would he think her dead with the others? Or would he wonder if she had been captured? Better that he would think her killed than to have come to this end, she thought morosely.

"So—they didn't kill you? I'm glad." The mocking voice could have only one owner and Honor tensed as she felt him draw near to her.

"You—glad? I didn't think I mattered to you," she said edgily, still toying with a blade of grass, desperately trying to

85

push the thought of them together near this very spot from her mind.

He laughed. "I knew you weren't a witch, Honor. Tutalo was sick with fever and the shaman's insinuations."

"You don't seem to mourn her," she put in, attempting to turn the talk away from anything more intimate.

He brushed her words impatiently aside. "That has nothing to do with you. Tutalo was a pretty little thing and would have made a good wife and mother. She—" He stopped abruptly as though loath to talk with her so personally.

"I am sorry that she is dead."

"Don't bother to express your condolences," he said, switching back so smoothly to his old arrogance that she might have imagined his softening. Then with a wicked grin, he moved closer to her so that he had caught both of her wrists in his hands before she could run away. "Missed me?"

She drew back like a jumpy mare. "Missed you! No, not at all, Brice Devlin. You see, Katala has filled in very nicely and—"

He shook her, not too hard. "Don't talk like a whore, Honor," he said softly.

It was her turn to laugh. "Why, that is exactly what I am in your eyes, isn't it—that is, until Katala can make arrangements to marry me." She ended on a forlorn note.

He seemed surprised. "Marry you!" He was silent for a moment, then went on, "Hell, I must say you have landed on your feet. Most white girls would have had the delicacy not to have survived the first man's attack on your sensibilities, much less have consented to marry the future chief of the village! There's something about you, Honor . . ."

He stopped and drew her closer. Honor watched him warily, unable to read his expression, thoughts of that other time running through her mind. She had wanted him to make love to her, she admitted. She had been fascinated by his strength, his arrogance, his sure masculine air. She had been like a starry-eyed child, willing to do anything to gain his attention. She had told him she loved him. At the thought she stiffened, feeling him probe between their clothing. She craned her neck back to avoid his mouth as it came closer.

Just as he was about to capture her lips, they both heard the sound of footsteps. Devlin released her and turned to peer into the darkness, his body alerting him to possible danger.

"My brother." It was Katala, and Brice cursed himself for

letting his senses trap him into desiring the girl yet again. Stupid of him!

"Yes, Katala, it is I," he answered steadily, knowing that showing fear would only increase his guilt.

"Ah, Devlin, I was not sure. The white one—she is with you?" The question was unnecessary and they both knew it.

"Yes, my brother, she is here."

There was a long silence and then Katala strode nearer. "You would dishonor me, Devlin, because of the woman?"

Brice shrugged. "I do not know why you speak of dishonor, my brother. Is she not destined to be village property? I have only exercised my rights as a member of the tribe. This woman is to be—"

"She is to be second wife to Katala."

Brice tensed. He damned himself for a fool, sniffing around the girl like a stray around a bitch in heat. Damn!

"You will stay away from her, Devlin, or there will be sorrow between us," Katala continued softly.

He moved to close his hand around the girl's wrist. Honor felt him tug at her, would have resisted, but her strength was nothing in comparison to the Indian's.

As Katala pulled her back, away from the stream, she turned her head to see Brice Devlin unconcernedly lighting a cheroot. By the glow of the light, she could see his hard, lean face, no more sorry over losing her than over losing his Indian wife, Tutalo.

He has no soul, she thought despairingly, then hardened her heart against him. She'd be damned before she'd soften toward him. He was a rogue, an outlaw, and heartless in his dealings with women. Good riddance to him! But her mind kept going back, maddeningly, to that night when he had made her a woman.

She had no time to dwell for long on Brice Devlin, though, for Katala was pulling her along to his lodge, where he pushed her quickly inside, ordering her to undress as though he wanted to lay claim to her without further delays.

Honor's pent-up emotions burst through her defenses and she glared at the Indian. "I will not disrobe for you or any other man! I've no wish to be your whore!"

Katala's brows flew up. He was still smarting from the subtle insult to his manhood from his blood brother's easy handling of this woman destined to be his wife. Now, to have that woman defy him angered him greatly.

"You await Katala's pleasure, white one!" he growled, his eyes threatening.

Honor was aware of Lianna, in the shadows of the lodge, probably listening avidly to the conversation between her husband and the unwanted white girl.

"Take off dress!"

"I will not!" she hissed back defiantly.

Disgusted, Katala punched her in the stomach so that she doubled over and fell on her back to the ground. She lay there, catching her breath, when she felt the blade of his hunting knife, cutting through the material of her shift. In short order, she was naked, but still glaring defiance at him.

"It is as it was on trail," Katala said angrily. "White one defies me!" He shook his head. "But Katala will let no woman disobey his command!"

So saying, he hurled himself on top of her, flattening her body to the earth. Grunting with his efforts, he pried her tensed legs apart with ungentle hands. With no feeling for her still delicate condition, he thrust his hand between her legs and explored her roughly, causing Honor to groan. Not to be treated such, she arched her neck and bit the hand that held her down. Katala cried out angrily.

"You lay for Katala before," he said through gritted teeth, trying to hold onto her wriggling arms.

"I have no more wish to be used if I am going to be your wife," she returned. Heedless of the consequences, she continued, "I will not bear you sons if you force me. I swear I shall kill myself before being so dishonored."

Katala reeled back. He stared at her incredulously and then, finally, a shamed look crossed his features. "You speak truly as one of our people," he admitted, his voice tinged with pride. "You have honor as even your name bespeaks. If you are to be my wife, I shall not touch you until you come to me after wedding."

He knelt between her legs and looked into her face. "You are, indeed, fit to be wife of greatest chief of Comanche," he said softly. His hard callused hand reached down to brush the hair from her face. "Hair of the desert sun, eyes of the mountain forest—you will be my wife before the new moon has passed."

Lightly, he got to his feet, then reached down to cover her nakedness with a deerskin. Amazed and a little worried at her easy success, Honor watched him tread to his own couch, where he called in the darkness for Lianna. A wave of revulsion swept over her at his perfidy and she turned on her side to try to hide from the sounds of their copulation.

Thirteen

Honor sat with her legs folded beneath her as she stirred the contents of the cooking pot slowly. She was aware that Lianna had her do the most mundane and dreary tasks of the Indian household because of this new development in the relationship between her husband and this white girl. Lianna resented deeply the fact that Katala would be taking another wife, although it was not considered odd for Comanche males to have three or four wives, and Comanche chiefs three times that number.

Of course, Lianna would still be his number-one wife with all the privileges and duties that the title required, but she had a hopeless feeling that Honor would prove strong and fruitful, while she herself suspected that perhaps she might not bear Katala another child. She had been many times to Magda's lodge in order to receive small packets of fertility charms.

The conversation that now passed between the two women was short and only when necessary. Aquita, too, had sensed his mother's deep dislike of this "foreign" usurper and behaved accordingly, throwing ashes in Honor's cookpot, leaving his arrows in places where she would prick herself, and even, one night, placing a slimy water snake beneath her deerskin blanket, nearly sending her through the top of the teepee. The two antagonists looked upon one another with mutual dislike, but Honor had little recourse against a boy of five who was his father's only son.

So life was not altogether blissful for Honor, although she was at least spared the further advances of Katala—at least for the time being. She stopped her stirring to consider. Only a week before the next full moon, she thought, and then she would be married to Katala in the Indian tradition. And with marriage came an open invitation to her bed—and probably children thereafter.

She hated to admit it, even to herself, but she missed Brice Devlin. At least he was of her own people and, if he had really been telling the truth about being from Savannah, they could have shared memories—but no—he would never have wanted to share memories with her, she reproached herself. Still, he had supplied a break from the monotony of the life of the village.

She had been surprised to find out that he had left two days after she had been acquitted of the witchcraft suspicion. Lianna had informed her that he had gone without the usual blessings and good wishes of Katala although Appina had visited with him in the great lodge the night before. She had hinted that Devlin might not wish to come back to Katala's village, especially when he took his place as chief.

"Because of *you!*" she had hissed venomously. "Magda was right—you have brought much sorrow to our friend, Devlin. He is well to be rid of you. If only Katala would see your true evil!"

"I would gladly leave today," Honor had retorted. "Just give. me a way to escape and you can have your husband all to yourself!"

Lianna had snorted derisively and walked away, leaving Honor exasperated that she would not bite at the bait she had held out.

Stirring harder now, she suddenly felt a sharp pain in her shoulder and turned around quickly to see Aquita dart behind the lodge. He and three or four other boys could still be heard laughing and whispering, but she was too tired to shout at him today. She picked up the sharpened rock he had thrown at her and hurled it in front of her.

"White one has anger in her yet again?"

Honor looked up as Magda walked over toward her. She didn't answer, but watched the old woman warily.

"You are unhappy. You have no wish to be wife of Katala. You want to run away from here—run after Devlin!"

Honor laughed scornfully. "He is to me as is Katala, toothless one."

The old woman laughed wisely. "Ah, Magda sees many things that you cannot, white one. But no matter, you should not be here. You do not belong."

Honor waited, wondering what the woman was getting at. Was this one of her visionary ramblings? Or was she ready to offer a means of escape?

"Lianna—she is unhappy too; and Katala—who knows the workings of men's minds? If you were gone, he would not sorrow long." She shook her head. "Such things should not be."

Honor had decided that the woman was just talking as usual and brushed her hands over her face to shoo an annoying fly. "Go away, old woman. I have things to do and cannot sit here listening to your ramblings."

Once more that eerie cackle that made Honor wonder if Magda had ever been accused of witchcraft. "Do not tell me to go away, white girl, or you will never leave this place." She winked with a conspirator's look. "You will do as Magda says and I will help you to your heart's desire."

Honor glanced up sharply. "My heart's desire is to escape this place, old woman. If you can help me, I will gladly do whatever you ask."

Magda sighed deeply. "If only you could give me your smooth, fresh skin, your clear eyes and your young body— but no, Magda has no use for such. Her power is too great for such worldly things. Listen to me, white one. Come to my lodge tonight after Katala is asleep and I will talk with you."

"But how will I be able to—"

"Tonight, white one, or the spirits will no longer be with me."

She tottered off, leaving Honor with a feeling of rising excitement. Could the old woman be speaking the truth? Or was she leading her into some sort of trap? And how could she possibly get past Katala at night? He tied the bearskin flap securely, and even should she be able to untie it in total darkness, there was still the probability that Katala would catch her. How could she fool him—or Lianna, unless the woman was Magda's cohort in this plan?

Honor gnawed her lips nervously and almost jumped when Katala laid a warm hand on her shoulder a few minutes later.

"The stew is ready?" he asked, allowing his hand to move slowly up to her neck to rub the skin with a caressing movement.

Honor swallowed. "Yes. You are ready to eat?"

She had not turned her head up and his hand came around to force her to look at him. "I am ready, Honor." His dark eyes branded her with his desire and Honor wondered how the old woman could be sure that he would not come after her should she try to escape.

Without speaking, she nodded and retrieved the pot from the fire to bring it inside the lodge. She was about to pour the contents into bowls when Lianna came up, her face looking flushed with irritation, and swiped the bowls away from her.

"I will fill my husband's bowl," she said between her teeth.

Honor glared back at her, but had no recourse but to wait until she was finished before filling her own bowl. She sat down and quietly began to eat, keeping her eyes on her food.

"We have had a great council, Lianna," Katala said after eating. He had relaxed with an aromatic-smelling pipe and Honor wondered at the resemblance to a "civilized" gentleman having his port and cigars after a meal. "We shall leave tomorrow for the great summer hunt. Our scouts have sighted many buffalo three days' ride from here. We shall hunt and then make ready to move on to our winter camp. We must leave tomorrow before buffalo use up grazing and leave for greener grass." He stopped and looked at Honor, who was listening with a constricted heart. "You will learn many things, Honor. How to be useful and be good wife to Comanche. Lianna will teach you." He looked at his wife, who dutifully nodded.

Honor very much doubted that she would receive any overt assistance from Lianna, but kept silent. Three days' ride! But in which direction? Would it be even farther into the desert, or north toward the mountains? Her hopes of escaping fled from her mind. They were leaving tomorrow. There would be no time in which to escape.

But perhaps Magda might have a plan in which Honor could slip away during the trek to the buffalo grazing grounds. If it were possible to leave the teepee tonight to consult with the old woman, Honor resolved to go. She looked up from her thoughts to find Lianna's eyes on her with a steady resolve that matched her own.

Honor had listened painfully to the sounds of fierce copulation between Katala and Lianna, wishing she could close her ears, but needing to find out when they slept. After no noise had come from their communal bed for some minutes, she raised her head to try to peer through the darkness.

She held her breath as a silhouette appeared inside the teepee, lit against the skin by the outside light of the moon. She relaxed upon perceiving the slender figure of Lianna, but kept silent as she watched the Indian woman go to the bearskin and deftly untie the flap with quick fingers. Was she actually aiding her?

There was no doubt when Lianna came to her bed and placed a finger to her lips.

"You must dress quickly and go to lodge of Magda."

"But Katala—?"

"He will not awaken for many hours," Lianna affirmed. "But there is still need for quickness. Go!"

Honor scrambled into her doeskin shift and soft moccasin boots that reached up to her knees. Her hair was already braided in a thick tail and would not impede her need for silence and speed. She started to say something to the woman, but Lianna had already returned to slip beside her husband, who mysteriously had not even shifted beneath the covers. Honor wondered if Lianna could possibly have attained some special herb from Magda to induce a deep sleep. If she had, Honor would be forever grateful, unless the escape attempt proved futile. Then, she was certain, Lianna would never help her again at the risk of her husband's wrath.

She hurried outside the teepee, where all was silent except for an occasional dog's howl. The moon and stars were obscured by a thin blanket of clouds that hung low over the earth and served Honor's furtive purpose well. It took her only a few moments to reach Magda's lodge, where she found the flap open to her.

"Come in, white one. I have been waiting." The thin smile that stretched the old woman's lips could hardly be called welcoming.

"I have come to learn how to escape," Honor reminded her. "Katala sleeps now, but—"

"Yes, I should know how well and truly he sleeps," the woman cackled, confirming Honor's previous suspicion. "But he no longer concerns you, white one."

She rummaged in an old skin bag and threw some sort of dust on her fire. The flames danced with a blue sheen for a moment, and she cackled gleefully again. Once more she threw something on the low blaze, murmuring an incantation. Her eyes closed as though in a trance and Honor waited impatiently.

"You must escape our village, white one," Magda said after some minutes. "The gods wish for you to be gone from here or you will hinder our buffalo hunt with your bad spirits. I must help you to escape."

Honor leaned forward eagerly, but a little afraid of this woman, recalling that it had been her own daughter who had

93

accused her of witchcraft. "Yes, I will do what you wish of me. But you know that tomorrow the village is moving to the pastures of the buffalo herds. Katala said that you must leave tomorrow—"

"Silence, white one. Magda knows of this. It is thus every year. But you"—and her craggy face grew even more shifty—"you will not be going, white one. You will be on your journey and leave our good spirits smiling at us. Katala will not find you in the morning."

Honor touched her throat. "You mean I must leave—tonight!"

"Yes, yes. You will leave tonight—now!"

Honor drew back from Magda's glittering eyes. "But how can I leave? I have no food, no—"

Magda smiled. "I have wrapped food for you—enough for three days and water for five days. There is a pony outside my lodge. He is yours."

"Food for three days, but I don't even know where to go. Which direction shall I take?"

Magda shrugged. "Your own spirits must guide you. You must leave now."

"But what will you say to Katala to keep him from following me?"

Magda stood up imperiously and led her outside the lodge to where the pony awaited her, shying nervously at his tether. Honor soon realized the reason for his skittishness as the carcass of a dead wolf appeared almost beneath her feet. She shrank back, startled.

"This is what I will tell Katala, white one. That you were the evil spirit of this she-wolf and that you were snared in one of my traps. You have died and that is a good sign for the buffalo hunt. His heart will be at peace then."

Honor did not care to dwell on such an outrageous lie, but she had to admit that, at least, the Indians would be superstitious enough to believe the old witch. And that suited her plans perfectly.

"I must thank you, Magda, for all that you've done—"

"I do not want your thanks, white girl. I only want you to be gone."

The woman's face was as hard as stone as she looked upon the girl. Honor bowed her head in acknowledgment and hurried to mount the pony. Magda untied him and Honor dug her heels into his flanks. The pony skittered away, only too glad to be gone from the unsettling smell of wolf. Honor leaned over the horse's neck and almost laughed aloud at the exhilarating freedom of the breeze brushing past her face. She was free! Free of the Indians!

"Thank you, Magda!" she called aloud to the quiet plains, the lowering clouds and the flying pony.

Fourteen

Honor had decided to follow a course that led her, roughly, in a southwesterly direction, remembering that the wagon master had talked of following that route to Santa Fe with the wagon train. Because of her ignorance of navigation, she had to travel by day, not knowing the direction of the stars at night. This caused her water supply to dwindle rapidly and her horse to tire more quickly.

By the end of the second day, there was less water left than Magda had foretold, and although she had eaten only sparingly of the food, there seemed hardly enough left for another meal. She began to wonder if Magda had devised the scheme merely to get rid of her—to send her to her death in the hot desert lands of the south. At least she was certain that the Indians would not be coming this way because she had seen no sign of buffalo, nor of any animal life for that matter. Only the lonely yipping of the coyote at night disturbed her sleep.

She had no idea if she would one day ride right into an encampment of the dreaded Apaches or come to an impassable river or range of mountains. All she could do was ride wearily onward during the heat of the day, using the sun as a fiery guide to wind her way through the ever expanding sandy desert. She wondered, despairingly, if she might continue riding too far south and find herself in Mexico, a prisoner of that land that was hostile to the United States after the recent war. If she got that far, she thought dully.

She rested fitfully on the second night and arose the morning of the third day with a heavy heart, barely making the effort to chew the food she forced into her body. She drank sparingly cupped some water in her hands for the pony and mounted after securing the thin blanket Magda had provided for her sleep. She felt miserable. Her face was sunburned and her thighs ached from riding the pony for long hours. She

95

licked her cracked lips and brushed pieces of hair from her face. Gently, she kneed the pony forward, feeling already the promise of another blistering hot day. The pony, sensing her lack of enthusiasm, plodded on, slowing their progress toward the range of mountains that she had seen, wavering in the far distance. She knew, with a sinking heart, that they must make some sort of watering hole soon or the sun would beat her—fry her to a crisp, or suck all the moisture from her perspiring body.

She was riding through a flat land of desert, shifting sands and little vegetation, a land cut here and there by jagged formations of rock whose shadow left little help in the way of coolness. It was as though a vast wasteland had suddenly taken over after she had left the green pines of the Indian village. God, how could a country change so drastically from one mile to the next, she wondered. What kind of place was this?

She plodded on, leaning on the horse's neck, keeping an eye on the direction of the sun's passing so that she would not swerve from her appointed direction. Suddenly the pony shied violently, nearly unseating her, and she was jerked forward. At the same moment, she heard the weird sound of rattles being shaken close by.

Horrified, she looked down, away to the side, and saw the biggest snake she had ever seen, staring back at her, its head uncoiled from its body and its tail emitting the curious sounds. She thought she remembered the trail scouts warning everyone about this type of snake—a rattler, he had called it appropriately enough. Its venom was deadly and Honor thanked the pony's quick reflexes. If it had been bitten, she couldn't have lasted a day in the treacherous desert.

She urged the horse forward, glancing backward to see the snake, no longer threatened, slithering slowly away. She couldn't help trembling.

The day wore on and her spirits sank deeper as the mountains seemed to continue to dance away from her weary gaze. Would she ever reach them? How could she continue without food, or water? She wished she could cry, but her body was so devoid of moisture that no tears trickled down her dusty cheeks. Would it have been better, she wondered, if she had remained with the Indians and taken her chances on escaping on her own—without Magda's help?

Well, it was certainly too late to change her mind about that, she reminded herself abruptly. There was nothing she could do but keep on, hoping that in this hot desert prairie there would be no roving band of Apaches to capture her.

She was grateful for the end of the day and decided to make camp within the dubious shade of a small formation of rocks and boulders. She slipped from the tired pony and patted him absently on his neck, then offered him water from her cupped hands. She tethered him to a tuft of tough mesquite and turned to lay her blanket on the sandy soil. A scorpion scuttled away, but she was too weary to be frightened of it.

Carefully she removed the moccasin boots and massaged her dry, hot feet. Her tongue felt her cracked lips experimentally and she didn't even bother to rebraid her hair. She looked and felt miserable. Hopelessly she sipped a little water and then sat on the blanket watching the sun recede behind the shadow of the far mountains. Tomorrow, she knew she must do all of this over again and the thought caused her shoulders to sag even more.

She lay down on the blanket and turned on her side, watching the pony for a time before her eyelids grew too heavy for her to remain awake. She fell asleep.

She was dreaming of the rattlesnake, tossing fitfully, when a big hand suddenly descended on her head, catching her by the braid to pull her up. She came awake groggily, her eyes taking a moment to become used to the semidarkness. Her breath caught in her throat when she focused on the broad, flat face of an Apache warrior. He leered crazily at her and when she started to scream, he jerked her by her braid, making her feel as though her scalp would crack off from her skull.

His voice made guttural sounds in the dark and another Apache came to stand beside him, staring down at her with curiosity mixed with a merciless glee.

Honor tried to find her voice. She wet her lips and summoned some halting words in the Comanche language. "What do you want with me?"

The Apache snorted derisively and said something to his companion. He looked back at her narrowly. His words came thick and contemptuously and she caught very little that made sense. That he was a warrior was obvious. He seemed to be some sort of scout. At any rate, she did gather that he and his companion were on their way back to the main village or camp and that they were alone.

She knew that there was a bitter hatred between Comanche

97

and Apache and knew that she had been automatically placed in the enemy camp when she had spoken in Comanche. She knew, too, that there was nothing she could do if these two decided to rape or kill her. She remembered the torture of a girl after the wagon train attack and felt an icy fear in her spine that seemed incongruous in the sweltering heat.

With a quick glance to the east, she discerned a pinkening in the sky and knew that dawn would be coming soon. Her attention was diverted back to the Indians when she was pulled to her feet, still held by her hair.

The two Apaches talked in a joking conversation for a few more minutes. The one who was not holding her pointed first to the pony and then to the sack of food and the jug of water. He babbled quickly to his comrade and picked up the food to rummage through what was left.

Honor cried out involuntarily as he spilled it contemptuously on the ground. She made a move forward to retrieve it from the sand, but was jerked back by her braided hair. She cried out angrily and swiped at her tormentor, heedless of her folly. With incredible speed, she felt the blade of a knife pressed to her throat beneath her ear and she squeezed her eyes shut in terror.

The Apache screeched something at her and took the knife away, shaking her derisively. His companion proceeded to take the water container and pour the remaining water after the food. Honor, who had opened her eyes, watched him with mingled hopelessness and hatred, swallowing convulsively at the irretrievable waste. She knew now that they were simply playing with her, mentally torturing her, but there was nothing she could do to stop them. She wondered if they had decided yet whether to kill her now or leave her without food or water to enjoy a slow death under the sun.

She found out quickly enough that they were not done with her yet. The one who was holding her placed his knife at the neck of her dress in back and split open the material to her waist. He did the same to the front of her shift while the other Indian watched with a menacing grin on his face. The two of them pulled the two halves from her arms and slashed at the material crazily with their knives. At first, Honor had thought they meant to sexually attack her and she had crossed her arms over her naked breasts, but as they continued only to shred the top of her garment she wondered what they were trying to do.

When they were finished, the first Indian grunted some-

98

thing to which the other laughed foolishly, then reached to pry her arms away from her breasts in order to fondle them roughly. Honor struck out at him and succeeded in scatching his cheek with one of her fingernails. He immediately drew his knife to plunge into her breast, but his companion intervened, said something in a deliberate tone, and the Indian put his knife away, still glowering at the white girl ,with unconcealed hatred.

The two of them backed away from her, taking her blanket from the ground and throwing it over the back of the pony. They led the pony away to where she could now see their own mounts tethered a little ways off. They clambered swiftly to their own steeds and, leading her pony, rode away at a steady pace.

Honor watched them go with some amazement, wondering that they had not killed her outright. She looked down at her half-nudity and shook her head, feeling lucky they had not raped her, but not knowing why they had chosen to rip the top of her dress to shreds.

She found out soon enough as she began walking in a steady direction toward the far-off mountains and the sun climbed higher in the sky. The strong, hot rays of the merciless white orb stroked her pale skin with the gentleness of a raging cat. Before noon, she could feel her skin turning hot on her back. Soon it would begin to blister and by nightfall—if she made it that far—her back would be a mass of ugly red burns. But she could not protect it, for she must hunch over to shield the even more tender skin of her breasts.

A raging thirst began to overtake her soon after midday and this coupled with the heat of the sun on her skin, made her think she would go crazy if she didn't find some shade. An idea suddenly hit her and she reached down to the waist of the Indian shift, pulling it up, squirming her shoulders into it, crying out as it seemed to scrape her sore back. The skirt was long enough to afford her some protection still, at least to her mid-thighs, and at least now she had covered the upper portion of her body. It was difficult to walk, though, with her arms confined to one position inside the dress.

"Hi-eeeee!"

She turned her head in alarm and saw the two Indians bearing down on her at full speed with their lances raised. They must have been trailing her through the morning and had been angered that she had found a solution of sorts to the problem of sunburn. She tried to run, but was greatly impeded by the lack of movement from her arms.

With horrifying quickness, the Indians were upon her. Only the fact that she stumbled and fell in the sand saved her from the lance thrown by the younger of the two warriors. His lance quivered in the ground barely two inches from her face.

Gasping, spitting sand from her face, she looked up to see the other Indian, sitting his horse, his lance raised to hurl into her prostrate form. She cringed, but could not close her eyes from the awesome moment of death. She gazed up at him, hearing nothing but the steady, fierce pounding of her own heart.

Suddenly it seemed as though the Indian wavered, his arm frozen as it swung upward. His dark eyes widened and a gout of blood spewed from his opening mouth. Without a sound, he fell forward onto his pony's neck and then slid to the ground.

His companion had turned around, seen his partner fall and let out a scream of hatred and revenge. He struck his horse savagely and pulled it up in front of the terrified girl. Springing with fierce agility, he pulled his knife and ripped the dress free from her body.

At the freedom Honor crawled away from him, rolling to her side and moving in striking resemblance to the scorpion who had scuttled away from her in fear the day before. The Indian grabbed her ankle and pulled her toward him, despite her repeated kicking and flailing of her limbs.

Honor could see the grinning, painted face looking down at her without mercy or lust—only an intense desire to maim and kill. She screamed as the Indian raised his arm to use his knife on her, rolling a little so that the blade scraped her shoulder. The pain was searing and for a moment, she was afraid she would faint.

From somewhere she managed to remain conscious and gather the strength to gain her feet and try to run. The Indian leaped up to catch her and, at the same instant, a shot rang out close by. The warrior crumpled in midair and came down limply, his hand dropping the knife he would have used to plunge into her body.

Breathing heavily, Honor looked around quickly to see if the man who had pulled the trigger was friend or foe. Dear Lord, could it be Katala? Could he have possibly trailed her this far?

Honor picked out the figure of a man on a horse rising eerily over a sand knoll in the distance, the heat shimmer causing him to seem to dance waterily in front of her eyes. He seemed to be alone and she struggled to get to her feet before he rode up to her.

As he drew closer, she sucked in her breath. The shadow of his hat shaded his face from her vision, but she knew that broad-shouldered, lean-waisted scoundrel before he even called to her and her heart constricted with a strange mixture of gratitude, elation and suspicion. He rode up next to her and leaned down from his horse, looking her over at his leisure, it seemed. A mocking grin curled the corners of his mouth and he nodded with a disdainful courtesy.

"Afternoon, ma'am," he drawled lazily, pushing his hat back on his head.

"Brice Devlin! I hate to admit it, but I've never been so glad to see anyone in my whole life!" she breathed, feeling an overwhelming need to crumple at his feet.

"I'm flattered, honey," he said, still grinning, letting those silver-blue eyes appraise her worth. "It seems you've gotten yourself into some trouble."

"I—I would have been all right if it hadn't been for those Apaches coming up on me in the night. I've been riding for almost three days and—"

"You escaped from Katala?" he questioned curiously.

"Magda helped me. She said I was—bad medicine for the tribe, that she would give me food and water and a pony. The tribe was leaving for the buffalo hunt."

He nodded and the look in his eyes deepened as they swept over her again. "It doesn't seem as though she equipped you very well for the journey." His indirect mention of her nakedness made her blush even under the sunburn and she swallowed hard to nerve herself to look him in the face.

"The Apaches ripped my clothes and took my food and water. My pony—"

"They've probably killed it since it came from their hated enemy, the Comanche. They would have known that from its markings. I suppose they thought you were connected with the Comanche too and decided to have a little fun disposing of you." He whistled sharply as she turned a little to shield her breasts from his disquieting gaze. "What happened to your back?"

"I've been walking since morning without anything to cover it. The sun—" She stopped and shrugged her shoulders.

101

Why was she standing here talking to him when any moment more Apaches could swarm down on them? Where there were two, there could be more.

He had slid from his horse and was pulling off his shirt. She cringed as he handed it to her. He smiled with amusement.

"Afraid to touch it, ma'am? You never know, do you, something might rub off on you."

His sarcasm spurred her temper. She swiped the proffered garment from him and hurriedly slipped it on, relieved that at least it fell below her hips so that it covered everything but her legs from his glance.

"Thank you," she said tightly. "Now, don't you think we'd best be going? There could be more Indians—"

He shook his head calmly. "I've been trailing those two for a couple of days. They've been scouting, on their way back to their main village. They won't be figured missing by their own people for some days."

"You've been trailing them for—" Her face reddened even further with anger. "You mean I've gone through this torture today and you knew—"

He shook his head once more, the silver-blue eyes assessing her as though trying to gauge the depth of her hysteria. "I didn't know they'd captured a woman, much less that it was you, Honor. You must admit, I had every right to think you safe and sound with Katala and his tribe. It was only an hour ago that I came close enough to get a good shot off at them, but I would have let them go peacefully enough if I hadn't seen them harassing you. I still didn't know that it was you until just now."

"But you must have known that it was a woman!" she retorted, still angry despite his calm, reasoning attitude.

He shrugged and let his eyes drift lazily once more over her figure.

After a moment, she shook her head. "*You*— you are the most exasperating man I've ever had the displeasure to know!" she flung at him.

When he was still silent, she took a deep breath and ventured to calm herself sufficiently to deal with him. "Are you ready to go?"

"Where are *we* going?" he asked indifferently.

"To Santa Fe. I have to get there so that I can—"

"Santa Fe! That's a long way for a young lady as inexperienced as you," he said softly. "I don't know if I'm taking along a bigger liability than I can handle." He seemed to be waiting for something.

She looked up at him, her green eyes flashing like fiery emeralds. She longed to slap his arrogant face, scratch her nails across the sun-browned chest, vent her anger on him in some way.

Finally, she said in a low voice, "If you help me to get to Santa Fe, I will see that you get a reward."

"You mean money?" he asked, laughing at her softly.

She looked up at him again. "What else? Surely a man like you would be interested in gold," she threw at him with bravado.

His smile was full and insolent. "I'm afraid not, Miss O'Brien. Gold doesn't do much for a man out here in the desert, especially when all he's got is a promise that he'll get it."

"All right then!" she exploded. "Go away and leave me alone. Just give me a pony and some provisions and I'll go alone!"

He shook his head, still with that insolent smile. "You've forgotten already that I'm a renegade, a trader between the Indians, the Mexicans and the Americans. I don't give things away for free, my lovely. Surely you know what a dishonorable brigand I am!"

She ground her teeth in her annoyance. *"What* do you want?" she screamed at him.

His silver-blue eyes assessed her lazily. "You."

She gasped. "I should have guessed!" she retorted when she'd recovered. "I should have known you would be low enough to—to ask me to do such a thing when you know very well—"

He interrupted her tirade impatiently. "Listen to me, Honor O'Brien! Don't mouth platitudes and put on that outraged virginal air that is the neatest trick among the Southern gentlewomen I know of. Let's be honest with each other. I've already known your—ah—considerable charms. You want to get to Santa Fe and I don't particularly have any business there—but I'm willing to sacrifice my own interests to help you—*for a price*. Look at it this way—you have nothing to lose and, I assume, a lot to gain."

"But you want to make me a whore—something I ran away from at the Indian village!" she protested futilely, already knowing she had no other recourse.

He shrugged. "Let's say we'll make a little business arrangment. You'll be *my* whore, Honor—and no one else's."

At her continued hesitation, he smiled arrogantly. "It's about 200 miles to Santa Fe—think about that."

She pushed the hair away from her face and looked at him with eyes like a cat—wary and seething. "You will promise to take me to Santa Fe?"

He laughed and nodded. "You have my word on that, Miss O'Brien, my word as a Southern gentleman."

She looked at him sharply, but was too weary to continue to fight him verbally. "Then I agree to your terms."

Fifteen

The days seemed to stretch endlessly for Honor as she sat on her horse, one of the packhorses that Devlin had brought with him. She was more than a little puzzled, even disturbed, by her companion's behavior the last few days. Ever since agreeing to take her to Santa Fe on his humiliating terms, he had not attempted to seal their agreement with proof of his interest. She couldn't understand him, although each night she awaited his demands with a shrinking heart, and was once more relieved when he curled into his own blanket, his gun at the ready beside him, his pistol beneath his hat.

They had come to the mountains, which had proven to be little more than a low range of foothills strewn with boulders and rocks. The sun still beat down with a fierce directness and Honor had already peeled twice from sunburn. Her honey-gold hair was streaked with light tresses and the freckles stood out in relief on her nose and cheeks.

They climbed through the foothills for nearly 200 miles, pushing their horses each day to make at least 25 miles. Honor thought she would drop at the end of the day, and after a while she even began to stop worrying about Devlin approaching her. He must be as tired as she was, she thought.

Then, finally, they hit San Miguel, a little town perched on the banks of the silvery Pecos River. They passed through quickly, following a trail that climbed up the Glorieta Pass until they could see the city of Santa Fe hugging the edge of the Sangre de Cristo Mountains on the end of a rolling plateau.

Honor was excited as she urged her horse to an even faster pace, until she heard thundering hooves behind her and Devlin was reaching out to grab her bridle.

"What are you doing?" she cried, trying to pull the reins from his hands.

"We'll make camp in the foothills tonight," he said softly, his eyes looking into hers with an unspoken demand.

"But Santa Fe is right down there," she protested. "My brother, Reid, might be there inquiring about me. We've got to go down there right now!"

"You'll not make me regret our agreement," he reminded her, still in that soft, intimate voice that she remembered dangerously.

It was the first time he had mentioned it and Honor had begun to think he would not force her into doing anything. She should have known better, she thought angrily. It was almost dusk and she supposed he would want to make camp right away.

They found a partially enclosed shelter of rocks where he built a small fire, a luxury they had not been able to afford in open country where an Indian might lurk. Honor had gotten so sick of the taste of cold beans and salted beef that her mouth had been watering at the thought of a hot meal and a soft bed in Santa Fe. Now the disappointment was all the greater for having been so close.

Honor sat gazing into the campfire after they had eaten, her mind on the possibility of being united with her brother again. She realized a little later that Devlin had already laid out his blanket and was preparing to settle down in that curious state of half-sleep that left him seemingly always on the alert for danger as he slept.

She stood up, shaking the dust from the shirt and pants he'd loaned her. She knew she must make a comical figure in the too big garments with an old hat jammed down over her hair. Perhaps that was why he hadn't approached her sexually before.

He had lifted his hat off his face in order to regard her, standing by the fire. "Come here, Honor."

She started nervously and remained rooted where she was.

"Come here," he repeated softly, leaning on one elbow as he spoke to her.

"What do you want?" Her blood felt as though it had

turned to ice and she could barely make her lips form the words.

"You know what I want, Honor," he replied smoothly, a hint of lazy mockery in his voice.

"But why now—why—when you haven't asked me to—"

He laughed softly. "Sorry not to have obliged you sooner, honey, but I had my mind on other things—like getting us this far through Apache territory."

Honor felt as though she wanted to cry and stamp her feet. She was tired, disappointed, bone-weary from the day's ride. She was dirty, sweaty and sticky and the thought of having him touch her in such a state made her cringe.

To make matters worse, he was grinning with that infuriating sarcasm, as though he dared her to defy him, to go back on her word. She would have liked to have been able to tell him to go to the devil, but she was, after all, at the mercy of his whims and he was perfectly capable of forcing her.

She willed her feet to move slowly toward where he lay, his eyes narrowing slightly now as though in anticipation of what was to come.

"Please—" she began and then caught herself, hating to plead with him. Slowly she sat down beside him, determined that if he was going to force her to assuage his baser desires, she would certainly not help him. He could undress her himself.

"Lie down, Honor," he said, and she scooted in beside him, stiff, her face turned away.

She lay there for several minutes. The minutes turned into a quarter of an hour, then longer, and she became both angry and embarrassed at his lack of attention. She turned her head to deliver a scathing remark—and was nonplussed to find him turned the other way, his hat once more over his eyes and his breathing deep and steady.

Despite herself, she flushed to the roots of her hair and clenched her fists in a fury. But the folly of awakening him overcame her anger and she settled down as comfortably as she could, without touching him, in order to go to sleep herself, although it took her several more minutes to calm herself enough to close her eyes and succumb to her weariness.

He awakened her early the next morning, and her mind, still groggy with sleep, took a moment to register the fact that he had unbuttoned her shirt and was fondling her breasts with easy familiarity.

106

"What are you doing!" she cried out, pushing him away and clutching the shirt to her bosom.

A laugh that was more a snarl broke in on the lazy humor in his silver-blue eyes and both he and Honor looked up in surprise at the two men that were standing over them, sighting down the barrels of their rifles.

"Well, lookie here, Pete, we got ourselves a couple of lovebirds," snickered one man, whose filthy clothes and straggly beard stained with tobacco wafted a smell through the air that would draw flies.

"Yeah, Gabe," the younger man said and then to Honor, "Don't be so skittish, honey. I'm itching to see more than a little tit."

Honor could feel Brice tensed beside her, the hand at her breast curved into a half-fist. He was silent at their railing, waiting for the right chance to make a move. His breathing was steady against her neck and the hand behind her back pressed her gently as though to give her moral support.

"Now, you two ain't too talkative, are you?" questioned the one called Gabe. He stroked the tobacco-stained beard reflectively. "We hate to disturb you, but my partner and I haven't had a woman in a spell. We'd be obliged if you'd hand her over without an argument." He pointed the rifle menacingly.

"Jesus, Gabe, she looks right pretty," Pete spoke up, setting his own rifle down in order to come nearer. "Come here, gal."

"Oh, Brice, what—what should I do?"

"I think you'd best do as I say, gal," Pete answered her, grasping her hand in his, "or your friend might find himself minus a few brains."

Honor shivered and took Pete's outstretched hand to rise to her feet. She caught her open blouse front in both hands to shield her bosom from the two men's avid eyes, but Pete slapped her hand away, allowing the shirt to gape open exposing the inner slopes of her breasts.

"Heh, now!" Pete cried out in excitement. "She's a decent one, Gabe. I get first go with her!"

"Bring the girl over here first, you damn fool!" Gabe shouted, excitement edging in his own voice. "We've gotta make sure he's got no gun hidden to blow your ass off when your back's turned!"

Reluctantly, Honor found herself held tightly by the older man, his arm pressed firmly against her breasts while he leveled the rifle at Brice's head. Brice was still lying on his side, his eyes watchful as the younger man rifled through his blanket for his gun.

"Here 'tis!" Pete shouted, brandishing the rifle.

"Check his hat, Pete," Gabe ordered, taking a moment to slip his hand inside Honor's shirt in order to pinch the tips of her breast. She jumped, but dared not make a move to run away.

When Pete recovered the pistol and rifle, he brought them over to his partner and reached greedily for the girl. Gabe held him back with a look.

"Aw, come on, Gabe, I'm as ready for her as I'll ever be!" protested Pete, his face tightening with anger.

"Dammit, Pete, you'll take your turn with her after I'm done!" Gabe said savagely. "I've a mind to take this little piece and rip her up the middle I'm so goddamned horny! Now watch that buck while I have a go."

The older man laid his rifle down and drew Honor into the relative privacy of a clump of mesquite. Pushing her down, he fumbled with his breeches, intent on the rape, a leering grin pasted on his wet lips.

Honor moaned in terror, covering her face with her hands to keep out the sight of him. She started as she felt his scaly hands move along her arms to pry them away from her face.

"I like my women to see what they're getting," he laughed.

Behind them a shot rang out and then a cry of pain. Cursing, Gabe twisted around, his hands slowed in the process of removing Honor's trousers.

"What's the matter, Pete? He try to run?"

"I'm afraid not," came a low, seething voice.

Honor's eyes flew open and locked into silver-blue fire that blazed from his eyes. Brice!

"Goddamn you, I'll—"

Before Gabe could finish the threat, Brice had whipped his arm up with the hand containing the small derringer that he had always concealed in his boot and shot him. Honor screamed in a reflex action as the man fell, dead, on top of her. Sobbing, she lifted her arms as Brice came striding toward her. He leaned over and picked her up, cradling her for a moment against his chest.

"Oh, Brice," she whimpered. "The other one—is he—dead?"

He nodded brusquely. "The bastards," he said quietly, with deep emotion.

She sobbed even harder and laid her face against his chest,

her eyes avoiding the body of the other dead man as he brought her back to the campsite. Quietly, he laid her on the blanket and set about pulling the younger man over to the mesquite clump.

When he returned, she was wiping her eyes, watching him silently as he broke camp. As he reached for the bedroll, she placed a hand on his arm. "Aren't you going to bury them?" she asked.

He stared hard at her for a moment, then, without answering, took the bedroll and tied it onto his horse. Still without speaking, he helped her onto her horse and they rode down the foothills to the plateau, toward Santa Fe. Honor was puzzled at his behavior, wondering if killing the two men had affected him that deeply. She had always assumed that, as a member of the Comanche, he had done more than his share of killing. For all she knew, he could have murdered someone in the white world of civilization, but perhaps she had been wrong. Still, she reflected, what else could he have done? They were going to rape her—might have killed them both afterward!

When they reached the outskirts of Santa Fe, he slowed his horse and she did likewise, although she was itching to find word of her brother. She looked at him inquiringly, wondering if he was thinking once more about the two men, if he should report them to the authorities.

Her question was answered as he said swiftly, "Those two men back there, Honor. They were nothing but scavengers, outcasts, probably thrown out of Santa Fe. I doubt that they'll be missed. We may have even done someone a favor by ridding these parts of them. Just keep your mouth shut about what happened. Understand?"

She nodded, more than willing to forget the whole frightful episode. She was sorry that two human beings had to die, but, realistically, if Brice hadn't killed them they would have raped and killed her, and killed Brice. Still, it nagged at her that they hadn't had a decent burial.

"Did you—did you have to leave them like that where the wolves and—things—could get to them?" she asked softly.

He gave her a cold look that chilled her soul. "I didn't like having to kill them, Honor," he said deliberately as though she were a stranger. "I did what I had to do—to save you."

He was silent so long that she wondered if he regretted saving her. The thought rankled and she kneed her horse

109

briskly. "I'd better ride on in," she said hurriedly. "I've got to find out about my brother."

He bowed mockingly. "Yes, first things first," he said, following her. But his thoughts weren't on her brother. He was remembering the look of surprise on the man's face as he'd bent down to pull his boots on, then come up with a loaded pistol. Before he could aim the rifle to shoot, Brice had already shot him clean between the eyes. He had hurried to the mesquite clump, his guts twisting inside at the thought of that animal rutting himself on Honor's body.

And then, after it was over, she had looked at him with those great green eyes, accusing him silently as though he had committed some heinous crime at saving her life—saving her honor, he thought, mocking himself with the pun. Well, dammit, she still owed him and whether she found her brother or not, which he highly doubted, he would exact full payment. Payment for having to kill two men.

He saw her riding eagerly forward into the city, leaning from her horse to question a woman about the place of authority. She looked like a ragged little urchin in those men's clothes, he decided after a while, not like the most desirable young woman he had ever laid eyes on. It had been an act of torture to keep away from her on the trail to Santa Fe, but his reasons had been twofold—first, because he had had to keep a practical eye out for Apaches and other vagabonds roaming the desert (witness Pete and Gabe when he had let down his guard) and secondly, because he wanted to prove to himself that what he considered a dangerous obsession could be kept under control by iron willpower. He had had to prove to himself that he didn't need her—even physically—and that when he finally did exact payment on her debt, his mind would not become involved.

She was looking back at him now, her eyes bright with excitement.

"Brice, I've found out where the authorities are. Hurry up! Maybe my brother left a message for me—maybe he's waiting for me to arrive! I'm sure he'll be here!" She kneed her horse down the narrow street, leaving him to follow at a more leisurely pace. He already knew where the presidio was. He could catch up to her later. Meanwhile, he'd have to think of a place where they could spend the night. A place, he thought, where she could have a bath and a good meal and a soft bed would be waiting for both of them.

Honor, unaware of her companion's thoughts, could only

think that she was on the verge of being reunited with her brother. How Reid would be surprised when she told him what she had gone through! His eyes would pop when she told him about Katala and about the Indian village—about everything, she decided, except Brice Devlin. She wasn't sure just how to tell Brice that she did not want him to meet her brother. No doubt, he had plans of his own, now that they'd arrived, but she wanted to make sure that he understood fully that her brother would take care of her now. Of course, she must tell him how grateful she was for all he had done in getting her here. Perhaps Reid would have a little extra money to give him for his trouble. The thought of paying him in anything else but gold had already escaped her mind. She only knew that she would be with Reid soon and he would help her to get to Monterey where Don Esteban awaited her. Surely now everything would fall into place!

She finally came to the large adobe structure that housed the offices of the United States Cavalry for the New Mexico territory and hurriedly tied her horse to a hitching post. Her heart throbbing with excitement, she flew up the wooden steps and into the relatively cool hallway. A man who looked like some sort of receptionist glanced up at her.

"Miss?" He seemed not quite sure what her sex was in her clothes.

"Yes," she smiled, her excitement causing her cheeks to bloom and her eyes to sparkle. "Please, sir, can you tell me where the officer on duty is? I have to see him as soon as possible."

"Why, that would be Captain Grayson, ma'am. His office is just down the hall, the second door on your left." The young man seemed bewitched by the beautiful smile he had just received from under the grubby hat.

"Thank you," she said quickly and knocked on the captain's door.

Brice had just tied up his horse and was standing on the steps, lighting a cheroot when he saw Honor coming out of the building, her face a picture of despair. He leaned casually against the hitching post until she caught sight of him.

"He—he's not here," she said in a small voice.

"He's not in Santa Fe, but has he been here?"

She shook her head. "The captain had no message, didn't know anyone by that name and had had no news of anyone looking for a Miss Honor O'Brien." She was fighting back the

111

ready tears. "Oh, Brice, do you think he decided not to come? Could he be back in Missouri still?"

Brice shrugged. "Listen, Honor, I think we need to check into a hotel here in town for the night. Maybe something will turn up in the morning. I'll help you check the inns tomorrow and go down to the telegraph offices. Right now, I think you need a hot meal and a hot bath. I've already spotted a nice, clean hotel that I think will be accommodating enough for you." If there was sarcasm in his words, he kept it veiled and she seemed not to notice.

Listlessly she nodded. "I—suppose you're right, Brice. Something's bound to turn up. If he's been through here . . ."

She mounted her horse and followed him down a winding street, past a missionary church where peasants were congregating for evening Mass. She thought of stopping herself and going inside to offer up a few fervent prayers for intervention from God, but she could sense that Brice was in a hurry to reach the hotel. It didn't occur to her to ask him to wait while she went inside.

La Posada del Gato, the Inn of the Cat, was situated on a quiet street. Inside all was cool and subdued and they were given the best room in the house. Honor had no time to think about sleeping arrangements before she was hustled up oaken stairs and shown into a charming room with white curtains blowing at the window and a brightly stitched counterpane on the huge double bed. The wooden floor was even covered with two sheep's wool rugs and there were fresh sheets on the bed.

"Thank you, Señora Moray. And if you would please have a meal sent up right away? And afterward a tub of hot water for the señorita." Brice was casual, sure of himself, winking at the broad-faced Mexican woman, who simpered slightly before bowing out of the room to attend to his commands.

"You do seem to have a way with women, Mr. Devlin," Honor observed dryly, taking off the dusty hat. The events of the morning could have been a dream as she stood in the room, unbraiding her hair to shake out some of the dirt.

"And you, Miss O'Brien, seem to have a way with men," he returned indolently, "So I think we are well matched."

She blushed at the backhanded compliment, busying herself with her hair as he watched her. She was instantly glad when a knock on the door preceded a dinner tray laden with wonderous-smelling fare that made her mouth water. Strips of roasted beef lay on a large platter with a bowl of frijoles and a dish of tortillas. A bottle of wine had been added and Honor sat down at the small side table to drink thirstily.

When the meal was finished, she wiped her mouth on the napkin that had been thoughtfully provided and gazed cautiously at her companion. "I'd like to have that bath now," she said tentatively.

He shrugged. "I ordered the tub," he reminded her.

"I mean," she faltered, "I would like to have some privacy while I bathe."

He smiled disdainfully. "I'd like to have a bath myself, Honor." The implication was clear in his words and she flushed deeply.

His careless insinuations began to anger her and she fixed a cool green gaze on him. "All right then, if you wish a bath, I'll be glad to let you have the tub. I suppose I can go one more day without washing. I'll just have to have one in the morning!" She rose, but his hand snaked out to catch hers.

"Don't be a prude, Honor," he said, and then, laughing a little, he released her. "Have your damn bath in private," he countered. "I'm sure the señora can fix something up for me elsewhere."

He stood up and bowed mockingly, leaving her to fume wondering just what he would be up to with the little widow who owned the posada. Her fretting didn't last long, though, when the tub arrived and the hot water was poured into it. She relaxed into it as soon as the servants had left the room, throwing her clothes into the corner. It was heaven!

Sponging herself lazily, she luxuriated in the warmth, soaping every particle of her skin. After she had finished bathing, she knelt at the side of the tub and washed her hair, using a fresh pail of water to rinse it. The maid had provided a fluffy towel, which she wrapped around her wet head, but she realized that she had nothing with which to cover her body. Spying the clean sheets on the bed, she wrapped the top sheet around her several times and sat in a chair by the open window to dry her hair.

She couldn't help wondering what Brice was doing, although she had an idea that he might be enjoying the favors of the widow. Angrily she told herself that she hoped he was. At least, it would keep him from attacking her the minute he came back to the room. She hadn't dared question him about the single room, knowing that he would give her one of those irritatingly mocking glances as though she knew full well why he had gotten only one room.

She was fluffing her hair furiously with the towel when he opened the door and she turned on him like a spitting cat. "Don't you believe in knocking?" she asked angrily. "I could have been bathing!"

He leaned against the closed door. If he was surprised at her angry air, he didn't show it, but his silvery-blue eyes roamed over the half-dried honey-gold hair and then narrowed with laughter at the mummy-like wrapping around her body. "I don't believe in knocking at my own room," he replied lazily, "and, to tell you the truth, I had hoped you still would be in the tub."

She huffed angrily and worked harder at her hair. She had noticed that he wore a new suit of clothes—a pair of clean buckskins and a dark-blue shirt with a brown leather vest. His hair was still wet from his bath and curled at the collar of his shirt. His shirt was half-unbuttoned, revealing a growth of black curls on his chest that were accentuated by the brown tan of his skin.

"I see you've been busy," she retorted acidly.

He shrugged. "You didn't want me in here while you were bathing."

"Well, you could have at least brought up some clothes for *me!* I'm sure you could have traded something for them!"

"I like you just the way you are," he replied smoothly. "Without the sheet, of course."

"Oooh! You scoundrel! Do you propose I put those dirty men's clothes back on?"

"I'm sure Señora Moray would be happy to wash them for you," he commented coolly, seemingly amused at her temperamental fit.

"Then go down and give them to her—and don't come back!" she flung at him, throwing the towel at him angrily.

He caught it and threw it to the floor. "Quit screeching like a banshee, Honor," he said with an edge of impatience to his voice. "Come here and let me see that sweet flesh of yours."

He walked across the room and abruptly pulled her into his arms. Before she could defend herself, he had already pulled the sheet down so that she was imprisoned in his arms, completely naked. Her hands were held behind her back as he pressed her closer, feeling every inch and curve of her femininity. He bent his head to kiss her and she strained away from his mouth.

114

"Stop fighting me, Honor," he murmured in softer tones now, nuzzling her arched neck. "Let me have you."

"No!" she threw out.

He tensed and she felt his steely muscles harden against her. She was afraid suddenly of the unleashed power of the man, the animal force that he could use to bend her—or break her. She shivered.

She felt him lift her up in strong arms and dump her unceremoniously on the bed. Opening her eyes wide, she saw him bending down toward her, a look of lust, fierce and impersonal, on his features, his silver-blue eyes narrowed to glimmering slits of determination, his mouth a hard line above the dark shadow of the beard he had grown during their journey.

Her eyes drew downward unwillingly as he undressed, touching the broad, muscled chest, brown as Katala's had been, the flat belly upon which a dark line of hair grew, and continued to his groin. Her eyes flickered quickly past the proof of his desire and she drew her knees up to protect herself.

"Don't try to close yourself to me," he said half-contemptuously, his strong hands prying her knees apart and leaning on them to keep them nailed to the bed. "This renegade will have himself one fine white lady to fire his animal lust," he mocked her.

It would do no good to plead with him, she knew. He was a lusting animal who sought a woman's body for his own comfort, she thought wrathfully. He did not care for her as a person with a mind of her own. He was all hard sinew and muscle, no softening anywhere to shield her own softness from bruising. He pressed her into the mattress, his hands tangling in her hair, pulling her head back so that her neck was arched and her mouth open to his kisses. His own mouth was hot, hard and demanding, his white teeth clashing against her own, until he succeeded in opening them.

He captured her lips, twisting them in a fierce kiss that held as much hurt as passion, allowing him the softness of her mouth while his hands captured and squeezed her breasts. His knees were sharp against the insides of her thighs, holding them open in a way that made her feel completely vulnerable.

Honor opened her eyes fearfully and saw his face close to hers, watching her with a savage expression that chilled her consciousness while it excited some deep, dark spark within

115

her. She told herself that he was using her as he would use a whore as a vessel to relieve his own tensions. She fought to keep the tears from sliding down her cheeks, for she'd be damned if she'd let him know he had hurt her.

He bent his dark head to kiss her breasts, laving the nipples with his tongue, arousing the tips to fire. Her back arched, offering her body to him involuntarily. Her breath was coming in gasps as her mind fought against her body's treachery. Determinedly she tightened her body against the eventual onslaught.

He sensed her tightening and it puzzled him, at the same time maddening him that she would still refuse him after all his careful treatment of her. She was withdrawing from him even in this, her most vulnerable position, and he was determined that she would feel something. The arrogant, well-bred little bitch!

Honor felt his rigid member press against the portal of her femininity and cringed even further. His hands had moved to either side of her head and she was powerless to move as he pushed into her without compassion. His merciless driving abused her flesh and she began to scream before he covered her mouth with his own.

Devlin was himself amazed at his reaction to her rejection. He was raping her, he knew it—the first time he had ever treated a woman this roughly, and he despised himself for it, even as he took pleasure perversely in bending her to his will. The awakened demon within him could not stop and the pleasure in her flesh was too much to make him want to stop. Her warmth, her tight, slick interior were driving him beyond his own will. He had thought too long of her tender flesh, had enjoyed it too well that first time in the Indian village. And he had denied himself for too many days to stop now.

He tasted salt in his mouth and realized she had bitten his lip. He only kissed her the more deeply as he felt his body beginning to build into wave upon wave of pleasure. Tremors quivered through the muscles of his legs and he increased his momentum despite a gnawing awareness that she was not sharing in his excitement, that she kept tightening against him at each surging thrust. She was not—refused to—open to him.

He looked down at her face, taking his mouth from hers, watching her expression with something akin to curiosity. He could see the long lashes trembling against her cheeks. Her mouth—her beautiful, soft mouth—was tightened with pain, her chin stuck out in hard determination not to give in to tears.

Suddenly his rage left him and he felt something close to shame—an emotion that had not troubled him before. How could he rape this lovely young thing, this perfect, womanly body that was made for a man to love, that cried out to be made love to, not abused like some cheap and tawdry prostitute on the docks of Savannah?

Gently, he slowed his feverish pace, willing himself to slow his own excitement, knowing instinctively that it would be better when she shared it with him. His hands released her head and began to caress her breasts, slow and provocatively so that she opened her eyes after a few minutes.

"Please—don't—hurt—me—anymore," she whispered jerkily.

Devlin ground his teeth, raging inwardly at himself. He bent his head to capture her lips once more and moved them exquisitely against his own, molding them until she opened them softly in almost shy response. The effect was electric on both of them. He could feel her blossoming open to him now, accepting him, adjusting her hips slightly to help his own pleasure. And that pleasure was breathless now for both of them as they helped each other to attain a glorious peak of culmination.

Devlin lay afterward cursing himself for a fool not realizing the potential of this child-woman to experience pleasure and to give him the same. He lay breathing deeply, hearing her own breathing in his ears.

But the feelings, the emotions, were too new for him— things that had been long buried inside of him rose once again to lock away the truth from him. Love was still something alien, something not to be trusted.

He disengaged himself from her and stood up beside the bed, looking down at the lovely face, the wealth of honey-gold hair spread upon the pillow, the enormous green eyes watching him with a shy wonder. Deliberately he allowed his manner to become brusque, arrogant once more—in control. He smiled down at her insolently.

"Thanks for the interlude, honey. Now I think we'd best fix the bed up a little and get some sleep."

Honor blushed. She had been feeling so happy a moment ago, fulfilled and sustained by his gentle ardor, but now the world came crashing back and she wanted to burst into tears at the cruelty of it. She had thought—she had really thought—but what did it matter? He hadn't changed, would never change, and she—she had a fiancé who was waiting for her in Monterey.

Slowly, she got to her feet, wincing a little at the unexpected tenderness. He noticed the movement and his smile was once more the same mocking twist.

"Forgive me if the passion of the moment overcame me, Honor," he said as he retrieved the sheet from the floor, where he had tossed it earlier. "I must admit your body is just too—volatile—for a man to keep his head. I must remember next time not to abstain so long."

Sixteen

"But you must have some message for me!" Honor protested, wishing she could shake the words she longed to hear out of the telegraph sender.

The man looked at her warily and shook his head once more. "Only had two messages left by non-Cavalry men," he repeated, "and neither of them mentions an Honor O'Brien. Sorry, ma'am." He tipped his hat and walked away from the sales window.

Honor sat dejectedly on a wooden bench and decided to wait for Brice Devlin to return. She hated to think that her brother had not come after all, or that he had come through and not checked to see if she had been on any of the wagon trains. She felt deserted, realizing that she had no one to turn to now.

No one but Brice Devlin, whom she wasn't sure whether she could trust or not. She thought about him for a moment, recalling the night of passion they had shared, passion that had been rekindled the next morning. She didn't know why or how she could respond to him so blatantly when she knew very well he was only using her. There were times when he could caress her and kiss her so tenderly that her heart would turn over with a feeling of weakness, but then he would gaze with that hateful mockery at her and say something to cause tears of rage to come to her eyes and all that had gone before would be as though it had never happened.

He was an enigma that she had long since ceased to try to puzzle out. He had a chip on his shoulder as far as women

118

were concerned, she thought, and he wasn't about to let her or any other woman twist him around her finger. Well, she would soon be saying goodbye to Brice Devlin, for if she could find no message from her brother, she would have to obtain passage with a wagontrain heading for California. There was nothing else she could do but ask Devlin to lend her the money, although she hated to be indebted to him once again.

She could feel his eyes on her, assessing her as always, before she even realized that he had ridden up in front of her. She looked up, meeting his glance with outward calm, although she was perturbed to find her head feeling lighter and her breath coming faster at sight of his handsome figure.

"Did—did you find out anything?" she asked to break the uncomfortable moment.

His eyes were inscrutable as he got off the horse and came toward her. "I located an inn where he stayed when the wagon train rolled into Santa Fe," he began.

Immediately she was hopeful, her eyes begging him, but she could see by the frown on his face that his news was not what she hoped to hear.

"He's not here. He decided to go on to the new gold discoveries in the Fraser River Valley in British Columbia."

"British Columbia! Why, that's way up north, in Canada, beyond the Oregon territory! Why would he go up there? Why would he desert me?" she cried despondently, unwilling to believe the facts.

"He didn't know where you were. For all he knew you were dead. Why should he have any reason to believe that you would be here now, looking for him? Your brother was an obvious opportunist, Honor. He went where the gold was." The words were cold, without emotion.

Honor knew he was only speaking the truth and yet she couldn't believe her brother would truly think her dead, would go on to a place where he knew he would never have word of her. She wished that she could cry, but no tears would come. It was clear now that she could only go on to California—to a fiancé who might or might not want her now.

"Well," she began with an effort, "I suppose there's no use staying here in Santa Fe any longer than I have to. I'll have to find passage on one of the wagon trains moving out to California." She started to go, then turned back to where he

119

lounged unconcernedly against the hitching post. "Thank you for—all you've done for me," she said wistfully.

"Honor," he began, "you can't go off on a wagon train by yourself! You have no money, for one thing, to hire out a wagon and a mule team."

"There's nothing else for me to do," she pointed out, her eyes steadily gazing at him. She waited, as though hoping for an alternative from him, but he remained silent, regarding her noncommittally.

With swiftness, she held out her hand for him to shake. "This is goodbye then, Brice Devlin."

He looked at her hand in amusement and then, without a moment to give her time to catch her breath, he strode quickly over to her and took her in his arms. His lips came down on hers, hard and masterful, drawing the kiss out until she was breathless. She was unaware of the romantic picture they made on the dusty streets of Santa Fe. She only knew that he was telling her goodbye in his own way and the thought somehow made her more miserable than the loss of her brother.

When he released her, she took a deep breath and would have said something, but he'd already turned away. Wearily she squared her shoulders in the new dress he had bought her that morning and tramped off to find the wagonmaster for the wagon train which had only arrived in Santa Fe last evening and would be leaving in two days. She was unaware of the slow trickle of tears that fell from her cheeks.

It had taken all her earnest energies to persuade the dour middle-aged man and wife to accept her services during the trek from Santa Fe to San Diego, in exchange for food and a place to sleep. The woman kept eyeing her distrustfully and whispering to her husband, who nodded in silent agreement. It was only her argument that they were her only recourse and that she was a good Christian woman who had fallen on hard times that finally persuaded them to take her in.

Ella Parsons admitted grudgingly that it was their Christian duty to take in such a woman, and after a moment of thoughtful consideration, Jim Parsons agreed.

"But you'll be expected to work for your share of food," Ella warned. "I'm not a woman who's used to laziness around here and I'll not tolerate it from a stranger either! You can help with the cooking and sewing and watch that the cow doesn't slip her rope from the back of the wagon."

"Yes, yes, anything you say!" Honor agreed eagerly, vastly relieved that they had actually accepted her.

"We'll start by taking that sinful dress away from you," Ella went on, sqinting dangerously at the low cut of the scooped neckline. "I've got a good gray dress that should fit you with a little alteration and you can keep it buttoned to your chin, miss!"

"Y-yes, of course, if this dress offends you—"

"It does offend us deeply, daughter," Jim Parsons broke in thunderingly, and Honor wondered if he was a preacher.

She meekly followed the wife and quickly changed the dress, although the gray was a bit too short in the arms. She would have to fix that later, as the woman was eager to familiarize her with their routine before the wagon train got under way.

The two days went by fast and Honor, who had hoped she would see Brice before leaving, was disappointed when the wagon train rolled out from Santa Fe. The familiar pattern was repeated that she still remembered from her days with Pearl and Vinny. Thinking about them brought a pang of regret that she would never again see Barbie Hampton.

They were moving along the Gila River, which would provide them with water until they reached the hot California desert. Honor had to learn quickly to manage the mules that were hitched six-deep to the wagon. Ella provided no gloves and her hands were raw and blistered after the second day out. The rough leather reins scraped at her palms and she felt as though her arms would be pulled from her sockets. She would fall asleep after attending to her numerous chores, filled with a sense of complete exhaustion.

The dawn would always come with the sounds of Zeke Smith, the wagonmaster, calling, "Catch up!" and then "Stretch out!" and she would pull herself from her bed with aching muscles and wonder how she would get through the day. At least her exhaustion helped to keep her from dreaming about Brice Devlin, she thought wistfully. But during the endless hours when Jim Parsons would hand the reins over to her so that he could read from his Bible, she couldn't help the unbidden warmth that suffused her when she recalled the three times that he had made love to her. Only three, she would think and wonder that it seemed like hundreds. She could almost feel his hand at her breast, his lips buried in her hair, his possession of her. A sigh would well unconsciously from her lips and she would glance in embarrassment at Jim

121

Parsons, who would be immersed in his Bible, thank goodness!

She would shake her head, attempting by physical force to blot Brice Devlin from her mind. Was he having this much trouble forgetting her, she sometimes wondered, and then would reprimand herself sharply. He had probably had no trouble at all when there were so many diversions in Santa Fe: she recalled the widow in the hotel as an example. She would just have to keep trying, she thought. He was gone now, as surely as Barbie was gone from her life. She had to look forward to the stranger at the other end of this journey—her fiancé, Don Esteban Sevillas. Desperately she hoped that he could wipe out the memories of Brice Devlin.

She concentrated on the mules ahead of her, feeling the drip of perspiration under the poke bonnet Ella had given her. Her hands were slippery with sweat and she had to tense her fingers tightly about the leather for fear the reins would get away from her and they would be obliged to stop the wagon in order to retrieve them from beneath the mules' hooves. She had already done this once and had been surprised to hear the considerable amount of cursing Jim Parsons had let out at what he considered to be her carelessness.

She glanced at him curiously now, wondering why he and his wife had elected to go to California. She knew very little about their background, only that they had started out from Illinois after selling their homestead for a pittance. Sometimes she thought she saw the light of missionary zeal in his eyes when he looked at her. Perhaps he had wild ideas about bringing Christ to the rakehells of California, she thought, and almost giggled.

Beside her, he must have noticed her movement, for he looked over, his craggy brows drawing close together. "Have you ever drawn comfort from the Bible?" he asked, startling her.

"No—well, that is, not for a long time," she amended. "When I was a child, my mother always read a passage to us after supper. It was a tradition with her, but when she died, the tradition sort of died with her."

He looked pleased, as though his own ideas about her upbringing were confirmed. "Then, my child, for so you still are to me, we will begin the tradition over again. After the last meal of the day, before you retire, we will read to you from the Bible." His tone brooked no refusals.

Honor cringed inwardly. After driving all day, then doing

her chores, she had no wish to be kept up even later by what he considered his Christian duty. Why, she thought suddenly, were people always trying to make good Christians out of lone women? Didn't they believe that a woman alone could have her own sense of moral and religious values without being forced into listening to others? It was a topic she didn't have the courage to discuss with Jim Parsons. Whether he had once been a minister, or was planning on becoming one, he would probably think her spouting the devil's own words.

Behind them, where Ella had been taking a nap—she had already explained to Honor that she had an ailment of the stomach that required her to stay out of the sun as much as possible with additional rest—Honor heard the woman stirring drowsily. She wondered if she was truly ill, or if it was a bald-faced lie concocted to keep her from having to sit next to her silent and boring husband. Surely there were times when Honor would have welcomed the respite of a nap instead of sitting next to him or fighting the stodgy mules with his eyes upon her in judgment.

"I presume you have been raised as a Catholic?"

She was surprised at his continuation of their discussion. So much time had passed since his last statement that she thought he had drifted off.

"Yes, my parents were Irish," she said, wondering at the necessity to point this fact out to him when it was obvious from her last name.

"A Catholic!" he hissed and she thought it sounded like a condemnation. "You have a lot to learn, my daughter."

"I wonder if it might rain today," she said to change the subject, although there was not a cloud in the blue-white sky.

"Do not be impertinent, child," he said severely.

She relapsed into silence as he harangued her on the wages of sin and so forth. Perhaps he was using her as a captive audience to test out his ability to become a minister. She listened to Ella's snoring, the clomping of the mules' hooves in the sand, the creaking of the wagon, anything rather than attend to his droning testament.

When twilight descended and the wagons formed a rough circle of defense, she slipped down quickly from the seat to attend to the cow that walked behind the wagon. Ella had insisted on bringing her, although her husband complained the animal was more damned trouble than she was worth. Still, her milk was a satisfying addition to their meals and Honor had quickly caught on to the job of milking her after a few instructions from Ella.

Now, as she patted the animal's rump in friendly fashion, she could feel Jim Parsons' eyes on her speculatively. She finished milking quickly and took the pail over to where Ella was beginning the meal.

"Wife, this child needs to be instructed anew in the ways of the Lord," Jim pronounced at the table.

Ella looked up inquiringly, then nodded. "As you say, husband."

After the meal, when Honor had finished cleaning up the dishes, she was made to sit for an hour on the wooden stool, her back smarting from the day's work, while Jim Parsons harangued in loud and angry tones of the sins of the flesh. A few others of the wagon train had come over to listen in respectful silence, but most of them kept to their own wagons.

Looking over when Jim wasn't looking, Honor caught a young man's eye in friendly salutation. He winked at her and thinking how horrified Ella would be if she noticed, Honor winked back. She was rewarded by a wide grin.

After the Bible lesson was over and Jim and Ella had gone to speak with the wagonmaster about what territory they would be covering, Honor saw the young man lounging at the back of her wagon, waiting for her with obvious expectancy.

"Hello," he said boyishly and she realized that he couldn't be more than a year or two older than herself.

"Hello," she responded, feeling suddenly, unreasonably shy as though she had not already known a man.

"I'm Ron Williams," he continued, taking off his hat and sticking his hand out.

She took it hesitantly. "I'm Honor O'Brien."

"Those two your parents?" he asked, jerking his head in the direction the Parsonses had taken.

She shook her head. "No. I was forced to ask them to bring me along. I was—stranded in Santa Fe after the wagon train I had been on previously was attacked by Indians."

"Too bad you didn't sign on with my folks and me," he said under his breath.

She smiled. "I know what you mean. If I'd known what I was getting into in Santa Fe, I think I would have felt lucky to have stayed behind!" She laughed with an ease she hadn't experienced since she'd been with the Parsonses.

He shrugged. "Where you headin'?"

124

"I—I have a fiancé waiting for me in Monterey. I hope to catch a ship in San Diego and sail up the coast."

"Oh," he said, as though her admission had caught him unawares. He had probably thought her a young girl traveling with her parents and, therefore, available for his attentions.

"I'd like to be friends," she said softly, desperately needing someone to talk to. "Tell me about yourself."

He shrugged. "Nothin' much to tell. My folks and my little sister and I come from Kentucky. My pa's aimin' to make us a fortune in the goldfields, but not from minin' the dust, mind you. He's a tailor, a right good one, too, and he knows men will be needin' shirts and pants and such. He's hoping to make us a good livin'."

"It's a wonderful idea," Honor agreed. "Are you going to be a tailor, too?"

"Don't know. Pa'd like it, but I've a hankerin' to see more of life than a clothes shop, you know? I just might go on to the Columbia territory and try my luck there."

"I wish you luck," she said, thinking of her brother, who had followed the same path, hoping for gold and glory.

"What about you?" He looked at her curiously. "This fiancé of yours know what you had to do to get to him?"

She shook her head. "I haven't seen him for six years. We were betrothed then and—well, things happened and I wasn't able to go to him as my parents would have wished. So, as I can't get to him any other way, I joined the train."

"Hope he appreciates the trouble," Ron put in.

She laughed. "Oh, I suppose it's not so bad. I—I just hope we don't run into an Indian raiding party."

He saw the haunted look in her eyes and he placed a hand gently on her shoulder. "If there's trouble, Zeke'll handle it," he said to bolster her courage and his own. "I'm right good with a rifle myself."

"I hope so. I'm not so sure about Mr. Parsons. I have a feeling he'd use his Bible as a shield and go out to them, delivering some long harangue about the wickedness of killing your fellow man."

Ron laughed appreciatively. "It might just work, you know. He could probably bore them to death!"

They laughed together, but were abruptly hushed as Parsons and his wife walked back toward the wagon.

"Child, what are you doing?" Ella questioned sharply, glancing at the young man as though expecting him to sprout horns.

"I'm talking with my new friend, Ron Williams," she replied steadily. "We've been discussing the effect of the Bible on the Apaches."

Beside her, she could tell Ron was stifling his laughter, but at a frown from Jim, he offered her a swift good night and went back to his own wagon.

"Daughter, you'd best keep away from that sort," Jim went on.

"What do you mean, 'that sort'?" Honor demanded, becoming annoyed at his inferences. "He seemed a very nice young man."

"Such things bring about the devil's handiwork," he muttered darkly. "No good will come of it, daughter. Best to stay away from temptation."

Honor would have retorted, but realized it would only prolong her need for sleep. She had to get to bed or she'd never get up in time to fix breakfast. With a curt good night, she went inside the wagon, drawing the makeshift curtain across the space allotted her. Fuming inwardly at the dour, fusty man and his equally stiff-necked wife, she finally got to sleep.

2

The California Coast

Seventeen

The days wound by endlessly, taking them alternately through scorching desert and barren hills until they had come to the edge of the California desert. Across the ninety-mile-wide land of sand and sun lay the town of San Diego, and Honor could hardly wait to cross it and book passage on a ship. She knew she would have to board with the promise of payment in Monterey and hoped she could find a captain gentlemanly enough to take her word that he would be paid.

The long days had passed with little respite from Jim Parsons' sermons and Ella's admonitions, but Honor had managed to keep up her friendship with Ron Williams. They had never exchanged so much as a kiss, although Honor was aware that Ron would have liked to have had more physical proof of her affection for him. But he didn't press her and she was grateful for that.

On the night before they would start their crossing of the desert, Honor had managed to slip away from Jim's watchful eye and had met Ron in a secluded spot a little bit away from the rest of the wagons. He seemed strangely quiet and she asked him what was wrong.

"Nothin'," he said aimlessly, and then looked up at her, "Just worryin' about you, Honor. I mean about when we get to San Diego and you sail for Monterey. You don't have any money, do you?"

She flushed. "That's no concern of yours, Ron. Once we arrive in San Diego, you've got the rest already planned out. What happens to me is—"

"I don't care!" he burst out emphatically. "I can't leave you stranded. I'd be less than a man. I just keep wonderin' if your fiancé—I mean, what if he already thinks you're dead? What if he—"

"Ron, I won't let you worry about me." Honor spoke sharply.

He shook his head. "I am worryin' about you, Honor, and I want you to have something of mine." He fished in his shirt pocket and brought out a small leather sack. As he put it in her hand, she heard the chink of coins.

Abruptly she pressed it back to him. "Ron, I can't possibly

take your money," she protested. "You'll need every penny you have to get to the Fraser River. Now, don't talk nonsense!"

"Dammit, Honor, I'd consider it an insult if you didn't take it!" he said quickly, thrusting the sack in her hands once more. "The money's mine to do with as I wish. It'll be easier for me to work off my passage, but I can't stand to think of you under the whim of any—Jim Parsons—who might come along!"

She had to laugh. "Oh, Ron, you really are the nicest man I've ever met," she said with warm feeling. Impulsively she reached up and put her arms around his neck to kiss him.

Despite her own warnings, she allowed him to take her lips, opening them under his pressure. His own arms wrapped around her, pressing her body to his own, and she had to admit that she felt so secure, being held and comforted this way. If only—if only she could erase the memory of Brice Devlin, the brief and painful interlude with Katala—she would be willing to give herself to this kind and innocent young man. But what would he think when he found she was not a virgin? She knew his illusions would be crushed and she couldn't do that to him. Gently she pushed her hands against his chest. He released her grudgingly.

"Sorry," he mumbled. "I didn't expect that as—payment for the money."

She winced. "I'm sorry too, Ron. Sorry that I can't do more, whether you had given me the money or not." With a coward's way out, she said, "My fiancé has waited a long time for me."

He nodded. "Well, at least take the money."

"I'll pay you back," she promised. "When you're fabulously wealthy, come down to Monterey and—"

"You don't owe my anythin', Honor," he said gently and she was amazed at the look of maturity in his eyes.

With a last, light kiss, she hurried away from him, afraid that if she stayed, her resolutions would be swept away by the inner urgings of her body. Oh, treacherous body! How it ached to feel a man's arms around it! Honor felt light-headed as she returned to the wagon, avoiding Ella's eyes and scurrying into the back. Her heart was pounding as though she had run a long distance. Ron's kiss had evoked a response deep within her, a cry for more. Her body was no longer virginal and she felt the cravings and need of a woman who had

130

known a man's body. She bit her lips and pushed her face into her pillow.

Ten days later, the wagon train rolled dustily into the sleepy town of San Diego. Honor looked forlornly at the humble cottages and buildings that comprised the village and burned to hurry away to the docks to see about booking passage on a ship bound north up the coast. She could see in the bay two tall-masted schooners and was glad that luck was with her. From the looks of this village, ships probably didn't stop often.

She had already bid a tearful and fond farewell to Ron Williams and his family, who had turned overland to follow the trail with their wagons. Several of the others had also decided this route would be cheaper and only two or three of the wagons had gone on to San Diego to seek passage on a ship.

Honor was irritated that Jim and Ella Parsons would most likely be on the same ship as she, but hopefully she would be rid of them in Monterey. She was sure they would go on to San Francisco, where surely the devil's work was widespread.

"I'm going down to the docks to talk to one of the captains of those two ships," Honor told Jim Parsons as she went to the wagon to get her money. Ella had already gone on to the one hotel in the village as her stomach ailment had begun troubling her again.

As Honor jumped down from the wagon, clutching the leather sack against her bodice, she noticed the look of surprise the man gave her.

"Where did you get that money?" he asked suspiciously.

His brusque manner irritated her and she started to walk past him silently, but he flung his arm out, barring her way.

"It's none of your business. It's my money and I intend to use it for ship's passage. Now, if you will step aside—"

"You had no money when you came to us," he went on relentlessly as though she hadn't spoken. "Where could you get money between here and Santa Fe?" And then as though the hand of God had touched him, his eyes narrowed, then lit with understanding. "Jezebel!" His hand cracked across her cheek, causing her to lose her balance and fall against the wagon. "You have taken money for your fornication with that young man! Haven't you, haven't you!"

She took a moment to clear her head and then glared up at him in disgust. "I have done nothing wrong in God's eyes

131

with Ron Williams," she said tightly. "He gave me the money because—oh, it doesn't matter now. Let me go!"

His eyes were suddenly crafty. "No, you'll not pass by me, young temptress. That money is not yours. Give it to me and I will accept it as offering for your salvation."

She looked at him in amazement. "You'll do no such thing, you old fool! I have paid for all my food and board by working my hands to the bone! If you had made your wife do all that I had to for what measly fare you allowed me, she would have died on the trail!"

His eyes blazed at her accusation. "Ungrateful wench! Your soul will be damned to eternal hell unless I force you on the right path! Give me the money!"

"I will not! Let me by!"

With a muttered oath, he slapped her again and before she could recover he had picked her up and thrown her into the back of the wagon. With the fervor of God in his eyes, he leaped up behind her and closed the flap.

Frightened by the light in his eyes, Honor tried to break away, but he caught her arm and turned it up behind her back to force her to her knees.

"We will pray," he intoned, keeping pressure on her arm. Quickly, he took the pouch from her nerveless fingers. "Pray, Jezebel, for forgiveness from God!" He pushed her head down with his free hand.

Pain spread outward from Honor's arm and collected in her shoulder. Her outrage was forgotten for the moment as she tried to think of a way to get away from this lunatic. He was pressing her head down in the attitude of prayer, but she was suddenly aware that he was pushing down into his own lap.

"Pray! Pray!" he intoned, keeping pressure on her arm while he pushed at her head.

For a moment, she thought she would faint from the pain and the nearness of his sweating body, but suddenly he released her arm, giving her some respite. When she realized why he had released her arm, she felt a wave of revulsion. With one hand still on her head, woven into her hair, he used his free hand to rip open the buttons of his trousers. Before her startled eyes, his rigid organ sprang to life, waving in front of her face.

When she struggled to get away, his hand went back to her arm, putting more pressure on it, while he pushed at her head, guiding her face toward him.

132

Not knowing what he wished her to do, she could only close her eyes against the reality of his desire. She felt the hot flesh bump her jaw, then her cheek and then nudge insistently at her lips. In horror, she realized finally what he wanted of her.

She struggled in earnest, but the pain in her arm was excruciating. His hand on her head was inexorable, and fruitlessly she tried to keep her lips clamped shut, but with an exclamation of sheer abandonment, he pushed his organ like a spear into her mouth. Horrified, she knelt between his legs, hating this man with a strength she had never known she possessed.

Hardly knowing what she did, she reacted in the only way she could. With deep and calculating hatred she bit into the turgid flesh as hard as she could. He let out a bloodcurdling yell and released her arm to clasp his abused flesh. With satisfaction, she watched drops of blood spread between his fingers and quickly she snatched the money pouch from the wagon floor.

"Don't try to follow me!" she warned, snatching a knife from the box where Ella kept them. "If you do, I swear I'll cut it off next time!"

So saying, she leaped from the wagon and ran down to the docks, hearing his oaths and curses behind her. Breathing hard, hardly believing what she had just done and said, she tried to quiet herself sufficiently to find directions to the captain's whereabouts.

A lone villager, sitting lazily beneath the shade of an evergreen, pointed in the direction of a tawdry-looking tavern. Hopefully Honor walked inside. There was only one man at the tables and one at a long bar. She walked to the man's table.

He was middle-aged, older than Jim Parsons, but her recent experience caused her to view him with distrust.

"Are you the captain of one of those ships in the harbor?" she asked with an edge to her voice.

He looked up, his wrinkled eyes moving over her thoughtfully. Then he nodded. "Captain Winston at your service, ma'am, of the *Lucille*."

Honor breathed a sigh of relief that seemed to well up from the very bottom of her vitals. "Captain Winston, I'm Honor O'Brien, badly in need of passage to Monterey. Can you help me?"

He eyed her quizzically. "I'm northbound up the coast,

ma'am, it's true, but I'm not used to taking on wild-eyed young ladies with no luggage about them."

"Please, Captain, the explanation is too long and too complicated to go into now. Just tell me if you will take me aboard for gold."

His eyes narrowed appreciatively. "For gold, ma'am, I'd take the devil himself aboard."

She laughed with relief. "Ah, Captain, you don't know how close you came to doing just that!"

Eighteen

Monterey was a sparkling gem of a city in that late fall of 1857. It lay on the tip of a peninsula that pointed out into the Monterey Bay, and Honor could see its gleaming white adobe buildings and red-tiled roofs from her cabin as she stared eagerly at the sight of land. She was excited and anxious at the same time, wondering what reaction Don Esteban would display when she presented herself to him.

It was a few hours later that she stood on the pier, anxiously searching the small crowd for someone who might seem to be looking for her. She had dispatched a short note to a small boy who promised to deliver it promptly to the hacienda of Don Esteban Sevillas. Whether the boy had been telling the truth remained to be seen, for she could only trust that he would return with Don Esteban as soon as possible.

She stood alone in the many-times-washed gray gown that was still too short in the sleeves and the equally uninteresting poke bonnet, which hid her face from the bolder stares. It was humiliating enough to have no luggage with her, no reticule, very little money left—but to appear to have no one waiting for her was even worse, especially with the dockhands beginning to edge nearer to her, ogling her shamelessly after looking furtively around for her escort.

"Waiting for someone, lassie?" a barnacled old man laughed.

"Yes," she said in her haughtiest voice, trying to dismiss him with a semblance of calm.

She moved away from the waterfront and toward the dusty street, searching for a carriage. She could see that the buildings here, which had seemed to gleam with a fresh coat of whitewash from the bay, were dingy gray and some were in need of repairs. There was nothing for her to do but start walking up the narrow, dusty street hoping to meet Don Esteban on the way to rescuing her from her predicament. She supposed now that she had really not thought about exactly how she was going to present herself to a man she had not seen for six years and whom she still presumed she would marry, despite all that had happened to her.

The walk up the street gave her time for thought and the problem became more wearying as she trodded along. Suppose the boy had lied and only wished the few pennies she had given him for his trouble. Suppose, if he did receive the boy's message, Don Esteban chose to disbelieve him. He might think her dead long ago, or perhaps her brother had stopped here on his way to the goldfields and told him of her disappearance.

Was she being an utter fool for coming this far, for believing that everything could go on as before? But after all, what else was there for her to do? She couldn't go back to Charleston, nor could she backtrack over the miles of Indian country to St. Louis. There was no one else to rely on. Her brother had left her destitute and she was certain she could not follow him, no matter what else happened. The chances would be more than a thousand to one that she might find him in the wilderness.

At a street corner, she saw a young woman with a basket balanced delicately on her head and she hailed her in order to question her.

"Can you direct me to the house of Don Esteban Sevillas," she asked.

The girl shook her head uncomprehendingly.

Honor tried again in a smattering of Spanish. *"¿La casa de Sevillas, D'onde?"*

The girl smiled and nodded, pointing to the basket on her head, which was filled with golden oranges. Then she began walking again, leaving Honor wondering what she was doing. Then, as the girl looked back and gestured to her to follow, Honor realized that she must be on her way to the Sevillas house now. What a stroke of luck! Eagerly she stepped beside the girl and followed her through the alleyway to what looked like the main square of the town. Honor looked about her with interest, feeling a little better that she was beyond the waterfront. She could see an imposing white structure

135

with massively carved stone decorations, above which flew the American flag. She pointed it out to the girl.

"*Presido*," she informed her shortly, hurrying on.

A buckboard was waiting for them at the edge of the square with an old man stooped over the front seat, the reins held slackly in his withered old hands. The girl chattered to him, pointed to Honor and then beckoned for her to get into the back of the wagon with her.

Tentatively Honor nodded and took her hand to help her up. "*¿La casa de Sevillas?*" she asked again nervously.

The girl nodded vigorously. "Tomás take us there," she said in painful English, putting a thick accent on the words.

"Thank you—*gracias*," Honor said with relief. She sat with her back against the side of the wagon, loosening the ribbons of the bonnet.

They were driving away from the town proper, taking a dirt road that led west and then turned north. She began to feel anxious again, wondering if she had been tricked, but her relief was overwhelming when they turned into a wide avenue along which grew broad-leafed trees, reminding her a little of the plantation drive she used to ride up when she was small. The thought calmed her spirit and she eyed the imposing hacienda at the end of the drive with a mixture of awe and appreciation. It was built in the Spanish style, of course, with thick adobe walls, a pale shade of pink, and a red-tiled roof. The facade was flat with no veranda as she had been used to seeing in Charleston. She suspected there would be a cool, tree-shaded patio somewhere in the interior of the house.

The buckboard stopped in the half-circle drive in front of the marble steps leading up to the front door. The old man waited patiently while Honor and her companion clambered down from the wagon, and then called a signal to the horses and drove away to what she presumed was the stables.

The girl indicated that she would be going around to the back of the house—the servants' entrance, Honor surmised. She felt suddenly afraid as the girl scurried away, leaving her to raise the massive brass knocker, which fell with a full, rich sound against the heavy, iron-decorated oaken door.

"*¿Sí?*" A gauntly thin, middle-aged woman answered the door, dressed impeccably in stiff black bodice and voluminous skirt. Her black hair, streaked with silver, was drawn over her ears and coiffed severely at her nape. She eyed the young visitor with disdain.

136

"Perdón, señora," Honor got out. "I would like to speak with Señor Sevillas."

"Señor Sevillas cannot be disturbed," the woman snapped back quickly.

"Please, let me explain," Honor said just as quickly. "My name is Honor O'Brien—you must let me speak to the elder señor if—"

"Don Diego has been dead for nearly a month now!" the woman retorted. "I cannot allow you to disturb the señora or the señor—"

She had already stepped inside and was preparing to close the door, but Honor would not be denied now. Throwing propriety to the winds, she pushed ahead, shaking off the woman's outstretched hand and nearly knocking her down. She rushed into the cool, mosaic-tiled hall, wondering what she would do now.

"Señorita! Come back here at once!" shrilled the woman in outrage.

Instinctively Honor headed for the door ahead of her, but upon opening it, she found that it led to the patio which she had expected earlier. Realizing her mistake, she would have turned back, but the housekeeper was right behind her, calling at the top of her voice for help from the menservants.

"Señorita, how dare you break into this house—"

Above her head, where a delicate wrought-iron railing traveled the length of the second story, providing a balcony for the rooms above, came an unhurried voice of authority.

"Señora Díaz, what is it?"

The housekeeper looked up, and following her gaze, Honor did the same, encountering the curious glance of a young man, perhaps five or six years her senior. His black hair was rumpled, suggesting that he had been pulled hastily out of bed at the commotion, a fact that was helped by his appearance, shirtless and barefoot.

"Señor Sevillas, this young woman has pushed her way inside like a wild person, insisting on speaking with you!"

The man laughed, his fingers idly pulling at the moustache that grew out on both sides of his face. "A young woman insists on speaking to me—why then send her up!" he commanded. "Rita has grown weary of my games."

The housekeeper colored with annoyance and gave the girl a look of offended superiority mixed with a kind of pity. "You heard him, señorita. You may take the stairs at the corner of the patio to the balcony." Without another word, the woman retreated quickly, leaving Honor alone with the man staring down at her expectantly.

"Come, come," he called down to her, scratching unconcernedly at his furred chest. "I am curious to hear what it is you wish."

Dubiously Honor walked to the stairway and ascended to the second floor. Could this man possibly be her fiancé, she thought in a kind of panic. Surely, it had seemed that Don Esteban was much more cultured, colder and, she was sure, more mature. Had it only been the visions of her youth? This man seemed somehow wild, careless and—yes—dangerous.

She had come up to him, stopping a few feet away to study him unconsciously while he openly did the same to her. A white grin lit his dark face, beneath the black moustache.

"Señorita, I would say, offhand, that you are not a native of our fair town," he offered sarcastically.

She shook her head. "I—am Honor O'Brien, señor. I—have—come a long way." The words seemed to stick in her throat as he stretched his lean, powerful body, his attention seeming to waver.

"Honor O'Brien," she repeated with more firmness. "Your fiancée!"

His look was one of open curiosity mixed with a kind of incredulousness. "My fiancée?" Then he grinned. "Señorita, what have I done to deserve this honor?" He laughed at his own joke.

She stamped her foot in growing annoyance. "I am not making a joke," she said angrily. "I am Honor O'Brien. I have traveled for a long time to come to you as—"

His eyes swept her searchingly, lingering longest on her waistline. "Señorita," he began in a complacent voice, "are you sure I am the one who has left the child in your belly? I swear I do not remember playing with you—and I think I would have recalled your face, *mi hermosa*."

She flushed with outrage. "I am not—with child!" she said, her temper flaring. "You were betrothed to me six years ago when I was 12. My father and yours signed an agreement, a formal betrothal which said that we would marry. I have come by wagon train from Santa Fe and have only arrived today. I had hoped for a more respectful welcome than this!"

He seemed genuinely surprised. "Honor O'Brien," he repeated frowning. "And you say you are engaged to me?"

She nodded, not trusting herself to speak.

He took her hand, a playful look in his soft-brown eyes.

138

"Then come and kiss me, lovely one, as a good fiancée should."

As she gasped for breath, he caught her hand and pulled her abruptly against his hard, half-naked body. His full mouth was hot and experienced on hers, plundering through her stiffened lips, careless as to her own lack of response. His hand was strong at the back of her waist, pressing her body inward to curve against his own.

When he finally released her, she was shaking with anger and a sensual awareness of him. He recognized her dilemma and smiled. "You are a hot-blooded tigress, Honor O'Brien," he said through half-closed eyes. "I would bed you now, for I do not think you remained a virgin for me."

She stared at him in disbelief. How had he sensed such a thing! What kind of man had her father promised her to? She backed away uncertainly.

He followed her with catlike steps, that uncompromising grin on his face. When she had backed herself to the far wall, he closed in on her, his hands sure and heavy as they fondled her breasts through the material of her bodice. Carelessly he ripped at the buttons at her neck, exposing her throat so that he could press wet kisses into the hollow of her neck.

Shaking with reaction, Honor could not move, nor could she cry out. This man was like some raving, sexual animal who took his lovers as people normally took wine with their meals. She was confused—and frightened.

"Let me go," she whispered hoarsely.

"Not until I have tasted your flesh, lovely one. Come with me now or I will lie with you here in front of all the servants!"

He was pressing her down on her knees, his hands heavy on her shoulders, when the sound of hurrying feet and the housekeeper's wailing stopped him. He looked up, releasing her so abruptly that she fell backward against the wall.

Honor could hear in the background the housekeeper's whining voice. "Oh, señor, I did not know. She said only that she wanted to see Señor Sevillas and I thought that she meant—. Forgive me, señor, your brother forced me to take him in while you were away in San Francisco making the arrangements. How could I have known? Oh, señor!"

"Get out of the way, María, before I lose my patience!" roared an angry voice.

With the speed of an alerted panther, the man who had

139

been about to seduce her only a moment before sped away down the balcony with a blown kiss in her direction.

At the same time, a taller, thinner, older version of him appeared in an archway leading to the inside of the house. "Jaime! Jaime, you won't get away this time, I'll have my men hunt you down!"

The younger man laughed. "Ah, brother of mine, if only you had waited a little longer I would have told you what a bargain you would have had in this woman who calls herself your fiancée. *Adiós, hermano!* Until the next time!" He leaped down the staircase at the far end and hiked himself over the patio wall and had disappeared within five minutes.

Bringing herself to her feet, Honor leaned against the wall, willing her head to stop its spinning. Had she come to some sort of lunatic asylum, she wondered. What in the world was happening?

The man who had entered and saved her from certain rape was turning toward her slowly, a look of puzzled wonderment on his face. "Who are you?" he demanded harshly, causing her to jump in alarm.

"I—I am Honor O'Brien, señor, and who are you?" she asked faintly.

His face seemed to whiten beneath its tanned exterior, but he was able to bow after a moment's hesitation with a smoothness almost inbred in him. "Señorita O'Brien, forgive me, I am Don Esteban Sevillas!"

"What!" She looked at him in surprise. "B-but your housekeeper, she led me to believe that—"

"María will be punished for her oversight. She should have known better. How could a young woman with your apparent breeding come looking for my brother, Jaime?"

"Your brother?"

"I am afraid so, señorita. Please accept a thousand apologies for—his rudeness."

Honor felt as though all the breath had left her body, as though someone had dealt her a blow on the head from which she would never recover. This man, dark and foreboding, was her fiancé! And the other—the one that had attacked her like a rutting stallion—was his brother!"

"If he was your brother, why did he run away?" she asked suspiciously.

Esteban laughed harshly. "Because he is a *bandido*—an outlaw. I never allow him in this house, but María . . ." He left the sentence unfinished, frowning darkly.

"Your brother has broken the law!" She couldn't imagine having a brother-in-law who was a fugitive from justice.

"He is a murderer and a thief," the man replied coldly.

A murderer! Honor felt her head spinning, whirling. With only the smallest of sighs, she slid down the wall in a dead faint.

Nineteen

Honor had awakened from the faint to find herself ensconced in a wide, soft bed, dressed in a silken nightdress with the covers firmly tucked under her chin. María was worriedly bending over her, her stern features pinched by fear of what her fate would be should the señorita prove to have been injured.

"Ah, señorita, thank God you have awakened!" the woman breathed with relief. "Señor Sevillas, he would have whipped my scrawny back if you had come to some harm!"

"Please inform the señor that I am quite well, but terribly tired, and I should like to remain in bed and go to sleep," Honor replied shakily, not wishing to have to face her fiancé so soon after all that had happened.

"*Sí*, señorita, I will tell him," the woman affirmed, nodding her head as she backed out of the room. She stopped for a moment and eyed the young girl with a hint of speculation. "Señorita, you—you will forgive me for my rudeness earlier, won't you?"

Honor nodded wearily. "Of course, María. How could you have known who I was?"

The woman smiled gauntly. "*Gracias,* señorita, and now I will leave you to sleep." She closed the door after her, leaving Honor to close her eyes and try to push all the disquieting thoughts from her mind in order to rest.

She had almost succeeded in doing so when the door opened quietly, allowing Don Esteban himself to enter. She sat up in surprise, clutching the covers like a frightened virgin, although she truly was upset that she should be subject to more questioning—and that he should enter her room without knocking!

"Señorita O'Brien," he said, testing the name on his tongue as he bowed.

141

"Señor Sevillas, I—I must apologize for causing so much commotion—"

He waved aside her protest with a languid hand and seated himself in a chair close to the bed. His black eyes moved slowly over her with an appreciative air that was lost on her as she picked at the cover nervously.

"You resemble your mother, señorita," he commented, looking at her over the tips of his long fingers which he had formed into a tower.

"Thank you," she said uncertainly. An uncomfortable silence lasted for a few moments until Don Esteban spoke again.

"I had received word that you were lost, had disappeared in Missouri before your brother had had a chance to join a wagon train."

"Then you have talked to my brother?" she asked eagerly.

He shook his head. "I received a brief wire from him—that was all."

"Oh." Her face fell.

"What *did* happen?" he questioned, his eyes narrowing slightly.

"I—I was kidnapped and found myself in a wagon train bound for Santa Fe. We—"

"Kidnapped! By whom, señorita?" he asked smoothly.

She flushed. "By a woman who wanted me to work for her in a house of—prostitution—once we arrived in California."

His eyebrow arched with haughty disdain. "Whorehouse?" he confirmed. "Señorita, what had you done to merit such distinction?" His tone was accusatory and she flinched.

"Nothing, señor! I was a total innocent and she had me drugged and bound and then taken to her wagon with two other girls."

"I see." But the way he was looking at her told her clearly that he thought she was lying.

Grimly she continued. "Some weeks out of Independence, the train was attacked by a band of Comanche Indians. I was taken prisoner along with several of the others." She hesitated, then plunged on. "The son of the chief wanted to make me his second wife, but one of the women of the village helped me to escape."

"And you came all the way from the Indian village to here?" he questioned in a mixture of amazement and heavy sarcasm.

"Of course not! I would have died in the desert before I

even got to Santa Fe, but—but someone helped me get there. Then I joined another wagon train to San Diego with a middle-aged couple who fed and boarded me in exchange for my services."

"Your services, señorita?" He was mocking her. "And were these services the same ones that you no doubt exercised in the first wagon train?"

She looked at him aghast. "Of course not. Señor Sevillas, I deeply resent such an accusation!" But she couldn't help flushing as the thought of what Jim Parsons had tried to make her do rose ugly in her mind.

As though he could read her mind, Don Esteban leaned forward. "You are a lovely young woman, señorita. You cannot tell me that no man molested you in all these months!"

"What do you mean! I—I survived everything—all of it—in order to reach you and fulfill the promise our parents made to each other! How dare you question me so—so intimately!"

"I dare, señorita, because I have every right, as your fiancé, to find out what manner of woman it is that I am bound to." He leaned back in his chair, regarding her flushed face. "You talk of being with the Comanche—I am well aware what they do to their women prisoners. As for the man who helped you get to Santa Fe—are you trying to make me believe he did it out of the goodness of his heart?"

She crimsoned and shook her head wordlessly, dropping her eyes at the intensity of his gaze.

"And what payment did he exact, señorita?" the don continued smoothly. "Your virginity, perhaps?"

Honor stared in surprise at his bluntness, thinking how alike he and his brother were, although this one preferred words to deeds.

Don Esteban was rubbing his jaw now, thinking to himself as he watched the young girl in front of him with interest. She was, he could tell even through the rather disheveled appearance, a very beautiful young woman.

"How old are you?" he asked suddenly.

"Eighteen," she whispered, deeply ashamed at his previous probing.

"Eighteen," he repeated to himself. Marianne Gordon was eighteen, he thought, but she was still a Dresden doll, an untouchable figure, well protected by her father's wealth and her mother's impeccable breeding. He wondered idly if she would have been able to survive the desert, Indians and a

143

man's lust to get to her fiancé. Probably not, he thought cynically, then brushed thoughts of her from his mind. His problem now was how to deal with this extremely delicate situation without endangering his own position. If this young woman found out that he was already affianced to another girl, after all she had been through, there was no telling what she might resort to. He had a feeling that she would exact revenge for his having dishonored their marriage contract.

"Señorita O'Brien—may I call you Honor, under the circumstances? I would have you call me Esteban." At her slight nod, he continued, "I must allow you to refresh yourself. Forgive me for neglecting your personal comfort, but I must admit all of this has come as a complete surprise to me."

"Of course," Honor agreed, but wondered at the same time why he had put her through such verbal torture. What sort of man was he really? Then, remembering her own manners, she said softly, "I am sorry to hear of your father's death, Esteban. María told me—"

"Yes, it was a long illness," he said shortly.

"And your mother?" she asked, finding it hard to understand this strangely indifferent man who was her fiancé.

He shrugged. "She is not well, but it is a different ailment." He touched his head meaningfully.

He studied her a moment more, then stood up. "I should leave you to sleep now, Honor. I think it would be better to leave more talk for the morning." He leaned over and, to her surprise, kissed her briefly on the forehead. "Good night."

"Good night," she said softly, watching him walk out of the room, closing the door firmly behind him.

Outside her bedroom, Esteban Sevillas felt a twinge of lust followed by a coldhearted, practical thought of how to get rid of her before his soon-to-be in-laws found out about her. It would be easy enough to keep her presence from his own mother, and the servants knew they would be punished severely if any indulged in idle gossip or speculation. But the girl herself? What to do with her?

Marianne and her parents would be arriving from San Francisco in two weeks' time to prepare for the wedding festivities. He had insisted that the ceremony take place at his ancestral home, but now he wished that he had let her have her way and had the marriage take place in San Francisco.

He walked to his study and seated himself in his favorite armchair, allowing himself the soothing effect of a cheroot. It helped to relax him as he thought of solutions to his dilemma. Needless to say, he had been shocked at the wire from her brother a month ago. But it had suited his plans perfectly, for he had really been hoping to extricate himself from the marriage agreement as soon as he had gotten word that the O'Briens were now virtually penniless. He hadn't counted on her showing up like this. Of all things! How many women would have made it, with or without help! Certainly not Marianne Gordon, or any of the other women he had known and used for his own purposes.

But now, he was not in a position to enjoy this unexpected delicacy dropped into his lap. He would not have married her in any case, since she was, after all, soiled goods, but he could have toyed with her, enjoyed her until he was finished with her. His black eyes gleamed and he stroked his moustache thoughtfully. There still might be a way to taste a little of what might have been his—and still could be if he was careful.

Walter Gordon, Marianne's father, was not a man to be treated lightly, for all his pomposity and big talk. He was largely, if not solely, responsible for Sevillas' own good fortune this past year. He had been dangerously close to losing the hacienda, his lands and his fortunes because of the fact that he had inherited everything under the Spanish-Mexican occupation of California.

California had been declared a state seven years ago and the Sevillas had held on only by the skin of their teeth. Last year, there had been grumblings by some of the United States citizens, wondering why the Mexicans were allowed to keep much of the land they had held before the occupation. The Sevillas family had been under attack by the American land-grabbers and it had been by the hasty, if somewhat underhanded method of becoming engaged to the daughter of one of the most influential men in San Francisco that Esteban Sevillas had managed to secure his holdings. By marrying an American, he was ensuring his own good fortune.

His father had abhorred the idea of voiding the honorable contract he had made with James O'Brien, but they already knew that he had died and Esteban had proceeded to persuade his father that the contract was no longer viable. His father, weakened by his illness, had made little protest when his son had gone ahead and arranged for the marriage to Marianne Gordon.

Sevillas had never dreamed that the girl and her brother would come all the way west by themselves. And that she

145

had, ultimately, come alone—she was truly a remarkable young woman!

He frowned and drummed the arm of the chair with his fingers. His wedding to Marianne was scheduled for the first of December. He had less than a full month to figure out what to do with Honor O'Brien. The task would be worthy of all his talents, but he was sure he would think of something.

Twenty

Honor had bathed and changed into a soft robe that belonged to Esteban's mother. She felt much better this morning after having eaten a light breakfast. The room she had been given was beautifully appointed and a far cry from what she had been used to of late. She almost smiled at the incongruity of this room in comparison to the Indian lodges she had shared, first with Magda and then with Katala and Lianna. God, but it was good to have survived it all and come home at last.

If she was anxious over Esteban's lukewarm reception of her, she was determined not to think about it now. Of course, it was a shock to him and—her frown deepened—he seemed concerned that she was no longer pure, but there were still many things she had to offer. She had learned many things in these past months—how to be independent, to cook, to be responsible—things she had never been required to prove as the spoiled daughter of a Southern gentleman.

In her feeling of happy lassitude, she felt positive that she would be able to work things out. Esteban would never regret marrying her. That she vowed.

She had washed her hair and was fluffing it out languorously, brushing it dry in front of the window as the mid-morning sun streamed prettily on her upturned face. She made a very fetching picture to Esteban Sevillas as he opened the door soundlessly, unannounced, and stood gazing covertly at her for a moment before knocking on the panel.

Honor called for him to come in, turning around to catch him looking at her with a kind of arrogant superiority that troubled her, although she wasn't sure why. For a moment, she could have sworn that he looked something like Brice Devlin when he— But now she had to stop thinking about

146

Brice, she chided herself. She couldn't compare her fiancé to Brice Devlin, the accomplished seducer, the notorious renegade! She shook her head to forcibly push out the notion. Nevertheless, she was nonplussed at having Esteban continue to step into her room without calling first for permission to enter.

"Good morning, Honor," he greeted her, bowing formally.

Honor noted the well-fitted suit of dark-blue broadcloth, the frilled, linen shirt, crisply starched. It made his skin seem darker by contrast and the black hair reminded her unaccountably of another's night-dark hair against the collar of his shirt.

"Good morning, Esteban," she answered, putting the brush down and turning fully to face him.

Esteban Sevillas could see, in one all-encompassing look, the honey-gold of her magnificent mane of hair, the emerald-green of her eyes, narrowing a little as they tried to guess the purpose of his visit, the perfection of her peachlike skin except for the sprinkling of freckles that served to make her look younger than her eighteen years. The curves of her figure were outlined through the material of her robe as the sun filtered through it, making him quite sure that she would fit perfectly into his arms. He could already feel stirrings of desire. He was certainly not the man who would deny himself the pleasure of a woman.

"Is everything satisfactory?" His voice was husky, already unconsciously growing more intimate as he anticipated her surrender.

"Yes, thank you," she answered. She moved away from the window and seated herself next to the dressing table. "I must put my hair up, Esteban, or what will you think of me?" she asked teasingly, trying to lighten the atmosphere.

"It looks lovely down, Honor,"

She blushed. "Thank you."

"Do not be embarrassed at my compliments, my dear. After all we will soon be joined in marriage, will we not?"

She nodded, then glanced up at him shyly. "Esteban, there are so many things I feel compelled to tell you. I—"

"Not now, Honor." He took a step toward her, his eyes black and piercing in his lean face.

For some reason, Honor wished desperately to run away from him. His eyes gazed so coldly at her as though anticipating that she would disgrace him. Was he so angry about her losing her virginity—so angry that she had managed to stay alive, despite having lost it? She shivered and looked away from his penetrating stare.

"Esteban," she said as lightly as she could, "I must get dressed now. I—I would like for you to show me the house," she reminded him.

He started, then smiled politely. It amused him to think that she felt so firmly entrenched that she could give orders to him already. He looked forward to ending her illusions, but not quite yet, he thought.

"Of course, Honor. I will await you downstairs. I believe my mother is about your size and I have taken the liberty of providing you with a few dresses until you are able to have some made."

"Thank you, Esteban, and—you will thank your mother for me?"

He nodded, although he had no intention of doing so. His mother was not right anymore. Her mind wandered too much for her even to hold a conversation with him. Besides, he doubted that the two women would meet.

He left her alone, calling sharply for a maid to come and help her. The maid, dark and pert, couldn't possibly have been more than fifteen years old. She curtsied swiftly to the don, avoiding his eyes, then introduced herself to the young woman who was watching her with a kind expression.

"Are you to be my personal maid, Elena?" Honor asked pleasantly, as the girl laid two dresses on the bed.

"*Sí*, señorita, as long as you wish."

"You are very young," she continued idly.

The young girl blushed as she smoothed the skirt of the gown Honor had chosen to wear. "*Sí*, señorita. The señor, Don Esteban, has done many things to help me learn to improve myself." This last was said with a trace of bitterness.

Honor detected it and watched the girl covertly in the mirror as she helped her to pile the heavy honey-gold mass of hair on top of her head. "Do you enjoy your work here, Elena?"

The girl dropped a pin nervously and quickly retrieved it to hide her agitation. "*Sí*, señorita, I am—grateful to the señor for all he has done."

Honor decided that this girl might prove to have some useful information. She was at a loss as to how to deal with her fiancé and she wanted to know something about him. "Elena, you may speak frankly with me. Is life here at the hacienda easy?"

148

The girl shrugged carefully. "Sí, when Don Esteban is away in San Francisco much of the time to visit his—" she stumbled over the word and quickly recovered—"his business friends. But he can be—he can be—" She started at the sound of footsteps in the hall. Quickly she finished the hairdo and went to the bed to get the gown in order to pull it over Honor's head.

"Yes, Elena?" Honor prompted, feeling as though the girl were about to admit a confidence.

"Nothing, señorita. Don Esteban provides for us all very well."

The girl stubbornly refused to say more even when Honor prodded her outright. Reluctantly Honor allowed her to leave after buttoning her gown. The girl must have been told to say nothing, she reasoned, else why would she appear so upset at almost divulging something of interest. It was absurd really! Why should Esteban seek to hide anything from her?

She was surprised to see her fiancé awaiting her on a bench in the upper hall. "Don't you trust me to find my way downstairs?" she chided him, hoping to keep the atmosphere light.

He laughed. "Certainly I did not want you to get lost," he returned, bowing and taking her hand in his. "My mother's gown suits your coloring perfectly, Honor. I am glad you chose that one."

"Thank you," she said, coloring at the compliment. "I should like to meet your mother as soon as—as soon as you feel she is up to it. She will be informed of my arrival?"

He smiled easily. "Of course, of course. But come, let me show you something of the house and the grounds. Do you ride?"

She nodded eagerly. "Oh, yes. It has been ages since I've really ridden, and the idea sounds wonderful."

"Good. We will ride this afternoon after lunch and tonight I have ordered a fiesta to celebrate your arrival. There will be wine and music and much revelry. You will enjoy yourself, Honor."

She took his hand delightedly, looking forward to the evening, unaware of the wicked sparkle in the don's eyes as he, too, looked forward to the night's festivities.

Honor could hear the soft strains of guitar and violin from the window of her room that evening as she prepared for the entertainment. A party frock had been hastily altered for her, and she now examined herself in the mirror with it on, pleased at the effect. It was of shimmering turquoise taffeta, the bodice cut very deep, baring the upper half of her breasts, her shoulders and her arms, and the skirts very full worn over a horsehair crinoline. The constricting garments felt odd after she had gotten used to so much freedom of movement and she found herself practicing how to walk in them as though she had never worn such clothes before. Perhaps the oddest feeling was from the lace-embroidered corset that pushed her breasts up high and whittled her already willow-slim waist until her breathing was nearly constricted—that and the white pantalettes that reached to her calves. She felt as though she must be wearing fifty pounds of clothing and hoped that the feeling would go away as the evening wore on. Really, she hadn't realized how she had almost been totally ruined by those savages!

She noticed that the girl who helped her dress was someone else, and wondered what had happened to Elena. Perhaps she had complained to Esteban about her mistress' stubborn curiosity and had asked to be replaced. Honor frowned at the thought, hoping she had not gotten the girl in any trouble.

But Elena was soon out of her mind as she descended the staircase on the arm of her fiancé, who looked splendid in a black frock coat and striped stock that accentuated his tall lean build. He wore diamonds at cuffs and shirtfront and she was more than proud that this elegant man had been promised to her as a husband. It was easy to forget the earlier unpleasantness of their meeting. She had carefully refrained from mentioning his brother again and he had not asked her anymore of her adventures on the Santa Fe Trail.

Theirs was an uneasy truce, though, as she heard him introducing her to the few guests as a very old acquaintance. She would have liked to ask him immediately why he didn't introduce her as his bride-to-be, but after the introductions he explained smoothly to her that the guests were no one important, only the servants and a few sharecroppers. He added that he was going to have a more gala affair to introduce her to his intimate friends and the important people of the town. Although Honor still felt miffed at his reasoning, she allowed him to go on with the charade. Certainly there was nothing else she could do!

Outside in the courtyard, torches flared as long tables were set up for the food. As the major ranchero in these parts, the Sevillas family had always held fiestas for their people and so no one thought it odd that Don Esteban had ordered an impromptu affair tonight. Honor was unaware of the curious stares among those gathered or the whisperings as to what exactly her position in the house would be. Never before had Don Esteban brought his mistresses so openly into public. He preferred to seduce the younger serving girls and keep them for a time before hungering for the high-quality kept women of San Francisco, which was only a three days' ride.

There was an odd assortment among the guests—from cowhands to serving wenches to María Díaz, the formidable housekeeper who no longer seemed so formidable to Honor. She spied her sitting alone under a lighted torch and resolved to go speak to her to lighten the dour look on her face. But before she could do so, Esteban caught her hand and pulled her over to where a space had been cleared for the dancing. Several couples were already clapping and twirling in the old folk dances of Spain. The contradanza, the jota, the bamba were executed with more enthusiasm than style and when Esteban pulled her into the circle, Honor laughingly tried to follow the steps, dipping and twisting, flinging back her head and snapping her fingers with the rhythm of the music.

The music became faster as skirts twirled, allowing flashing glimpses of bare legs, and men threw off their jackets to dance in their shirt sleeves as sweat beaded their brows. Honor laughed and clapped and drank the wine that Esteban pushed into her hand. Her hair was falling from its pins, her dress was damp with perspiration as her lips parted revealing her even, white teeth. She turned, laughing, to say something to Esteban, and then her face froze and her eyes widened in shock.

Standing not ten feet away from her, an infuriating smile on his handsome face, was Brice Devlin!

"What is it, my dear?" inquired Esteban easily. "You feel unwell?"

"N-no, Esteban, I—I thought I—" She shook her head, attempting to regain her composure. "Nothing." She drank the wine in her glass in one gulp, causing her eyes to smart and her head to spin for a moment.

"*Querida*, you really have had too much to drink for the time being. Let me take you to your room," Esteban said with soft expectancy.

"No, I think I just need to sit down," she said, moving to an iron bench beneath the spreading branches of an old cottonwood tree. "Go on and dance, and I will watch you for a

151

moment," she urged him, scared to death that Brice Devlin would come up to confront her. She glanced uneasily behind her, but he had disappeared.

She sat folding her hands, trying to quiet the pounding of her heart. How could he possibly be here, now? He should be in Santa Fe, or with Katala! Not here! How dare he come into her life again when she was about to become the wife of one of the most respected men in Monterey! Her concern gave way to anger as she thought of Brice deliberately trying to spoil her wedding. He was just the scoundrel to do it! And she had almost thought—had almost forgiven him for having taken advantage of her weakness in the Indian camp!

She tried to remember. Had she told him the name of her fiancé? She did recall she had told him what her destination was, but could it be mere coincidence that made him turn up here tonight? And why was he here? Surely Esteban would have mentioned a guest.

When her fiancé returned to her side, she was fanning herself furiously, for she had caught sight of Brice Devlin again, his arm casually about the shoulders of a young Mexican girl. She pointed her fan discreetly in his direction.

"Esteban, who is that man over there?"

He looked over unconcernedly. "Why do you ask, *querida?* Has he done something to offend you?"

She shook her head unsteadily. "He—he looks something of the desperado, a renegade—an outlaw, perhaps. I don't think he should be here!"

Esteban laughed as though she were a child and didn't understand the ways of men. "Honor, I think he is only having a good time. Perhaps he will drink too much tonight and then I shall have the servants send him home to his quarters."

"His quarters?"

"Yes, I have hired him only this afternoon as a vaquero."

At her dubious look, he explained with a condescending grin. "A vaquero—in your language, *querida,* a cowboy. You will have no cause to meet him if he displeases you, as he will be out on the range during the day, but I have invited all of the vaqueros to the fiesta tonight."

"I—I see. He is an American, is he not?" she asked, trying to keep her voice calm.

"Yes, I think so, although he does not act like most gringos—forgive me, *querida,* I did not mean an insult to you," he hastily amended.

She smiled weakly, hardly hearing him. All her attention

was on Brice Devlin as he leaned toward the servant girl and whispered something in her ear. The girl laughed and nodded, then went to join another beckoning vaquero on the dance floor. Honor watched as Brice Devlin's silvery-blue eyes followed the dancers unconcernedly. He was dressed in typical cowboy attire—black pants, dark-blue shirt with a black vest, and kerchief knotted casually at his throat. His black hair seemed a little shorter than she remembered it and he had shaved off the beard he had been growing, but had kept a neatly trimmed moustache that seemed to Honor to draw attention to the full, sensual lips. She remembered those same lips on her own and looked away quickly, fearing that he might turn and catch her staring at him.

But her curiosity impelled her to find him again a little later in the evening and anger bubbled nearly to the surface as she spied him walking away from the patio with the same serving girl he had been talking to earlier. She told herself she was being foolish to get angry over such a trifle. He was nothing to her anymore—had only used her body for his own gratification. Whatever tender feelings there may have been between them were one-sided on her part. The thought that she had actually told him she loved him galled her so that she ground her teeth in irritation.

"*Querida,* I think you must be tired," Esteban was saying as he caught her arm possessively, causing her to swing around to face him. "Come, let me escort you to your room."

Honor would have protested, but his grip was strong and she really hadn't the heart to remain any longer at the fiesta. She allowed him to lead her upstairs, hardly aware of him, her concentration on Brice Devlin as she fumed at the turn of events.

"Honor, you have not listened to me," Esteban was saying chidingly as they entered her room. With the snap of his fingers, he dismissed the servant girl who had been waiting to assist Honor to undress. The girl hurried out of the room, closing the door behind her.

"What? Oh, I'm sorry, Esteban," she said contritely. "I was thinking of—of the arrangements that will have to be made for our wedding."

He knew she was lying, but couldn't pinpoint the reason for her inattentiveness. Surely she couldn't be homesick. Had one of the servants filled her mind with gossip? He frowned and stepped close to her.

"Do not bother yourself with trifles." he commanded

153

softly, pulling the light shawl from her shoulders and throwing it carelessly on a nearby chair. "Come here to me, Honor, I have not yet greeted you properly."

His arms went tightly about her, swinging her around to press her body against his own. After a slight hesitation, Honor dutifully lifted her face for his kiss. She was not prepared for the sudden plunder of her mouth as he forced her lips open and scoured the interior of her mouth with his tongue. She pushed at him to release her, but was aware of his hands on her back, pulling at the fastenings of her gown.

Freeing her mouth, she gazed up at him in surprise. "Esteban, what are you doing!" she cried. "Please let me go. How can you try to take liberties when the banns have not even been published yet?"

He looked at her incredulously, and she thought he was about to burst into laughter, but with an effort he controlled himself. *"Querida,"* he said gently, "I would think you would wish to show your affection for me. Do not deny me now," he urged.

Her eyes widened. "Esteban, you actually expected me to—to go to bed with you before our marriage?"

He could not believe her indigant reaction. How many men had she already lain with, given her body to? And now she dared to refuse him! It was inconceivable, but he could feel the tenseness in her body, the tightening within her that told him clearly she would not receive him without a struggle. Esteban Sevillas had never had to fight for a woman. The young servant girls he took, especially those under sixteen, were in awe of him, did what he wished without question, as though they were blessed to be allowed to please him thus. The high-priced women in San Francisco were professionals and, if they had seemed coy, it was always part of an act which ultimately ended in bed. Marianne Gordon—she was in a different class, an untouchable now, but once married, she would do her duty as a wife and accept him whenever he desired. Already she had allowed his hands to please her, although she would not let him enter her yet. He ground his teeth in frustration that this little American chit should defy his desires.

"Please, Esteban, I am tired and I would like to go to bed." Honor looked at him steadily, sensing only dimly the struggle within him.

Finally, he let her go reluctantly, touching her lips with a brief kiss. *"Querida,* I—you must forgive me for my

154

hastiness. You spur my desire with your beauty and I forgot myself." He leaned closer and whispered caressingly, "You make me yearn for the wedding night, my sweet." He was satisfied at her shiver of anticipation and released her slowly.

After bowing to her, he quit her room, standing for a moment in the hallway, trying to regain his control. The servant girl he had dismissed earlier had remained in the hall and his eyes beckoned her imperiously. She came to him, her head bowed in abject submission.

"Were you, perhaps, listening at the keyhole?" he demanded in Spanish.

The girl shook her head quickly, her eyes downcast.

Esteban regarded her for a moment. He thought he recalled having taken her already, but she was young and lithe and her hair was long and thick. Shrugging, he caught her hand and led her down the hall to his own room, pushing her roughly inside so that she tripped and fell on the floor.

"No, do not get up," he said, excitement in his voice, as he ripped at his own clothing. "Only lift your skirt, *chica*, and spread your legs for me."

As the girl obeyed and turned her face away, he knelt on the floor and plunged into her body, finding the solace he needed so badly after that cursed little chit had defied him. There would be, he decided coldly, time to enlighten her later.

Twenty-one

Honor breakfasted with Esteban early the next morning. She wanted to know more about the circumstances of Brice Devlin's hiring, but knew it was foolish to arouse her fiancé's curiosity.

"Your home is truly lovely," she commented, referring to the tour of the house he had given her the day before. "How large are the grounds?"

"Two Spanish leagues," he said, then at her confusion, "Nearly ten thousand acres of land, *querida*."

"You must employ a great number of—vaqueros for so vast an estate, Esteban," she continued.

He nodded. "Almost two hundred men to ride the range

boundaries, herd the cattle and keep off vandals," he said with little interest.

"Two hundred! But there weren't nearly that many here last night for the fiesta," she went on, fishing for any details of Devlin's whereabouts.

"I did not invite all of them, my dear," he said condescendingly. "I doubt that you would be interested in some of them. They are half-enslaved Indians, mestizos and poor Mexican half-breeds. Not the sort for you to have to entertain."

"I see—but then, the ones who were invited must be on a slightly higher level?"

"Sí, they sleep in the bunkhouse a few yards behind the stables. They are the men I rely on to keep the peace among the illiterates."

Honor finished her questioning, wondering whether or not she really wanted to talk with Devlin. She was burning to ask him why he had chosen this rancho to find work—why he even wished to work at all! She was sure that Esteban did not pay his men well—and Brice had never seemed the type to put himself under another man's authority. She couldn't understand it—if she hadn't known him better she might have thought he had followed her.

Their breakfast was interrupted by the majordomo, who doubled as Esteban's personal valet, bringing in a salver upon which rested a crisp white note, scented, Honor noticed sniffing appreciatively, and immediately she wondered who could have sent it. She was not to be enlightened by her fiancé, who read the note quickly and folded it into his pocket.

"Good news?" she inquired curiously.

He shrugged. "Business, my love. I must go to San Francisco on a—legal matter. I hate to leave you, *querida,* but I may be gone all week. Do you mind?"

Honor seized at the chance to get away from Devlin eagerly. "Of course not, Estenban. Why couldn't I go with you? Oh, I would so love to see San Francisco!" Her eyes sparkled like emeralds as she leaned forward eagerly.

Esteban groaned inwardly. *Dios,* when she looked like that with her lovely face shining, he was hard put to keep himself from ripping the clothes from her body. Could he take her to San Francisco? But how could he when Walter Gordon had insisted upon him coming to straighten out last minute details of the marriage contract? Marianne had written him, asking him to come as soon as possible, "for Papa's wishes and

156

mine," she had said. He knew he would be spending a great deal of time with her—he couldn't leave Honor in the hotel room, she would begin to wonder. No, he couldn't take her. It would be stupid!

"I'm sorry, *querida*. Although I would love to take you, I will be tied up every day with these legal matters and wouldn't have the time to show you the city. Of course, I wouldn't allow you to sightsee alone. You do understand? I promise you that after the wedding I will take you there on our honeymoon." The lie came so smoothly to him, he surprised even himself.

Her disappointed face hid her panic at being left alone here while he was away. They had had only two days together and she felt as though she needed more time to get to know this strange man. She was afraid, too, that his brother might decide to pay another visit when he heard that Esteban had gone back to San Francisco. She shivered at the thought of that animal, that murderer coming near her again. And then too, there was Brice Devlin, who must have seen her last night—who would know that Esteban would be gone.

"Oh, Esteban, must you go now?" she asked desperately. "We—we haven't even read the banns in the church yet. We really haven't discussed a date for the wedding. I haven't met any of your friends—what will they think if they come to call and they find me here?"

He patted her hand reassuringly. "I will send a few of my servants over to the closest rancheros, telling them I will be away on business. Do not worry about discovery, my dear."

She blushed. "I didn't mean it like that," she amended hastily.

He smiled. "I realize that you are still nervous. I promise that as soon as I return things will be straightened out." His eyes gleamed at the thought.

"All right," Honor sighed at length, "but I will be lonely until your return, Esteban."

Her fiancé had been gone seven days and Honor felt as though she would go mad if she remained in the big house another minute. She had resolved not to set foot outside its walls, as a protection to herself, but found that her voluntary incarceration was preying too much on her nerves. She longed to get out in the beautiful autumn weather, to ride a little, observe the people and lands that would soon be hers to share with her husband. There was no one to talk with in the

157

house, for the serving girls kept their distance and María Díaz was endowed with an unusual reserve that allowed no companionship.

She was sitting listlessly in the front parlor, curled in a chair reading, when she thought about Esteban's mother, whom she had never seen. She had wondered if the old woman really existed, then chided herself at the idea. Esteban wouldn't lie to her about such a thing. Possibly she was confined to one of the rooms on the third floor, which was seldom used. Getting out of the chair, Honor resolved to go and find the woman herself. Perhaps she was lonely too and they could comfort each other.

Instinctively, she knew that María would disapprove of her actions and so she checked first to see where the housekeeper was. She found her in the kitchen supervising the cleaning of the wine cellar, which would keep her occupied for hours. Resolutely Honor made her way upstairs to the third floor.

Once there, she stood at the end of a long hallway, on either side of which doors were lined—six on a side. She opened the first to find old furniture stacked inside. The second, third and fourth doors revealed guest rooms which needed only new linens and a good dusting to make them livable. At the fifth door she tried, she was surprised to see a collection of paintings and artifacts, some of which looked very old. Curiously she studied a portrait of a regal-looking lady, her black hair swept up grandly with a diamond comb. A silver lace mantilla spread outward from the comb in the Spanish style, covering the woman's shoulders. Her black eyes looked imperiously down from above the thin, straight nose and her lips were folded into a thin, almost arrogant line. She seemed truly formidable. Inscribed on the frame was the name *Yolande*.

Passing out of the room, Honor went to the last door on that side and turned the knob.

"Who is it?" called a harsh voice.

Honor jumped at the human sound and peered into the semi-gloom. "Who—who is there? Señora Sevillas?"

"Of course it is, you fool," came the voice again. "Have you brought more tea?"

The voice came from the depths of a curtained bed and Honor stepped hesitantly over to it. "I am not a servant, señora. My name is Honor O'Brien, engaged to your oldest son, Esteban. Has he not told you about me?"

"What? What did you say? Come here, young woman, and let me look at you."

"First let me open the drapes, señora, for I doubt that you can see anything in this gloom," Honor replied with spirit.

"Impertinent, too!" cried the señora, but with a hint of amusement in her voice. "I simply must tell Diego about this. Have you met my husband yet?"

Honor shivered. The woman did not know her husband was dead? Or, perhaps, she refused to know. She walked to the bed to draw back the bed curtains and gasped in surprise. This was Yolande, she was sure of it! But—how different from the portrait in the next room. Only the diamond comb and the silver mantilla had brought the likeness to her mind.

Yolande Sevillas was now only a wasted old woman, although she hadn't thought her this old. She looked nearly eighty with her white hair and paper-thin, wrinkled skin. Her eyes were cloudy, no longer the piercing black of her youth. The imperious look was only a travesty of her former youth.

"So, you say you are Esteban's bride," the thin lips were saying. "Young woman, you can't fool me. I know my son's appetite for the female sex. Another doxy, I'll be bound!"

Honor flushed in embarrassment, but reminded herself that the woman was not herself. "It is true, señora, I am to be your daughter-in-law."

"Pah! How can this be when Esteban has already dressed me up once and allowed me downstairs? You are not the girl he introduced me to! Go away!"

"Señora, perhaps you only thought—"

"Don't you tell me what I thought, young woman," she said regally. "My son tries to tell me I think things that I do not see, or that I do things I don't remember, but he tries to make me believe I am crazy."

Honor was at a loss, realizing that she should not have come up here on her own. Esteban had been right to keep the old woman away from her. The poor thing was out of her mind. To think that Esteban had already introduced her to his betrothed—when how could he have? She tried to soothe the woman by patting her reassuringly on the hand. Instantly Doña Yolande snatched her hand away suspiciously.

"You have come to steal my jewels, haven't you? Ah, now I know who you are—a thief! Leave me or I shall call out and you will be killed!" She put her hand protectively over the glittering diamond comb in her hair. "Diego!" she screamed. "Diego, help me!"

Honor backed away, afraid that if the servants came they would wonder at her presence up here. "No, señora, please do not alarm everyone. I am not a thief. If I were, I would not have stopped to talk with you," she said reasonably.

The old woman hesitated, then nodded. "*Sí*, you are right." She took her hand away from her head and played absently with her beringed fingers. "You—you must forgive me, my dear. I am—I have not been well for a long time and I'm not used to—to having visitors."

"Perhaps if I came another time for a visit—" Honor began, feeling pity for the lonely woman.

"Oh, yes, yes! But do not tell my son. He thinks I am crazy and he is afraid that I will hurt myself, he says."

"Don't worry. He is away in San Francisco and he will not be back for some time."

"Ah, he must be visiting his betrothed. She is a lovely girl, my dear, really. Oh, not as lovely as you—I can't understand what you are doing here if Esteban—"

"Doña Yolande, I think I had better go now," Honor said firmly, "but I promise to come up tomorrow and visit a little longer." She did not care to hear about Esteban visiting his betrothed in San Francisco, even though she knew he had gone on business.

"Well then, go if you must, my dear," the old woman sighed. "But do not forget me tomorrow."

"I won't," Honor said firmly. She took the wrinkled hand and pressed a kiss to it.

The woman seemed pleased at the gesture and she smiled softly at the young girl. "If only Esteban could find such a one as you to marry," she said brightly. "He chooses too willfully."

Honor smiled and left the room. Outside in the hall, she wondered what to do next. The visit to the mother of her fiancé had only made her more restless, longing for Esteban to return quickly. She walked downstairs to her room and paced to and fro for nearly an hour, wrestling with herself, wanting, on the one hand, to go riding, and on the other, to keep away from any place where Brice Devlin might be.

Finally, her restless nature took over and she called for a serving girl to help her change into a riding habit. There had been little time to have anything appropriate made up, but she had altered one of Yolande's gowns, dividing the skirt so that her legs had more freedom of movement. The short jacket was half-sleeved, allowing the softer material of her

160

blouse to show to the wrist. The servant girl divided her hair on either side and pulled it back in a ribbon, allowing the long tail of honey-gold to cascade down her back.

Eager now, determined not to think of what might happen should she meet Brice Devlin, she hurried out to the stables to ask one of the grooms for a horse. The man looked at her doubtfully.

"*Caballo*," Honor repeated insistently, pointing to a lovely white mare that seemed as eager as she for a ride.

The man shook his head. "*No caballa*," he proclaimed. "*Señor Sevillas no está aquí.*"

Honor felt her temper rise at this oaf who refused to saddle a horse for her. "Saddle that white mare or I will saddle her myself!" she ordered angrily.

He shook his head once more and they stared at one another furiously.

Going to where the livery was kept, Honor began to take off one of the saddles, a bridle and bit and walked back to where the man was regarding her stupidly.

"Stand aside, I am going to saddle her myself."

His dark eyes flashed, but he dared not touch her. "*Puta*," he hissed.

Honor hadn't the slightest idea what the word meant, but she was sure that it was meant as an insult. Disregarding him, she heaved the saddle onto the mare and tightened the cinch. She put the bit between its teeth and placed the bridle over its head. She had never before saddled a horse herself, but she was so angry, she was determined that she would not ask for help. Hoping that she had done everything correctly, she led the mare out of the stall and outside where the mounting block was. She already knew it was useless to ask for a leg-up from the groom. She could only comfort herself with the thought that as soon as Esteban returned, she would inform him of the man's disrespect and see that he was punished properly.

Mounting the mare, she realized too late that she had saddled her with a man's saddle, but she was determined not to go back into the stables to make a fool of herself. Besides, she did have the divided skirt and could ride astride if she had to. She urged the horse forward with her heels, the action reminding her suddenly of when she had ridden astride with Brice Devlin. Truly, if she had had her way, she would have ridden astride with Esteban, but he had assumed that she would ride as a lady should and had ordered a sidesaddle put on her horse. Not for anything would Honor have brought up the fact that she was more used to riding astride now.

She headed the horse in the opposite direction from the bunkhouse, leaning far over the animal as it stretched out, feeling the power in the little mare's long legs. She had chosen well, and for a moment, she wondered that Esteban hadn't let her ride the mare before. She would be sure to ask him for the horse for her own as soon as he returned.

It was glorious, riding on the surefooted mare, the wind and sun beating against her body. She felt the restless feelings begin to leave her and she cried out with joyful delight as the mare jumped over a screen of bushes. It was almost like flying for the tiniest moment.

Off in the distance, to her right, she caught sight of a group of men riding herd on grazing cattle. Abruptly she veered to the left in order to avoid them and headed for a wooded area which would shield her from inquiring eyes. She slowed the mare down, trotting it toward the copse of trees. She wished she had brought some food along, for it would have made an ideal place for a picnic. Then she laughed at the foolish thought—a picnic, with no one else along? Still, she would remember to suggest it to Esteban when he returned.

She was abruptly brought out of her daydreaming by the sound of hooves behind her. Curious, she turned her head and saw a horseman approaching. She wondered idly if he had news from the rancho—perhaps Esteban had returned already! She guided her horse under a tree to wait for the caballero. From this distance, she could see that he was dressed in the style she had become used to seeing—the wide-brimmed hat, held by a thong under the chin, the striped serape thrown carelessly over one shoulder, under which was worn a full-sleeved shirt and dark trousers, belted tightly at the waist. Calf-high boots were worn to protect the legs.

The mare had begun to graze idly and Honor was patting her neck, watching the man come closer. Only then did the idea come to her. Putting her hand to her mouth, she jerked at the bridle, causing the mare to jerk her head up angrily. Trying to recover herself, Honor dug her heels into the mare's flanks and turned her into the trees. Who else would come riding after her, she thought furiously. Why hadn't she realized it? Now he was too close, and she knew that he could catch her easily. Desperately she weaved among the trees, hoping to lose him. Too soon, though, the wooded

162

cover disappeared, leaving her stranded on flat grassy land which sloped gently upward to a hill.

Determined that Brice Devlin should not catch her, Honor leaned low over the mare and guided her up the hill. From the top, she turned around and could not see him. Relieved, thinking she'd lost him in the woods, she cantered along the ridge of the hill until she came to a small valley, carpeted even this late in the year with blue and gold meadow flowers. Enchanted, Honor began negotiating the hill carefully. She would rest for an hour in this little valley where she was sure she would not be disturbed.

As the mare slipped down the hill, Honor felt the cinch beneath the mare's belly giving way. With a cry, the saddle slipped and she was thrown to the side, thinking that she had not tightened the cinch enough—but soon there was no time to think of anything but catching herself in the fall, for now she was rolling down the hill, unable to get any leverage to stop herself.

Helplessly she rolled to the bottom of the hill, lying quietly as the dizziness made her head spin. She closed her eyes tightly and tried to sit up, but fell back. A nagging pain in her right ankle made her clench her teeth.

"See what happens, señorita, when you try to run away from me."

Putting a hand to her forehead to shade the sun from her eyes, Honor looked into the sun-browned face of the man she had been trying to avoid. His silver-blue eyes deepened in mockery and his mouth was grinning impudently in a way that made her grind her teeth helplessly.

"Let me help you up," he was saying, trying to keep the laughter from his voice.

"No, thank you!" she shouted at him angrily. "I am quite capable—" She winced as she raised herself on her elbows. A small pain shot up her ankle as she tried to move her legs.

"You've hurt yourself, you little idiot!" he exclaimed angrily. "Be quiet or I'll leave you here!"

"Someone would come looking for me," she said haughtily. "I'm sure by suppertime—"

He looked at her and she thought she saw pity in the silver-blue eyes.

Gritting her teeth against the pain, she sat up and leaned forward to massage the injured ankle. "I've only twisted it," she said. "You—you may go. I don't need you."

He laughed, a mixture of contempt and more pity that she

163

couldn't understand, but knew she hated coming from him. "You need me more than you think, little fool," he said in an undertone, his hand brushing hers aside as he felt along her ankle.

"Don't do that!" she commanded.

He ignored her, sliding up her gown a little and taking off her riding boot. He felt along her ankle and calf and pronounced, "I don't think you've broken anything. It may be only a small sprain."

"You see," she said in exasperation. "I'll be all right. Now please leave before someone comes by and sees us. They might tell—"

"No one will come by and find us here, Honor. And who would they tell? The señor of this estate? He is away—on business, is he not?"

"But when he returns, you can be sure I will tell him what you have done," she snapped. "You will be lucky to leave the hacienda in one piece."

He laughed disdainfully. "What have I done, Honor? So far, I have only been playing the Good Samaritan." His eyes narrowed reflectively. "Perhaps you were hoping for more?"

She flushed. "How dare you! It—it was bad enough to have to put up with your—your mauling when you had me under your control, but now, I won't stand by and let you think you own me!"

He was laughing in earnest. "Honor, I seem to recall that you didn't mind being 'mauled' at the time."

"Oooh! What else could I have done? I had to pretend to—to—"

His hands caught her arms and made her look up at him. She could see the silver-blue of his eyes, deepening until they seemed like blue smoke. "You had to pretend to love me," he said quietly.

She turned her eyes away from his look—so different, somehow—searching, yet guarded. Taking a deep breath, she regained her composure enough to face him. "I—I didn't know what I was saying," she said in a low voice.

The blue smoke in his eyes seemed to freeze and his face hardened. "I'll tell you what you said, Honor O'Brien. You said you loved me."

She struggled and broke free of his hands. Angry at his probing, angry at herself for provoking this meeting, she glared at him, ready to fight. She had to protect herself, she had to retain some measure of her own self-respect. If he

164

ever thought she had meant those words, he would use her and use her until he was finished.

"My emotional outburst then was that of a child," she snapped sharply. "I—thought I was supposed to say that I loved you to make everything that had happened right. I was only deluding myself and you! The—words—meant nothing to me." It cost her an effort to say that and she refused to look him in the face, afraid that he might read her inner struggle.

He whistled softly and pushed his hat back on his head. She didn't see the look of regret that appeared briefly on his features, only to be pushed firmly aside, replaced by a cynical disdain at his own gullibility. "You almost had me fooled, Honor," he said caustically.

"The renegade, Brice Devlin, admitting to being a fool!" Honor laughed harshly, determined to break off any ties between them with her cruelty. "How was it that you let an untried virgin turn your head?"

She was trying to get to her feet, to test the strength of her ankle, when she felt him catch her leg and pull her roughly beside him. She was flat on her back, staring up into his furious face. "That's mighty funny, Honor, coming from you. I mean, you call me a fool when you can't see the trick that's being played out right in front of your nose."

"What do you mean?" she demanded, trying to raise up on her elbows.

He forced her prone again and held her arms down while he leaned over her, the cruelest look she had ever seen on his face. "I mean, little fool, that your fiancé is passing you off as his *puta* to the whole ranch."

Honor remembered the groom in the stable using that same word in reference to her. "I don't know what you're talking about," she said haughtily. "I've never heard the word."

He laughed. "Well, you'll be hearing it quite often around here, no doubt," he returned sardonically. "It means 'Whore' Honor. Whore! That's what your station is in the eyes of everyone on this ranch—including your erstwhile fiancé!"

She flushed and then whitened, freeing one hand to slap his cheek. "What are you saying? You don't know what is between Esteban and me! We—we are to be married very soon. When he returns from San Francisco—"

"Ah, yes, the city where his true fiancée lives," Brice interjected, hurting her wrists as he pressed on them. She could see the imprint of her palm, pale against his brown skin. "Señorita Marianne Gordon, the daughter of a wealthy speculator who came to California on the tails of the gold rush, I've heard. You'd be surprised, Honor, how the ranch hands love to gossip, almost as bad as the kitchen help." His eyes raked her cruelly, "They've got bets going on how long you'll be around to amuse the señor until he tires of you—as he has of every other *puta* he's brought here."

Honor wished she could make him stop—make him stop telling these lies! They were lies, weren't they? She remembered her visit to Esteban's mother, when even *she* had assumed that Honor was only another in a long line of available women! The thought shamed her to the bone that the woman had thought her a prostitute. Hadn't she even mentioned already meeting Esteban's betrothed! And she had thought it only a crazy wandering! Could Brice be telling her the truth?

"You—you must be lying," she finally said shakily. "Brice, I can't understand why—why you would—how you could be so mean to me," she continued.

The trembling voice cut Devlin to the quick, but he couldn't afford to go soft toward her, he told himself stiffly. She had already proved what a bitch she could be, how she could make him feel worse than a fool for thinking that she—ah, what the hell! If she was only a *puta*, he could think of a few things to reduce her to just that in his own eyes.

One hand slid up her arm, pulling up the sleeve of her blouse. His fingers caressed her skin, while his other hand began to unbutton the front of her riding jacket.

Honor, realizing suddenly what he wanted of her, struggled to free herself. He pulled her jacket apart and his hand fastened on the softer material of her blouse, ripping the buttons off with his impatience. It was easy for him to pull down her chemise with one quick swipe, uncovering her breasts to his gaze.

She would have screamed for help, but his hot mouth covered hers, forcing it open, caressing her tongue with his own, sending shivers of awakened sensuality coursing through her. She stopped struggling, her arms going around his neck as she sobbed once in despair at her own weakness.

Brice, aware of her quick surrender, lost himself in her flesh, feeling the texture of her breasts against his palms as he kissed her open mouth. Impatient to claim her more fully, he pushed the divided skirt down to her ankles and then threw it to the side, tossing her chemise after it. His silvery-blue eyes blazed with liquid fire as he looked at the perfect body laid out beneath him for his pleasure. Her breasts were not large, but they fit his hand completely, and he could feel the stiffened points stabbing his palm eagerly.

Softly, he let his hands slide down her ribs to her waist, then downward across the gentle swell of her belly and the honey-gold curls that gathered between her legs. Her thighs were firm, smooth, and the muscles jumped beneath the quivering skin as he caressed them.

"Honor, Honor," he breathed in her ear, his hands continuing to caress her, bringing small shivers and little cries of pleasure from her. "Why do we fight this thing between us," he went on, kissing her cheeks, her eyes, her lips.

He felt tears as he kissed her cheeks again and glanced down at her in surprise. "What is it?"

She sobbed and shook her head vehemently. "Nothing, nothing, Brice. Don't stop," she begged him brokenly. "Don't stop now—I couldn't bear it."

Her admission startled him. Had she been lying before when she had denied feeling something for him? When she had said she loved him, had she really meant it? Or, and his brow furrowed, could it be that she enjoyed the act of sex so much because she had become used to it under Esteban's tutelage? The thought made him grit his teeth and push her thighs apart with rough impatience.

Despite his roughness, though, her arms entwined themselves around his neck, pulling his face down to hers as she kissed him softly. Groaning inwardly with his own need, Brice lowered his body to her eager one, feeling her clasp him tightly as her legs rode high on his waist.

At his first thrust, Honor had to stifle a cry that bubbled in her throat. She felt as though the breath had been pushed from her body, but as he continued she relaxed against him and let her passion take over. Their kisses were as hard and thrusting as the movements he made inside of her. Their passion took them on wings and they soared high above everything but the deep need they held for each other. Honor wished that he would never stop, never leave her, but as they struggled together to reach the peak of their sexuality, she thought she could not stand it if he didn't finish soon. Her back was arched, fitting her body tightly to his.

"Oh, Brice," she whispered brokenly, "I am a fool."

He was beyond hearing her though, for he could not get

enough of her warm, slick wetness, her hands pulling him against her silken skin, her mouth responding to his kisses with a passion that overwhelmed them both.

Honor felt him exploding inside of her at the same time that a delicious feeling of satiety overwhelmed her. She shivered and clutched him tighter, closing her eyes as the intensity of their shared passion flowed around them, then, finally, ebbed and receded.

Wearily she turned her head to face him, aware of their perspiring bodies, their ragged breathing. She arched her neck and caught his mouth with hers as she kissed him deeply.

"Brice, I—"

His mouth silenced her. "Not a word, Honor. Just—say you'll come with me."

For the first time, she caught a note of sincerity in his voice. He wanted her! Wanted her enough to take her with him, wherever he was going! And she realized that she didn't care where he was going—where *they* were going—as long as they would be together!

Thoughts, doubts all flew from her mind as she contemplated being with this man who, despite everything, wanted her with him.

"Yes, Brice, I'll come with you," she murmured softly.

He relaxed against her and kissed the tip of her nose. "I can't promise you that it will be like this always," he cautioned, feeling as though he ought to warn her before she put her life in his hands. "Honor, I can't honestly say that I love you. I've put up this hard shell around me and I've never wanted to remove it before. You'll have to put up with me." He grinned teasingly. "You know full well, we'll still fight."

She laughed softly. "We're both stubborn, Brice, but I want to come with you. Whether or not Esteban is truly trying to trick me or not, I can't stay with him when I feel this way about you."

"What way?" he grinned again, catching a gold curl in his fingers and letting it slide softly through.

She blushed. "My God, after what just happened," she began to fume, then realized he was teasing her and shook her head ruefully. "You're right," she went on, "we'll still fight."

He stood up and brought her up to stand against him. She laid her head on his shoulder, unmindful of her nakedness. There was no one to see but their two horses, who were grazing placidly nearby.

"When shall we leave?" she asked, feeling nervous at the thought of having to confront Esteban.

"Tonight," Brice said firmly.

"But Brice, I can't just leave without—without telling him why!" she objected.

He shrugged. "You can tell him in a letter," he said.

"But—but what if all the talk about his having a fiancée in San Francisco is just—gossip! What if he really intends to marry me—in good faith!"

Brice's dark brows arched sarcastically. "Honor, he never intended to marry you," he said, being harsh because he realized she needed that now. "He only wanted to use you. After all, he thought you were dead. What would have stopped him from becoming engaged to someone else?"

She could see the logic of his words and nodded slowly. "All right, then, Brice, but I—"

"Come on and get dressed," he said brusquely, reaching for her clothing. "You'd best ride back alone and gather your things."

"I—have no things," she said forlornly.

He sighed impatiently. "Just take what you'll need for a few days. I'm sure Esteban won't begrudge you that much." He helped her to dress, after dressing himself, and gave her a hand up to her horse.

"When will you come for me?" she asked, and he was pleased by the tenderness in her tone now.

"An hour after sundown. Everyone will be eating and you can ask for a tray to be brought to your room, then slip away. I'll wait for you at the end of the stableyard."

"All right," she agreed. She bent down and kissed him, then pushed her heels into the mare's flanks, guiding her up the hill, out of the valley.

As she reached the crest of the hill, she thought she saw a flash of color disappear into the wooded area she had come through before. For a moment, she felt an icy shiver of dread run down her spine and she turned to go back down and tell Brice of her suspicion that someone might have been spying on them. But Brice had already reached the other side of the valley and was circling around, ostensibly to go after straying cattle so as not to alert anyone.

Shaking off her fears, Honor resolutely pushed the mare down the hill and through the woods, peering through the trees for sight of anyone watching her. But there was no one

169

that she could see and decided it must have been a brightly plumaged bird she saw flitting through the branches.

Her thoughts turned toward Brice and a smile lit her features. God, she did love him, she thought happily. Despite what she had tried to make him believe, she really did love him—and she was sure that she could make him love her. Already, the battle was half won.

She noted that the sun was nearly sitting on the horizon now and realized that she wouldn't have much time to complete her preparations. Wistfully she wished she could go up and say goodbye to Yolande, but realized that there would be no time for it, and she would probably be attended by a servant with her meal anyway.

She urged the mare faster now, her mind on what lay ahead of her. Thinking of Brice nearly took her breath away. He was surely the handsomest, the most daring, the most intelligent of men, she thought dreamily. She felt it would be easy to let him, strong and experienced, take control of her life from now on.

She rode into the stable, calling sharply for the startled groom to attend to her horse. She hurried into the hacienda, passing through the cool patio and upstairs to her own room. She had just begun to tear off her riding habit when a sixth sense made her swing around swiftly.

"Honor, *mi chica,*" came the caressing voice of Esteban Sevillas.

Honor stared at him as though he were some evil apparition looming before her. "What—what are you—doing here?" she asked with an effort, her voice coming through choppy and hardly audible.

He smiled at her, his black eyes going over every detail of the torn gown, her tumbling hair and flushed face. "Why, this is my home, señorita. I have a right to be here."

"I mean—I didn't expect you home so soon," she amended, taking control with strength she drew from somewhere.

He laughed. "I thought to surprise you, *querida.*" He paused. "It seems that I have."

She colored. "You—must excuse me, Esteban. I will get out of these clothes and join you in the dining room in an hour or so."

"Yes, do get out of those clothes, *querida,*" he agreed silkily.

She stopped at the look in his eyes. "If you will excuse me?"

170

He laughed again as though delighted at her innocence. "Honor, *querida*, you have no secrets from me, do you?"

She glanced inquiringly at him. "Esteban, I could ask the same of you," she said smoothly, countering him at his own game.

He had the grace to pale, but then he smiled, once again in control. "Of course I have no secrets from you, *querida*, but some things I may choose to reveal to you later—for your own good."

Honor would have retorted something, but realized that she was wasting time standing here talking to Esteban. She suspected now that he had been lying to her about his purpose in going to San Francisco. Something about him—everything about him—suggested the ferret or the fox, outwitting the slower hound. She knew a moment of unease as he walked toward her.

"Come, come, Honor. Change your gown and join me at the dining table. If you loiter here much longer, I will think you have other things on your mind." His black eyes gleamed like cold, polished onyx.

"Then leave the room, Esteban," she commanded softly, "so that I can refresh myself."

He chuckled and came even closer, causing her to take a step backward. His eyes were dangerous now and she could see no mercy there.

"We are to be married soon, *querida*," he said just as softly. "Surely there can be no embarrassment between us now. Many couples introduce each other to the pleasures of the marriage bed—before they are married." His eyes slid meaningfully down her body and Honor cringed.

"Esteban," she said as steadily as she could, "please get out of my room. I should not like to have to call for assistance when—"

"Assistance from whom, *chica?*" he said and now the danger was in his tone of voice, challenging her—and with an awful dread, she knew that she had not seen a bird in the woods earlier, but one of his men, sent out to look for her. He must have told Esteban about her and Brice. But surely he had not been close enough to hear their promise to meet tonight and go away. She must get rid of Esteban somehow—to give her the time she needed to meet Brice.

"All right," she said with resignation in her voice. "If you wish to bed me, Esteban, I will not keep you out, but only let me have something to eat first. And wash up. I would not receive you like this."

Watching her, Esteban had to admire the way she fought for control. Did she think he did not know she had already given herself to one of his hands—a common vaquero! Did she think he would wish to mix the seed of a Sevillas with such common scum? He stared at her accusingly and his nostrils quivered. He did not know yet why she had coupled with the man. but he would find out soon enough, he thought gleefully.

"As you wish, *querida,*" he said, bowing and backing toward the door. "I will expect you within the hour."

Honor nodded shortly and waited until he had shut the door and she could hear his footsteps going down the hall. Panic threatened to reach up and engulf her as she frantically thought of how she would meet Brice without giving Esteban time to catch them. He knew that they had been together this afternoon! For a moment, she thought of telling him that she knew of his deception and had decided to leave him without compromises on his new marriage contract. She would get out of his life and they could both find peace with their new partners.

But somehow she knew that he would not let her go so easily. There was a cruel streak in the man that genuinely frightened her. He would go to great lengths to gain revenge for a dishonor done to him.

Of course, she had no intention of meeting him in the dining room. Once there, it would be too difficult to get away and she would have to think of some vague excuse which Esteban would see through immediately.

"Oh, God," she whispered softly to herself, "why did this have to happen?"

She didn't bother to change, only threw cold water over her face and braided her hair quickly in one thick tail to keep it out of the way. She made a compress by soaking a few handkerchiefs in the wash water and packing them beneath her riding boot against her twisted ankle. It throbbed a little as she walked and she didn't want the pain to impede her in her escape.

Softly she walked to the door and peered outside. As she suspected, a servant was lolling uneasily in the hall awaiting her appearance. Biting her lip in frustration, she went to the other side of the room, which opened out onto the balcony,

172

leading down into the patio. She chose this route as she could see no one about.

Moving swiftly she crouched close to the balustrade and found herself in the interior courtyard within a few minutes. She circled through the greenery until she came to the gate which led outside the house to the grounds. Quickly she slipped through, realizing that very soon, Esteban would have someone come for her as he would wonder at her tardiness.

It took her only a moment to orient herself outside, and she made for the stables with all speed. Her heart was bumping fearfully against her ribs and her breath was coming in gasps. She searched the area, straining to see the tall, lean figure of the man in whom she had placed all her faith.

With a sigh of relief, she saw him, leaning against the stables, calmly smoking a cheroot. Rushing forward eagerly, she nearly fell into him.

"Oh, Brice! Esteban, he knew about us today in the meadow. He knows—he knows about you and me—what we mean to each other. I'm afraid he's going to try to stop us!"

He turned to her sharply and she wished she could read the expression on his face. "How could he have found out about us, Honor?" he asked her calmly.

Surprised at his self-assurance, she burst out. "He had a man follow us. A spy! And—and Esteban has returned only this evening from San Francisco. Oh, Brice, why are you standing there? Hurry!"

"I'm afraid, señorita, that there is no longer a need for us to hurry," he stated flatly. And then in a low, intense voice, "Honor, why didn't you leave well enough alone? Why did you have to betray my trust like this and tell him!"

"What—what do you mean?" She gulped audibly. "I never told him—"

For the first time, she noticed that Brice was standing with a tenseness that she hadn't sensed at first. If he was this wary of something, why did they stand here, talking nonsense and wasting time?

Impatiently she caught his hand. "Come on, Brice, do you have the horses ready?"

"Honor, there is no longer any need to finish our charade," he said bitterly, jerking his arm away from her grasp.

"Our—charade!" What was wrong? "Brice, Esteban is in the dining room this very moment awaiting my presence and—"

173

"Why did you have to tell him?" he whispered viciously again as though he hadn't heard her words.

Suddenly a dark shadow stepped from behind the end of the stable wall. Honor tensed and gathered her strength in order to break away, but she realized that Brice had not moved, had not given her any indication that he was concerned.

"Ah, *querida*, as you can see I went on with dinner without you."

"Esteban!" Honor thought she was going to faint. "What—"

"*Chica*, as you can see your confession earlier—"

"My confession!" she cried. She turned swiftly to Brice's impassive face. "Brice, what did he tell you?"

"Only the truth," Sevillas cut in viciously. "Your tearful confession, how your upbringing forced you to tell me you were going to run away with him out of spite because you thought I was to be married to another."

"Brice, I—"

"I almost forgot," Brice said quietly as, at Sevillas' nod, four men came out of the shadows to hold him, "that you were only a woman."

Twenty-two

Honor had been locked in her bedroom, after screaming and struggling in Esteban's grasp as he half-dragged her back to the hacienda. In her room, she faced him, her anger raising her voice to near-hysteria.

"What will you do with him? What are you going to do to him?"

He smiled coldly, a reptile's smile. "Nothing—for the moment, *chica*. I have instructed my men to lock him up in the barn for tonight. I believe it will do him good to think about what may happen to him tomorrow."

"What do you mean?"

"We Spaniards are not known for our leniency when someone has gravely dishonored us," he explained patiently. "The man has had carnal relations with you, *querida*. He has dared to take my woman—"

"I am not your woman," she spat at him, her eyes flashing

like emeralds. "You never had any intention of marrying me! I was only to be your—your *puta!*"

He smiled at her bravado. "I'm glad you understand the word, *querida*. It will help you to understand your position."

"I will not stay here! I am leaving tonight!" she announced. "You cannot hold me!"

"If you go now, I promise you, your lover will bear your punishment tomorrow. Can you bear to think of him without that part of him which you seem to love?" His cruel taunt took her breath away.

"You would kill him?"

He shrugged. "Not quite, *chica*. I could have my men cut his manhood from him and then bury him to the neck in the sand so that the worms could eat at his wounded flesh." He smiled darkly. "He could possibly live through it. He seems a strong man."

Honor screamed in abject horror. What sort of devil was this man?

"Those blue eyes of his—no doubt they helped to attract him to you in the first place. I could slit his eyelids and leave him staked out in the sun for the vultures to—"

"Enough! Why do you torture me with this?"

"Because, *chica*, I want to see you squirm. I want to see you repay me just a little for the dishonor you have done me—for the humiliation you have caused me in front of my servants, chattel which must not be allowed to laugh at me behind my back!"

"Pride! Your pride has been hurt! And for that, you would torture a man who has done nothing to deserve such hatred! Punish me, instead, and release him."

He shook his head. Then the black eyes glittered as though a new plan had formed in his mind. "Beg me to punish you, *chica*—and perhaps I will consider it."

Honor reared back, her own pride bubbling to the surface. "You devil! You snake! You—"

"Spare me the words of your hysteria, *chica*," he said in a bored tone. He turned to leave the room.

"Where—where are you going?"

"To check on my prisoner—and then I will return, my sweet, to see just how well you can beg."

And so he had left her. Honor had roamed about the room distractedly, her mind crying out at the injustice that had been done. How could this have happened? She realized that she herself had placed Brice in his present danger because of

175

her deep-seated desire to see him. If only she hadn't gone riding! If only she hadn't given in to her passion! And then, to see the accusation in his face, in his voice! Sevillas had lied to him—had made him believe that she had gone to him and confessed everything—a feminine weakness that Brice would consider a test of her love for him. She had failed the test!

Restlessly she stalked back and forth across the room, staring out the window into the garden below, wishing that somehow she could get to Brice—tell him what had really happened. But she already knew she would not be given the chance. The only thing she could do was submit to Sevillas' demands and hope that he would not injure Brice too badly.

Perhaps if he released Brice, after feeling his pride assuaged, Honor could meet him later. Yes, that was the best plan, she thought. She held onto the idea desperately, willing herself to believe in it.

She had succeeded in calming herself sufficiently to face Sevillas' sneer as he returned to the room, locking the door carefully behind him. She knew already what he would require of her and she was prepared to let him make love with her—anything to free Brice from his evil intent.

From beneath his coat, he produced a bottle of wine and set it carefully on a low table. He had stuffed two glasses in his coat pockets and poured the wine into them slowly. Impatient at his deliberateness, Honor turned her back on him. It was meant as a snub, but it allowed him to pour a powder into her wine which dissolved on contact. He allowed himself a smile as his victory came closer.

"Your wine, *chica*," he said with a note of affection.

"I am not thirsty, Esteban," she shot back. "I only wish to conduct our—business and be done with it."

"Our business! My dear, what kind of blackguard do you think me? Do you believe I would take a woman against her will? Take her only as a recompense for another man's crime? Come, come, have a drink with me and then we will talk."

Reluctantly she sipped at the wine. He seemed to be waiting for her to finish it before speaking and so she downed the rest quickly in one gulp. She coughed slightly and then leveled her green gaze at him haughtily.

"Good, my dear. Now, I want you, first, to tell me how it is that you know this man."

She hesitated, but realized it would do no good to lie. Perhaps she could appeal to him somehow. "When I was captured by the Comanche, this man was a part of that tribe. He—he took my virginity as payment for helping me to escape."

"But you told me that an old woman of the tribe helped you to escape," he reminded her sharply and Honor cursed herself for forgetting what she had already told him.

"That's right," she admitted, "but then he—he helped me to get to Santa Fe. He saved my life." He had saved her life, she reflected, and now it was her turn to save his. "When we reached Santa Fe, we parted. I had no idea that he would come to this rancho to hire himself out."

Thoughtfully Sevillas stroked his moustache, watching the girl's face, looking for signs that the drug was beginning to work. "Perhaps he followed you," he suggested.

She shook her head and was amazed at the effort it cost. Her limbs seemed to be melting like that time when Pearl had— She looked over at Esteban, her eyes widening. "You—you drugged me," she said.

"Only a little, *chica*, not enough to put you to sleep. Only to make you submissive to me." He stood up and began to take off his clothes.

Horrified, she watched him until he was naked. She seemed not to be able to take her eyes away. A languor was seeping through her veins. She seemed to be on fire and there was a strange tingling between her legs.

Sevillas stood before her, lean and brown, his male desire obvious to her dilated eyes. Slowly, with infinite patience, he began to undress her, making her stand before him as he stripped the clothing from her heated body.

Unable to help herself, Honor moaned deep in her throat and arched her back toward him, thrusting herself against his eager flesh. Her arms closed behind his neck and she was pulling him toward her, sinking her teeth into his shoulder. She heard him laugh victoriously and thought she heard a door open, but was oblivious to it as Sevillas picked her up abruptly and carried her to the bed.

"Now beg for it," he said in a whisper, licking her ear with hot, wet kisses that seemed to be driving her mad.

"I—" She hesitated, concentrating on the delicious tingling all over her body.

"Beg!" he whispered again, louder.

"Make love to me, Esteban, please, I—I can't wait any longer," she gasped, writhing beneath him.

"Beg harder," he breathed, enjoying her torture.

177

He rose on his knees, taunting her with the sight of his member before her eyes. A part of Honor was crying out at this humiliation, but the drug he had given her was incensing her, making her crazy with some terrible need she couldn't understand.

Helplessly she grasped his organ and guided it urgently to where it would appease her hunger. Still he would not satisfy her desires.

"No, I'm afraid it is impossible, my love, after what you have done with that gringo lover of yours," Esteban sighed, his eyes flinty.

Honor sobbed and threw her arm across her face, holding herself back from a desperate urge to impale herself on him by force.

"Don't do this to me," she cried out. "Do not make me suffer with wanting it. Do it! Do it now!"

Esteban smiled, immensely pleased at the performance so far, but his cruelty sought to add one more touch. "Renounce your gringo and I will satisfy you, *chica.*"

Honor tossed her head from side to side. She couldn't renounce Devlin—she couldn't. But her sexual urges were almost too much to bear and she ground out painfully, "I renounce him. I—I never loved him. It was only a physical thing."

"Just another man to satisfy you, *chica?*"

"Yes, yes! Now, now, please, Esteban!"

"Ah, but look, my little one. Look who watches you with such burning eyes. Hold him, vaqueros, or I'm afraid he might try to strangle my little *puta.*"

He moved his body aside and Honor registered the shock of blazing blue eyes, touched with liquid silver that seemed to burn to her soul.

"Puta! Puta!" Sevillas repeated joyfully. "You are my *puta,* Honor O'Brien!"

With all her strength, Honor tried to resist the drug and the struggle nearly caused her to faint. No, she mustn't faint! She must tell Brice, must explain what a horrible thing . . .

"I've seen enough, Sevillas," came a deadly voice that surely could not be his. "Take me back to the barn where her screams of passion will not penetrate."

Sevillas shrugged and nodded to the men to take him out.

"No!" Honor shouted, but it was too late. The door had closed and he was gone.

"Now, *puta,* shall we return to our pleasant pastime?" Sev-

178

illas said, catching her around the waist to pull her up to meet his thrust.

But before he could complete his revenge, Honor arched her neck and sank her teeth into his cheek. He drew back and the flesh tore raggedly, causing blood to drip down. Rage burst through him as he brought his fist crashing down into her face.

"Bitch! For that I will let you suffer your desire alone tonight!" he shouted at her in fury. "And tomorrow, you will watch your lover suffer also!"

Honor awoke with a throbbing ache in the whole left side of her face. Her cheek was swollen and her jaw felt as though the bone had been broken. Carefully she felt along the flesh for cuts and then got to her feet to look into the mirror. Her skin was puffy and bruising already. Luckily, he had missed her eye with his blow, but the skin beneath it was swollen.

Her glance fell on the bottle of wine, and with angry strides she wept it to the floor, where it did not break on the carpet, but spilled onto it, making a stain. She was still naked and hurriedly she went to the armoire to bring something out to wear. There was nothing.

Fury swept over her. A hatred was born against Esteban Sevillas that would not be quenched until she saw him humiliated and abused as she had been. Her only consolation was that he had not finished the game on her drugged body.

She was standing, wondering what to do next, when the door opened and Don Esteban himself stood regarding her soberly. His cheek still bore the mark of her teeth and it, too, was swollen.

"*Buenos días,*" he said, contempt edging his voice.

"I do not wish to speak with you!" she shouted at him. "Get out before I kill you!"

"With what, *puta,* your bare hands?" he laughed arrogantly. "No, little one, I must insist that you come with me." He threw a robe he had brought with him at her feet.

She picked it up and slipped it on, only so that she wouldn't be naked in front of him. "I have no wish to go anywhere with you. I only want to leave this place!"

He shook his head. "You will leave when I decide I am finished with you. Now follow me if you would like to see your gringo lover once again."

She hesitated, wondering what horrible trick he had up his

179

sleeve, but her impatience to see Brice, to try to explain what Sevillas had done, decided her fate and she followed him out of the room and down the corridor. He led her outside to the stables into a small yard that was corralled and used to break wild horses.

Inside the corral, tied to a pole with his face pressed to the splintery wood, was Brice Devlin, stripped naked. At sight of him, Honor wold have hurried to his side, but Esteban held her back wih a strong arm across her breasts.

"Let me go to him!"

"He wants no part of you, *puta!*"

"No, he doesn't know what happened. He—"

Sevillas hesitated, then shrugged. "All right, go to him."

Instantly she was flying across the yard, coming around the pole, her hand reaching out to caress his cheek. He flinched away from her and his eyes held that same accusing stare she had seen before.

"Brice, let me explain," she began breathlessly, aware of approaching footsteps. "What I said last night—"

"Do not repeat it," he said slowly, hatred seething in his voice. "Leave me alone and go back to your lover, *puta!*"

She winced as though he had struck her. "No, no, Brice, you don't understand."

"I understand that you crave a man's rod inside of you— that you tricked me with your tender words and those soft green eyes that can haunt a man's soul. I understand, finally, that you are as he called you—nothing more than a *puta!*" He spat at her, hitting her on the chest. "Now go away—or perhaps you had hoped to watch the fun begin!"

"No, Brice, I—"

Beside her, Sevillas had her arm and he deliberately snaked his hand inside the robe to caress her bosom. Honor would have struck his hand away, but something in his eyes stopped her.

"You only make it harder on your friend," Sevillas was saying.

Honor knew what he meant. If she resisted him anymore, Brice would only be punished longer. Stoically she tried not to think of his hand, pinching her flesh, cupping her breasts inside the robe.

Brice could not help but see what was happening within only a few feet and he let out an exclamation of disgust. "Must I be put through a repeat performance of last night?"

180

he asked contemptuously, and then, noting her bruised face, "You play rough, señor."

"*Si*, the *putas* like it that way, gringo!" Sevillas laughed evilly. He continued rubbing her breasts until Honor thought she would scream. "Let's see now. What punishment would fit such a crime of dishonor?" Sevillas continued, contemplating. "To cut off your bag of jewels, eh! Then you might find work somewhere as a gringo eunuch!"

Honor whitened and her eyes sought Brice's face, but he seemed not to care what was said. His face was impassive, his expression turned inward.

"No, I suppose that would be too much," Sevillas went on slowly. "He has a handsome face, *chica*, and perhaps that was what brought you to him at first. Too handsome, did you say? Perhaps you are right." He stepped forward and lifted Brice's face from the pole, regarding it solemnly. Then with swift action, he punched him solidly in the jaw, causing a stream of blood to spill from his cut lip and cheek. "There, is that better, Honor? Not quite?" Again he punched the tied man, giving him a cut over one eye, closing the eye almost completely. "I don't know, maybe if I broke the nose—"

Honor wished she could scream or faint, or kill Sevillas. She could hardly stand this slow torture, watching the man she loved being turned to living pulp by the man she hated. By now, Brice was groggy and Sevillas ordered a bucket of water thrown over him.

"Lash him twenty lashes!" Sevillas ordered.

"No!" Honor couldn't help the cry that escaped her. Tears were streaming down her cheeks—tears that Devlin could not see for the blood in his eyes.

"No? Not enough, you think, my dear? Of course, you are right. Thirty!" he ordered.

Honor would have said more, but a look from Sevillas warned her that more words would only bring more lashes on Devlin's body. Feeling as though her heart had turned to stone, she allowed Sevillas to grasp her arm and draw her to the side while one of the vaqueros began the whipping. She was forced to stand through it all, her own body cringing with pain even as the lash fell on the man she loved. It seemed it would never end and the vaquero had to be replaced by another as his arm tired. Honor had bitten through her lower lip, but was heedless of the blood or the salt taste in her mouth. She could only stare in horror at the bloody mess that once had been Brice Devlin.

181

Finally it was over and Sevillas ordered the man cut down. He slumped unconscious in the dirt. Through it all, he had not uttered a cry of pain and Honor almost wished he had. His cold, unfeeling hatred of her seemed to emanate from his body. Beside her, Sevillas caught her hand and pulled her against him. She struggled and tried to bite him.

He grinned nastily. "Turn him around, Diego, and give him twenty more on the front," he ordered.

Honor froze. Her eyes pleaded to him, her voice tried to speak, but no words would come. He was going to die, she thought dully. Brice Devlin was going to die. She hadn't saved his life. She had killed him.

"Wait!" Sevillas was watching her face. "Perhaps I will be lenient," he said, "if the señorita can find it in her heart to follow all my wishes."

She looked into his dark, burning eyes and nodded slowly. She doubted that Devlin would live through this, but at least he wasn't going to be pounded into a broken body before her eyes.

Sevillas nodded to the vaquero, who untied Devlin's hands and feet and picked him up to carry him.

"Take the dogmeat into the barn!"

"Sí, señor. ¿El doctor?"

Sevillas shrugged. "He is beyond that. Give him a decent burial. Do not trouble me about him anymore."

Taking Honor's numb arm, he pushed her forward, back to the hacienda, where gaping servants scuttled quickly to get out of their way. Honor's face reddened at his careless humiliation of her. Her eyes slid away from the servants, focusing on the doorway, the hall, the staircase . . .

When they arrived at the door to her room, Honor felt her heart turn over with dread. How could she let this man touch her after what he had done to Brice—and to her? Shame washed over her in horrible waves as she thought of the night he had drugged her. She wished he would drug her now. It would, at least, have made it easier.

Sevillas gave her no time to think as he pushed her into the room and closed the door forcefully with his foot. The catlike smile that crossed his face caused deadened rage to well up inside her.

"You—animal!" she shouted at him. "You're nothing but an animal!"

He glided swiftly toward her and caught her shoulders, shaking her. "You remember your promise?" he questioned,

182

hissing the words softly. "There may be something still left alive in your gringo lover that can still feel pain—"

She looked up at him in horror, then pushed her face into her hands, succumbing to great, wrenching sobs.

Sevillas frowned. "Stop crying!" he commanded, releasing her. He turned away in disgust. "I will not have you playing the martyr with me!"

Honor could only continue sobbing even harder. The cruel brutality she had been forced to watch, the knowledge that Brice might die hating her, and the wicked deception that Sevillas had played out, pretending to honor their marriage contract—all pounded at her consciousness until, in order to keep her sanity, the mind protected itself in the only way it could . . . she fainted.

Sevillas looked down at the huddled form on the carpet with a sneer. The stupid gringa! Did she think she could fool him with this woman's trick?

"Get up!" he shouted, and when she did not respond, he prodded her impatiently with the toe of his boot. Finally, he pushed her inert body over with his foot.

The whiteness of her skin made the bruise on her face seem even more vivid. Sevillas contemplated her still form a moment longer, then shrugged. So, she really had fainted—what did it matter? She was useless to him in this condition, and he began to wonder if he even desired her anymore.

Perhaps he had made a mistake. Perhaps she was, after all, like all of the rest of his women, who finally learned to cower and bow to his passions. Her strength—that determined strength he had grudgingly admired—seemed to have slipped away from her with the loss of her lover.

Sevillas turned on his heel, leaving the unconscious girl on the floor, her upturned face bone-white except for the bruised purple flower on her cheek. With a rasping voice, he called for a servant and strode to his room in a simmering anger.

Upstairs in her bedroom which faced onto the stable side of the hacienda grounds, Yolande Sevillas had heard the commotion outside and, for no reason she could think of, had decided to go to the window to peek out. She really hadn't been too interested, but she remembered that the young señorita had not come to visit her as she had promised and thought, perhaps, she might see her below and draw her attention in some way.

She could see a young man tied naked to a pole in the cor-

183

ral and wondered briefly what his crime was. Then she saw the señorita she remembered and her son coming across the yard. The rest of the exchange was easy to follow even from her high vantage point. She could sense the hatred that was exchanged between the girl and her son. And then, she could not believe the punishment that was inflicted on the young man tied to the pole. Her mouth gaped at such cruelty. Diego must be informed immediately! But—and she closed her eyes in defeat—they kept telling her that Diego was dead! Surely, he must be dead, for he would never have allowed such a thing!

Distraught now, her hands shaking, she could see the look of despair that the girl kept giving the bloody mess that had been the young man. Yolande felt hot bile rise in her throat, but she watched as the man was taken into the barn and the girl was led away by her son.

It was plain, even to her saddened eyes, that the girl was in love, not with Esteban, but with the man who had been punished so frightfully. Remembering the girl's kindness, she resolved to reward that kindness with one of her own doing. In a high voice, she called the serving girl to her that usually hovered outside her room while she ate to await the dinner tray. Only recently, she had been served by a new girl, Elena, who had seemed only too glad to get away from her son's influence. She was young, but she would have to do.

"Elena, I have just been watching outside. Can you tell me something about it?"

The girl shook her head, but was amazed to see the cloudy eyes begin to darken and take on an old, almost forgotten imperious look that brooked no refusals.

"That is one of the new vaqueros. I have heard gossip that he and—Señorita O'Brien were found to be lovers. Don Esteban was furious at such—such impunity and—"

"Impunity! Child, you have learned much for a serving girl."

Elena nodded proudly.

"Then, Elena, since you are so intelligent and capable, I have a task for you to perform. I want you to go to the barn and provide the man a means of escape."

"Señora!" she gasped. "How can I do such a thing? If the señor found out, he would kill me!"

Yolande's dark eyes grew even more ominous. She had never realized what a monster her son had become. To punish a man for a crime was one thing, but to so frighten a

184

child such as Elena by talk of punishment by death was another. "Have you no one to help you?"

Elena thought for a moment, then nodded. "I—I have a friend. He is strong. He could carry him to a wagon. We could—we could steal horses and take the man into town to see a doctor."

"Excellent, Elena," the woman smiled. "You must go to your friend without delay and—and tell him of our plan. You and he will take the man into Monterey to see the physician immediately. If there is a chance he will survive, you must keep him there until he is well enough to travel. You must hide him, Elena, for I have an idea my son will not rest until he has discovered where he is hidden." Her hand went to the diamond comb she always wore in her hair and, shaking a little, her fingers pulled it from her hair. "Here, this is all I have of value now. I'm only sorry I don't have more."

"Oh, señora, you are too kind. This is worth much more than—"

"Than a man's life, Elena? Nonsense! Now go!"

She walked to the bed and leaned against it as if her efforts had cost her dearly. "I think I shall rest now, Elena. But I must know that you have gone before I can sleep. Go!"

The girl scampered out and, minutes later, Yolande looked out her window once more and could see a thin stream of light from the barn as the door was opened to allow two figures to enter. It seemed hours later that she heard the wagon roll out of the yard.

"*¡Vaya con Dios!*" she called out to the night. She only hoped that God was with the señorita downstairs.

Twenty-three

Brice Devlin was conscious only of intolerable pain. He recalled that someone had carried him to the barn—at least he thought it was the barn—and laid him on a stack of hay. When his back hit the dry straw, he thought he would scream as innumerable tiny prickpoints seemed to be biting into the raw flesh. His throat was tight from holding back the shouts of pain that he had held back only by his own strong will not to give that bastard Sevillas the satisfaction of hearing them.

Now it seemed a thousand fingers of fire were jabbing into

his back. His face was one huge throb of pain from his eyes to his chin. He had no idea if he was going blind or if it was only the blood and pain that clouded his vision. His nostrils were thick with blood and he opened his mouth to breath noisily, spitting out blood to keep himself from choking on it.

He lay alone, for unless he was deaf, he could hear no one else about. He was alone with only his thoughts for company—a worse torture than the physical one he had just gone through. For he wasn't sure he could survive the whirlwind of thoughts that filled his tired mind.

Honor! How could she have betrayed him, he wondered dully. He should have been warned—should have known when she protested at leaving Sevillas without telling him where she was going and with whom. The stupid bitch had confessed to that devil, as though he were a priest! Damn her for her betrayal!

Last night, he thought he would go mad at seeing her panting, heaving beneath the man who had done this to him. He had watched, trying to keep his mind blank, trying not to remember what had happened between them only that afternoon, but he had not been able to keep the pain and hatred from boiling through him. If he could have gotten to her, he would have strangled her lying throat.

And then today, to see her, allowing herself to be mauled by that black bastard! He had concentrated on that, rather than the pain that kept coming, and he had been able to blot out the pain as he fed on his hatred. Even now, he tortured himself with thoughts of Honor with Sevillas, in his bed, most likely giving him her body, which he, Devlin, had thought belonged only to him.

It seemed that hours had passed. He was thirsty, nauseous from the blood he had swallowed, and the pain seemed to be closing him in a ring of fire that would not let go. The idea of dying now had never occurred to him. He couldn't imagine not obtaining revenge on those two in the hacienda someday. He must live in order to kill both of them.

Suddenly someone was reaching down, pulling his arms up to grasp his neck, lifting his pain-wracked body up as gently as possible. But there was no way that Brice could stand the close contact, and he would have screamed with the pain if someone else had not stuffed a rag in his mouth. God, what did Sevillas have in mind now, he wondered dully. Hadn't he finished with him yet?

He was carried outside and laid in something hard that had

been cushioned somewhat with blankets. At least he was laid on his side, which did not hurt nearly as badly as when he had been placed in the barn. The ball of cotton was taken from between his jaws and he found he could breathe again. Still, the pain was not receding and he prayed for unconsciousness as the wagon began to move.

He must have blacked out, for the next thing he saw was a strange man's face bending over him inquiringly, his spectacles threatening to fall off the end of his nose. Brice found himself nearly mummied in bandages, even his head, so that he was allowed only slits through which he could see out.

"Ah, he is awake," the man said softly, smiling to himself.

A young girl he had not seen before was leaning over him anxiously now. "Sí, señor, I think he is wondering where he is," the girl said in a whisper.

"Time enough for that, my dear. First we must see if he can hear us—if he can see us clearly." The man looked at Brice and called, "Can you hear me, Devlin? Nod if you can."

Brice nodded, but the effort cost him a streak of pain through his jaw.

"Good, and can you see me too?"

Again a nod, though not as swift.

"Ah, I am pleased at your progress so far then, Devlin. I know you are wondering who I am and where you are. Many questions must be going through your mind, but I do not wish to tire you out. Just rest a little longer and we will talk later."

Gently the man forced some liquid in a spoon between his bruised lips and Brice was soon asleep again.

"Now, we'll just take some of these bandages off and see what your face looks like," the man was saying as Brice opened his eyes, allowing a stream of late afternoon sunlight to dilate the pupils.

"Who—are—you?" he whispered, the words coming with difficulty.

The man smiled benignly. "Dr. Isaac Cooper, at your service, young man. You're in Monterey and I've been treating you for about ten days."

Ten days! Brice could hardly believe he had lost so much time. And this man was a doctor.

"How—" he began, but the doctor shushed him.

"You were brought here by a young girl, Elena, and a

rather large young man, both of whom said they work for Señor Sevillas. Now, no more questions until I finish taking off these bandages. I want to see if that cut has healed properly. And the nose—I can tell you, young man, you were the worst mess I've seen in some time and I've been a doctor for nearly thirty years. Quiet now, while I cut this last bandage."

Brice waited, not worried about his appearance. He could care less whether he was still handsome or not. A man usually relied on looks for only one thing—attracting a female—and Brice Devlin had enough self-confidence that he needed no outward attractions to feel secure around the opposite sex. Although, he thought wryly, it didn't help when a man was the ugliest thing next to a polecat.

"There now," Cooper was saying to himself. "Yes, I think you'll be all right—a few scars, but that's to be expected after the punching you went through. Your back now—" He frowned slightly. "Boy, you've got enough marks back there to stripe a dozen skunks."

"It doesn't matter, Doc', I'm not in the habit of going around without a shirt on." It was still difficult to move his mouth.

"Good thing or someone might think you're an escaped convict. I've seen scars like these on the bodies of men who didn't last through the night." He held up his hand as Brice started to speak. "No, I don't want to know how or why you got 'em, son. I'm just the doctor. My duty begins and ends in healing your body, not hearing your confession."

His choice of words sent Brice's mind plummeting back to her—to the woman who had caused his torment. He frowned and the motion hurt his forehead, but he was oblivious to it as he lay in the bed, wishing her a thousand torments to make them even.

Honor had remained in bed for two days after Brice's whipping. She had been allowed a servant girl to bring her food and see to her cleanliness. Occasionally Sevillas visited her, his dark eyes sweeping over her with haughty indifference.

She had been locked in her room to impede any plans of escape, especially after the day in which Sevillas stormed in in a black rage, spitting out the fact that Devlin, by some miracle, had managed to escape. He had questioned everyone on the ranch, and no one could tell him a thing. Only one servant was missing, and that was Elena. He had not bothered to question his mother about her disappearance, knowing full well the old lady didn't know what was happening around her most of the time. Unfortunately for Honor, she was obliged to bear the brunt of his rage as he verbally abused her whenever he came to her room. She wished she had the strength to laugh in his face, to taunt him that Brice had escaped the fate Sevillas had planned.

Unknown to Honor, Sevillas was truly worried. He knew that Marianne Gordon and her father would be arriving in the next two weeks and the thought brought him no joy as he tried to think what could be done to get rid of Honor O'Brien before that time. It would not bother him unduly to see her turned out without money or a place to go. After she had deceived him with Brice Devlin, any feeling toward her that resembled human caring had been snuffed out. He would have perhaps used her to gratify his sexual urges, but the look of indifference in her eyes put him off more powerfully than any words of hatred or further tears.

After two days of visiting her, trying to break through her icy remoteness, he began to tire of her docile contempt and visited her no more.

Sevillas much preferred the spice of the younger servant girls, even the knowing sensuality of the older ones. The gringa, he told himself, was cold and her green eyes glittered with some hard, impenetrable feeling that filled him with unaccustomed unease.

Honor felt nothing but relief when, after a few days had passed without a visit from Sevillas and his biting derision, she realized that she need no longer fear a breakdown of his reserve. She had been in agony that he might rape her and the thought of him performing the same act of love on her body that she had enjoyed with Brice filled her with revulsion.

The man, she decided, would not be capable of making love—he was only capable of destruction.

Honor's mind was her worst enemy as, night after night, it conjured up nightmares of Devlin's broken body, of his hatred of her. Her eyes grew red with continual weeping and her body thinned out as her appetite waned. She could have cared less if she died, for if Devlin was still alive somewhere, she was sure he wouldn't rest until he had hunted her down and killed her with his own hands. Better to die now than have to stare into his cold hatred while he took her life. She couldn't bear thinking that he might, after all, have died despite his escape.

One morning, toward the end of November, Sevillas entered her room, his manner alert and purposeful. His cold, black glance passed over her as she sat dejectedly at the window in a long robe, her back deliberately turned toward him.

"You look terrible," he commented sarcastically. He strode toward her and whirled her around to face him. "You have grown ugly, Honor O'Brien."

Truth to tell, he thought objectively, she wasn't ugly. Her bones were too fine, her eyes too beautiful ever to be called ugly—but her face had thinned, showing those fine bones at cheek and jaw and hollowing out shadows beneath the beautiful eyes. She looked almost spirit-like as the magnificent honey-gold hair tumbled softly around her face.

"Do you hear me?" he asked, reaching down to shake her slightly. "Even the lowest of my servants would not wish to warm your bed, *puta!*"

"It is the least I could wish for," she replied coldly.

"Hah—and what is the most you could wish for? That Brice Devlin would come riding back and take you away from here?" His smile was ridiculing. "You are a fool!"

"I know," she remarked, after sighing against her will.

He regarded her, then a new thought came to mind to ease the irritation of her indifferent defiance. "You asked me once if I had any secrets from you," he said, his eyes becoming almost mischievous.

"I don't care about your secrets any longer," she said despondently, wishing only that he would release her so that she could turn away from his smug expression.

"Ah, but you may be meeting her very shortly," he said, satisfied to see a note of questioning in her eyes finally. "Yes, the woman I am to marry should be arriving within the next few days and you can see for yourself how highly I have aspired."

"The poorest drab would be high for you," she retorted and felt his hands squeeze her arms painfully.

"Now, now, mustn't let that sharp tongue put you into trouble," he said, his voice holding countless promises. "My, you have become somewhat of a coldhearted bitch. Perhaps we would never have made a very loving couple, no matter what the circumstances."

She looked up at him with a wealth of cynicism, but said nothing.

190

Goaded, he shook her. "But unfortunately you have turned into something of a problem. You see, I wouldn't really want you to meet Marianne. She might wonder at my moralities. You do understand?" At her silence, he continued, "So, I'm afraid I must find a way—to get rid of you."

His coldness filled her with dread. So, he would actually kill her, she thought—and realized that she really didn't want to die. As long as there was a chance that she might someday see Brice again, she didn't want to die.

He laughed at the look of apprehension that she could not quite hide from his observant eyes. "My dear girl, I am not *that* much of a reprobate," he assured her, as he enjoyed her discomfiture. "Despite your feelings to the contrary, I have never killed anyone in my life."

You only have your henchmen do it for you, Honor thought coldly.

"At any rate, I must have you out of the hacienda as soon as possible. I admit there will be little regret on my part, as I'm afraid only sheer boredom would ever draw me into your bed."

For which I thank God, she thought fervently.

"So, I have come to a decision." He waited for her to ask him what that decision was, but she only looked coolly into his eyes, awaiting his words. He had to admire her courage—perhaps the breeding really did mean something. "You will be leaving tonight."

"Where shall I be going?" she inquired, determined not to let her fear show in her voice.

He laughed. "You will find out soon enough. I will come for you this evening, late. Choose one of the sturdiest dresses in your wardrobe. You will need it."

Honor was dressed in a fine worsted gown of russet-brown, her hair braided and pinned around her head, her riding boots on her feet, when Sevillas returned for her that night. She said nothing when he greeted her, only swept him a cold look from beneath her long-lashed eyes.

"The marble statue," he said approvingly. "So effective when you wish to spurn a man's advances."

She inclined her head, rising to follow him out the door.

"I'm afraid, though, that my brother might break the marble statue," he warned carelessly. "You see, he is less able to control those urges than I am." He seemed hard put to keep the sarcastic laughter from his voice.

"Your brother!" The words came bursting from her lips incredulously. "That animal! Why, you do not even want him on your property!"

He nodded, smiling ruthlessly, pleased that he had put life back into the statue. *"Verdad,"* he agreed, "but that does not mean that he doesn't come in useful now and then. And I'm sure he would be only too glad to take you off my hands."

"But he is an outlaw—a murderer!"

"Even so, he may also be your lover very soon," Sevillas returned.

Honor's face whitened further and she shivered.

Twenty-four

Don Esteban dispatched three of his vaqueros to "escort" Honor O'Brien to the appointed place where she would be given over to Jaime Sevillas. The moon was high and lit the path brightly that they must take. With a painful tug of memory, Honor could see the little wooded area where she had tried to escape Brice Devlin. Over the next hill, she knew, would be the valley where they had made love to each other. She felt tears in her eyes at the thought of how such a wonderful love discovered could turn into bitter hatred only a short time later.

But she couldn't dwell on what had gone before. Brice's love was lost to her and now she could only thing of remaining alive so that, one day, she might find him again and—at least—explain how they had been tricked by Sevillas' jealous pride. It might not bring back his love, but at least he might not hate her.

Their little party rode swiftly through the darkness to the edge of the lands belonging to Don Esteban Sevillas. Ahead, she thought she could make out the dark shadows of men on horseback, awaiting their approach.

"¡Hola!" called out one of the vaqueros testily.

"¡Hola!" responded one of the awaiting riders. "Have you the girl?"

"¡Si!"

Honor was guided to the top of a short ridge, where two men on horseback watched her approach curiously. "This is the one?" they asked.

192

The lead vaquero nodded and then gathered his men and rode off hurriedly, as though fearing they could be shot in the back. Honor was immediately aware that these men were rough, ignorant peasant types who had little interest in her.

One of them took the bridle of her horse and attached a lead rope which allowed him to make sure she would follow his swift pony without trying to break away. They rode northwest until they came to a natural barrier of sandstone that formed a small opening through which they rode, coming out into the open on the other side into a plateau area.

They had been challenged twice by sentries at the entrance to the plateau from the sandstone mountains and again after climbing through the passage and coming out on the other side. Honor couldn't help but be impressed at the operation of this man whom she had previously thought only a mindless animal. It seemed he was not as stupid as she had thought.

They rode a little way onto the plateau, and she could see bright campfires ahead where rough cabins had been constructed. She was amazed at the layout and thought it reminded her of a small village—of Katala's village—except for the visible absence of children. That there were women was evident in the sweet, clear notes from some woman's throat as she sung in accompaniment to the strains of a guitar.

Honor was led to the largest of the cabins and hurried inside. She adjusted her eyes to the light of the roaring fire in the grate and saw, to her surprise, that several men were playing cards at a table while the woman she had heard earlier was singing in one corner as she played the guitar. One man was writing a letter and another was squinting through dirty glasses as he attempted to read a book by the firelight.

"Jaime, we have the girl," spoke one of the men to someone at the card table.

The face she recalled dimly looked up from concentrating on his cards and nodded absently. "Give her to Christabel. She can see to her for now."

And that was all! Honor couldn't believe that she was not immediately thrown to the floor and raped in front of everyone! She couldn't help her sigh of relief and thought she detected a small smile tugging at the mouth of this enigmatic outlaw she found herself bound to.

The woman in the corner, upon hearing her name, got up quietly and came over to this stranger girl who looked, she

193

thought, to be an uppity gringa. She frowned to herself, but signed to the girl to follow her.

As they stepped out into the night air and then walked to a nearby cabin, Honor felt obliged to introduce herself. "I am Honor O'Brien," she said as the girl pushed open the cabin door. "You're Cristabel?"

The other woman shrugged as if such things hardly mattered. "You may wash there, behind that screen," she said, pointing with her sun-browned arm. "When you have finished, if you are hungry, there is food in that cupboard. You may sleep here tonight."

"I—will—not be bothered?" she asked, a slight strain in her voice.

Christabel's white teeth flashed with laughter. "You are safe, gringa, until Jaime has won back his money at cards."

Honor could see that the girl was closemouthed, not one to gossip, and hurried behind the screen to wash. She wasn't hungry and asked Christabel, who had remained, where her bed was.

The woman pointed to a small alcove where a cot had been placed. There was only one blanket.

"Thank you, I am tired," she explained. "Goodnight."

The woman's brows drew up. "Sleep well, gringa."

"Where—where will you sleep, Christabel?"

She shrugged again. "If I am lucky, with Jaime. If I am not so lucky, I will return much later, after they have finished playing."

Honor nodded and went to the cot, keeping her clothes on. She had learned, in a very short time, that she could trust no one in this wild, savage land. Although the woman did not seem to view her with hatred, she had displayed no liking at seeing her arrival in camp. Her mention of sleeping with Jaime might mean that she was his woman now and it would be natural for her to be jealous of another woman brought in for his pleasure. For his pleasure! The words swirled in Honor's brain despite her weariness. Lord, she was tired of being at the whim of every man she met. First Brice, then Katala, Esteban and now, she supposed, Jaime Sevillas. Even Jim Parsons had considered her fair game. Wistfully she recalled Ron Williams, who had given her the money to get from San Diego to Monterey. If she had been able to look into the future then, she might have elected to go with him and his parents on to San Francisco and the goldfields. But try as she might, she couldn't bring Ron's face into focus. She could never lie to herself and pretend that she would have been wildly happy with Ron—but at least, she was sure, she would never have known degradation.

With that dubious thought in her mind, she fell asleep, dreaming no nightmares for the first time since she had lost Brice Devlin.

She would have been surprised to know that Brice Devlin was, at that moment, not very far away from her. After his recovery from his ordeal, he had bade farewell to the doctor, thanked Elena profusely for her help and begun to make his way up to San Francisco, where he should have gone in the first place, he thought, as he lay in the hotel room on the northern road. It was not really a hotel, more like an inn, but the bed was soft enough and the room halfway clean.

He was smoking a cheroot as he lay with his arms folded behind his head, staring up into the timbers of the ceiling. His back still ached, especially after the long ride today, but he tried to put the pain out of his mind. His face was almost healed, although he had the scars from a cut over his left eye and where his cheek had split open from his temple to his jawline. His nose had set well in the doctor's opinion, though Devlin hadn't even bothered to check it in a mirror. He recalled that Elena had seemed pleased enough when he had offered her the use of his bed for the night.

"Oh, señor, I can see how the señorita could love you," she had whispered passionately in his ear after the act had been consummated.

Her words had made him jump, as though in pain. She had almost ruined his pleasure in her. His words were drenched in insolence as he replied, "The señorita is a good little actress, Elena. She fooled even you, I see."

The girl knew enough to keep quiet at his tense words and they had finished the night in each other's arms. She had wanted to go with him the next morning, but Cooper had told her she could stay with him for a while when Devlin firmly denied her.

He had thought about riding out to the Sevillas hacienda immediately and shooting that black bastard, after first strangling Honor with his bare hands. But he thought better of it when he realized that he was in no condition to fight, and that neither of them would be going anywhere. He assumed that Honor would become Sevillas' mistress after his marriage. There would be time enough to settle that score.

For now, he had decided to go to San Francisco. He needed the change, and the excitement and newness of the coastal city would probably give him a fresh outlook. He did not like the change he had undergone since meeting Honor O'Brien. Perhaps it was best that things had worked out this way. He had found himself dangerously close to committing himself to one woman—and the idea was as alien to him as running from a good fight. He had been close to falling in love with the little bitch! What a fool he had been to forget his own best advice! Never let a woman dominate him. From now on, he would use them as they were meant to be used—on his terms, or on theirs, if they were sensible.

He drew on his cheroot, still staring at the ceiling, and couldn't help thinking of Honor. Had any other woman in his life had such power to conceal her thoughts from him? He recalled the wide-set green eyes that had softened to the color of a summer pool when they had made love in the little valley. He had really thought she loved him then and, although he had admitted even to her that he wasn't sure of the outcome, he would have taken her with him that day.

His teeth clenched unconsciously against the cheroot as his mind unwillingly remembered the way her honey-colored hair swung free down her back and curled coyly around her shoulders, the way her hips swung with unconscious grace when she walked, and the way her laughter could rise with delight at some small thing. God, he groaned in a kind of pain, why did she have to betray him like that?

Angrily he took the cheroot and ground it against the floorboard. Damn the bitch for keeping him from his sleep, he thought. Determinedly he pulled his hat over his eyes and started to snore.

Twenty-five

"Get up, Gringa, the sun is already high in the sky."

Honor roused her sore limbs from their cramped position on the narrow cot and looked out of the alcove at Christabel's impudent look.

"You are a lazy one, gringa. I can see already that I will have to teach you the ways of bandidos."

"Oh, not now, please," Honor pleaded. "I think I shall never sleep on this cot again."

"Eh, you sound like a *puta* already," Christabel approved.

Honor flushed at the inference and deduced that Christabel must have spent the night in Jaime's arms to put her in such a good mood.

"I'm famished," she put in, changing the subject.

"Get up then and you can have lunch with me!" Christabel laughed. "Come on and I'll teach you how to cook, little gringa."

"I know how to cook." Honor defended herself stoutly.

"Hah! Have you ever cooked for thirty men at once?"

She shook her head.

"Then, gringa, you do not know how to cook."

After Honor had smoothed the wrinkles from her gown and washed her face, Christabel took her outside, where a whole steer was cooking slowly over a fire. Honor could not believe the size of it and looked inquiringly at her companion.

"What we do not eat, we will dry or salt for long journeys," she explained. "Nothing is ever wasted, but we do have plenty to eat. Cattle, goats for milk, even a garden for vegetables. We are not as primitive as you might think, gringa." Her voice was defensive again. "The cattle are only the best," she chuckled.

Honor realized that all their animals were probably stolen. "How long have you been here—with them?" she asked curiously.

"Maybe two years."

"Two years!" She couldn't imagine living like this so long. Didn't the woman miss civilization? "How can you stay here all the time when there is so much else—out there?" she went on vaguely.

Christabel laughed. "I do not suffer, gringa. Jaime takes me to the city with him sometimes and we have much fun, drinking, gambling and picking the rich men's pockets."

"Which city?"

"San Francisco, of course, *idiota!* Jaime goes there often, for he has the gambling in his blood. It is almost a sickness with him. He goes at least ten times a year."

San Francisco again! She recalled that Esteban's fiancée, the girl he had called Marianne, lived there too. She pushed

197

that out of her mind, but the thought remained that she would like to go to the city with Jaime.

"Do you think I could go the next time?"

Christabel shrugged. "It depends on whether or not Jaime thinks he can trust you." The woman grew somber. "If he thought you would try to run away, he would kill you."

Honor was reminded of her position here in the camp and of the nature of those who were in it. She followed Christabel silently around the camp as the woman explained its operation to her. They passed Jaime, leaning against a tree to get out of the sun, his sombrero pulled back to watch them pass.

"Christabel, I see you have taken our guest in hand," he said derisively, whittling absently on a piece of wood. "Does she seem to like her new home?"

Christabel smiled and rolled her hips suggestively. The man's brown eyes darkened with remembered passion. "Do not worry about the gringa, Jaime. I will take care of her."

"Hah! I think she would rather I take care of her," he commented. His eyes looked at Honor as though they shared some secret.

"You men are all alike," Christabel snorted, hurrying her charge along.

"Thank you," Honor whispered once they were out of his hearing range.

"For what?" Christabel asked in surprise. "Do not deceive yourself, gringa, I cannot protect you if Jaime decides to warm you up tonight."

Honor held that thought as she ate her lunch, chewing reflectively on the highly seasoned beef that was washed down with quantities of wine. The men and women ate with relish as though the meal were their last—and Honor supposed that with their life-style they would certainly have to consider that possibility.

She was introduced carelessly to those present to the accompaniment of much winking and laughter. Apparently they already knew why she had been brought. She bristled at the indignity, and then wondered that she could still feel such emotion after everything she had already gone through.

Later in the afternoon, while everyone was taking siesta, Honor thought about her plans. The best course to follow, she surmised, would be to gain Jaime's confidence so that he would take her to San Francisco. Then she would find some means of escaping him.

In the evening, as darkness gathered around the outside

cookfires, she calmed herself with determination when Jaime caught her arm and took her out of Christabel's cabin. She was surprised when he led her away from the campsite toward the two great sandstone mountains that guarded the entrance to their hiding place. It seemed a great distance to walk, but before long they had reached the first low ridge and he helped her climb up a narrow pathway to a large shelf of rock. They had not spoken to each other.

"Up there," he pointed, "one of my men is stationed to watch for unwanted intruders. Do not make too much noise, gringa, or you will find yourself being shot at."

"Then why did you bring me here?" she wondered.

He laughed softly. "To make sure you would not make too much noise." Then he sobered. "And to ensure that we would not have unwanted company."

He indicated that she sit beneath an overhang which would provide some protection against the late November wind. In California, the seasons did not change very much, but the wind and fog could be chilling in the winter, and already Christabel had given her a woolen jacket to keep out the wind.

They sat together in silence for a moment. Her blood was pounding through her veins and she thought her heart would surely be heard by him, sitting so close.

"Tell me why my brother would not marry you," he finally said.

Surprised, she turned to him warily. "He did not tell you?"

He shrugged. "Esteban does not like to tell me anything. We are—as much as brothers can be—enemies. He only sent a note, saying that he wanted me to take you off his hands."

She blushed at Esteban's lack of gentility. "He did not marry me because he was already engaged to someone else."

"But you told me you were his fiancée," he reminded her. "I recall it well." His grin flashed whitely beneath his full moustache in the darkness.

"I was, but he thought I was killed coming west and had already chosen another girl to take my place," she said with bitterness. "At least, that is what he told me."

"Well then, I suppose he cannot be blamed for thinking you dead."

She looked at him angrily. "He can be blamed for many things, Jaime. He lied to me at first and made me believe that we would still be married when all he really wanted was to—to—"

"Bed you?" he supplied knowingly.

"Yes! And when I found someone—someone I had known before at the ranch, I decided to go with him, to run away together. But Esteban found out and nearly killed him. For all I know, he may be dead!" She suppressed the sobs that welled up. "He had no right to stop us, when he was already engaged! For what reason could he be so cruel?"

He shrugged. "Pride, gringa, does strange things to a man."

"Your brother is evil. I would like to see him hanged for what he did to me." She gulped unsteadily. "He almost—he would have raped me, cold-bloodedly."

"Rape!" Jaime shrugged. "The word is overused, it seems to me. Whenever a woman finds herself with a partner she doesn't particularly like, or in a situation she hadn't reckoned on, she thinks it is rape."

"He would have raped me!" she insisted. "Your brother is not a kind man—he delights in suppressing his women."

"That is my brother's way," Jaime put in lightly. "No doubt, his real fiancée will be subjected to much the same."

"And you are like your brother," she said in the tone of an accuser.

He laughed. "Many men are alike in such things. Some are afraid of women and so they mistreat them in the bedroom. Others simply enjoy making love. I am one of the latter." He leaned closer. "But you, conveniently, brought up my lack of attention, *querida*."

"Don't call me that!"

"*Querida*—it is only a word that means 'dear one,'" he assured her softly.

She shook her head desperately. "Esteban called me such—and ended calling me much worse."

He laughed soothingly. "Very well, *hermosita*. That means 'little beauty.' Does that suit you better?"

She looked at him distrustfully.

He laughed again, pleased with this young woman who had fallen into his hands so easily. "*Hermosita*, you must learn not to be so sad. I have not noticed your face filled with laughter."

"Life—has not gone at all the way I had planned—had hoped," she said with a kind of wistfulness, looking into his brown eyes, which seemed, despite what she knew of him, kind.

"But you are still young, little one," he pointed out reasonably. "How old are you?"

"I will be nineteen in the spring," she replied softly. He had surprised her with his concern and she felt herself relaxing her vigilance a little.

"Nineteen is not a vast age, *hermosita*. Life will be better to you now," he promised.

He moved toward her a little, pressing her arm with his hand. Honor flinched at his touch.

"Do not be afraid, little one," he calmed her. "It is true, I would like to make love to you now—and I would not be gentle, for I enjoy women too much. But I would not rape you, little sweet," he whispered in her ear, bringing his hand up to her arm to toy with a honey curl that swept against her shoulder.

Honor tensed and closed her eyes, preparing herself to have the clothes torn from her body. She recalled the savagery of his brother and panic threatened to choke her. Desperately she brought her hands up to push him back.

He caught at them and forced her chin up. "Why do you fight me?" he asked her, still in that softly reasonable tone. "You must know that I can have you whenever I wish—that to fight would be foolish, and would, perhaps, result in your causing yourself injury." He chuckled. "And then you would call it rape, would you not?"

"You laugh," she said bitterly. "Why do you torment me like this? Why did you bring me out here and talk so kindly to me—when in the end, it all comes out the same way?"

He shrugged. "As I said before, I do not like my women unwilling. I have tasted rape before and it has left an unpleasantness in my mouth." His words were colder now and he took his hands away from her. "You accuse me of things in your own mind, *hermosita*. You are a foolish woman not to enjoy the time I can give you."

"I do not ask for it," she replied, defiance creeping into her voice.

"Hah! You would *beg* for it if I had not chosen already to offer you my protection. My men are not hungry wolves, but they take a woman when they feel the need, and I do not stop them. They would take *you* if I did not stand in their way."

"You threaten me now," she put in, as though she had won her point.

He watched her with a slight frown as though he were disappointed in her for some reason. The wind whirled around the little overhang and Honor could feel the chill of it down into her bones. She stared at the man who had brought her to this place and wished she were far away.

He sensed that no amount of sensible talk, nor threatening, nor silky words designed to soften her, would relax her mood. Was she so cold a woman, he wondered. He remembered her once, for only a moment in his arms at the hacienda, and she had warmed a little after the first stiffness had passed. What had his brother really done to her? The cold kiss of the wind touched him and he felt his own desire slowly ebb away. Christabel's bed seemed warm and inviting and he longed for a woman that he understood and could enjoy.

"Let us go back now," he said with a note of urgency.

Honor looked up in surprise.

"Let us go," he repeated, standing up and reaching down to pull her to her feet. "It is cold—colder than I thought—here."

He pulled her along behind him and as they neared the campfires, he stopped her and his voice was harsh. "You will stay here, in my camp." His words were hard, to the point. "You have been brought here against your will, but I cannot let you go now. You know of this camp. I cannot risk you telling the authorities of its whereabouts should I release you."

She was confused at his sudden mention of release, but caught at the words hopefully. "But I would promise . . ."

He shook his head. "I have not come so far by clinging to the promises of women," he commented sagely. "Whether you enjoy our company or not, you will be obliged to remain with us." He looked her up and down and there was a sardonic pity in his glance. "I do not care if you wish to keep your favors to yourself, or if you decide to bestow them wherever you desire."

"Then you will not offer me your protection any longer?" she wondered, feeling a slight jolt of fear.

He laughed and shrugged. "If it is your wish, I will tell the men that you are my property, señorita," he said. "If it is your wish . . ."

"I—I do not want to sleep with you," she whispered, glancing away from him.

For a moment, Jaime thought he might lose his control and slap her stupid little gringa face. But he calmed himself with an effort. It is not worth it to aggravate himself over this girl, when Christabel probably waited for him only a few feet away.

"All right then, I will give you time," he finally ground out. "Honestly, señorita, I do not want to hurt you, but you try a man's patience. There would be many who would have forced you. At least, remember that."

He is not going to hurt me, Honor thought angrily, following him into Christabel's cabin, where she was relieved to see him lead the other girl outside, and yet, he will not let me go. She would have liked to have trusted him to help her. She would not be so foolish again.

Twenty-six

Winter passed slowly. Honor was not singled out by any of the men in the camp, and she assumed that Jaime still protected her from the rest of his men, although he had never again tried to sleep with her. There was Christabel—and others—to satisfy his sexual urges, and Honor was grateful for them. For their part, the women thought Honor was crazy, especially Christabel, who privately thought that Jaime was himself crazy to let the little gringa have her way. But she shrugged philosophically—after all, she would rather not share Jaime with anyone else.

Honor looked forward to those days when Jaime led his men on numerous raids into Monterey and the surrounding haciendas. She was able to relax completely in the camp only when the men were all gone. She was glad that Jaime enjoyed his work so thoroughly, and that women were really only a secondary pleasure to him when he was caught up in the excitement of a raid—or a card game. To Honor, Jaime was much like Katala, the camp much like the Comanche village she had known before. It was almost as though she were reliving that part of her life—except that now, she had no one like Brice Devlin around.

She could still work herself into a fury when she thought of Esteban—by now, surely married to his bride from San Francisco. She wondered if the young woman might regret marrying him. The scandal of divorce was unheard of among the Spanish-Mexican element of the state—and Honor could only feel pity for the wife of such a man when she had no recourse against him.

Sometimes, when Jaime was in a receptive mood as he

203

half-dozed, lazily, under a tree, Honor would sit by him and suggest suitable revenge to be taken on his brother. Jaime would shrug or laugh and wave her anger away, or he might frown and nod and agree that his brother was, in his way, as bad as himself.

"Why should he have the hacienda to himself?" she would whisper rebelliously.

"Because he is the eldest—and he doesn't have the law after him," Jaime would reply practically.

"The eldest? Such a poor excuse for giving him everything—while you have nothing!" Honor would retort.

"I have things my brother doesn't have," Jaime murmured, reaching out to caress her cheek, and then laughing when she moved out of reach. "Esteban is confined in his big hacienda with his cool little wife, while I have the open sky and spicy women who are hot for me." He looked at her with derision. "Do not try to make me carry out your own personal grudge against Esteban, *hermosita*. Would you truly wish brother to go against brother?"

"I would wish anything to see that devil brought to justice!"

"Ah, but you see how differently I view it, little one. It was Esteban who enabled me to have you for myself. If he had been an honorable man, he would never have sent you to me. Why, right now, you would have been his contented, rich little wife with a child in the making."

His sarcasm jabbed at her and she colored hotly. "But he is not honorable and—and I can only wish for the worst to happen to him!"

"All right, all right, *hermosita*. You have been a good little *chica*, I suppose. I will have a few of my men steal cattle from Esteban. Will that suit you?" He was yawning, tiring of the conversation.

Honor, frustrated at his inattention, did not even trouble to answer. Such a small thing to steal Esteban's cattle, when he had stolen her life and her love away from her.

The skills that Honor had begun to learn from the Comanche were honed anew in her captivity with the bandidos. Christabel taught her how to cook for the men, how to sew heavy sheepskin into garments and how to trail. By the end of winter, there had been a substantial change wrought in the young woman who would be only nineteen in April.

Honor had regained the golden tone to her skin that she had first acquired among the Indians from being out-of-doors so much. Her hair was streaked from the sun and the effect of her hair and skin made her green eyes seem larger, deeper. There was not an ounce of fat on her body, only lean curves and firm contours that made her seem almost boyish with her small breasts. She wore the dress of the Mexican peasant women of the camp—a white or red *camisa*, full at the sleeves and scooped at the neckline, and a brightly patterned skirt that was very full and reached only to her ankles. Her feet were usually bare and the soles had hardened from running over the hard-packed earth.

Sometimes, when she thought about Charleston and the girl she had been, she couldn't believe that she had changed so much, from the mindless, flirting, harmless socialite to a young woman who could think like a man, shoot a pistol with a fair degree of accuracy and ride a horse better than anyone else in the camp. It was a metamorphosis that had almost caught her unawares. Sometimes she would weep for the lost innocence of her life in Charleston, but was honest enough to admit that she had probably fared better than most women would have in her situation.

She rarely thought of Brice Devlin, preferring not to remember the hatred in his face, the accusation in his voice. There were times, in her dreams, that a pair of silvery-blue eyes would haunt her sleep and she would awaken with a yearning inside of her that could not be quenched. She almost wished she had given in to Jaime's indifferent flirtation, but Jaime liked his women full and soft, round of breast and hip, not slender and hard like the young woman he still called *"hermosita"* and gave his protection to so that his men would not devour her.

Jaime would watch her covertly at times in the cabin or around the campfire in the evenings. She moved with a lithe grace that was more suited to a lioness than to a woman. Her slender body, outlined in the light of the fire, did not promise a yielding softness to him—rather it reminded him of a startled deer who would flee from his embrace if it was possible. She had become adept at using a pistol and a knife in order to defend herself, and, he thought, he wasn't so sure that she needed his protection from his men any longer.

He knew he would not find the mindless pleasure with Honor that he felt in Christabel when he made love to her, and so he became used to seeking Honor out when he felt the need for conversation before a good night's sleep. It wasn't that she was no longer desirable. It was more that she had put herself above the usual woman's notions and sometimes he felt as though she would only endure sex with him if necessary, but she would obtain no real pleasure.

It was too bad, he thought objectively. She was still beautiful, still a woman, but it was as though she rejected these things. As though she sought to hide from them—perhaps she was afraid of being hurt again.

Watching her by the light of the fire, one evening, he wondered if she might perk up if he took her to San Francisco for a few days. He knew her birthday was in April, only a few weeks away. It would be a nice surprise.

Honor couldn't help the rising tide of excitement as she mounted her horse and guided it forward behind Jaime's. He had waited until last night to tell her that he was going to take her with him to San Francisco. She had been almost absurdly grateful. San Francisco! She couldn't believe he was going to take her with him. It had been in the back of her mind so long, and she had never thought that she would be able to go—leave this bandido camp that had been her home for so long. She wouldn't be coming back, she wouldn't! She would make her escape as soon as she could. Surely it would not be hard in a city the size of San Francisco.

She was aware that besides herself and Jaime, Christabel would be along as well as two or three others, but that would not deter her. She could think as coolly as Jaime under pressure and could ride even better than he.

As they rode north, a journey of some three days, to San Francisco, she tried to formulate a plan. They would make camp every night on the road, deeming it too risky to stay at an inn as Jaime now had a substantial price on his head. Honor had been surprised and, despite herself, concerned, when Jaime had shown her the wanted poster. The likeness had been very good and the reward was up to five hundred dollars.

Jaime had made the mistake of stealing horses from a nearby ranch, and in the process, one of his men had killed the overseer. The owner, a hard-bitten gringo, had vowed revenge, and hence the uplift from a twopenny thief (who, she had found out, had murdered one of his own men in a barroom brawl) to a full-fledged outlaw, the subject of greedy bounty hunters.

Jaime had not minded the added notoriety. It had only increased his recklessness. This trip to San Francisco had come about directly as a way to thumb his nose at all those who wanted his hide, he said. He could still travel freely, he insisted, without interference from the bounty hunters, and he could still live it up with stolen gold in the gambling saloons of the city. It was an act of bravado that was lost on Honor, but she was fervently glad he had thought of it, and was taking her along.

They arrived in the coastal city in the afternoon and Jaime led them to Portsmouth Square, which had been the old plaza in the Spanish-government days. Honor's eyes widened at the influx of people everywhere in the square. All sides of it were lined with shops, gambling saloons and a few hotels which catered to the low life by offering dice games, cards and whores.

She could see the excitement on Jaime's face at the prospect of getting into a card game that very evening. He paid for their rooms and dispatched the two women upstairs with the little luggage they had brought. Actually, only the women had brought an extra change of clothes, as the men could have their shirts sent out to a Chinese laundry while they took an afternoon nap.

"It's certainly no castle, is it?" Christabel smiled, flopping unceremoniously on the bed, the sheets of which were a dingy yellow.

Honor sat on a stained chair gingerly. "Do they actually call this place a hotel?" she asked incredulously.

Christabel shrugged. "It's only one dollar a day for all of us for two rooms. Remember, Jaime would much rather spend his money on gambling than worry about our comfort."

"Ugh! And I had actually looked forward to this trip," Honor bantered.

"You're lucky! I remember the time Jaime put us up in a hotel in Sydney Town along the coast of the city! I lived in fear of my life the whole time!"

"What's Sydney Town?"

"It's a bad area, Honor. You never want to be caught there without some male protection. Even the police don't like to go in unless there's five or six of them. They call it Sydney Town because most of the people who started it are Australians. The worst of the lot, too. Mostly convicts, murderers, thieves and whoremongers." She shivered. "They're the dregs of the earth."

"Then why don't the city fathers do something about it?
207

Don't they have a system of law and order around here?" Honor demanded.

Again, the sarcastic shrug. "The 'city fathers' are all political fat cats," Christabel explained contemptuously. "They'll take a fat bribe from any one of the disreputable types in this town—and there are plenty of them. There used to be a Vigilance Committee that took it upon themselves to try to oust all the murderers and other criminals from power. They used to hang anyone they found committing a crime, but the authorities finally persuaded them to lay their arms down and graft and vice came in faster and stronger than ever. The whole town is one big bed of sin!"

"You mean there's no one to stand up for their rights?"

"Very few who don't end up on the payment end of a political scheme," Christabel said. "Law and order is something that happens only when it suits someone with power in the city. Of course, there are bankers and big merchants and railroad men who strong-arm the criminals through their money and sheer force—but they always use their own bullies."

Honor shook her head. "I can't understand how the city survives." She remembered the domed capitol building in Charleston, the political figures in their black cutaway coats and gray-striped ascots, the elegant balls and dinners that she had attended with her parents. Authority had seemed all-seeing and swift to punish those who offended it. She supposed, now, that there must have been those who took bribes and looked the other way when a crime was committed. But things had looked so different then.

"The city survives because of one thing," Christabel put in. "Gold. There is so much that flows through here and changes hands every day, I'll bet no one has any idea of the actual amount."

She grinned at Honor's stupefaction. "Anything else you want to know about the history of San Francisco?" she asked teasingly.

Honor shook her head. "Only—what are we supposed to do while Jaime gambles?"

"We can do just about anything we want if we take Luis and Paco along. What would you like to do?"

"I'd like to see the ocean!"

"All right, you wash up while I go and ferret out our two unwilling escorts."

In no time, Jaime had hired them a hansom and they were

on their way north toward Golden Gate. From there, they would swerve west to avoid the waterfront district.

Honor was breathless with awe as they stopped on a high knoll and looked out over the ocean. It was nearly sundown and the bright red ball of the sun was dipping into the water, causing rays of red and pink to highlight the waves. A low fog was beginning to move in with the evening darkness and reluctantly Honor agreed with Christabel that they should be on their way back to the hotel.

Because of a disturbance on their route, they had to go down Pacific Street. Peeping out from the window curtains, Honor could see the wooden sidewalks crowded by all manner of people, including drunken sailors who disappeared inside groggeries that lined the street.

"You can smell the Chilenos from here," Christabel said, wrinkling her nose in distaste at the scents of garlic, chili, outhouses and whiskey.

"What are the Chilenos?" Honor asked avidly.

"The Latin peoples up from South America and Mexico," Christabel explained. "They call them 'greasers' up here."

"You mean they're considered one of the disreputable types," Honor amended.

"Yes, and they—"

Before Christabel could fully explain, there was a sudden commotion outside, followed by a rocking of the coach, causing Luis and Paco to finger their Colts nervously.

Honor exchanged an anxious look with Christabel before glimpsing outside. A small group of sullen-looking men were pulling down the driver and starting to whip him with short quirts, as though in playful teasing.

"Riffraff," Christabel snorted. "They won't play long when they see the iron our two companions are carrying." She nodded to the two men, who opened the door and stepped out, menacing revolvers at the ready.

In a few moments, the men had quit their game, skulking back into the shadows while brazenly painted whores blew kisses at the two Mexicans and invited them inside their clapboard houses. Luis helped the driver back to his seat and the two men climbed back into the coach. They would have liked to have taken the whores up on their promises, but knew that they had to get the two women back to their hotel first, or Jaime Sevillas would have their hides on a stake.

"Whew, I was afraid we were going to get a firsthand look at what I was talking about!" Christabel breathed after the

209

hansom had resumed its course. "After they finished playing with our driver, we would have been next if it hadn't been for our two gallants." She nodded at the two men.

"I think I'll stay around the hotel tomorrow," Honor put in nervously.

She was wondering how in the world she was going to be able to escape Jaime when, without him or the protection of his men, she would probably wind up robbed, raped or murdered. It wasn't going to be easy to get away from Christabel's watchful eye anyway, for Honor had the feeling that Jaime had charged her with looking out for her during their stay. She slumped back in her seat, her brow knit in thought. San Francisco was not at all what she had expected. Perhaps she would be better off to stay with Jaime for the time being.

Twenty-seven

Despite the restricting circumstances, Honor found time to tour parts of the city with Christabel, both of them always escorted by Luis and Paco. They prudently avoided Sydney Town and the waterfront, but drove boldly through the Chinese quarter of the town, shying away from the sinister alleys where Chinese "cribs" operated at twenty-five cents per customer for half an hour with the Chinese girl of their choice. They did see the more elite Chinese parlor houses on Grant Avenue and Waverly Place which exuded the odors of musk, sandalwood and a sweet, cloying scent that Christabel explained was opium smoke, a drug that made one a mindless zombie if one indulged too long in it.

They shopped at some of the better stores, including a small store owned by Levi Strauss, who specialized in blue serge trousers which were called "denims" by the local miners, who were his biggest customers. They climbed Telegraph Hill and gazed in awe at some of the monstrous houses that were already being built on Nob Hill.

They toured the whole of Portsmouth Square and passed by the notorious Bella-Union, a high-class gambling and whore house that catered to the best clientele. They dressed up one day and drank Madeira at the Virginia City International Hotel restaurant, where tailcoats and cowboy boots seemed to mix incongruously.

Avoiding the dangerous upper part of Pacific Street, they rode through the lower part, enjoying the colorful sights. On almost every parlor house and gambling saloon, they saw signs printed with "No Irish" or "No Greasers." Christabel and Honor had to laugh a little since Honor was one of the former and Christabel, unashamedly, one of the latter. At any rate, they were not about to go in any of the places.

On their last night in the city, Jaime, who had won consistently at the tables, exuberantly presented them with two new gowns he had purchased in a ready-made store. His taste was a trifle gawdy for Honor's sensibilities, but she accepted his gift with heartfelt thanks. It was the first time a man had given her a present with no strings attached, except for Ron Williams, and she was grateful.

She and Christabel dressed in their new gowns, which were thankfully pretty true to size. Christabel's flame-red dress suited her dusky complexion and Honor's pale blue taffeta brought out the color of her eyes and hair. They dressed their hair carefully, as Jaime had promised to take them someplace special tonight.

He arrived at their door (the two women had stayed in one room, the men in the other) promptly at eight, dressed neatly in black broadcloth and string tie. He hired a hansom to take them to Seal Rock House, which was newly built and already a favorite place of sporting gentlemen and their ladies. There was a restaurant where one could eat while watching the bay and Honor was excited at the prospect. She only wished Jamie had thought to buy them gloves and slippers, but she would have to make do with her riding boots and bare hands.

They were shown to a table by the window after Jamie gave the maître d'hôtel a generous tip, and all three gazed out to the bay as they talked lightheartedly of their stay in the city.

It was not until the last morsel of glazed pheasant was eaten that Honor felt uncomfortably that someone was watching her. The feeling persisted through the last glass of champagne, and finally she turned her head to catch a pair of cold black eyes gazing at her burningly.

Honor choked on the Dom Perignon, and when Jaime asked her what was wrong, she could only gasp, "Your brother . . ."

He nodded thoughtfully. "Yes, I know."

"You know! But—"

"What was I to do about it, *hermosita*? He has not bothered us."

"But after what he did!" she exclaimed, beside herself. The evening was ruined for her and she only wanted to return to their hotel. She hated that man and it was all she could do to remain poised at their table.

"What would you have me do?" Jaime asked uncomfortably.

"I wish—I wish there was some way to expose him for the cheat and the liar that he is!" she answered vehemently.

"And have him expose me, *chica*? You do not think wisely." Jaime's tone held a note of warning in it and Honor realized he wanted no scene in this public place, but she couldn't help looking again at Esteban, a look of disgust on her face.

Beside him, she noted, sat a frail-looking young woman of about her own age with enormous blue eyes and fair hair that was curled impeccably about her heart-shaped face. The eyes watched her with curiosity mixed with a certain anxiety and Honor knew this must be the girl he called Marianne, his wife. She could only feel pity for her. She did not look the sort to be married to a blackguard such as Esteban Sevillas.

To her utter chagrin, as they were leaving the restaurant, Esteban and his wife were also collecting their capes. There was no way to avoid a confrontation, and Jaime hastily pushed Honor behind him.

"Ah, *mi hermano*, we meet in strange places, eh?" Jaime said easily.

"*Sí*," Esteban replied blandly, turning to help his wife with her evening cloak.

"But Esteban, you forget your manners," Marianne said, more than ever curious about this man her husband called brother. "Will you not introduce me?"

It was easy to see that Esteban had no wish to introduce his wife to his brother, but after a moment's pause he did so hesitantly.

"My brother, Jaime—my wife, Marianne." Brief and to the point.

"I confess that Esteban has never talked much about you, Jaime," Marianne said lightly, "but now that we know each other—"

212

"Jaime and I do not see each other often," Esteban cut in quickly. "Come along."

Twirling his moustache and smiling wickedly, Jaime bowed low to his brother's wife and introduced his two female companions. "Señora, allow me to introduce my friends, Christabel Sánchez and Honor O'Brien."

Marianne's pleasant smile froze for a moment and a look of puzzlement appeared on her features. "Honor? Forgive me, but I have heard the name before—from my mother-in-law." She smiled nervously. "A coincidence, I suppose."

Good for Yolande! Honor thought wryly.

"Have you—do you live near Monterey, Miss O'Brien?" Marianne pressed, aware of her husband's fingers digging cruelly into her arm beneath the cloak.

"Yes, I do," Honor replied boldly, avoiding Esteban's eyes. Let him sweat this one out, she thought angrily. "As a matter of fact, I was engaged to someone who lived in one of the haciendas outside of Monterey."

"That *is* a coincidence," Marianne laughed, but her smile was still anxious as Esteban's fingers tightened even more.

"I suppose then we might have been neighbors," she continued softly as Esteban tugged forcefully at her arm, leading her outside.

"I think not," Honor said to herself as she watched the fury on Esteban's face. And then aloud to Jaime, "Perhaps we shouldn't have irritated him like that, Jaime. He might—"

Jaime laughed securely. "You forget, *chica,* that he is my brother. And brothers do not betray brothers."

Honor shrugged, but she said nothing more. Christabel gave her an understanding look as she drew her arm through Jaime's, and the three of them left the Seal Rock House and returned to their hotel.

The next morning, Jaime wanted to get a good start and both girls awoke early to breakfast downstairs before beginning the journey back. Honor chafed sullenly as they mounted their horses and Jaime turned in his saddle to give her a wink.

"Ah, *hermosita,* I am surprised you are still with us, eh? I had expected not to see you this morning."

"And where would I go?" she retorted angrily. "Perhaps to Sydney Town, or the Chinese quarter?"

He stroked his chin thoughtfully. "Or perhaps to one of the gambling halls to learn the trick of the cards. Or," and he

213

grinned engagingly, "into the lap of one of these fine millionaires that seem to abound in this city of sin."

"It seems I am to be stuck with a foxy bandido instead," Honor replied, with a hint of laughter.

"You could do worse," he said.

They urged their horses into a quick canter and San Francisco was soon well behind them and they were on the open road to Monterey. The journey back was quicker than their journey to the city as Jaime was anxious to get back to his camp, where he knew fights may have broken out in his absence and some of his men may have been apprehended by the law or killed by other bandidos.

They arrived at the camp in the blaze of a spring sunset and Jaime was pleased to see that all were safe and the home fires burning for his return. He ordered a grand fiesta and everyone stayed up the whole night, drinking, gambling and wenching. Alone, Honor watched from the cabin she shared with Christabel as the others danced the wild fandango dances that exuded a sensual awareness of the body that could drive men wild. Christabel was dancing in a ring of clapping people, her skirts flying around her thighs and her arms damp with perspiration. In another moment, she knew Jaime would leap up and join her and afterward he would collapse with her in his bed. She did not mind being left out. Despite her closeness to Christabel and her fondness for Jaime, she felt like an alien—and there was still the nagging worry about Esteban in the back of her mind.

"Why do you walk around with such a frown, *hermosita?*" Jaime asked her lazily one day when he returned from a successful raid with several horses and steers.

"I am still thinking of your brother, the snake," she informed him, her chin in her hands.

"Do not worry about him, *chica*. Look, I have only just now returned from stealing some of his herd. That will make him angry, no?"

"Yes! I don't trust him, Jaime. Perhaps—perhaps you should stay away from his ranch."

He laughed. "Ah, do not tell me what to do, my little gringa, or you will anger me. For your remark, I will raid him again tomorrow—and you shall come with me so that you can work out your anger on his cattle."

"I? Ride with you on a raid?" Honor shook her head. "Jaime, I don't want a price on my head."

214

He seemed delighted with the idea. "A reward for twenty-five dollars for the outlaw woman with hair of gold and eyes of the sea. I am sure, *hermosita*, that many men would try to capture you." He winked slyly. "And not for the reward alone, eh?"

She blushed and eyed him hotly. "No doubt you would collect the reward yourself?"

"But of course, and then I would come to break you out of jail," he assured her, still smiling.

"Oh, Jaime, must I—"

His brow raised slightly in the beginning of a frown. "You will not refuse me, *hermosita*, or perhaps I will think you need a strong man in your bed to tame that willful nature," he threatened in a low voice.

Again her cheeks bloomed. She considered him a friend, but had no interest in him as a lover. In fact, she had told herself ruefully, she hardly cared whether she ever had a lover again. Men were too treacherous and too greedy. She was really better off by herself.

"All right, I will ride with you, but only if you let Christabel come," she said, feeling safer if another woman rode with them.

He nodded graciously. "Although she would not make as good a robber as yourself," he said under his breath.

He rode away, leaving her annoyed and angry and ashamed all at once. All right then, if he insisted, she would ride with him and carry out her vengeance on her enemy's cattle. It would be a little thing to him, she knew, but it would help to ease her anger.

The next morning, she was in the saddle, dressed in a man's breeches—a pair of denims she had bought from Mr. Strauss—and a checkered shirt and neckerchief. She wore a serape over her shoulder and a large sombrero under which she pinned her hair.

Upon seeing her, Jaime laughed his approval. He helped Christabel to mount her horse and then gave the signal to ride out. They rode between the blocks of sandstone and into the beautiful morning, the grass still dew-kissed.

"We shall take twenty cattle for you, *hermosita!*" Jaime cried exuberantly.

"Thirty!" Honor shouted back as she leaned over her horse's neck.

"Agreed!"

They circled the unfenced portion of the Sevillas land and

215

stopped on a crest to survey the land. There were no cattle this far out and so they moved in a little. Finally they spotted a herd of Angus grazing placidly in one of the many small dips between knolls. There were about fifty and only two men riding herd.

"This will be an easy snatch!" Jaime laughed. He signaled his ten men to split up and surround the herd, keeping close to some cover so as not to alert the vaqueros.

"You will stay close to me," he ordered the two women.

"Will there be any shooting?" Honor wanted to know, feeling the gooseflesh on her arms at actually breaking the law.

"You mean those two hombres down there?" Jaime shrugged. "Not unless they feel like heroes today. And that is usually not the case."

He raised his pistol and fired once in the air, causing his men to tighten their circle. Instantly the vaqueros split in two different directions, leaving Honor to wonder at the ease of it all. No wonder Jaime thought this a wonderful way to make a living. She had to admit it certainly seemed so.

"Pick your thirty, little one," Jaime offered.

Honor turned to him saucily, but before she could open her mouth, she caught riders out of the corner of her eye. Surprised, she turned in her saddle and saw ten men coming at them. A strange feeling of fear welled up inside of her and soon turned to a fateful dread as she saw ten more men gather on the other side. More men appeared to the east and west until they were snugly surrounded by the Sevillas vaqueros.

"*Hermano*, we meet again!" came a voice that held no emotion.

Jaime whirled in surprise to confront his brother, who was riding calmly toward him with three of his men. Then he laughed.

"Brother, what are you doing here? You try to spoil my fun, eh?"

Esteban laughed, showing white teeth that seemed to Honor to resemble the fangs of a hungry wolf. She tensed in her saddle, awaiting Jaime's signal to fire and make a run for it. He did neither.

"Surrender, Jaime!" The command was light, almost playful.

"Brother, you ruin my reputation as a bandido." Jaime laughed again.

"Jaime, he has surrounded your men," Christabel hissed. Even she had begun to worry.

Jaime shrugged. "He is my brother. We will talk this out between us." He called out, "All right, Esteban. I am yours. What is it you want of me?"

"Come with me to the hacienda, Jaime."

Everything in her warned Honor against such a course of action. Esteban Sevillas was a snake, a wolf, a man without honor. Desperately she tried to caution Jaime, but he would not listen, dismissing her fear as a woman's prerogative. Raising his hand, he gave the signal to his men to follow him to the hacienda.

"I trust *hermano*, that you will provide good food and wine for my men and me?" he asked Esteban lightly.

The older man snickered softly. "Of course." His eyes touched briefly on Honor, met and held her eyes for a moment, then slipped away. A slight smile appeared on his face and Honor shivered. She would have wheeled her horse and tried to run for it, but Sevillas' men were hemming her in on all sides now and it was impossible to escape. Oh, Jaime, Jaime, she thought. How could he be so foolish?

"And how is your lovely *esposa?*" Jaime asked politely as they neared the hacienda.

Esteban smiled. "She is well. She remained behind in San Francisco with her parents."

"Her parents—they are wealthy, of course?"

"Of course, *hermano*. Her father is one of the richest of all the speculators. Would I have countenanced a penniless bride?" His words made Honor wince and then redden in anger.

She remained silent through sheer determination not to invite further harassment. They dismounted in the yard and Jaime's men were dispatched to the barn for victuals. Honor watched them go with a feeling of dread she couldn't shake. They entered the hacienda. María Díaz ushered them in, but her eyes would not meet Honor's in salutation.

"In here, Jaime," Esteban was saying, as he threw open the door to his study.

Inside, three men stood up, their guns held ready in their hands. Jaime gazed first at them, then at his brother, openmouthed. "What is this, *hermano?*"

Esteban nodded to one of the men. "This is your man, sheriff. Jaime Sevillas. Take him."

The two other men swiftly moved to tie Jaime's hands and

217

when he struggled to pull out his pistol, one of them knocked him out with a hard knock of his pistol to the temple. Christabel cried out and bent to help him, but was kicked away.

"And this is his whore, sheriff," Esteban calmly went on, pointing to the distraught Christabel.

"Bastard! Spineless bastard! I will kill you!" Christabel screamed, trying to lunge for Esteban, but she was quickly subdued by one of the sheriff's men. She struggled as they tied her hands behind her. "Jaime's men will come for him and I will see you roasted on a spit!"

"His men have been tied up neatly by now in the barn by the rest of the posse, *puta!*" Esteban said bitingly. "And I doubt you will see anything, with your eyes bulging out of your skull at the end of a rope!"

"No!" Honor stepped forward, her hand a blur as she pulled out her pistol and leveled it at Esteban's chest. "Untie both of them and let us go, or I will put a bullet through you," she warned through her teeth. Her green eyes were stormy, her tongue held between her teeth as she met his cold gaze.

"You! Who would have believed it? My brother has taught you something, I can see," Esteban said jeeringly. His gaze was contemptuous. "Put that away, Honor, before you, too, seal your fate at the end of a rope. They have nothing against you now," he reminded her.

She shook her head. "Let them go," she repeated with deadly calm.

The sheriff stood undecided, his men holding each of their prisoners. Jaime was still unconscious, slumped in the arms of his captor, but Christabel's eyes shone at her companion's bravado.

"She can kill you, batard!" Christabel hissed ominously. "She can put the bullet in your heart or between the eyes. Let us go, as she says."

For a moment, the resolve in Esteban wavered, but he quickly collected himself. He could see, coming down the hall, one of the sheriff's deputies. His eyes flickered as he relaxed. "You remind me of a lioness protecting her mate," he said scornfully, eyeing the slender girl with a ridiculing glance. "You have grown up, *querida,*" he added softly.

Honor cocked the pistol and returned his glance as coolly as she could. She wasn't at all sure she could pull the trigger and actually shoot a man cold-bloodedly, but she was sure of

218

one thing—that she couldn't allow this man to hang Jamie and Christabel, the only people she had left. He had killed her lover already; she could not let him do more harm to her.

"Put the gun down, miss," the sheriff spoke gruffly.

Honor looked at him with contempt. "Are you afraid of losing your reward money, sheriff?" she asked.

The sheriff reddened, but he, too, had caught sight of his deputy and his brows lifted in silent signal to the man, who was slowly sneaking up behind the girl. Christabel caught the sheriff's look and her mouth flew open in alarm.

"Honor, behind you!"

Honor whirled, but the deputy had already pounced and had hit her with a glancing blow that knocked the gun from her hand and sent her to the floor on her side. She struggled to get up, but the man held her down grimly. He knew what these greaser whores could do with a knife or a gun, and this one seemed to mean business.

The sheriff heaved a sigh of relief and motioned to his men to take his two prisoners outside. "And this one," he began, pointing to Honor, "will have to be taken in too for threatening an officer of the law."

"The law!" Honor spat. "You mean an officer of Esteban Sevillas! Did he pay for you to be voted into your office, sheriff?" she asked sarcastically, wriggling beneath the deputy, who seemed to enjoy keeping her in her ignominious position on the floor.

"Shut your mouth, you damned greaser," the deputy yelled at her, swiping her across the cheek.

Honor saw stars for a moment, but regained her sensibilities to realize that she was being dragged to her feet and propelled out of the room. She slumped against the deputy, hoping he would think she had fainted, but the man did not trust her enough to release her.

Esteban was arguing with the sheriff. She could hear their voices from the hallway, but they no longer interested her. She wondered briefly what the inside of a jail would be like. She had never even been in one to visit. Well, she could face it, if she had to. She steeled herself to remain stiff as the deputy tried to make her walk down the hall.

Finally the sheriff stalked out, his round face reddened even more as he strode toward Honor. "Take this woman to the barn and tie her up!" he ordered the startled deputy.

"But sheriff—"

"Goddammit, Lawson, do as I say!" he yelled and walked

outside to where Jaime, Christabel and his men were tied together, awaiting their next orders. Most of them were slumped awkwardly over their saddles, their hands tied behind them, and Honor felt pity for them.

Pity and an intense desire to go with them. More than anything else in the world, she did not want to be left behind—with Sevillas. She shuddered. He was having her put in the barn. Where he had put Brice before— But she mustn't think about Brice now, she mustn't, or she would never be able to bear up. Stoically she walked in front of the deputy, who was still muttering under his breath.

The barn was fragrant with hay and she was ushered into a boxlike stall and made to sit down while the deputy tied her hands and feet and, as a further precaution, placed a gag over her mouth. She knew he was only doing it because of the trouble she had caused him. He stood back from his work, regarding her with a pleased eye, then spat and left her alone.

Honor sat in the warm half-light, gagging on her kerchief and chafing her hands as she tried to work them loose. It was no use. The deputy had tied them so tightly that she felt them numbing almost instantly. Wearily she leaned her head back against the wood. She could hear the rumble of horses as the sheriff, his posse and hostages left the hacienda. Two tears trickled hopelessly down her cheeks as she thought of Jaime's fate.

Her ears picked up the sound of booted feet entering the barn and she steeled herself to regard her captor without flinching. She was only sorry that she could not wipe the tears from her cheeks, for he saw them instantly and was pleased.

"Sad over your fate, *querida?*" he asked her disdainfully.

He watched her eyes, green emeralds blazing defiance at him. Every line of her body spoke her hatred of him and his eyes gleamed at how he would subjugate her to his will. He had been able to tame Marianne so easily, he had almost forgotten how this one had heated his blood with her defiance. Oh, Marianne had tried to defy him for a while. She had been surprised at this new husband of hers, who was determined that she would obey him in all things. She had fought back for the sake of her own self-respect, but he had crushed her brief rebellion with ridiculous ease. Marianne was such a mewling kitten. He suspected that she might tell her father how she was treated and had viewed her wish to stay behind

220

in San Francisco with suspicion, but after a night's stay with her, he had made her see a glimpse of the wrath that would await her should she attempt to have the marriage annulled. Even her father, with all his wealth, could not do that. Without evidence.

Now she was away and he had this young woman here now—one who was all fire and blazing defiance. Impudent *puta* who would test his will with her own, only to come out the loser ultimately. But the game was the thing—and he was sure that she would give him a good one. Still, better to let her stew for a while in the barn. He had plenty of time and could afford to take some of the spunk out of her.

Deliberately he walked toward her and leaned over, his face close to hers. With all her might, Honor wished she could spit in his face, but the gag prevented her and she could only dart hatred at him with her eyes.

"You are not glad to see me again, eh, *querida?*" he asked softly. "Ah, but you should never have defied me so brazenly in the city. Perhaps, if you had not tried your luck, I would have forgotten about you." He was taunting her, making her think it was all her own fault—Jaime's capture, his ultimate death, her fate in his hands.

She shook her head vehemently, denying his charge. He laughed at her frustration. "Ah, *querida,* I wonder how much you have changed in—how long?—five months? Did my brother spread your legs often, *puta?*"

She was still as his hands lifted the serape from her chest and threw it over her shoulder so that it fell to the ground behind her. The only sign of her agitation was her quickened breathing as he calmly and deliberately began to unbutton her shirt. Slowly, so slowly, he pulled aside the two halves and assessed her breasts before cupping them in his hands experimentally. His thumbs rolled the tips, watching them thoughtfully as they stiffened at his expertise.

Esteban felt his crotch filled, stiffening with his desire. He would have liked to have vented his urges on her then, but forced himself to wait. She had closed her eyes, renouncing the betrayal by her own flesh. He laughed low in his throat. To her horror, he bent his head and placed his mouth on her flesh, nibbling and sucking with his teeth and lips. Her whole body tensed, stiffened with hatred and a flash of desire that she was helpless to quell. Her body grew warmer as he continued to nuzzle at her breast and she shut her eyes tighter.

She hated him, she told herself over and over. Nevertheless, she couldn't help the relieved sigh as he took his mouth away.

"Do you want me now?" he asked her, breathing hard.

She could see the bulge in his trousers signaling his raging desire. But she knew this game from before. The pleading for him to take her, the holding back, the humiliation. Before he had used drugs to stimulate her and now it had been her own body, starving for a man's expert touch, that had betrayed her. And she had thought she no longer needed men! She hated herself—and him for making her see her own need.

But she did not need him. She did not want him. She gazed into his eyes and defied him with all her strength. He smiled condescendingly. He pulled her shirt together and straightened.

"Mustn't let my men be tempted," he said to himself, still looking at her thoughtfully.

Without another word, he walked out of the barn and she could hear him bawling for one of the kitchen wenches. She was filled with disgust. If she could only free her hands, but it was no use. She fell back, panting from her exertions, feeling as though she would strangle on the tight gag around her mouth. She forced herself to breathe slowly, allowing the panic to recede.

She had no way of knowing what Sevillas would decide to do with her. That he would rape her was obvious, and although she cringed at the thought, she was more concerned with what he meant to do with her afterward. From a man who could turn his own brother over to certain death, she expected no mercy.

She suffered throughout the remainder of the day and the night, barely sleeping from the pain in her swollen ankles and wrists. Her throat was sore from the dryness caused from the gag and she almost wished for death to relieve her from this torture. All through the next day, she tensed at any unexpected sound, but no one came to her. Her relief gradually turned to panic again, as her hunger overtook her. She had a raging thirst and began to fear that her hands and feet would fall off from lack of circulation. She had not even been allowed to attend to her personal needs and was sitting in a pool of wet straw.

Finally, toward the end of the second day of her torture, Esteban entered the barn, his nose wrinkling with distaste.

"*Querida*, you have soiled yourself—how disgusting!"

Honor looked up at him through a blur of her vision. Dear God, she would do anything if only he would untie her!

He was pleased at the subdued look about her. Her eyes were haunted from lack of sleep and her lips were bruised from the cloth that bound them. He reached over to untie it and saw the tears of relief well up in her eyes as she worked her mouth experimentally. Realizing that there was no longer any danger, he took a knife and cut the rope at her ankles and wrists. A cry of sheer pain jolted from her dry throat as the blood began to flow more freely in her hands and feet. It felt like a thousand needles pricking her flesh, and for a moment, she thought she would faint.

"Come now, *querida,* how would you like a hot bath? Quite frankly, *chica,* you stink worse than one of my cows."

His insults bounced off her numbed brain and she followed him haltingly, falling to her knees more than once from the pain in her feet. Impatiently he pulled her along to the kitchen, where a frightened serving girl waited next to a tub of steaming water.

"Strip her and burn these clothes!" Esteban ordered.

The girl did as she was told and helped Honor into the tub. Slowly but surely, as she soaked in the heated water, Honor felt life coming back to her. Esteban had almost beaten her, she thought, but now she felt nearly well enough to defy him again. The fire in the kitchen warmed her even more as the girl dried her with a towel and then pulled a thin silk shift over her arms.

"You are hungry?"

Honor nodded weakly. She felt as warm and snug as a newborn kitten. She would have liked to have curled up somewhere and fallen asleep, but she was hungry and she knew she would need the strength against Esteban. The girl kindly brushed her hair as Honor ate the bowl of soup she set before her.

"Much, much better." Esteban was watching from the entrance to the kitchen, his eyes picking up the glow from the fire. "You will come with me now, *querida.*" He was commanding her and for a moment was surprised to see resistance in her eyes.

Honor quickly veiled her fiery defiance. It would be better to let him think he had won for now. There would be time for revenge very soon, she thought, getting up to take his hand. His arm wrapped possessively about her shoulders and she allowed herself to sway against him to help the illusion of weakness.

She remembered the stairway by heart, knew where his room was. He was taking her there now and as she entered, the sight of the turned-down bed was so inviting that her resolution wavered by a fraction. But, she reminded herself, he had not brought her here to sleep and her determination hardened once more.

A table had been laid out with fruit and wine and cheese and he bade her sit down while he stoked the fire. He was already dressed in a rich, velvet dressing gown and so there would be no chance to retrieve a weapon from his person. Her eyes roamed the room and came to rest on the fruit plate, which held a small knife used to peel the fruit.

Hesitantly she slipped it closer to her, then turned quickly as she heard him speaking to her.

"Come to me, *querida*. The refreshment is for later."

Honor slipped the knife inside a pocket of the shift and went toward him slowly, as one mesmerized. Her mind worked feverishly as she assessed the room, his state of mindless desire. She picked at details—his suit of clothes thrown carelessly over a chair, the key to the locked door on his dressing table.

"You are too slow, Honor. Hurry—I do not wish to be kept waiting," he commanded softly.

He was sitting in an armchair by the fire, his arms outstretched to fold her fragrant flesh against him. Still standing, Honor felt him press his hands against her hips to bring them forward as his head bent so that his mouth could devour her bosom, then travel slowly downward, parting the thin silk as he went. She started as his wet tongue traced glistening patterns on her belly and then began to delve even lower.

Now was the time, she thought, using her hatred to force herself to retrieve the knife from her pocket. Her fist closed around it and she raised her arm to strike him between the shoulder blades.

The sudden tenseness in her body was the only thing to give her away, but Esteban, sensing it, lifted his head for a moment to reassure her. His eyes caught the gleam of cold steel in the firelight and, instinctively, he moved sideways to avoid the death blow.

Honor's downward swipe caught only his shoulder, but it was enough to make him release her with the sudden pain. She stepped back and watched him slump slowly forward to the floor, but she knew that the pain would not keep him there for long. Hurriedly she glanced around the room and found a porcelain vase on a shelf. Without a second thought, she rushed to it and brought it back to where Esteban was groaning in pain. She felt no guilt as she brought it forcefully down over his head. With a final sigh, Esteban passed out on the floor, pieces of broken vase in his hair.

Honor quickly stripped off the shift she was wearing and went to his suit of clothes to pull on his trousers and the shirt. His boots were far too big for her, but she would have to make do. She found a sombrero lying close by and jammed her hair inside of it, pulling the thong up under her chin tightly.

With a last glance of triumph at the prone figure of her enemy, she hurried out into the hallway and down the stairs. She hoped that she would be able to find a horse without any trouble and was in luck as one of the vaqueros had left his mount standing in the corral.

She tightened the cinch and mounted swiftly, leaning low over the horse's neck as she heard a shout from the stableyard. She urged the horse into a fast gallop, making for Monterey. She knew it would be ridiculous to keep to the open roads tonight as, when her escape was detected, they would be sure to ride after her. She would have to go to Monterey and hide there for a few days. She recalled the name of a man whom Jaime had told her might help in case of need. Many of the outlaws had gone to him for stray bullets caught in the arm or other sicknesses that plagued them from bad food or contaminated water. Dr. Isaac Cooper! Yes, she would go to him in Monterey and hope that he would put her up until the chase died down.

Twenty-eight

"But of course you may stay here," Dr. Cooper insisted after Honor had breathlessly explained her danger. "A friend of Jaime Sevillas' is indeed a friend of mine."

"Thank you, Doctor," Honor breathed, nearly collapsing into his study. She had had some difficulty in locating the doctor's residence at this time of night and had almost given up hope. She glanced gratefully in the direction of the fire.

"Come in and sit down, my dear," Isaac offered, closing the door and bolting it firmly behind her. "Would you like some hot tea? Elena!"

Honor's mind barely registered the dark-haired young girl who came to the door of the study to receive the doctor's order for tea. Isaac was leading her to a chair and patting her hand comfortingly.

"That devil, Esteban Sevillas, should be drawn and quartered for the troubles he has caused. Why, I can still recall a young man that he— Ah, well, you don't need to hear about that, my dear. Tell me, what—did he do to you? I mean have you any physical—"

"No, Doctor," she said, shaking her head vehemently. "I wish I had killed him!" she added on a note of hysteria.

"What happened?"

"I—I stabbed him in the shoulder with a fruit knife and then broke a vase over his head. Oh, if only he had not moved!"

"Child, child. I know he must have done something terrible to have deserved your hatred, but do not wish another's death. If you had killed him, it would have been my duty to turn you over to the sheriff." His kindly eyes had hardened with truth.

"But he is evil, Doctor. He—he killed someone very close to me and I—"

Ah, yes, the doctor thought to himself, shaking his head sadly, thinking that she was referring to Jaime. "He was hanged this morning."

Honor looked up, startled. Then she understood and sighed softly. "Poor Jaime—he really wasn't the terrible bandido I had thought. It's hard to believe that his own brother could betray him like that." Her expression hardened. "For five hundred dollars—a pittance compared to what he has!"

Cooper shrugged expansively. "They had never been friends, Honor. It was bound to happen sooner or later—either Jaime would have killed Esteban or this would have come about."

She nodded thoughtfully. She stared into the fire, trying to revive her hatred for Esteban, but somehow she felt only a great emptiness, a sudden loneliness. All her life, it seemed, she had had someone to protect her, take care of her. First her father, then her brother, Reid, even Pearl Holliday had taken care of her in her own way. Brice Devlin had kept his word to take her to Santa Fe, where she had come under the care of the Parsonses, and then Esteban for a time and Jaime. Now she had no male dominating her life and she felt at a loss. She would have to go on alone.

The girl had returned with the tea and she was setting it carefully on the sideboard when Isaac smiled in her direction and gestured her over.

"Forgive me, my dear. Honor, allow me to introduce my wife, Elena."

At first glance, Honor could only think that the girl was much, much younger than the doctor, but after a moment's contemplation, something began to nag at her memory—something that obviously affected the other girl, as she had paled at the meeting.

"Señorita O'Brien!"

There, she had it now! Elena, the girl that had served her for a short time at the Sevillas hacienda. But she recalled that the girl had disappeared without an explanation.

"Elena, how—how did you leave the hacienda? What happened to you?" Honor was instantly eager for news. Although she had not known the girl well, she had felt an instant friendship for her even in so short a time.

"Oh, señorita, that terrible *diablo!* That wicked man punished me because he thought I was going to tell you about his fiancée in San Francisco! I was thrown in the wine cellar for three days and then, when he forced me to grovel and beg his forgiveness, he banished me to the third floor to help with his mother."

"Yolande! Is she well?"

The girl shook her head. "I do not know, señorita. I have not been with her for many months, ever since she ordered me to save the señor's life."

"The señor's life—"

"*Sí,* Señor Brice Devlin."

"Brice!" Honor's eyes shone with joy. "He's alive!"

The girl looked puzzled, then quickly veiled her curiosity. "*Sí,* the señora saw from her window all that had passed between her son and Señor Devlin. She felt pity for the señor and ordered me to find help to free him from the barn and bring him here to my husband for treatment."

"Dr. Cooper, was he—were you able to—"

The doctor, who had been watching the two young women thoughtfully, broke in with a kindly smile. "It took some time, but we pulled him through. It was then that I first met Elena and discovered her natural talent for healing. She

227

helped me with Devlin from the moment she brought him here torn to pieces. He'll have those scars on his back for life, but we managed to put his face back together."

"Oh, my God! And all this time . . . Is he here? In Monterey? Oh, you must tell me where he is, Doctor."

"He left as soon as he was able to ride," Cooper responded sympathetically.

"He went to San Francisco," Elena provided quietly, her eyes not quite meeting her husband's. "He was—a bitter man, señorita, and much of the bitterness was against you."

"Of course, he thought—he thought . . . Oh, it doesn't matter what he thought now—only that he's alive!" She was unaware of the tears on her face or her hands clasped together before her lips as though in prayer.

Dr. Cooper urged her to be seated again and poured her tea, pushing it into her hands. "My dear, you mustn't allow yourself to become too excited. You've just been through an ordeal . . ."

"Oh, you don't understand, Doctor!" She laughed, on the verge of hysteria. "I thought he was dead all these months! I had taught myself to believe he was dead so that I couldn't be tortured by his—his last memories—of me." She stopped her wild laughing suddenly and abruptly. "But it doesn't matter, I suppose, that he's still alive. He hates me—doesn't he, Elena?"

The girl said nothing, but veiled her eyes against the other's probing.

"In San Francisco!" Honor went on after the import of Elena's silence weighed too heavily. "Imagine, I was only just there! What a coincidence if I would have seen him. Why, I thought I had toured almost the entire city! I wonder what he would have said, would have done? Nothing? Oh, if only . . ." She was babbling tiredly now, the cup of tea shaking badly in her hand.

"Come now, Honor, I think it would be best if you went to bed. You're tired and things—will look differently to you in the morning."

"If only they *could* be different," she sighed softly.

Cooper nodded to his wife, who led their guest to an extra bedroom. Inside the room, Honor turned to the girl gratefully.

"You—you have my heartfelt thanks, Elena, for what you did for Brice."

The girl looked at her levelly, her large, dark eyes potently expressive. "I did not do it for your sake, señorita."

Honor blushed. "Well then, for Yolande's sake . . ." She stopped as the girl continued to gaze at her with a kind of pity.

Honor turned and fumbled at the nightgown Elena had provided which was lying on the bed. "Please tell your—husband—that I will be leaving in the morning," she said, willing her voice not to shake.

"As you wish, señorita. Shall I tell him your destination?"

"I don't think it is necessary to tell him," Honor said, deliberately meeting her gaze.

3

The Wicked City

Twenty-nine

Brice Devlin sat at the faro table, leaning back a little, relaxed, with a lighted cheroot between his teeth. He let his silvery-blue gaze sweep the assembled players casually as he waited to see how they would play their cards. Out of the corner of his eyes, he could see Babs mingling among the customers, the aigrette feather waving constantly above the bevy of heads. He smiled to himself and then caught her eye and winked.

The play ran smoothly and he stifled a yawn. He really didn't like to play faro, let alone deal it. It was a complicated game, not as risky as some of the others. Poker was more his style, but few of the miners and gentlemen cared to play that game and so, after Carter had called in sick this afternoon, he had been forced to cover for him. In a few more hands, he would change places with Schneider, a red-faced German, who was sitting in a high chair right now so that he could oversee the game and make sure that everyone who played, played fairly. Should any of the men dare to attempt to cheat, they would soon be eternally sorry when Schneider got his beefy hands on them.

After twenty more minutes, Brice called it quits and stood up to stretch, indicating to Schneider to take over. But before he could climb into the chair, Babs was touching him lightly on the shoulder.

"Honey, no need to go on. I see Carter standing rather sheepishly at the front door. Probably wasn't even sick tonight—just more trouble with his wife." She shrugged expressively, her large brown eyes, velvety soft, smiling into his. "Should we give him another chance?"

He laughed in a low voice. "Schneider wouldn't know what to do without him," he agreed. "I can tell he doesn't think I'm good enough for the game."

"All right then, I'll go over and set his mind at rest." She blew him a kiss and sashayed over to the front door, wiggling her bottom in her tight dress in a way that Devlin could appreciate. He whistled to himself and pushed through the crowd to order a drink.

Leaning lazily against the bar with one elbow as he sipped

the house whiskey, he let his eyes stray around the gambling saloon that he had owned for only three short weeks.

It had been a stroke of luck that he would be eternally grateful for. After arriving in San Francisco, he had wandered aimlessly about the town for several days, striving to forget both the physical pain he had suffered and the mental torment. He had not completely forgotten about the little witch who had betrayed him, but his thoughts were filled with black rage alternating with a cold, mocking indifference that wished her luck in her venture with Sevillas. They certainly belonged to each other.

He had barely escaped being shanghaied on a boat to China, but whatever they'd given him to drink had worn off too quickly so that he had been able to escape through a window. He had finally found work in the Bella Union, a high-class gambling saloon that catered to only the richest of the miners. He had been employed as a dealer and there he had met Babs—a woman he had come to admire for her courage. She had told him a little about her past, how she had gotten to San Francisco through the dangers of the unfeeling West, how she had persevered in the face of each frustration. He admired her strength and soon the admiration had turned into a mutual respect that had enabled them to trust one another in a business scheme.

Babs had wanted to break out of her rut as part-time dealer, part-time prostitute at the Bella Union. She had already conceived the notion of saving enough money to build her own gambling hall. With Brice's help she had achieved that dream. They had acquired the lease to one of the older clapboard saloons at the end of Montgomery Street, which ran along the waterfront. In three months' time they had made a huge profit and only three weeks ago had moved into the more genteel location along Portsmouth Square. Babs' Den had proved, in such a short time, to be well on its way to becoming one of the better establishments.

Babs had entrusted Brice with handpicking the dealers and the bouncers. He had been careful to recruit no Sydney Town men—they were hard and not to be trusted with either the cash or the women who would be employed. Babs had agreed to allow a little female companionship, for without it, the saloon would have folded the first day. The men who frequented such places, especially the miners, wanted a pretty, clean woman to tell their troubles to and to make them feel like men again. Whores were a necessity in a town like San Francisco and Babs had reluctantly given in.

As equal partners in the saloon, both Babs and Brice had made it clear that they could sleep with whomever they wished. Babs took no paying customers, of course, but she had had her eye on a certain railroad man ever since he had begun frequenting Babs' Den. For his own part, Brice took only the best of the women, and took them often. It was as though by sheer numbers, he sought to erase the memory of a sole woman. He had never told Babs about Honor. There was no reason to do so.

Now, if not one of the respected peers of the town, he was still doing very well, had more money than he needed and had found that he had a definite flair for business concerns. His father, he thought ironically, would have been proud of him.

"He was ready to kiss my shoes, Brice," Babs giggled, breaking in on his reverie. She noticed and put a hand on his arm. "Anything wrong?"

He grinned wickedly. "Nothing that a pretty woman couldn't fix, as they say," he replied, shaking his temporary melancholy away.

"Who says?" she said saucily, the brunette curls shaking beneath the aigrette plume. "Brice, you need an understanding woman in your bed tonight. And—I volunteer," she continued, her eyes twinkling.

For a moment, he remembered that he'd half-promised some of the boys an all-night poker game, but he shrugged philosophically. Babs was offering herself on a platter—and he wasn't the man to refuse such a tempting dish.

"My room, or yours?" he asked, touching a curl by her ear with an intimate gesture that sent a tiny thrill of pleasure through her backbone.

"You've got the bigger bed, sir," she replied, laughing. With a teasing look, she dug her sharp nails into his hand and pursed her lips. "About twelve, when it's died down a bit," she whispered.

He watched her walk off and couldn't help admiring her. She was a real woman—no pretense, no coy tricks. She said what she wanted and stuck to her word. Lord, it was good to know such a woman, he thought mockingly. She reminded him unaccountably of an Indian girl he had known in San Antonio. He found himself looking forward to the evening.

* * *

"Honey, you're a hard worker. Maybe you should take a little rest for a while," Babs was saying as she slipped beneath the covers to wriggle against his naked, expectant body.

"You work just as hard as I do, Babs," he whispered, bending his head to kiss her ear, punctuating it with his tongue.

"Whew! Don't do that or I swear I'll go weak as a kitten on you," she protested, letting her hand stray down his chest caressingly.

He continued his ministrations, turning his body so that his arm could go around her, gathering her closer to him. She was taller than average and fit against him perfectly at breast and hip. Her flesh was warm and silky smooth and when she unpinned her hair as she had done before climbing into bed, it lay about her like a velvety-brown fan. Her large brown eyes gazed up into his mischievously as she arched her neck to bite the skin of his shoulder.

"Ouch! Bitch!" he said affectionately.

"Bitch, is it! Well, mister, nobody calls me a bitch unless he wants me to act like one!" she snorted teasingly.

With that, she flung her body against his, nipping his neck and chest with strong, white teeth while her hands raked his back as she pulled him closer. He laughed, enjoying her abandon, but as she continued, he stopped laughing and his silvery-blue eyes narrowed in growing desire.

With an impatient oath, he brought her mouth up to his and kissed her deeply, completely, their tongues twisting against each other as their hands moved slowly and then faster over their bodies.

Brice took his time, not wanting to hurry their joining. He was not like most men, Babs thought, who wanted to get to their own gratification and to hell with what the woman felt. He caressed her and kissed her from her head to her feet and, in between, she felt the first pinnacle of release.

"Oh, Brice," she breathed in his ear, "I'm primed, honey. You just slip on in now."

Brice laughed again, a little wildly at the realization of his reward, and positioned her for his entry. She was a good lover and together they soared into mindless oblivion.

Afterward, as they lay together, a light sheen of perspiration covering their bodies, he heard her chuckle softly to herself.

"Something so amusing?" he asked lazily, reaching over to the side table for a cheroot. He enjoyed smoking in bed after making love.

236

"Not really," she replied casually, turning to look at him by the light of the whale-oil lamp. She studied him for a moment, with her head cocked. "It's just that while we were making love you mumbled something about 'your honor.' " She let one of her brows rise in mock surprise. "Honey, I didn't know you had any."

Thirty

Honor had left the Cooper household early the next morning. She had been grateful to the doctor for providing her with a change of clothes, and more importantly, with enough money to get her to San Francisco and enable her to stay there for a few days before having to find work. The goodbyes had been short between her and Elena, with Honor only asking to be remembered to Yolande should Elena or the doctor ever be called out to the hacienda.

Isaac had suggested she spend the nights on the road in an inn since it would be highly dangerous for a woman to camp out alone. There would be no protection against cutthroats and she would be making herself an open target for any of Sevillas' men who might stumble upon her.

So, on the first night out, Honor turned in to Breen's Tavern, an old house belonging to the Castro family before the American takeover and converted into an inn. Patrick Breen was a kindly man and gave Honor a guest room close to his own living quarters. The charge was minimal too, only a dollar for the night, plus fifty cents for a bath and dinner. Honor relinquished some of the precious money, but felt it left for a good cause and settled down into a soft bed after feasting on roast beef and frijoles.

The next morning, she rose early, breakfasted in her room and went to get her horse, which had been stabled and fed for ten cents. She felt much better, hoping that fortune had finally turned in her favor. Her thoughts were on Brice Devlin—she couldn't get him out of her mind. He was in San Francisco! She had been so near to him—perhaps had even gone by him, not knowing—but she would have known!! Yes, she was sure she would have felt something! Oh, Brice, please don't hate me too much, she prayed. Give me a chance to prove that everything that Sevillas said was a lie.

The second evening of her journey found her at the Plaza Hotel, an old house, originally built in the late eighteenth century by the Spanish and bought only recently by Angelo Zanetta, an Italian cook. Through the years, it had turned into a regular stopping place for the stages and had become well known for its good meals and well-stocked bar.

Honor had learned all this from Angelo himself, who had personally brought her dinner and proceeded to entertain her with stories of the old inn and the surrounding countryside.

"You are very beautiful, Miss O'Brien," the jovial Italian remarked with a twinkle in his dark eyes. "Angelo would be most appreciative of—your favors for the night?"

Honor was nonplussed at his directness, but felt no alarm. It was commonplace for pretty women traveling alone to receive unwanted attentions. She had known that at the beginning. She felt sure she could handle any intrusions and gently steered Angelo away from the thought of bed and into the kitchen. His culinary instincts immediately took over and she was saved having to make an embarrassing scene. They parted congenially with Angelo promising to feed her a good Italian breakfast in the morning.

Alone in her bed in her room that night, Honor lay staring up at the ceiling, thinking about Brice. What would he be doing when she found him? A nagging thought entered her mind that perhaps he might have moved on, but she deliberately put it out of her head. It was too wonderful to find out that he was actually alive, but to think that he had gone, that she would never be able to find him— She wouldn't let such thoughts spoil her excitement. She knew she would find him, she knew it! She would scour every inch of the city if she had to.

Practically, she knew she would have to find a job of some kind. There weren't too many positions open to women, except for dealing and prostitution—and neither appealed to her. With a sixth sense, she felt that Brice would have gone into something to do with the gambling saloons, but she knew nothing about dealing cards. She couldn't sing or dance well enough to hire herself out as an entertainer—perhaps a waitress at one of the better restaurants? She had seen very few women serving at tables, but it was worth a try. She would be willing to take Chinaman's wages if they were enough to keep her in a hotel until she could find Brice.

And when she found him—what then? It was a question that frightened her with its possible answers. She hoped that she could persuade him to listen to her and afterward—oh God! Could it be possible that he might just sweep her into his arms and take care of her forever after! She grimaced—it wasn't true to form, of course. Things like that only happened in fairy tales. More likely, she could imagine him taking one look at her and telling her to stay out of his life. Perhaps he had a lover in San Francisco. She totally rejected the idea of him being married. If there was one thing Brice Devlin was, it was an independent man!

Well, she would just have to deal with the situation when she found him. She could be as persistent as hell, she thought grimly. She would force him to listen. And, if she could somehow manage it, she'd seduce him as well!

Her heart beat faster at the thought of lying again in Brice's arms. It had been so long! Perhaps she was turning into one of those fallen women, but she couldn't help the thrill that flashed through her at the thought of sharing Brice's bed. There was no other man like him. She admitted to herself that Jaime, for all his fondness of her, had not been able to stir her emotions like Brice had. Certainly Esteban had done nothing but incur her disgust and hatred. She was fervently glad that Esteban had not been able to consummate his lust on her after her capture. The thought made her sick. She hated Esteban and would give almost anything to be revenged on him—but if she got Brice back, she would gladly forsake her revenge and devote herself to being a good—wife?

Honor smiled dreamily and closed her eyes, falling asleep with the contented look of a child.

The morning sun had just burned through the fog when Honor rode up to the edge of the city in late April. She took a deep breath and gazed down at the sprawling city below her as she thought of her next plan of action. She knew no one in the city, knew very little at all about where to stay. She supposed she could go to the same hotel that she stayed at with Jaime and Christabel. The proprietor seemed reasonable and the rooms had been fairly clean. And Portsmouth Square would be a good place to start looking for Brice.

By all means, she knew she must stay away from Sydney Town, the most dangerous part of the city. Christabel had told her the area was bounded by the waterfront, Pacific and Broadway streets and the steep climb up Telegraph Hill. With these coordinates in mind, she was sure she could steer away from that most sinister part of town.

Feeling better with the knowledge of a base from which to start, Honor urged her mount forward into the city. Deliberately she patted the little derringer in her pocket. Dr. Cooper had pressed it into her hand as she was leaving and she was glad of its company now.

Despite the fact that she was dressed in men's clothing, it would not be hard to discern that she was a woman. The shirt clung to her in the morning mist and revealed the swell of her breasts, and the trousers could not conceal the rounded curve of her hips. She had pinned her hair up and jammed the sombrero over her head, and now she draped the serape over her bosom to help to conceal the obvious.

She had little difficulty in finding Portsmouth Square and the hotel where she hoped to obtain a room, but to her dismay, the place was filled with guests and the owner had no choice but to turn her out. Dismally she gazed around the square, noting the names of the various establishments—El Dorado, the Alhambra, Águila de Oro, Ward House, Dennison's Exchange, Babs' Den. The last one sounded fairly American and she was about to cross the square when a small Chileno boy came up to her shyly, his huge brown eyes darting away from her questioning gaze.

"Señorita," he began slowly, "you look for *posada*—hotel?"

"Yes—*sí.*" He was an endearing little soul, but she could see that the shirt on his back was threadbare. "Do you know a good place? One of these?" She gestured around the square.

He shook his head. "Ah, no, señorita. Too much *dinero*. Come with me, *por favor*. I will show you cheap place."

"Where?" she asked, hating to be suspicious of a small boy, but recalling another time when she had trusted a seemingly harmless old lady.

He grinned, showing decaying teeth that took her heart. "Come with me, señorita." He grabbed her hand and was about to pull her along when a shout nearby caused him to turn white and then run swiftly into the crowds.

Honor looked around curiously for the owner of the voice and her eyes encountered a pair of snapping blue ones that, for a moment, took her breath away before she realized that it was not Brice Devlin. Dejected, she grasped her horse's bridle and prepared to seek out information on a room at Babs' Den. But the blue eyes were suddenly in front of her.

Above them, a thick shock of pale blond hair was revealed as the man took off his flat-crowned hat.

"Morning, ma'am."

"Good morning," she said and proceeded to go on, but he remained in front of her, hat in hand.

"Can I be of some service, ma'am? It looks as though you're lost."

She shook her head quickly. "No, not really. I'm just going to find lodgings. I've only just arrived in the city. Now, if you'll excuse me?"

"The name's Riley Tate, ma'am—and you're—"

Honor looked him over carefully, noting the dusty, travel-stained appearance of his clothes. "I don't believe that's any of your business, sir." Her tone was cool and once again she attempted to move past him, to no avail.

"Ma'am, you know that little Mex boy who was just here? He was about to get you fleeced. Don't you know that those Chilenos send out their little ones just to trap pretty things like you? He would have led you down an alley where you would have been cracked over the head and thrown to the whoremongers in Sydney Town."

"Why would they want to do that? Why me?" she asked, feeling rising panic begin to fill her at her own vulnerability.

He shrugged laconically. "They do it for the money, ma'am. The Sydney ducks—they give them maybe ten dollars for each girl they bring in. You're a prime target, ma'am, seeing as you're all alone."

"Well—thank you for your help, Mr.—"

"Tate, ma'am."

"Yes, well, thank you, Mr. Tate, but I really am in a hurry."

Honor began to walk in the direction of Babs' Den, something about the man nagging in her memory. Where had she seen him before? Had she seen him before? There was something about him . . .

"If you'll allow me, ma'am, I'll be glad to help you out."

Lord, he was persistent! "Mr. Tate, I must say you're quickly becoming a boor. Now, if you don't mind, I—"

He laughed. "Now don't let that Irish temper catch fire here in the square, ma'am," he said softly. And then continued, "Listen, I'm a dealer over at the Bella Union. It's not too far away and I could get you a room pretty cheap."

The Bella Union—she remembered Jaime having mentioned it as one of the better establishments in San Francisco.

If this Mr. Tate was telling the truth—perhaps she had seen him while they were in the city before.

"I'm not sure I should trust you, Mr. Tate," she said thoughtfully, losing some of her previous irritation. The prospect of getting good sleeping quarters at a cheaper rate did intrigue her. "How do I know you deal at the Bella Union?"

He laughed again. "Why, ma'am, you can follow me there now and ask anybody inside. Riley Tate's one of the best dealers they've got. Come on, follow me and I'll take you there."

She hesitated. "I don't know, I—" She didn't want to make a mistake with this man. He looked trustworthy, she supposed, but if her judgment was wrong . . .

"I'll go with you, as long as we stay on the main streets," she decided.

He chuckled. "As you say, ma'am. Just let me get my horse and I'll lead the way."

When he returned, she noted absently that his horse hadn't been brushed in a while and its coat was dusty and sweat-rivuleted. She mounted her own horse and followed behind him as he led her through the square and down a crowded street. They had to get down and walk their horses after a few minutes, though, because of the press of people. Honor was forced to walk closely to the man to make sure none of the crowd tried to steal her horse from under her nose.

"How—how long have you been dealing at the Bella Union?"

He shrugged. "Oh, since it opened. I'm a natural-born gambler."

He was leading her down a side street, then through a short passage and into an alley. She stiffened, her senses alert for danger. She desperately needed a room, but she wasn't going to be trapped again. When they broke out of the alley, she was quite relieved and was even more glad when there was room to mount her horse.

"I'll ride the rest of the way," she announced, beginning to mount.

He looked back carelessly. "No need to, ma'am, we're almost there."

"I'd still like to ride. I'm tired."

"I know what you mean," he agreed readily, "those Southern roads up to the city need lots of work."

Honor felt her blood freezing in her veins. "How—did you know I came from the South?" she asked quickly.

He turned around and she saw, before he masked it, the quick surge of frustration. "Just a guess, ma'am. Ah, we're almost there. If you'll give me your horse, I'll lead it for you and you can rest."

Honor jerked the reins, making the horse wheel sideways. "Who are you?" she said angrily. And then it came to her. He had made reference to her Irish temper. How could he have known that she was Irish? He must be—he had to be—one of Sevillas' men! She must have seen him the day Jaime was captured! That's why he looked so familiar!

Quickly she dug her heels into her horse's flanks and without a word, headed back the way they had come. Behind her, she heard him shout and risked a look around to see if he had had time to mount and follow her. The crowds were already surging around them and it would be hard for him to catch her if she could get a head start.

Her heart pounding with fear, she urged the horse forward, careless of passersby, who jumped to get out of her way, cursing and swearing at her as they tried to catch her jacket to haul her off her horse. Honor bent low and continued her mad dash. Thrice a fool! she thought furiously. Pearl, Esteban and now his man Tate. How could she hope to survive if she couldn't trust her own instincts?

She had forgotten the way to the square in her hurry to get out of reach of Tate. She could always go back there later—right now, she had to put as much distance between herself and her pursuer as possible.

Buildings, people rushed by in a blur. She realized the streets were becoming less crowded, giving her more time to rush past. Suddenly, though, she was brought up sharply by the brick wall that stood in front of her. She had gone down a blind alley!

As she jerked at the reins to wheel the horse around, something hit the side of her head with enough force to throw her out of the saddle. She hit the dirt pavement with a sickening thud, feeling blood dripping down the side of her face from a wound in her scalp. Dear God, had she been shot?

A drab gray light was slowly closing in on her, like the fog that enshrouded the city at night. Slowly, slowly, she was sinking into blackness and the last thing she heard was something like excited children jabbering childishly as she lost consciousness.

*　　*　　*

"She waking, missus."

Honor, still groggy and with a shooting pain in the side of her head, tried to sit up, but fell back again against a hard, level surface that she thought, at first, was a bed. Upon reaching her hand out tentatively, she realized it was a dirt floor. She flinched as a spider crawled curiously over her fingers, and shook her hand to get it off.

"Missus, she still sick!"

Honor tried to locate the person who belonged to the high-pitched feminine voice, forcing her eyes to focus. They finally made out a very young girl, perhaps twelve years old, her shining black hair swinging forward over her eyes—eyes that slanted upward and narrowed in the middle. She was an Oriental!

"Where—where am I? Who are you?" Honor croaked. When she spoke her head felt as though it would split and she slumped dejectedly back on the ground.

"See, missus, she awake now," the girl was saying to someone at the door.

"Thank you, Pia. You may go now."

Both feminine voices were thin and accented, but their grasp of English was good enough to enable Honor to follow the conversation.

A short, rotund figure stepped over and leaned down next to her. Her moon face with its heavily slanted eyes and short, thick mop of black hair reminded her somehow of a doll she had once owned.

"You still velly sick," the woman said as though to herself.

Making an effort, Honor leaned forward on one elbow and asked her, "What happened to me? You must tell me where I am."

The woman chuckled softly. "You in Chinese crib, round eyes. Ling Chow velly lucky to find you."

"But how—"

"Man use rock in slingshot. You—ah—stunned!" She seemed pleased as she explained it carefully to Honor. "He go now to sell you to Hoy Tai for much gold! Much gold!"

"But you can't sell me! I'm an American citizen—not a slave! What are you talking about? I need a physician immediately and I want to be taken to Portsmouth Square without delay or—or I will have the law on you!" She fell back after the exertion of venting her anger, her frustration and her fear.

Ling Chow shook her head, still beaming placidly. "You in crib. No one come for you here in Little China."

Little China! How had she gotten here! She recalled the furious ride to get away from the man called Tate and then finding herself in the alley. Then the blow to her head—from a slingshot, this woman had said. And now she was supposed to be sold! Uneasily, she looked around.

The room couldn't have been more than eight feet wide and perhaps the same long. There was little furniture, only a dresser and a chair and a rather ragged-looking screen that closed off another part of the building. She remembered Christabel telling her a little of the Chinese cribs—the lowest of the brothels in the city. The cribs knew no color line and accepted Chinese, Negroes, filthy old men and others that the higher-class houses turned their noses up at. She shivered at the thought, but her attention was drawn back to the woman as she clapped her hands loudly.

The girl she had called Pia entered solemnly, bowing low. "Yes, missus?"

"Pia, you stay with woman. I go now."

The girl sat down obediently and Ling Chow left. Honor stared up at the girl.

"Are you a prisoner here, too?"

The girl shook her head, then nodded. "I bought by Ling Chow at age of eight to serve in clib."

Honor noticed how the girl pronounced her r's and remembered that the Orientals had great difficulty with some of the English words. It was still easy enough to understand her and she continued their discussion, determined to find out where she was and if there was a way to escape.

"How long have you been here?"

"Five years."

"Five years!" Honor gasped. Surely the girl could not be prostituted so young. "You—you have served Ling Chow all that time?"

The girl veiled her eyes. "One year I serve men for Ling Chow."

"Oh, I'm sorry!" Honor felt tears of distress come to her eyes at the thought of this young girl sold into slavery at the age of eight and required to sell her body to men at twelve years of age. The thought sickened her and her heart went out to the delicate waif, who was regarding her curiously.

"You cry for Pia?"

"It's just that—when I was a little girl, about your age, I

did nothing but play with dolls and explore our plantation with my brother, Reid. I learned to ride a horse and—" She could see the girl did not follow her. "Oh, Pia, how I wish I could get you out of here!"

The girl shrugged with a worldly air that sat ill on her young shoulders. "I no different than other girls. Some made to serve sooner than Pia. I have nowhere else to go. You cannot escape Ling Chow—she will beat you with bamboo rods."

Honor gulped at the thought of the brutality this girl had known. As the minutes wore on and she continued her talk with Pia, she became more and more obsessed with the thought of escaping with the girl.

"Pia, listen to me. I must escape here. I came to the city to find someone. If I could get word to him, I know he would help us both. Wouldn't you like to get away from Ling Chow?"

For a moment, she saw a gleam of terror in the girl's eyes, replaced slowly by hope, then despair. "But you cannot help Pia escape," she said sadly. "You will be sold to Hoy Tai. He very rich, very rich. He like white women as slaves."

Honor bit her lip thoughtfully. She was sure that if she could get word to Brice he would help her to escape—but she didn't even know where he was! It was pointless to pin her hopes on his help. She would have to think of some way to do it herself. And she was determined now to take Pia with her. How could this be happening in an American city? Girls of twelve and under being sold as slaves for prostitution! Uneasily she wondered if the Negroes on her father's plantation had been used for such purposes. No! Her father would not have allowed it. She pushed the thought out of her mind.

"This Hoy Tai. Tell me more about him."

"He Chinese merchant, very powerful. He bring in girls from China to be slaves. He pay money to white men to let him work so. He—"

"Pia! You will be silent or I shall whip you soundly!" Both of them glanced quickly to the door, where Ling Chow's figure stood threateningly. "You will go to the other room and get customers! Go!"

The girl scrambled to her feet and hurried out, leaving Ling Chow to scowl blackly at her white captive. "You no talk to Pia!" she commanded abruptly.

"She is only a child!" Honor objected. "How can you brutalize her so? Have you no heart?"

Ling Chow stared at her as though she were insane. Then,

246

shaking her head, she left the room, leaving Honor to her own thoughts. She would find a way to escape, she vowed, and Pia would go with her!

Thirty-one

Hoy Tai was not a patient man and he stamped his foot with irritation against the rough stone that made up the floor of the waiting room to Ling Chow's crib on Washington Street. He had been told that a white girl had been captured, riding alone in the adjacent alleyway, and that she was as beautiful as he could wish, with honey-gold hair and eyes as green as the spring grass. He had found his appetite whetted at the thought of possessing her.

Hoy Tai had come up fast in the world of cribs and grog shops and dives that was part of San Francisco. As a boy of fifteen, he had been brought in a slave ship from China to the United States in 1850. At the age of twenty-four he was already independently wealthy.

He had become rich through the greed of others. He had learned much from working as a houseboy at one of the saloons for the first two years of his service in America. The miners, the gamblers, all of the whites yearned for things new and exotic. He had made a daring gamble himself that had paid off.

He had commissioned a ship with money he stole from his employer to bring back ten Chinese girls on his next trip to the Orient. The captain had kept his word and brought back ten of the most attractive girls he could find, not being too particular as to their ages. As Hoy Tai had expected, the miners went wild over these new toys. He watched in disgust as they paid any price to lie with them. After a few years of this, he became wealthy enough to have his own ring of trade, using "overseers" to run his string of cribs and brothels while he raked in the enormous profits.

He now lived on Dupont Street in a two-level house with rich furnishings and elegant appointments that defied the shanty-looking exterior. He did not want his white contacts becoming too suspicious, he thought. For he knew that, while they did condescend to trade with him, they hated him for his power and would like to see him topple so that they could

247

take over his trade. It was never good to show signs of too much wealth, for their greed might overtake their good judgment and Hoy Tai wanted very much to continue with his profitable business schemes.

Besides the parlor houses and cribs he owned several Chinese laundries and took a percentage of many of the Chinese houseboys' wages, in return for his protection against unsympathetic whites. Hoy Tai hated and despised the whites even while he worked with them—and for this reason, he enjoyed prostituting white girls for his own pleasure. He normally gave them enough opium to get them hooked on the sticky, gumlike substance and after he was finished with them, the poor souls would die from their withdrawal symptoms or be killed trying to steal money to buy the stuff.

Now, as he waited impatiently for Ling Chow to bring the white girl to him, he felt desire building within him at the thought of shaming yet another of the round eyes.

"Sir, here is white woman we spoke of," Ling Chow called as she came into the room, dragging a reluctant girl by the arm.

Tai looked at her speculatively. She was not as young as he normally liked, although she had not seen her twentieth birthday he was sure. Her hair was, indeed, splendid, long and silky with the look of polished brass. The eyes were rebellious, blazing emeralds in her pale face.

He wanted to throw her on the floor and take her immediately, but controlled himself with an effort. He was not overfond of sulky women. He would rather they be passive, pliable to his every wish. In this he was like most Chinese males. A woman with any fire or spirit to her did not treat her man as master, and that was an insult!

"Does she please you, my master?" Ling Chow was practically beaming as she observed the man's face.

He nodded quickly. "You are sure she was alone? There is no one to care for her absence?"

Ling Chow shrugged. "She was alone, her horse well traveled, when we came upon her. I do not think there would be trouble, master."

"Good. Bind her hands and I will take her with me now."

"As you say."

"No! I will not go with you!" Honor shouted, kicking at Ling Chow's shins. "I am not a slave to be sold like this!"

Tai smiled thinly and nodded to Ling Chow. "Hurry up. This one needs to be shown who is master."

248

Ling Chow called for help while she tied Honor's hands behind her, taking care the knot was too tight for her to slip out of it. When she was through, she stepped back, regarding the flushed, angry girl as though she were her own handiwork.

"She is yours, master."

Honor paled. This was ridiculous, impossible! "I will not go with you! You cannot force me."

But he was forcing her, prodding her like a balky mule with the gold-headed walking stick. She noted he was dressed like an American businessman in a tailored suit and white shirt. The derby on his head gave him a grotesque look and she wondered just who this man was.

She was pushed into a carriage and the shades were drawn after he climbed in beside her. He did not speak to her as they moved away from Ling Chow's and Honor remained silent, trying to think of how best to get away. It was awkward sitting in the carriage with her hands tied behind her. There would be no way to jump out the door and run away from him. She eyed him silently.

Hoy Tai knew she was studying him, knew she was, beneath her facade of righteous indignation and anger, quite frightened. This Tai could deal with. Fear was an emotion that he had long ago learned to use and channel in his own behalf. He smiled contentedly to himself and leaned back against the well-cushioned seat to think on his good fortune.

Honor, studying him covertly, saw a man barely taller than herself, with a tinge to his skin like old, yellowed lace. He was very slender; his wrists looked almost fragile above the starched white cuffs which were fastened with what looked like diamond cuff links. His face in repose reminded her of a contented cat's. His rounded forehead and chin were at odds with the angular boniness of his cheeks. His eyes were narrow, slanted upward at the corners, and the mouth was thin at the upper lip, but oddly full at the lower, giving it a very sensual appearance.

She could not help but curse herself for making such a stupid blunder as to fall into the hands of this Chinese overlord. She had been lucky enough to have escaped from Sevillas' man, Tate, but wondered now if she wouldn't have been better off being delivered into the hands of Esteban Sevillas.

The carriage stopped several times before they reached their final destination. Each time, Hoy Tai would come back with a bag of gold dust, a wallet of bills or a pouch filled with clinking coins. He must be, she decided, as rich as Ling Chow had indicated.

Finally they reached their destination. The carriage stopped and Hoy Tai called for someone to come out and carry Honor into the house. A brawny Chinese, his long pigtail swinging below a wide straw hat that looked like an inverted saucer, picked her up as easily as though she were a feather and took her inside what appeared to be a most miserable two-story house which badly needed painting.

Upon entering the outer door, they walked down a short corridor and then turned to the right, where Tai unlocked a door allowing them entrance. Honor gasped at the luxury that filled the place.

The Chinese servant set her on her feet and she felt as though she might sink into the thickness of the carpet. Her eyes widened incredulously at the burnished oak panels which ran the length of the walls. Paintings and objets d'art lined the walls and thickly cushioned furniture covered in bright velvets and satins seemed set like jewels amid the splendor.

Tai signaled the servant to follow them after slicing through the cords that bound the girl's hands. Honor rubbed her wrists and felt her arm taken by the Chinaman as he led her through this entry room into an arched doorway that opened out into another room, and then another. Stairs curved gracefully to the second story, where more splendor greeted her bedazzled eyes. A sitting room with ornately carved furniture and gold inlaid table tops was complemented by a russet and blue patterned carpet. More pictures and expensive bric-a-brac were scattered about in random spots.

From the sitting room, they entered what must be his study, for a large oak desk took up much of the room. Books lined two of the walls and another wall held maps and charts of some sort. Through a curtained archway, they came into the bedroom, a huge area, carpeted and furnished in almost garish decor. Orange-reds and golds seemed to dominate and Honor closed her eyes for a moment to recover from the vivid glare.

Hoy Tai clapped twice and the huge Chinese servant bowed and left them alone. Honor tensed and waited to see what this strange man was going to do. He clapped once again and a small, slender girl hardly older than fifteen shuffled into the room, a tray in her hand. On the tray were different food dishes, all of which tickled Honor's nostrils as she realized how hungry she was.

"Sit."

It was a command and Honor walked over to a small table, looking around uncomprehendingly for a chair.

"Sit—on the floor," Tai said, suppressing his mirth at her ignorance.

Dubiously, Honor did, tucking her folded legs beneath her. She found that the table was now at exactly the right height. The serving girl was setting the succulent dishes out before her and she could hardly wait until she bowed and left before attacking the nearest one. She was famished!

Behind her, Tai chuckled to himself and left her alone for a moment while he went behind a silk screen, only to appear some minutes later relieved of the uncharacteristic business suit and dressed in a more comfortable long, flowing robe patterned in green and blue silk. His long pigtail, which he kept tucked beneath the derby, fell down his back and swayed gently as he walked in bare feet over to the table. He noticed the round-eyed one had consumed at least three of the dishes and was now drinking the wine experimentally.

"You are satisfied?" he asked softly.

She whirled around, nearly upsetting the contents of the table, her green eyes widening at the sight of his changed appearance.

"I—I was hungry and I ate without asking your permission," she said quickly.

He was surprised at her humble attitude. He hadn't expected an apology from her and it intrigued him that she would offer it of her own accord. Her hand still held the glass of wine and he noted it was trembling slightly. He nodded to her.

"Drink, it is not drugged," he assured her.

He watched her drink the wine, noting the slender arch of her throat as she tilted her head back slightly. Her long, unbound hair nearly touched the floor and he felt a sudden urge to run his hands through its glory and rub it against the length of his own body. He touched none of the food himself, preferring to wait until after the act of sex had been performed.

When she had finished, he casually brought out a long-stemmed pipe attached at one end to an ivory mouthpiece and at the other end to a flattened bowl filled with some darkish liquid. Honor watched him curiously as he lit the pipe and began to inhale from it. Soon a sweet, cloying scent began to permeate the air and she felt her eyes filling with

251

tears. She coughed, trying to rid her throat and nostrils of the oppressive smell.

Tai smiled and offered the pipe to her. Honor shook her head instinctively, backing away a little as though afraid he might force her to smoke.

"It is only the fruit from the poppy, little one," he spoke gently, continuing to hold the mouthpiece out to her. "How can something that comes from such a beautiful part of the earth hurt you?"

"I—I do not wish to smoke. Please, I—"

"Smoke only a little," he assured her, "and it will relax you." He held the mouthpiece against her lips. "Only a little," he repeated softly, and then in a more dangerous tone, "You will do as I say, or I will find other ways of dealing with your stubbornness that may not be so pleasant!"

Honor pressed her lips tightly together at first, then relaxed them as she looked at the man's expression. She needed time to think of a plan, and if acceding to his commands would give her time, then she would do as he told her.

Nervously she inhaled the sweetish odor into her lungs, coughed violently, then inhaled again at Tai's urging. She saw him watching her with a smile, then he took the mouthpiece and blew a smoke ring into the air. She waited for what he might do next.

Several minutes passed and the thick scent of the opium seemed to be filling her lungs, her throat, her eyes and nose. A fog seemed to be descending slowly in front of her eyes so that gradually she could no longer see Tai. She felt herself lying backward, sinking into the carpet that was suddenly, magically turned into a warm pool that swallowed her into it, allowing her to come up for air. Multicolored flowers swam around in the pool and dazzling goldfish swam up to her and nibbled at her toes and fingers. It seemed that she was suddenly stripped naked and golden honey was being poured over her skin, soothing it as strong hands kneaded the flesh, smoothing out her weariness. She lay back, totally relaxed, breathing deeply.

She closed her eyes and a myriad blend of colors surrounded her. Reds, yellows and vivid blues swam around in her vision and she felt as though she were suspended in mid-air in a sea of color. Splashes of orange and green burst in on the other colors and then cooled and darkened and

252

she was floating away from the colors into a void that was black as night.

She awoke suddenly, completely, from the effects of the opium and looked around her wildly. She had thought hours must have gone by, but the paper shades that closed the windows were still letting in rays of thin sunshine which fell on the carpeting in warm pools of light. She was, she realized, in bed, and beside her lay the strange Chinaman, Hoy Tai, watching her with a benign smile on his oddly shaped face.

"What—what did you do to me?" she asked, bringing her hands to her cheeks to steady the dizziness inside her head that still lingered.

"Nothing, nothing, little one. I have only introduced you to the greater joys of opening up your consciousness. Do you feel hurt or abused? I can assure you that I have not touched you except to loosen your clothing and place you in bed."

Honor realized then that her bodice was unbuttoned, revealing the inner slopes of her breasts. Oddly, she felt more ashamed that he had seen her without the modest benefit of underclothing than that she was lying on his bed. She sensed that Hoy Tai was naked beneath his robe.

"Let me go," she said, but the words seemed not to sound convincing even to her own ears. She felt as though she had never been so relaxed in her life. It was pleasant to lie here without having to worry about why she had come to San Francisco. The pillow beneath her head was satin and the covers were soft and smooth, sliding almost caressingly against her bare skin.

"I shall call you green eyes," Tai was saying to himself. "You will please me greatly, I know. Do you really want to leave, green eyes? I can offer you fine clothes, soft living, good food and more of that aphrodisiac that takes away those little irritations of life. You would not be my slave—except in that you must come to my bed whenever I call for you."

Like a harem girl, Honor thought, but couldn't bring her anger into focus. It was just too heavenly to lie here as he talked softly in her ear while his hands were doing such marvelous things to her pliant body. Then she remembered her earlier vow and struggled to get away from him.

"Where are you going, green eyes? There is no way out of here for you! Haven't I just told you . . ." He calmed himself visibly. Mustn't let his anger betray him, he thought, until she was completely within his command. "Come back here, little peach."

"No, I—I must save Pia from that horrible place. I must go back for her—I almost forgot! She—she is only twelve." She began to cry brokenly.

Sensing that the effects of the opium were rapidly wearing off, Tai brought the girl forcibly into his arms. He began to stroke her passionately while his voice soothed her with promises, "I will go tomorrow and bring you back your Pia. You say she works at Ling Chow's? Then she is, truly, my property. I will bring her back to wait upon her benefactress. Will that please you, green eyes?"

"Y-yes, I would be pleased," Honor breathed, thoughts of Pia flying from her mind as Tai stroked her neck and pushed the hair back soothingly from her forehead.

She squirmed a little, wanting to be free of his arms, fighting her lethargic reactions. Tai moved closer, his long fingernails tracing small patterns inside her opened bodice.

Suddenly a frightening dream seemed to overtake the tiny, beginning thrill of pleasure and she opened her eyes wide, looking past Hoy Tai's slick black hair into the doorway beyond. For a moment, time flew back and she was once again in Esteban's arms, drugged out of her senses, on fire with a perverted passion that could not be quenched. And there! There, into the room came a tall, lean figure with eyes like a thunderstorm, accusing eyes seeing the proof of her faithlessness as she tossed on Sevillas' bed, begging him to make love to her.

"Nooo!" She put a hand before her eyes to blot out that accusation. "It was not me, Brice, it was not me!" she pleaded brokenly. "Don't leave me again!"

The figure was receding into the mists of memory, leaving her suddenly coldly sober, looking down at the careless, evil man who would very soon try to vent his drugged lusts on her body. With a cry of revulsion, she brought her nails down to rake at his back, his face, his hair. Heedless of the danger she might be putting herself in, she continued to pummel him with all her strength.

"Get off me, you disgusting pig!" she screamed, nearly beside herself.

Hoy Tai, taken aback by this flare of rage, hurriedly jumped off the woman's body and clapped his hands. The tall Chinaman who had brought her upstairs appeared as if magically brought. Hoy Tai railed in his native dialect and the big man scooped the still thrashing Honor into his arms. By now, Tai was nearly speechless with his own rage. The girl was a shrew, a banshee who would never fit into his scheme of living. His hatred for the round eyes flared anew and he rubbed his hands fitfully as he thought of a fitting punishment.

"Take her downstairs and lock her in the still room!" he ordered the servant as he secured his robe with the belt he had previously loosened. "I shall have to think of what I am to do with her!"

Thirty-two

Honor sat on an overturned butter churn and contemplated her fate. Hoy Tai would be slow to punish, she knew instinctively, allowing her to sit and fret and fume about the stupidity of what she had done. She had, after all, put herself in a position in which there was no longer any hope of escape. The room in which she sat had no windows and only the one door which was locked from the outside. A half-gloom pervaded the room from the feeble light shining from a whale-oil lamp in the center of the ceiling.

She had been sitting here for hours, unaware of whether it was still day or night. She was glad she had stuffed herself in Tai's room, for she would probably be allowed no food as part of her punishment.

The room itself must be partially underground as it was reasonably cool and there was moisture on the walls, which were a sort of dried adobe. Barrels and crates, most of which were empty, were tumbled about in disarray.

Finally, since no one came to the door, she leaned back against the wall and nodded off to sleep. Her dreams were filled with visions of Brice, and Esteban and Tai all mixed up into one monstrous, evil devil who pummeled her body as Brice was helpless to save her. She woke up, her mouth open to scream for help. But only the darkness greeted her, as the lamp had gone out. It was pitch black in the room and she couldn't even see her hand in front of her face. She shivered with dread, her eyes opening wide, straining to see through the darkness. She prayed aloud that someone would come to take her out soon.

* * *

Several hours later, the door opened and Honor was ready to kiss the feet of whoever had come to take her out. It was the big Chinaman and she stayed her exhibition of passion as he came toward her to push her outside. He nudged her forward, through the kitchens, where a cook and two scullery maids cowered in fear, and out into a small courtyard at the back of the house which was bounded on all sides by high walls over which no one could see in.

Tai was standing to one side, bringing up his hand so that the servant held her firmly where she was. His smile was a mixture of contempt and ruthlessness. He walked slowly over to the girl and lifted her chin with his long fingernails.

"I think you will find your new master much more suited to your tastes, green eyes," he began softly. "He is of your own race and presumably will know how to please you better than I."

She held her head high, already knowing that whoever this new man was, he could hardly be any worse than Hoy Tai, who wanted to keep her under his control by using drugs to dominate her senses. She waited for him to go on.

The narrow, slanted eyes were laughing at her studied nonchalance and he clapped his hands. Quickly, before she could defend herself, her hands were drawn back and tied and a thick blindfold bound over her eyes. She was propelled forward, a heavy hand on her shoulder to guide her direction. She heard the squeak of an iron-hinged gate and then she knew she was outside the courtyard, for she could smell horse and heard the groan of an unsprung wagon as someone climbed out.

"She's the one?" Rough hands began to feel her body as a doctor might feel for a broken bone. "She seems in good health—not sure she's worth the price, though. Kinda skinny."

Humiliation washed over Honor as she realized this man was bartering for her.

"She no fat to slow you down," Tai said in the humble speech he used when talking to whites. "She strong, not too young. Price set at two hundred dollars."

"Nope, I just don't think it's worth it, mister. Hundred dollars about right, I'd say, no more than that."

For a moment there was silence as neither man gave way. Finally, with an exasperated sigh, Tai spoke again. "Hundred seventy for her. Very cheap!"

"Hundred twenty. I'll meet you halfway."

"Hundred fifty, then."

"Damn! You slant eyes are awful tight with your purse strings! All right, hundred and fifty, but you throw in another one."

"Deal made for this girl only," Tai reminded him, slowly losing all patience. Then a thought came to him and he bowed. "All right, one other girl added, but she not here now. I send her."

"Listen, chink, I'm not about to trust you as far as I can spit! I wanta see that girl now!" The man's manner was ugly and Honor wished she could tear off the constricting blindfold and assess him.

"Very well." Tai clapped his hands angrily, realizing he had backed himself into a corner. "Cudow, you go for Pia at Ling Chow's. Chop! Chop!"

Honor's heart lightened. Pia would be going with her! It was more than she could have dreamed! She waited tensely, still standing with the man's hand on her back until Cudow returned with the girl.

"Nah! She's a goddamned whore by the look of her—been used too! How do I know she ain't diseased!"

"Pia good girl, only whore for year. She no used up! Good bargain."

With a disgusted oath the man moved away from Honor and she assumed he was putting Pia through close inspection. After a few minutes, he snorted and said, "All right. The pair for one fifty. Gold, it is."

The clink of metal exchanging hands and Honor felt herself pushed into a wagon. The soft weight of Pia's body came down on top of her, but the girl rolled away and Honor was allowed to sit upright with her help.

"You're not tied?" she whispered.

"No, I will untie," Pia whispered back, her hands working nimbly on the rope at her wrists.

When she had unbound them, Honor hurriedly tore the rag away from her eyes and looked up anxiously at the bearlike man who was sitting on the buckboard. From the back, he had to be the biggest man she had ever encountered. His hair was long and greasy, tinged with gray and falling halfway down his back to mingle at the sides with his filthy beard. His rough cotton jacket was near to bursting at the seams and the armholes had already partially torn away. He was hunched over the reins, possibly contemplating the loss of his hard-won gold. It was obvious that he was a miner in town to enjoy the fruits of his diggings.

"You're mighty quiet back there," he threw back as they emerged out of the district known as Little China and began following Montgomery Street along the waterfront. They would be passing through Sydney Town, but Honor had the feeling that they would not be bothered by any Sydney ducks.

"Where—where are you taking us?" she asked him soberly.

He turned his head and she nearly gasped. His face was a huge, fleshy mass, one side of which was covered with a purple birthmark that extended from his nose to his jawline. One eyelid hung limply and his mouth revealed rotten teeth which needed to be pulled.

She realized the extent of Tai's revenge. To have sold her to this half-man, half-creature would be his ultimate vengeance. She wished she had the strength to weep. And she had been glad that Pia had been allowed to come with her! She would probably be suffocated the first night under that man's awesome weight! At the thought, Honor felt nauseous. She hung her head dejectedly.

"I'll be taking you both to the goldfields with me in a couple days," the man was saying almost to himself. "Lord, the men'll envy me—maybe I'll share you with some of them, for a price of course!" He smacked his lips at the thought of more gold. "An easy way to make a living, macking two of the best-looking little kitties I've seen in a while." (Mack was the common word for pimp.)

"Will we be staying at—at a hotel here in the city before we leave?" Honor asked, shying away from the thought of the fields, where men would go crazy at the sight of two available women.

"Sure, the best in town, I'm told! Bastard owner wouldn't have me in his hotel until I threw a bag of dust in front of his face. Then he was all simpering and cozy, telling me I'd get the best room in the place."

Honor wondered which hotel he might be talking about, then caught herself. What did it matter which one it was? Any one was the same to her. She gave Pia a wan smile and patted her hand comfortingly.

"Pia most grateful to leave Ling Chow's," the girl said softly, her black eyes lighting up with relief. "Pia owes you much." She hesitated, "Your name?"

Honor laughed mirthlessly. "Honor."

* * *

The clumsy wagon rolled up in front of the Bella Union. Honor was infinitely surprised. The man hadn't been lying when he boasted of being at one of the finest hotels in the city. His strike must have been pretty rich. He still hadn't told them his name and they jumped down from the wagon silently, following him into the building, which combined sleeping quarters upstairs with a gambling saloon downstairs. The Bella offered everything from faro to poker and staged lavish entertainment for the benefit of the woman-hungry miners.

Their new owner shoved his way through the rows of gambling tables, knocking over two chairs and sending a tray filled with glasses crashing to the floor. He glared at the houseboy who rushed to clean up the mess, as if daring him to say anything.

Upstairs, he pushed open the door, barely squeezing his girth through the opening. The two girls followed silently, Honor closing the door discreetly behind them. She dreaded the prospect of this man pouncing on either one of them and wondered with bitter amusement if the bed could even hold his weight.

"Sit down and make yourselves to home, ladies," he quipped, laughing to himself as he promptly went to a sideboard where a tray of half-eaten food was being buzzed by flies. "You hungry?"

Honor shook her head quickly and Pia followed her example, although the shreds of the meal whetted her appetite.

"Well, dammit, don't you have a tongue?" he growled, coming threateningly over to them.

"I—I am hungry," Honor said truthfully, "but a bowl of good soup and a cup of tea would do me better than—" She nodded to the tray.

He snorted in disdain. "No wonder you're so damned skinny. Girl, you'd better eat high while you can. The goldfields don't hold much in the way of delicacies."

Honor wondered, then, how he maintained his huge girth, but decided it would be best to keep quiet.

"Your names?" he went on, the limp eye nearly all the way closed as he scanned their features appraisingly.

"Pia."

"Honor."

"I'll be damned! With names like those I'll haveta charge double the price!" he laughed, slapping his thigh. Despite his large torso, Honor noticed that his legs and arms were incongruously thin.

"Can we order something to eat?" Honor asked tentatively, not wishing to rile him, but hoping that the idea of food might deter him from any sexual activity.

He nodded. Going over to the bell-pull, he jerked at it and Honor was afraid he might pull it off the wall, but the slender piece of twined silk held and in a few minutes a Chinese houseboy knocked smartly and entered to take their request. He eyed Pia with obvious surprise, but said nothing as his mind was filled to bursting with the man's food requirements.

"Now, what say we get a little better acquainted," the man said, rubbing his hands together in anticipation. He pointed to Pia meaningfully. "You, come into the bedroom with me, gal, and let's see you do some of your whore tricks on me."

Pia nodded and followed him silently, padding on bare feet into the room. He didn't bother to close the door and Honor was forced to sit on a chair agonizing, aware of every sound that came from the other room. Soon a huge bellow of satisfaction filled the room and she assumed that Pia was finished. She hoped desperately that the big bear had little stamina. She knew that the time would come for the inevitable, but any time left was precious indeed.

Pia returned, a gamine's smile on her mouth, and at Honor's questioning look, she giggled softly. "He too big to go inside. Pia use hand!"

Honor had no chance to respond before the man followed Pia, buttoning his trousers brusquely. He gazed around for the food.

"What the hell?" His purple birthmark seemed to throb angrily. "It's not here yet?" Disgusted, he started toward the door, then stopped as though remembering something. "Come on, you two, I'm not about to let you run away while I'm gone. We'll go down to the kitchens and see what the hell has happened to our dinner!"

Brice Devlin leaned lazily against the outside door leading to the kitchens. His hands were in the pockets of his trousers as he leveled an intimidating glance at the cook, whose fat arms were folded mutinously.

"Mr. Brice. I know you asked me to come work for you two days ago, but I can't do it! Old Grizzly Alice would have my hide—and yours too, if you took me away from her!"
260

The dimpled cook preened slightly. "You know half the city knows about my cooking!"

Brice smiled slightly. "Quite true, Lolly," he nodded toward the pink-cheeked woman, who had, before coming to San Francisco, been highly rated in the moneyed world of New York City. "That's why Babs and I would love to have you join our establishment. You'd be taking your reputation with you, sweetheart." His silver-blue eyes flashed with deliberate purpose. "We'd be more than grateful, Lolly."

She sniffed with pretended disdain. "I've built up a reputation here. The clientele expect me to be here to serve 'em. I can't just leave Alice flat like that." Her round blue eyes gazed at him with a disarming air. "You'd be asking a lot, Mr. Brice." She hesitated and went on, "Babs' Den is a good place, but it's just getting started. I'm not sure I could—"

"Double the salary you get here, Lolly," he interrupted swiftly, still leaning nonchalantly against the door.

The cook's gulp was audible. "You say double the salary?" she repeated, her eyes rounding even more. "Why, Mr. Brice, I—I hardly know what to say. I think—"

"I think you'll let Alice know today, Lolly, and I'll see you at the Den first thing in the morning. Just wrap your things and I'll send someone over to pick them up. We've already arranged for a room for you—away from the customers." He knew that she had always been upset by having to room upstairs, close to the clientele she had just praised. He had made sure he knew everything about her, so that if the money hadn't worked, he would have had something else up his sleeve. "Is it a deal then, Lolly?"

She gulped again. "I—I suppose it is, Mr. Brice. I'd be a fool if I didn't go with you now. Besides, Alice has done me dirty a time or two and I'm not really beholden to her."

"That's my girl," he said silkily, tipping his hat with his two fingers. "I'll send a hansom for you around nine." He had already started to leave when a sudden commotion seemed to roll in from the servants' corridor.

"Where's my food, woman! Damn your fat hide, I want service right now or I'll see the manager throw you out!" The huge man looked almost grotesque with the purple side of his face reddening like the other side with his anger.

Lolly looked at him incredulously, then her face took on a thunderous expression of her own. "Who's talking fat, mister! And don't bother to talk to the manager, you'd only be doing me a favor!" She whirled around, sniffing disdainfully as the man began to sputter helplessly.

"Why you—you . . ."

The rest of his words were lost on Brice Devlin as he saw the girl who remained behind the man, her face looking as lost as a child who never hoped to see her mother again. Damnation! Could it possibly be the same!

Brice took a reflexive step toward her and she looked up, her eyes widening in shocked recognition. Those same lovely green eyes, hollowed now with purple smudges under them which only enhanced their enchanting quality. The mouth, full and vulnerable, rounded now in an "oh" of surprise, and the hair tumbled down her back in unruly honey-gold curls that asked for a man's fingers in them.

"Honor!" The name broke from him before he could stop himself, but instantly, as though uttering it had shaken off the spell, he veiled his expression of surprise and surveyed her with a curious disdain.

"Brice, is it really you?" she said, tears filling her eyes. She made a tentative move toward him, then her arms fell at the quick look of disgust that shaped his features. "Oh, Brice," she whispered with the finality of one who had lost all hope.

"What are you babbling about, gal?" The man had turned and was glaring first at her, then at the man she was looking at as though he were God Almighty. "Get away from him," he snarled angrily, his frustration at the cook venting itself on the girl. His huge paw came out and smacked the side of her face, causing her to reel backward against the side of the doorway.

Brice controlled his impulse to go to her. After all, no doubt, she was in the company of this beast through her own manipulation. She no longer concerned him and he shut out the flare of emotion in his chest. What a coincidence, though, to see her, here in San Francisco, obviously no longer with the wealthy Esteban. He wondered who had tired of whom first.

The big man was glaring at him, waiting for him to make a move, Brice realized with a start. He shrugged his wide shoulders and grinned lazily at the man.

"Not interested," he commented insolently.

The man huffed for a moment, then turned his attention back to the stout cook. Honor risked a quick glance at Brice's impassive gaze, but turned away almost immediately. She did not look at him again.

262

Brice became aware of his own agitation. He wished never to see her again, while at the same time he was incredulously angry that she would not look at him. He needed to vent his wrath on her, if not verbally, at least in the disdain, the contempt of his gaze. But she would not lift her head, like a hurt child who has been punished and has finally learned the lesson.

Damn! She was still lovely, despite how many men, he wondered tightly. The thought of her with that ugly man caused his stomach to rebel, but he quelled the feeling sternly. She was, after all, no longer his concern. Let her lie in whosoever bed she chose—and he would do the same!

With a quick pivot on his heel, he turned back to the door, opened it and walked determinedly into the street.

Thirty-three

To her owner's surprise, Honor would eat nothing when they returned to their room. Her appetite had left her; all she wanted to do was crawl away and be alone with her grief. She had seen him and he hadn't wanted her! She was powerless to go to him, for his contempt held her back more firmly than the huge man who looked at her as he wolfed down his meal. Brice! Oh, Brice, I do love you, she cried out in her heart, burying her face in the sheets, where she had flung herself upon their return to the room. The material was already soggy with her tears.

Pia had wisely said nothing. She had also wisely set aside some food for the inevitable time when she knew her friend's hunger would rise to the surface. She hoped with a kindness oddly mature for her twelve years that the big man would not try to trifle with her friend tonight.

It was not to be, though, for the man had little sensitivity in him and considered it the girl's duty to pleasure him. Hadn't he paid good money for her to do that? He'd be damned if he'd be suckered by that Chinaman!

"All right, gal, strip off those duds and let's be at it," he growled impatiently, flopping his weight abruptly on the bed, causing Honor to roll into the indentation he had caused.

She looked up, her face red and tear-stained. "Leave me
263

alone," she said miserably. "I don't think I could stand your gross body on me!"

The look of shock on his fat features slowly changed to anger and then rage. "What did you say! Listen, you stupid whore! You'll do as I say or I'll break your goddamned neck! Do you hear me?"

Pia, looking covertly through the crack in the door, saw the man close his huge hands around her neck and begin choking her, shaking her body back and forth like a limp doll's. Biting her lip, Pia wondered worriedly if she should risk going in and trying to placate him for Honor's sake. Quickly she made her decision and opened the door wider.

The man released Honor's neck abruptly and the girl fell back on the bed, her hands on her throat, gasping painfully as ugly purple bruises began to appear on the pale flesh.

"What do you want?" the man demanded, maddened like a raging bull.

Pia smiled with trembling lips. "Lookee, feelee, doee," she said, shaking her hips in the manner that Ling Chow had carefully taught her. "I not use hand, sir, if you want me tonight."

The man, eased a little from his rage, chuckled to himself. "So—you liked it, enough to want more, eh? That little box of yours itchin' for a man to fill it, eh?" He glanced down in disgust at the other girl and his brows knit in a frown. "Well, she gets it tonight, slant eyes. Damn her, I'll teach her to insult me!" He leaned over again to grasp her arm, jerking it roughly.

Pia searched the room for a weapon, something to stop this terrible thing from happening. She sensed that Honor would not give in to the man and he would surely kill her. Looking around desperately, Pia noticed the gleam of metal on the dressing table. It was the man's gun, a Colt revolver. Pia had never in her life handled a gun before. It looked heavy, menacing even as it lay innocently on the furniture.

She took a deep breath and glanced warily over to the man on the bed. His hands were going around Honor's throat, throttling her.

"Damn you! You'll spread your legs, whore, or you won't have nothing to spread!" he was yelling. His hands snaked from her throat, pushing her backward and then going to her legs.

Pia was at the table, her slender hand reaching for and closing around the heavy, cold metal. She lifted it up—it was oddly foreign in her hand. Her fingers closed around the butt and she was pulling it up in front of her, turning to the two struggling forms on the bed. His, of course, was the larger— and it was on top as he clawed at his trousers. The bed squeaked and groaned under the weight and looked as though it would collapse any minute.

Honor screamed softly as one of the man's legs kneed her stomach and Pia's hand jerked as she tried to steady the gun. She wasn't sure if she could pull the trigger, but as Honor began to groan steadily, she cocked and fired.

After the shot, all seemed to grow still and freeze. Pia could see the hole in the man's shirt and jacket, small and black, beginning to seep red blood. Suddenly he was turning around, roaring with pain, his dilated eyes fixing themselves on her. A cruel madness promised her she would pay dearly and Pia's hand trembled so violently that she barely got off the second shot. The report seemed to fill the room and now there was another hole in the front of the man, but still he kept coming—within inches of her now, it seemed. She closed her eyes and fired again.

She opened them to see him crumbling in front of her, the roaring having ceased after the third shot. In horror, she dropped the gun and ran to the bed, reaction setting in so that she could hardly speak.

"Honor, I've—I've killed—him," she whispered, shaking the girl to her senses.

Honor opened her eyes and looked first at Pia's horrified face and then at the man on the floor. She wanted to scream, but caution told her not to. They must get out of here, she thought, but found she had no strength to move. She could only stare back and forth between Pia and the dead man. She hadn't even known his name.

"We—we must run. Hurry," Pia was urging, dragging her off the bed. She got Honor on her feet and pushed her forward, out of the room, into the corridor, where the curious were already poking heads out of their rooms. Pia caught Honor's hand and ran with her down the stairs that led to the kitchens.

Pia knew they had to get away. But where to go? Oh, if only her friend could think for her! But Honor seemed in a daze, going as one in sleep. She stumbled twice on the stairs and Pia had to help her up. They were in the kitchens now and Pia remembered with sudden vividness the man whom Honor had seemed to recognize. He was their only hope!

Fighting to keep her presence of mind, she flew at the cook, waving her arms frantically.

"Please, you must tell me where man lives who was here before!" She searched her mind frantically. "Brice!" Her dark eyes pleaded with Lolly.

"Brice Devlin? Why—why he'd be at the—at Babs' Den in Portsmouth Square just down the block. Why do you—"

But Pia had all the information she needed, and grasping the stupefied Honor, she hurried out the door into the crowded street, pushing her way past people who were too stunned seeing a Chinese girl pulling a white girl by the hand to stop her.

Honor hardly knew what she was doing, where she was going. Her throat was bruised and throbbed achingly. The arm that Pia held hurt dreadfully from being jerked up forcibly by the man who—who . . . She gulped. Pia had killed him! She stared at the small, shiny black head in front of her forging ahead through the crowded street like an avenging angel. Pia had killed a man—because of her!

Honor knew instinctively that the courts would not take the time to judge a Chinese girl. Pia would be hanged instantly! And she was only a child! Then the harsh truth struck her—Pia hadn't been a child since the age of eight, when she had been brought over from China and sold like a piece of furniture . . . She wished she could weep for her— but there was no time! Pia was dragging her swiftly through the crowd past curious bullies and slobbering drunks and dashing gamblers who looked after the golden-haired girl with a spark of interest. But the two were soon lost in the crowd.

Finally Pia knew they had come to Portsmouth Square. She had come here often on her outings, which she had been allowed once a month, from the crib in Little China. In frustration, though, she realized that she would not be able to read the name. Searching frantically for help, she spotted a Chinese houseboy, hurrying on his way to work.

"Please, can you tell me where Babs' Den?"

The boy nodded and pointed to a building on the other side of the street. Pia made for it with a new surge of strength, imagining the police right behind her! She knew, as well as Honor, that she would be hanged for the crime. But she couldn't think of that now. They must get to the man who would protect them.

She rushed into the twin doors leading into the lower level of the saloon, her eyes jumping wildly from table to table.

"I'll be goddamned!" someone said.

"Look at that China girl barging in here as proud as you please!" another voice answered.

"Throw the little whore out!"

Pia could have wept. She couldn't see the man anywhere, but she did see a tall woman, dressed elegantly, sweeping toward them, the plume in her hair waving gracefully.

"My dear child, what are you doing in here?" she asked, keeping a rein on the anger in her voice. "I'm afraid the likes of you aren't allowed in here. If you have a brother or cousin who works here—"

"Brice—is here?" she asked, interrupting the woman, whose mouth fell open at the question.

"No, I'm—afraid he's not, but I am the co-owner if you wished to discuss—"

"Missy, please, my friend is hurt. She—she know—"

Babs drew herself up stiffly. "There are hospitals for that—now go away. If you have business with Brice Devlin you'll just have to conduct it somewhere else!" She waved her arms as though to shoo the girl away.

"Brice! Brice!" Honor, hearing the name, lifted her head to stare at the woman, who was returning the stare coldly.

Suddenly the cold stare turned to shock and then incredulous surprise! The woman bent down as though, Pia thought, to kiss the girl, whom she still held protectively by the arm.

"Honor! Honor O'Brien! Jesus Christ!" The blasphemy burst through Babs' lips before she could stop it.

Honor, blinking rapidly, thinking she was looking at a ghost, nearly fell to the floor. "Barbie Hampton!" she whispered.

Thirty-four

"Honor, I can't believe it's really you!" Barbie was saying for the upteenth time as she sat at the side of the bed, holding her friend's hand.

Honor smiled back from the pillows, squeezing her fingers happily. "I can't believe it either, Barbie—"

"Babs," she corrected, laughing a little at Honor's curious look. "It sells better to the customers around these parts."

"You—you have to tell me everything," Honor went on,

267

her eyes filled with pain at her last memories of Barbie being dragged off from Katala's village after being sold to Pawnee warriors. "I can only remember when you rode off on one of the Pawnee ponies with that terrible look on your face."

Babs sighed. It was something she didn't like to recall, but she supposed Honor couldn't be put off. "I was taken to the Pawnee village, farther north from the place where you were. It seemed years, but actually only a few weeks passed, before the warrior who bought me made me his third wife!" She grimaced at the recollection.

"He treated me well, I suppose, but I hated the place. His other wives were bitches and it seemed as though I could never get along with anyone else in the tribe. I was a loner, an outcast. I suppose I became so miserable that Texaca became bored and ill-pleased with me. One day, a white trader came through the village and Texaca sold me to him for exactly three rifles and four jugs of 'firewater.' " She hesitated, glancing at Honor's worried expression.

"It wasn't as bad as you might think with Bill Tyler. I called him 'Old Horseface' because that's what he looked like, but he never abused me except when he got drunk. He was heading west over the mountains. His trading days were over, he told me, and he was fixing to come to California and sell the rest of his pelts and settle down—doing what, I couldn't guess! Anyway, we arrived in Sacramento and poor Old Horseface got himself shot in a poker game with some high-spirited miner who claimed he was cheating. I didn't wait around to see who was going to lay claim to me! I hightailed it out for San Francisco with nothing but the clothes I had on and a few coins that Bill had given me for safekeeping."

"And you bought this place?" Honor asked with wonder, admiring her friend for her perserverance.

Babs laughed gently. "Well, I wasn't that lucky, honey," she said warmly. "First, I tried my hand at waiting tables at the International, but management frowned on their customers sticking their hands up my skirts, so they blamed me and I was thrown out on the street, so to speak, with nothing to pay my rent. As a last resort I applied at the Bella Union as a dealer, although I didn't know a damn thing about cards!" She saw Honor blink at her vocabulary and grinned. "I'm no angel anymore, Honor," she said softly. "I learned a long time ago that my father meant well, but men just aren't ready to give women the independence he tried to teach me. I had to go with the tide or end up in Sydney Town with a mack who'd stripe my back once a day and a hovel to live in and turn the tricks that would enrich his pockets!"

"I—I do understand," Honor said quickly, thinking of the fate that would have been hers had not Pia killed the man who would have seen her prostituted for his own gain.

"Well, I learned fast enough that you can't be 'just a dealer' at the Bella Union. I was expected to entertain the gents too. It was just part of the job after a while and all I worried about was contracting some disease, although the Bella usually screened its customers. Well, I finally found a partner who was willing to go halves with me on a small saloon in the cheaper district. We did well enough to sell it for a profit and buy this building which became— *voilà!*—Babs' Den."

"A fairy-tale ending," Honor sighed.

Babs shook her head with a worldly air. "Hardly, my friend, but I would almost admit to my partner being a veritable prince among men. If it hadn't been for him—" She hesitated and glanced at the other girl sharply. "But your friend, the little slant eyes, tells me that you already know Brice Devlin."

Honor resisted the urge to confide in Babs at that moment. She had no idea if Brice had told her anything about her, nor did she know if the two were lovers. So she shrugged noncommittally, although it cost her a tremendous effort.

"He used to work on a ranch near Monterey."

"Your husband's?"

Honor blushed and looked away from Babs' probing look. "Oh, you don't know what a farce that entire episode was," she sighed. "After I had escaped from the Comanche through one of the women of the village, I came to Santa Fe and hired myself out to a couple who were coming west to San Diego. When we arrived in San Diego, I—we parted company, and I took a ship to Monterey, where I met my 'fiancé' Don Esteban Sevillas, who had already reaffianced himself to someone else."

Her breath came faster as she stared at the bedcovers and relived all the sordid details, except, of course, for Devlin's part in it. "When he realized his fiancée was going to arrive any day from San Francisco, he conveniently 'lent me out' to his brother, Jaime, who was an outlaw."

"What a bastard," Babs put in thoughtfully, her chin cradled in her hand. "Was this Jaime good to you?"

"In his own way, yes," Honor replied truthfully, "but I

269

couldn't imagine living with him in his bandido camp for the rest of my life. I was spared the danger of escaping after Esteban handed him over to the authorities and kept me at the rancho for his further use." Her eyes glittered with remembered rage. "I wanted to kill him, Babs. I wanted to kill him desperately, but—as it was I wounded him enough to escape to Monterey and—from there I came north to San Francisco."

"The hand of God," Babs commented laughing. "He knew there was someone waiting for you up here."

Honor blanched, then relaxed as her friend went on.

"And I'm certainly going to make sure that nothing further happens to you, Honor. We're together again—a trifle soiled and a little wrinkled at the corners, but we've weathered everything so far, right?"

Honor smiled bleakly. "Right."

Babs stood up and smoothed the skirt of her dress absently, then glanced in the mirror to check her coiffure. Casually she glanced at Honor, who was pressing her hands to her temples as though trying to relieve a headache. "Ummm, you didn't tell me how all this happened—I mean with your little friend a murderess and all."

"I—I don't think I'm up to discussing that right now, Babs, if you'll forgive me?" Honor pleaded. "Do you think the law will come for Pia?"

Babs shrugged philosophically. "Hard telling. Sometimes someone puts a bee in their bonnets about the crime running rampant in the city and they start rounding up overy offender they can. Otherwise, they all sit in their plush offices and tell each other dirty jokes while the bribe money rolls in."

"But if they arrest Pia—?"

"All it takes is a little money in the right place," Babs assured her, patting her cheeks as she glared once more into the mirror.

"Bribery? Even you, Babs?"

The woman turned to her with a faint disdain on her face. "Would you rather she hang without a decent trial?" she asked.

Honor colored and shook her head. "I'm sorry—I shouldn't have tried to judge you like that. I would do the same thing."

Babs smiled again and patted her shoulder. "Don't worry about Pia, Honor. She's sleeping comfortably in another room. She was terribly upset, but wouldn't lie down until she knew you were all right." She looked at her steadily. "That's a good little friend you've got there."

Honor nodded shakily and lay back on the pillows as Babs made her exit, promising to come back later after hours. It was hard to think of Babs running a gambling saloon—and with Brice Devlin as a partner! They must be lovers, Honor thought, torturing herself needlessly. How could she ever admit to Babs that Brice Devlin had been in Katala's village the very day that she had been traded to the Pawnee warriors? In fact, that he had been the very one who had held Honor back from trying to aid her?

She stared glumly at the covers. It would do no use to bring up the past at any rate—it was obviously dead according to Brice. She would have to take her cue from him and not mention their earlier relationship. It would be better for everyone concerned, she decided. She knew that Brice would want it that way.

She fell asleep a long time later, listening to the muffled sounds from the saloon below.

"Missy Honor feeling better?"

Honor looked up from the tray where she was buttering a roll and smiled at the impish face framed in the doorway. "Pia! Come in!"

The girl hurried inside and sat on the bed. Inpulsively Honor reached over and kissed her. "Did you sleep well?"

The girl nodded. "Pia killed man, but no evil spirits haunted her dreams. Does it mean the gods are pleased?"

Honor was taken aback at the girl's forthright question. "The man was evil, Pia, but it is not a good thing to take another's life. Still, you did it to save me and I—I can't sit in judgment of your actions when I would have done the same thing, if I'd had my wits about me."

"Pia will hang if white men catch me," the girl said soberly, fingering the fringe on the bedspread.

"They will not come for you, Pia," Honor assured her. She tried to explain the system of corruption in San Francisco, but failed utterly. Pia could no more follow her explanation than if she was teaching her complicated mathematics. Finally Honor gave up and patted her head. "Don't worry. You killed in self-defense and no one will hurt you for that."

"I am glad. I do not wish to part from you." She bowed her head as though in servitude.

"I am not your master," Honor said sharply. "You will be

free to do as you please from now on. Tai relinquished his hold on you when he took money for your body. You can do as you wish."

Pia shook her head uncomprehendingly. "Chinese girl cannot go about the city without concern, Honor," she said simply. "Pia would be taken back to crib to work again. I stay with you—here."

"Why, I'm—I'm not sure I will stay here much longer, Pia. You see, I—"

"Woman your friend. She not let her friend leave now. You will stay." Pia was confident, the ordeal of last night determinedly swept from her mind.

Honor had to remind herself that Pia was no ordinary twelve-year-old. She was mature far beyond her years. Because of the circumstances of the last five years of her life, she had developed a knack for keeping a hard shell of non-emotion about her which enabled her to get through life without being hurt. This shell kept her sane after the trauma of committing murder. Honor wished she could pull the same kind of protective shell around herself.

"I—I must think on it, Pia. It is true that Barbie—Babs is an old friend of mine, but she has a different life now—and so have I. I'm not sure we can live together now and remain friends." She was thinking of Brice, but told herself that she was grasping at straws.

"We shall see," Pia returned wisely. She picked up a roll and buttered it for herself. After chewing hard and swallowing, she commented briefly, "If we stay here, Pia will work as crib girl again."

"No!" The word was short, almost vicious, and the girl cringed involuntarily. "You won't even think of such things!" Honor told her angrily. "Never, never again will you allow a man to—to degrade you like that—or I shall never again call you friend."

Pia looked up in surprise, then shrugged and grinned. "Missy Honor will work as crib girl then?"

"No, neither of us shall do any such thing. We'll find decent work. If we do stay on here, perhaps Babs can put us in the kitchen or working as chambermaids."

Pia sighed. "Easier to work as crib girl," she said to herself, then at Honor's expression, she sobered and took her hand to hold it tightly. "Pia swear to do as you ask, Honor." Her face was somber, as though she were repeating an oath.

"Good, I—"

A swift, hard pounding at the door brought both of them to their feet, the tray spilling unceremoniously on the floor. Honor, her heart knocking against her ribs, thought for sure it was the law come to take Pia away from her. Pia obviously felt the same thing, for she pressed closer to her friend for protection. As the knocking was repeated, Honor realized she must answer.

"Who is it?" Her voice was hardly more than a croak.

"Dammit, Honor, do I have to announce myself before coming into your bedroom? Unlock this door—I want to talk with you!"

It was Brice! Honor's hand flew to her mouth and she looked down at the nightgown Babs had loaned her. It was very sheer and the tips of her breasts could probably be easily discerned through the material.

"Just—just a minute. I'm not dressed," she called out.

"I don't give a damn. Let me in now!" He seemed very angry.

Pia was looking at her with worried eyes, but Honor nodded quickly for her to unlock the door. "And you may leave then, Pia," she added. "I think Mr. Devlin will want to speak privately."

Pia hurried to obey, slipping out the door as the tall man entered with a swaggering arrogance that was reflected in the expression in his silver-blue eyes. He closed the door abruptly with a kick from his boot. He stood for a moment lounging against the door, obviously trying to control his anger. After a pause, he walked toward the bed, where Honor had taken refuge under the sheets. He grabbed a chair and swung it around to straddle it and lean over the back. His eyes were questioning, the brows drawn up in sardonic crescents as he assessed her silently.

"What is it you wanted of me?" Honor asked, glad that her voice was steady.

He smiled with mock surprise. "You mean you can't guess?" he asked insolently.

She shook her head, her lips held between her teeth.

He laughed. "I want to know how come you're here! Why you chose this particular place to seek refuge from the police! Don't you realize that your stupidity could cost Babs her whole investment? She could be arrested for harboring criminals!" The words came so fast, Honor could only stare at him, temporarily speechless.

When he was done and watching her speculatively, she

found her voice. "Are you really worried about Babs' investment—or your own, Brice Devlin?" she queried impudently. "For your information, Babs invited me to stay as long as I wished. She—"

"Does she know everything about you, Honor? About you and me?" His mouth uttering the words was hard and contemptuous.

"What do you mean—about you and me? Certainly, I never told her we were lovers—I'm not that mean-hearted!"

"Lovers! What an interesting choice of words you use, my dear." He was mocking her deliberately, baiting her.

"Well, we did —Oooh!" she fumed suddenly, recognizing the trap. "Get out of my room immediately before I—"

"—call the owner," he supplied sarcastically. "You're talking to him right now, I'm afraid, and he's sorely tempted to have you thrown out!"

"I'm not causing you any trouble!" she defended herself quickly. "I have done nothing wrong, except shelter a young girl who saved my life by killing a man who was more beast than human!"

"I'm assuming you knew that before you tagged along with him," Brice put in pointedly.

"I had no choice," she said soberly, her green eyes narrowing with anger. "I was sold to him!" She was fiercely glad to see the look of shock that temporarily swept his features. "Yes, I was sold to that—that monster for the sum of one hundred and fifty dollars—with Pia thrown in, of course."

The shocked look was replaced by cold brutality. "So, you were in the habit of servicing more than one man?" he asked and his eyes glittered like ice. "I must admit, I didn't think Sevillas would tire of you this quickly. What's the matter—did you threaten to expose him to his wife?" He snickered abusively. "So you came to San Francisco—the best place to be for a born whore!"

Throwing caution to the winds, she flew out of the bed, her fingers curved to rake his eyes out. Surprised, he was hard put to keep the furious little hellcat from accomplishing her purpose. He swung his legs over the chair and caught her arms with his hands, throwing her back onto the bed.

"Damn you, Honor, will you ever be anything but a willful bitch?" he swore, his own anger igniting. He stood above her, his chest rising and falling rapidly as he attempted to maintain control. He was afraid that he might just throttle the little deceiver right then and there!

274

"Go away!" she shouted, gazing up at him, spitting like a cat.

He caught her roughly, pulling her to her feet, catching her chin to force her to look at him. "You'd best learn to control that temper of yours, Honor, or I'll have to sell you myself—just to get you out of my hair."

She kicked him on the shin, her expression stormy. "You're as bad as him—as Hoy Tai!" she shouted. "You—"

"Hoy Tai! What are you talking about?" He gripped her waist, his strength threatening to squeeze the life out of her. "How do you know of that yellow son-of-a-whore?"

She blinked rapidly. She had let her tongue get the best of her wisdom. Oh, God, she didn't want to tell Brice about her degradation. She—she couldn't tell him! She averted her eyes and tried to calm herself.

"I—I've heard of him through—"

"Dammit, you know him, Honor. You'll tell me how, or I'll wring your neck! Better yet, I'll ask your little Chinese friend—is that where you met her, in one of his cribs!"

"Yes!" she screamed at him. Then her face fell and her shoulders shook with her sobbing as she covered her eyes with her hands. "Yes, yes, yes! It's true, I met Pia in one of Tai's cribs. Now are you satisfied?" She looked up at him with tortured eyes.

His expression seemed engraved on the stone slab of his face. He shook himself forcibly and took a deep breath. "How could you have stooped so low?" he almost whispered.

She gazed back at him defiantly. "Because I was trying to get away from Esteban's men—the ones he sent after me when I escaped from him and came to San Francisco to find you!" She sat back abruptly on the bed, her hands twisting the stuff of her gown. "I thought—surely you were dead! I—I didn't think anyone could live after—what he did to you, but—but I found out you were alive and here, and I came to find you, but I—I was kidnapped by one of Tai's men and brought to him to be his—whore." She winced at the word, but went on. "He drugged me and I fought him. So—he—sold—me . . ."

"To the man I saw you with in the Bella Union?"

"Yes, I had only been with him a day, but when I saw you I went into the bedroom and cried and cried! When he wanted to—bed me, I couldn't stand the thought and he attacked me. Pia killed him with his own gun and we fled from the hotel. I'm not sure how she knew to come here, but when

Barbie and I recognized one another . . ." She shrugged. "Now you have it, Brice, the whole terrible truth. Are you glad?"

"I'm not sure I can believe it," he said honestly. Looking at her, her face so sad, her eyes filled with tears, he wished desperately that he could hold her, caress her, but he hardened himself.

"That still doesn't explain why you sold me out to Sevillas," he said darkly, feeling any tender emotions sufficiently squelched at the reminder of her betrayal.

She laughed tiredly. "I never told him anything. He returned unexpectedly and one of his men told him that we had been together that afternoon. He suspected we would try to run away. He—he lied to both of us, Brice."

"It didn't look like a lie when I saw you in his arms that night, panting and raving like you'd never had a man before!" His teeth ground together in renewed disgust and rage. "You were willing enough with him, Honor, admit it!"

"Didn't it occur to you that that was part of the cruel trick he was playing on us, Brice?" she asked him softly. "He drugged my wine and I—"

"You seem to fall back on that story quite a lot," he said sarcastically. "Wasn't that how you first came west in the beginning?"

She started to say something, then shrugged. What did it matter? He was determined to hate her. Nothing she could say was going to change his mind.

"Think what you wish," she said.

"I doubt that I will waste sleep on it," he said, turning to go, as though he could no longer stand to be in the same room with her.

"Brice!" She couldn't help the cry torn from her heart. When he turned, she could barely see him for the tears distorting her vision. "Please—please don't hate me," she said, holding her hands out in a gesture pathetically recalling defeat. "I couldn't bear it."

"I'm afraid, Honor, that is *your* misfortune."

And he was gone.

Thirty-five

It was May and people were arriving in San Francisco faster than the city could swallow them up. Babs' Den was making remarkable profits off a lot of the overflow and the owner and namesake went about the saloon with a perpetual smile of bliss on her handsome features as the money continued to pour into the coffers.

Brice Devlin, on the other hand, went about short-tempered and irritable most of the time. No one thought to associate his bad attitude with the arrival of the two new laundresses who worked in a separate room in back of the kitchen, washing and ironing the costumes of the women and the shirts of the men dealers. Pia was cheerful and sang odd fragments of Chinese songs as she pressed the never-ending flow of shirts with a hot iron. Honor worked steadily with the same expression of determination on her face all the time.

Babs would drop in on them during their five-hour workday, chiding Honor on not accepting her offer to deal cards in the main saloon, but Honor would shake her head quickly. She had no wish to be where Brice was all the time—she couldn't stand it. Babs would try to wheedle her, telling her the washing was too menial a task and her hands and back would suffer from it sooner or later, but Honor was steadfast. She would work for an honest day's wages and had even put up a fight when Babs cut her working hours to only five. But on this, Babs remained firm.

"I wish you would talk to Honor," she put in to Brice one afternoon as they began setting up tables and getting ready for the night's action. "She insists on remaining in the washroom when, with her looks and figure, she'd be dynamite in our card room! I can't understand her—it's not like I'm asking her to whore for us!"

He shrugged tightly. "Maybe if you did ask her to whore for us, she'd accept more readily." Then he sobered at Babs' puzzled air. "I'm sorry, Babs. If she doesn't want to deal, it's up to her. I doubt that I could talk her into it if you can't. After all, you two were friends." He shrugged again.

Babs bit her lip. "She's being so damned stubborn and silly, I could wring her neck!"

A mutual coincidence, Brice thought with amusement as he went around laying out packs of cards on the green baize cloths of the tables.

"Maybe she just doesn't like working evenings," he put in sarcastically. "Maybe she likes to save them for gentleman callers."

Babs laughed and tugged playfully at the hem of his jacket. "She has no gentleman callers, my friend," Babs said wickedly. "After she has dinner downstairs, she goes to her room and reads or sews or—thinks, or something! I have an idea she kneels down and prays for our sins!" She laughed again roguishly. "I would never have thought dear Honor would qualify for a nun, but she seems to be heading that way."

"A nun? Her?" It was Brice's turn to laugh with bitter cynicism. "She's a whore down to her toes, Babs, and don't you think otherwise."

Babs' brown eyes looked into his innocently. "What makes you think so, Brice?" she asked.

The silver-blue eyes flashed dangerously. "She's got that look about her," he hedged and bent to pick up a card that had fallen to the floor.

"You've got to be kidding!" she replied incredulously. "If a man comes near her, she flits away like she's afraid he's going to step on her toes! I've never seen a woman so skittish around the opposite sex!" She frowned to herself. "I really think that what she needs is a real man to show her how much fun they can be." She eyed her friend cockily. "You'd make a hell of a teacher, Brice."

He laughed with an amused look at Babs' face. "Now, I thought you'd be jealous if I'd go sniffling around the 'hired help,' honey," he said, chucking her lightly under the chin.

She put her hands on her hips and stuck out her tongue. "Brice, I know I don't own you," she retorted sharply. "You can play with whomever you wish—and I expect you to allow me the same freedom." She cocked her head and her brown eyes turned thoughtful. "Listen to me, honey. We both know that we can never get serious with each other. We're just not cut out to do anything but give each other a little pleasure now and then."

Brice looked at her in surprise. Then he whistled softly. "Babs, you're the damnedest woman I've ever had the pleasure to know."

She shrugged airily. "Thanks for the compliment. Now—will you do a favor for me?"

He nodded, grinning.

"Wheedle our little laundress into learning the cards with you?"

The silver-blue eyes narrowed, then she saw an amused admiration creep into their expression. "If it will help business—I'll try," he answered finally, grudgingly.

Babs smiled sweetly. "You just do that, my friend," she said softly as he departed the room.

Brice hesitated at the door to the laundry room, telling himself he was a fool to let himself be talked into this. He cursed Babs silently, then pushed open the door.

The first thing he saw was Honor bending over a hot iron as she smoothed the wrinkles from one of his shirts. The moist heat put a sheen on her forehead and caused her hair to curl and wave out of the pins that she had put in to keep it carelessly piled in a knot on top of her head. Her bodice was unbuttoned to the cleavage in her breasts and perspiration pearled the skin at her throat. Brice thought that she had never looked so appealing.

She hadn't looked up at his entrance as she pressed the iron against the shirt, a tiny wrinkle marring the smoothness of her brow.

"There's another load here to wash, Pia," she said.

"Sorry, I don't do wash."

She looked up, startled, her green eyes widening in surprise, "What—what are you doing here?" she asked after a moment.

He smiled lazily. "Making sure you do your job."

She frowned. Then she bent over the shirt and slammed the iron down on it as she pulled at the sleeve to straighten it out.

"Wishing I were in it?" he asked indolently.

She didn't answer, but continued to work furiously.

He walked closer to her and she stopped to look up at him, her eyes narrowing in anticipation of an argument. As he moved around the padded board, she put the iron in its dish and backed up a little.

"Pia will be back in a moment," she said, as though to waylay him from making any overt moves toward her.

He shrugged. "I didn't come to talk with Pia. She's doing a fine job."

She bristled. "And I'm not? Are you trying to find an excuse to send me out into the streets?"

He shook his head, trying hard to hold on to his own temper. This girl was maddening—why did she always think he was about to attack her? "Listen, Honor, I came to talk with you because Babs told me she can't persuade you to deal for us."

Honor looked puzzled at what she considered a change in tactics. "You came to talk to me?"

He nodded mockingly. "Were you hoping for something else, perhaps?"

Her eyes grew stormy. "I was hoping you would leave and let me get on with my work."

He laughed, then shrugged. "This work isn't for you, Honor. You could do a great deal more for me—and for Babs—if you'd consent to deal for us. We have other women dealing for us. Most of the houses do."

"I know," she replied defiantly, "and they're also expected to supplement their dealings with other entertainments."

"I believe Babs has already told you, you wouldn't be expected to take the men upstairs. Just to deal. You'd be paid the usual salary."

"I've already told Babs, I just don't want to do it!" she returned hotly.

"Why?" he asked her bluntly.

She reddened. "I—I just can't stand to—to—"

"—to have a man look at you with desire?" he guessed, his eyes turning silvery.

She looked as though she would burst into tears at any moment and Brice would have put an arm about her shoulders, but she stepped back, avoiding his arm. "I'm surprised at this sudden change of heart from you, Brice," she said. "I can't help wondering why you'd want me around so much when you obviously despise me."

He shrugged. "I don't despise you, Honor."

"I seem to recall that the last time we met, you gave a very good impression of that emotion," she retorted.

"I was angry," he said. "I'm sorry."

His apology completely threw her off guard and she could only look up at him with wide, soft eyes.

At the look, he was hard-pressed not to take her in his arms and crush the spunk out of her stubborn little body. As it was, he grinned enticingly. "Honor, I promise you won't be disturbed by any of our customers. You know damn well you're not suited for this type of work." He indicated the steaming iron.

She pressed her hands together uncertainly. Why was he being so nice to her, she wondered uneasily. Did it hide some ulterior motive that she could not figure out? Was he only doing it on Babs' behalf? Or was he really interested in her welfare, her happiness? She sneaked a look at him through lowered lashes. Lord, he was handsome! She thought her heart would melt when he first came into the room. She had thought—she had thought . . .

He doesn't love me, he doesn't love me, she repeated to herself. I mustn't let him lead me into a trap.

"If I took the job," she began, licking her upper lip, "who would teach me?"

His eyes mocked her. "I would."

"Couldn't someone else?" she pleaded.

He laughed. "What's the matter, Honor, afraid I'll chew you up?"

She glared at him, stung out of her nervous indecision. "Of course not, Brice Devlin! Neither you nor any other man is ever going to get the best of me again if I can help it!"

"And what if you can't—help it?" he asked softly, moving nearer to her.

She gazed up at him and felt a trembling in her legs, she sought desperately to quell. "I can," she whispered.

What would have happened next, she didn't want to guess, but fortunately Pia arrived just then, halting Brice's ominous advance.

"Pia," she breathed on the end of a sigh.

Pia looked uncertainly between the two and set her basket down. "You have more wash?" she asked.

"Yes, yes, over there." Honor pointed, turning her body so that her shoulder brushed against Brice's chest. She could feel the crispness of his shirt against her skin.

"Do you agree then?" He was impersonal again, reaching in his breast pocket for a cheroot, which he proceeded to light up calmly.

"I—I really should think about it."

"I need an answer right now," he said quickly, "or we'll have to look for another girl." He smiled to himself thoughtfully. "I know just the one, too. A big-bosomed gal at Dennison's Exchange who's looking for a change of venue."

Honor tightened her mouth. "I'll do it!" she almost exploded, taking the bait in one gulp.

Brice smiled secretly to himself. "Good girl," he said, "Wise decision."

Now that she had agreed, Honor wasn't so sure she had done so by her own choice. "When do we start lessons?"

He shrugged. "You can finish my shirt first. There'll be plenty of time later on."

He walked out, whistling to himself, closing the door just in time to miss being hit by his own half-ironed shirt.

Thirty-six

"It's impossible! I'll mess it up, I know I will!" Honor said woefully into the mirror as Pia buttoned the back of her gown.

"No, no. You do as Mr. Brice tell you—you be fine," the girl assured her calmly, stepping back to clasp her hands at the lovely picture her friend made.

Honor, too, looked at her reflection worriedly. She saw a tall, willowy young woman with honey-gold hair piled in rich burnished curls on top of her head with glittering black sequins placed at strategic points. A black sequined gown clothed her body, the bodice tight and low, revealing fully half of her perfectly formed breasts, the sleeves very short and puffed at the shoulders. The skirt, by her firm insistence, was full and reached to the tip of her satin slippers. Long black gloves sheathed her arms to the elbows and diamond earbobs swirled enticingly below her ears, nearly brushing her shoulders. Her green eyes looked back at her with concern.

"Oh, I know I'm going to forget everything," she said, biting her lips.

Tonight was her debut as a dealer and she felt more nervous than at her coming-out party at sixteen in Charleston. Her palms were wet beneath the gloves and her heart was jumping like a rabbit. There was a becoming flush to her cheeks.

She tried to recall everything Brice had taught her, chewing her lips with worry. She had been surprised at his objectiveness as he taught her the different games—nothing too fancy, just the basics to get her through the easier tables. He hadn't once touched her, except to take the cards. In fact, he had shown a reserve that she wasn't used to and it puzzled her. But, after all, what had she expected him to do? She blushed at the answer.

282

She reached abruptly for the black, glittering fan. It had been Babs' idea to dress her all in black to highlight the gold in her hair and the unusual color of her eyes. She would be, Babs had insisted, the rage of all San Francisco if she—no pun intended—played her cards right!

"Honor, you ready!"

"Yes, Babs, ready as I'll ever be," she called back, catching the tassel of her skirt to walk out of the room. She gave Pia a nervous smile. "Now, don't you wait up for me, Pia," she smiled reassuringly. "We can talk all about it tomorrow over the dirty shirts!"

Pia laughed and clapped her hands, blowing her a kiss for good luck.

"My friend, you look marvelous!" Babs exclaimed enthusiastically. "I just know you'll be our star performer tonight."

"I'm nervous, Babs," Honor admitted. "Will you fire me if I make a mistake?" She was half-joking, half-serious.

Babs laughed. "Everyone's allowed a mistake, Honor. Come on, I've put you at one of the monte tables. You think you know the game well enough?"

Honor nodded. "I hope so."

Babs linked her arm in the other girl's and they sailed downstairs, where the room was already beginning to fill. Honor took her seat at the round table, glancing up at the high chair behind her which would seat the man who would be watching for cheaters. She glanced at one of their bouncers, who was lounging at the bar, for reassurance. Then, with a deep breath, she began to shuffle the cards.

She played at the monte table for most of the night, and as the hours wore on, she realized she was doing well, keeping her cool and gathering a fair number of unwanted admirers. She shuffled, dealt and passed out chips with a sureness that surprised even herself. But she kept telling herself that at five other tables there were women doing the same thing and the thought gave her some comfort.

Once, during a short break, she felt a warm hand on her bare shoulder and, looking up, gazed into enigmatic blue eyes that were smiling thoughtfully.

"You're doing fine, Honor," Brice assured her, letting his hand stay on her skin a moment longer.

"I'll be glad when the night is over," she confided, choosing not to read anything special in his offhand caress.

Later in the evening, when her table was closing, she was

glad she hadn't read too much into it, for she saw him go up-stairs, smiling and talking, with one of the other dealers. For a moment, she felt a quick stab of painful jealousy, but deter-minedly turned away and gathered her remaining chips.

"You're new here, aren't you?"

Honor looked up into the quizzical blue eyes of an older gentleman whose brown hair was graying at the temples. She noted that he was dressed very well and there was a black band on his arm signifying he was in mourning for some-one.

"Yes," she answered briefly.

"I didn't think I'd seen you before—and I come here at least once a week, although"—he hesitated—"I've missed a few weeks lately because of my wife's death."

"I'm sorry," she said quickly, impatient to go now, her mind filled with pictures of Brice and his companion.

"Fine woman she was," the man was saying to himself. Then brightening, he was laying a confident hand on her arm. "Would you like to have a late dinner with me, my dear?"

She shied away. "No, thank you, I have to go."

The blue eyes twinkled. "You've already promised someone else your company?" he guessed.

She was about to shake her head, then thought it would be the best way to get rid of him. "Yes, good evening."

He released her with a bow. "Perhaps another time then?"

She didn't answer, but hurried off to turn in her chips. Babs hurried over to her. "I see you were talking with Walter Gordon, my dear."

"He neglected to introduce himself," she said dryly.

"Dear Walter, he is getting a trifle absentminded, but he still knows a pretty girl when he sees one," Babs trilled.

"Despite his wife's recent demise," Honor put in, no less dryly than before.

"Oh, but that was weeks ago and Walter's not one to ig-nore the women for long. You should be nice to him, Honor, he's quite wealthy," Babs observed.

Honor shrugged. "I was nice to him, Babs, I just wasn't about to encourage any ideas he might have to bed me tonight."

"You could do worse."

"Babs! He's—he's too old for me and he—"

"He's only forty-five, the prime of life for rich speculators like himself. That's when they can lie back and enjoy the fruit of their younger days." Babs sighed. "I wish I could sink my teeth into him. I'd get a good sum out of him before I'd let go."

"Well, I don't think he has anyone to go out with him tonight," Honor said archly. She turned back to where the middle-aged gentleman was still eyeing her. With a furious flounce of disapproval, she hurried upstairs, leaving Babs to wind her graceful way through the tables to meet him.

The next evening, she played the monte table again and this time found Mr. Walter Gordon playing with her. She met his eyes and he winked at her.

"Your manager told me you went upstairs to bed—alone—last night," he whispered when the hands changed, leaning toward her.

"That is my business, Mr. Gordon," she said stiffly, shuffling the cards.

"So, you know my name. I'm pleased that you took the trouble to find out, although I was remiss in introducing myself to you last night. Will you forgive me, my dear?"

"Of course," she said lightly, beginning to deal.

"Then you won't be angry if I took the liberty of learning your name?"

She looked up at him exasperated. "Mr. Gordon, are you playing this hand, or not?"

He smiled. "But of course, my dear, I wouldn't think of playing anywhere else."

During a break in the play, Honor went to a small room behind the bar where the hired help was allowed to relax and drink non-alcoholic beverages. Before she could slip through the door, she felt a hand on her arm detaining her, and she looked up to see Walter Gordon grinning confidently.

"Miss O'Brien, I would be most pleased if you would allow me to buy you a drink." He bowed, still holding her arm.

"I'm afraid we're not allowed to drink with the customers, Mr. Gordon, during working hours." she replied, fighting to remain calm. Really, the man simply did not know when he wasn't wanted. "If you'll excuse me, I'd like to freshen up before the next round."

He released her arm promptly, bowing again. "As you wish, my dear, but I can assure you I do not give up easily when I've found something that definitely excites me."

With that oblique promise, he rejoined the other gamblers in the saloon, leaving Honor gritting her teeth in exasperation. She could tell the bouncer on duty about his unwanted advances, but, really, he wasn't being obnoxious, nor was he truly bothering her with any lewd attentions. There was really nothing she could pinpoint to warrant having him thrown out. She would just have to fume silently and get through the evening somehow.

It became increasingly hard, though, to ignore Mr. Walter Gordon, for every night she played, he made it a point to wager at her table no matter what game she was dealing.

One evening, after he had lost heavily, he leaned toward her and slipped a small package down the décolletage of her gown. Honor caught her breath in outrage, but there was no way she could retrieve the package without making a spectacle of herself, so she fumed the rest of the way through the evening, darting looks of fury at him from beneath her lashes.

After the evening was finished, she hurried upstairs to dig down for the package, which had slipped below her breasts. Furiously she ripped the tissue from it and gasped at the perfectly matched emerald earbobs.

"They're beautiful," Babs said, entering her room as Honor stood in the center of the floor gazing at the gift. "From Mr. Gordon, of course?"

"Yes, but—but, Babs, I can't possibly accept them. He would think—" She bit her lip. "Why did he do it?"

Her friend shrugged. "He likes you, Honor, don't get so upset," she said sagely. "If all the girls had such polite admirers as you, they'd consider themselves very fortunate."

"Fortunate!" Honor cried helplessly. "But I don't want his attentions, Babs!"

"I don't understand you, Honor," Babs said frankly. "He's rich, he's attractive, he likes you! Why not enjoy his attentions while you've got them? Who are you saving yourself for?"

Honor stared at her and the green eyes flashed as brilliantly as the emeralds. "You're right, Babs, who *am* I saving myself for?" she said to herself. Certainly not Brice, she thought, for he hardly knows I'm alive for all the attention he pays me. She resolved to wear the earbobs the next evening.

Thirty-seven

"Ah, I see you approve of my little gift." It was Walter Gordon, at her elbow, leaning toward her ear, making a caress out of the statement.

Honor turned, flushing slightly. "They're beautiful," she agreed.

"And they match your eyes exactly when they sparkle as they're doing now," he added, delighted at the softening in her mood.

"Mr. Gordon, you really are too kind. I—I shouldn't accept them, but they were so lovely . . ."

"I'm glad you like them, Miss O'Brien. May I call you Honor?" His blue eyes were confident, sure of the ultimate conquest now.

She nodded shyly. "I suppose, under the circumstances, I would be foolish to say no."

Walter Gordon felt a pleasant tug as she gazed at him with that little-girl look. It fired his imagination coupled with the sensuality of her perfect figure and he found himself itching to feel the length of that form pressed tightly against his own. He amazed even himself, for he was not one to feel this deeply about a saloon girl, a dealer.

He had loved Mary very much while she was alive. She had come from a well-bred background and it had taken a lot of willpower for her to leave her family to come with him to California on his wild schemes of speculation. They had both been ecstatic when Marianne had been born to them.

He had turned to entertaining pretty women when Mary's disease had progressed into the final stages, but he hadn't felt he was cheating on her, for she was in no condition to receive his embraces, and Walter Gordon was not the man to abstain from a woman's company.

But he had treated them as toys, to be played with, then cast aside. This one, though, was different. There was something . . .

"Are you playing, Mr. Gordon?" Her clear voice cut through his thoughts.

"Yes, I think I am," he said.

The play went smoothly and Honor was beginning to feel

confident in her new role. The threat of the bouncer's fists kept the rowdy miners and the other gentlemen in line and a cool look would turn most of them away if they tried anything naughty at the table. Except for Walter Gordon, she had no admirers—or if she had, they were silent ones.

As the evening wore on, she regained her good spirits. Her nightmare with Hoy Tai and the miner was beginning to fade into the back of her mind. She felt eyes on her and, looking up, found Brice staring at her with cool speculation that sent a shiver down her back. She knew he spent his nights with no one particular girl—in fact, she was the only dealer at Babs' Den who had not shared his bed. She threw him a dazzling smile. She would show him that she could care less if he deigned to bless her with his company, she thought determinedly, and dealt with renewed vigor.

"Drinks, gentlemen?"

It was one of the Chinese houseboys, tray in hand, asking for orders from her table. Honor suppressed a shiver at sight of the long pigtail and black satin skull cap that reminded her of Hoy Tai.

When the boy had taken the order, he bowed correctly, returning later with the drinks. The slanted black eyes slid quickly over Honor, not meeting her gaze, and an uncomfortable feeling assailed her for a moment before she returned her concentration to the game and forgot about the boy entirely.

Walter Gordon sat on her right, eyeing her above the cards with a question in his eyes which she chose to ignore for the moment.

"Cards?" she asked him, not quite meeting his gaze.

He nodded, leaning toward her once more with an intimate smile on his face. "Will you meet me later this evening and have supper with me?"

She took a deep breath. "Mr. Gordon, I really can't accept," she began, choosing her words carefully. "I have no wish to compromise myself by making such a promise."

"Miss O'Brien, you sound like a prude," he said disapprovingly, clucking his tongue as he looked at his cards.

She glanced up swiftly, retorting, "I would rather you label me thusly, Mr. Gordon, than to call me something much worse."

"Or think it?" he countered.

"Naturally."

He laughed. "You play the game well, my dear," he said

almost absently as he frowned at his hand. "And I'm not talking about the cards."

She blushed and continued to deal, aware of his gaze directed on her throughout the rest of the evening. It was clear that Walter Gordon was not the type of man who would give up without a struggle. She felt certain she could look forward to a long and difficult battle of wits with him.

But when the play was over and she was closing her table, it was not Gordon's arm that brushed against hers as a hand reached out for her wrist, but Brice Devlin's. She looked up in surprise.

"Honor, you've been doing beautifully," he said approvingly, at the same time noting the emerald earrings. "It's time I rewarded you."

She started and was silent, waiting for him to explain.

"How about dinner tonight?" he asked softly, leaning toward her as his finger tapped at the earring to set it swinging.

"Well, I don't know," she answered slowly, glancing down to where Gordon was collecting his winnings.

He followed her gaze and smiled, then shrugged. "If you've already promised someone else, Honor, I wouldn't think of intruding," he put in sarcastically, straightening up with an expression of suppressed anger on his face. "I wasn't aware you had other things to do."

She glared up at him, ready to retort something, but bit her lip and managed to answer him calmly. "I hadn't promised Mr. Gordon I would go with him, Mr. Devlin," she said clearly, noting that Walter Gordon had come closer upon hearing his name mentioned. "But since you insist it is part of the policy, I will gladly accept." She threw a smile at Gordon, who returned the grin.

"Excellent, my dear." He looked over at Devlin, who was hard put to keep control of his own anger. "Mr. Devlin, I do owe you a favor, for I admit I was beginning to despair of persuading this lovely creature to dine with me."

"Think nothing of it," Devlin murmured between clenched teeth. He had turned to go when Honor stopped him with a hand on his arm.

"Must I be in by any certain time?" she asked him with a deceptively innocent look on her face.

"Just be at the roulette table at eight tomorrow night!" he ground out and hurried away.

Honor gazed after him for a moment, feeling a sense of

289

loss while at the same time telling herself he needed to be taught a lesson. She did not belong to him and she had no wish for him to think that she was only waiting for him to take her back to bed with him.

"Mr. Gordon, if you will excuse me while I change?"

He nodded. "I'll send round for my carriage and will meet you in—say, twenty minutes?" He looked at her questioningly.

She nodded. She could feel his eyes on her as she swished her skirts behind her and made her way through the tables upstairs. She went into her room, beginning to feel the tension in her neck developing into a headache. She looked around distractedly for Pia to help her undress, but realized the child was already in bed and set about undressing herself and slipping into a fresh gown of soft lavender taffeta that helped only a little to lift her spirits. She freshened her coiffure and dabbed on a little cologne water to drive away the scents of men's tobacco smoke that lingered from the night's entertainments.

She slipped a light shawl around her shoulders to protect her from the night's mists and was walking hurriedly down the hall when she saw Brice coming up the stairs with one of the other dealers, laughing drunkenly on his arm. He glanced at her indifferently.

"Enjoy yourself, Honor," he said, bowing gallantly, before turning the girl toward his own bedroom.

"Thank you!" she huffed to his back and wished she had a knife to stab him with at that moment.

With more determination than before, she descended the steps and walked toward the front of the saloon, peering out to find the carriage awaiting her. She called out to Walter Gordon, already knowing the risks of entering a strange carriage. But then she saw his face, smiling at her, and then he was getting out to escort her inside.

"I like a woman who doesn't dawdle at her toilet," he said, kissing her hand as he seated himself opposite her.

She inclined her head. "Where are you taking me, Mr. Gordon?"

He laughed. "My word, all business, aren't we? Well, if you're that famished, Honor, we can go to the Virginia City International Hotel. They have some excellent cuisine and serve only the finest champagne." He leaned closer. "I can order a private room so that we can dine at our leisure." He cocked a haughty eyebrow. "After all, you don't have to be back until tomorrow night."

She smiled. "Yes, Mr. Gordon, but I do have to get some sleep or I'm afraid I'll fall into the roulette wheel tomorrow and probably lose my job."

"Please, call me Walter," he interjected quickly.

She nodded. "Of course, Walter. After all, I suppose it is safe to assume that we are, by now, friends?"

He laughed in delight. "Very safe to assume, my dear. I've only been watching you for the past several nights, hoping to seal that friendship." But at her look of withdrawal, he amended hastily. "I mean with an evening's dinner, Honor, since I would never presume to more—unless—you wished it."

The light blue eyes were challenging her and she hadn't the strength to meet his look. Idly she glanced out the window, the curtains of which were drawn back to allow her the view. She saw a small buckboard pass and her gaze sharpened. The boy was Chinese and his visage seemed familiar, but Walter was catching her hand, turning her back to face him.

"I think it would be wise if we got something cleared immediately," he was saying earnestly. "I admit to enjoying women, Honor. In fact, you might call me something of a bounder if you knew of some of my exploits."

"You don't need to tell me all this," Honor assured him. "Let's just enjoy the evening." She certainly had no wish for him to reveal his past to her—why should she want to hear it, when this would probably be the only time they would go out together?

He shrugged. "I suppose you're right. It's just that I wouldn't want you to form a bad opinion of me through others' gossip."

"I promise I would never listen to gossip about you," she said, teasing him a little to bring him out of his somber mood.

He relaxed. "You really are a remarkable young woman, my dear," he said, leaning away from her now in his seat. "I hate to think you're probably around the same age as my daughter." He laughed lightly, but she knew it had cost him a lot to say such a thing.

"Does she still live with you?" she asked, hoping to keep the conversation light until they reached the International.

He shook his head and for a moment she saw a look of frustrated rage appear on his features. "No, she is married."

"Have you other children?"

"No, only my daughter." He shook himself visibly. "But tell me about yourself, Honor. What have you been doing with your life up until the time I spotted you at Babs' Den?" He seemed genuinely interested.

She veiled her eyes and looked down at her hands, which clasped and unclasped nervously. "Surprising as it may seem, Mr. Gordon—I mean, Walter—I was born in the cream of Southern society in Charleston. I was raised on magnolias, mammies and outdoor barbecues with nary a care in the world."

"I knew it!" He leaned forward again, his eyes gleaming. "Something about you gave you away, my dear, for I sensed you were from good background."

She laughed. "Background hardly counts when one is dealing cards in a saloon in San Francisco," she put in dryly.

He shook his head and caught one of her hands. "It makes all the difference, my dear," he said enigmatically.

They had arrived at the International and soon found themselves upstairs in a private room, tastefully, if opulently, decorated. Gordon ordered their meal and sat back to sip the Dom Perignon as he allowed himself the luxury of assessing his delightful companion.

"So, tell me, Honor, how did you leave the one coast and arrive at the opposite end of our fair country?"

"It's a long story, Walter, and would probably only bore you. I'm sure the life of a speculator is much more exciting than the tale of the trip west on a wagontrain."

"Well, I must admit, I didn't take the wagon train. Mary and I—" He paused and reddened a little. "Mary was my wife," he said softly.

"Please go on," she said quickly, wanting to put him at his ease.

"We bought passage aboard a clipper around the Cape. The journey was long and there were times when I was certain the storms were going to do us in, but it was all worth it. We found a nearly virgin land, rich with promise and ready to yield her fruits to the man who could tame her." He looked at her deliberately and noted her blush. "Of course I used tactics which were deemed hard, even cruel at times, but it takes a man with strength to reap profits when there are so many others who wish to share those profits. I did what I had to to make a decent life for my family."

"More than decent, I've heard." She couldn't resist needling him a little.

He shrugged. "Mary was from good stock, but I had very little in the way of financial security to offer her. It took great strength and courage for her to break away from her family and follow me west. I was determined to reward that courage and prove myself to her family."

"I admire you for what you did," she said honestly.

He relaxed. "You remind me a lot of Mary," he said simply. "You, too, must have left the safety and security of your home to come out to the temptations of the West. Was it because of a man?"

She flushed and shook her head. "Please don't think of it as being noble, Walter. Actually, I did it because I had no other choice. My brother was intent on coming west to make his fortune after he had lost my father's money through bad business deals. We—got separated and now all I know is that he's up in the Fraser Valley, still looking for his fortune."

His face was earnest now. "If we could find him, perhaps I could find an honest job for him with my company and he could come back here to San Francisco. Would that please you, Honor?"

She was taken aback at the idea. "I have no idea where Reid is now. It would probably be next to impossible to bring him back now. Besides," hesitation filtered through her voice. "I'm not sure he would want that."

"But surely, he would want to be reunited with his sister!"

She laughed bitterly. "My brother is an opportunist, Walter. He would not appreciate my mixing into his affairs. We have not seen each other in over a year now. He is still my brother and I love him, but I realize that he must do as he wishes and I—"

"—must do as you wish."

"Yes."

For a long moment, they looked at each other. He was about to speak when the waiter arrived with their meal. They ate in silence, neither wishing to upset the delicate balance of harmony between them.

When she had finished, Honor sighed in satisfaction and wiped her mouth with a fine linen napkin. "Oh, I have to approve of that meal," she said. "It was fit for a king."

"And a queen," he added. Then he picked up his glass of champagne and motioned her to do the same. "A toast?" He thought a moment, then looked her straight in the eye. "A toast to you and me, Honor O'Brien, and to what may yet be."

293

She hesitated a moment, then drank the rest of the sparkling liquid. When she had finished and the remains of the meal had been taken away, she looked to Gordon questioningly.

"It's late," she said pointedly.

He sighed. "I was hoping you wouldn't notice, Honor."

She laughed. "I do have to get some sleep if I'm to appear tomorrow night without smudges beneath my eyes."

"They would still be beautiful," he observed, deliberately moving closer to her on the settee.

She was aware of his movement and felt her heart beginning to beat rapidly. Her hands trembled and her nervousness was apparent even to him.

"Are you afraid of me?" he asked incongruously.

"I'm—I seem to find myself getting uncomfortable if a man—if a man—" She trailed off in embarrassment.

He sat next to her and pressed her hand. "I'm too old and too experienced to ravage you, Honor," he said plainly. "I wouldn't expect you to 'reward' me with a favor for this evening's entertaiment."

"Thank you, Walter. I really do think we should be getting back."

He smiled tightly. "I said I wouldn't press you," he reiterated, "but I can't help hoping that you might offer—"

She stood up, her green eyes suddenly ablaze with fire. "Offer what, Mr. Gordon!" she said angrily. "You hoped for what?"

He stood up also. "Please don't be angry, Honor. I didn't mean—"

"I know what you meant, Mr. Gordon, and it disgusts me! I don't care how old you are or how experienced! You want the same thing any other man expects of a girl without protection!" She grabbed her shawl.

"Honor, please believe me, I wasn't imagining that you would go to bed with me!" he pleaded. "I only thought that some show of affection, of pleasure in our evening spent together, might—"

"Please, Mr. Gordon, I would like to go home now!"

"Dammit, Honor," he said, angry now too and striding toward her to grab her arms and shake her. "I'm not letting you go home until we've resolved this misunderstanding! I was speaking about a kiss, a sign that you enjoyed my company! Is that too much to expect?"

His eyes were so sincere that she wavered in her tirade.

"Well, I had no intentions of bestowing a kiss," she said on a somewhat calmer note. "If you can't accept my verbal thanks for the evening—"

"Good God! That's enough for me, if that is what you want," he interjected quickly. "Do you forgive me for any imagined wrongdoing?"

She eyed him seriously, then smiled a little. "I forgive you," she said finally, "and I hope you forgive me for flying off like that!" She was almost impudent now. "Now you can see how horribly my background has slipped in the last year," she went on. "I suppose you think I'm some sort of hoyden."

He smiled in genuine relief. "Not at all, my dear. I'm simply delighted at seeing you so strong in your—er—convictions." His smile was unabashed.

"I suppose I could blame it on the champagne," she sighed and smiled back at him. "I really must get back now."

He nodded. "My pleasure, Honor."

They returned to the carriage and rode back to the saloon, each intent on his own thoughts. When they arrived, Honor declined his offer to escort her to her door, but he insisted and she finally had to relent or risk making a spectacle of herself again. She pulled out the key to the side entrance and the two of them made their way through the dimly lit downstairs to the upper hallway.

"It was a lovely evening, Honor," he whispered at her door, capturing her hands to press a kiss to the palm. "I would hope for another?"

She looked down demurely. "Perhaps, Walter," was all she would say, and he had to be content with that.

With regret, he watched her close the door firmly to her room.

Thirty-eight

"Your little friend seems to be missing, Honor." It was Babs coming in her room after knocking lightly.

"Missing?" Honor stretched and yawned sleepily, wishing Babs would go away and let her go back to sleep. She was tired from last night and resented the intrusion. "What time is it?"

"Half past noon."

"Half past noon!" Honor pulled herself out of the depths of the bedcovers and wiped her eyes. "I had no idea it was so late!" She glanced over to Babs questioningly. "How do you know Pia is missing?"

"Because there's a stack of ironing downstairs and she's not in her room," the other answered her calmly. "Do you think she could have gone somewhere—on an errand, perhaps?"

Honor shook her head, trying to think. "Pia would have told me."

"Maybe a note?"

"She can't write! I wonder . . ." Honor got out of bed and went to the armoire to search for something to wear. "She doesn't know a soul around here," she commented into the closet.

"Perhaps she's found herself a boyfriend, Honor," Babs laughed. "Anyway I thought you should know since you two are so close. I know you worry about her, but if she's just gone off to get out of doing her work, I'm not going to be too happy with her."

"Pia wouldn't do that," Honor objected, bringing out a gown of light yellow muslin. "I can't think where she would be . . ."

"Well, I'll leave you to get dressed," Babs said, opening her door to leave. "By that time, maybe she'll show up with some glib excuse about forgetting the time—like her friend!" She laughed and left her to dress.

Honor's mind was working as she washed herself and donned a clean chemise and stockings. She tried to think where Pia could be, chiding herself for not checking on the girl last night before going out with Walter Gordon. Was she gone even then? A horrible suspicion began in her mind and she caught her breath at the possibility. Could someone from the law have come to take Pia away—without her knowing it? But surely Babs would have known! And yet, the law was corrupt, and there were vigilante committees who specialized in kidnapping their victims and hanging them without a fair trail. The possibility was frightening. Perhaps the miner who had been killed had had friends in high places. He had, after all, had plenty of money.

By the time she was fully dressed, she was shaking at her thoughts of Pia's fate. She rushed out of her room and downstairs to the kitchens, where a dining room was set up where the hired help ate their meals. She looked around frantically for Babs and saw her, drinking coffee and talking casually to Brice Devlin.

"Oh, Babs! Have you heard anything about Pia yet?"

Babs looked up in surprise. "Of course not, Honor. What are you getting at?"

Honor wrung her hands nervously. "I think—I suspect that someone might have kidnapped her," she got out, her eyes jumping from Babs' face to Brice's.

The latter looked back at her incredulously. "Who would want to kidnap a twelve-year-old China girl?" he asked slowly.

"The law, for God's sake! She did kill a man—in self-defense! But they won't be thinking about that! They'll hang her—you know they will, Brice!"

"Hold on now, Honor. Pull yourself together," he cautioned. Then his look became indolent. "Perhaps if you had not been so wrapped up in your evening with Walter Gordon, you would have thought to look in on your friend last night."

She swung on him furiously. "Well, if you hadn't been so—so arrogant last night, perhaps I wouldn't have even gone with Mr. Gordon!" she countered.

He grinned mockingly, then took another swallow from his coffee. "Look, Honor, I'm really in no mood to banter with you this afternoon. If you want me to check with the authorities, there are ways of finding things out."

"Oh, Brice, would you? I would be so grateful!"

His silver-blue eyes narrowed. "If you're that worried, Honor, I'll go over to the courthouse as soon as I finish my coffee."

"Oh, thank you, Brice!" She hesitated. "Do you think I should go with you?"

He shook his head. "I'll go by myself. There are ways of dealing with corrupt officials which I'm sure you wouldn't approve of, sweetheart."

He got up from the table and was out the door in a few minutes. Honor watched him go, biting her lip in trepidation.

"Do you think he'll find out something?" she asked Babs worriedly.

The latter shrugged. "If there's anything to find out."

"What do you mean?"

"I think you're making too much of this whole thing, Honor. I hardly think the law would suddenly decide to come and pick her up after letting the thing go this long. What about her old connections?"

"Her old connections were in Little China, Babs," Honor put in quickly. "Pia would never go back there. She hated the cribs. She—"

"She was a whore for a year, Honor. She had to be pretty used to men and—ah—their charms. Maybe she got homesick for—"

"She wouldn't! She promised me that she would never go back to being a crib girl! She hated that life!"

"What did she have here, Honor?" Babs said softly. "She worked every day in the laundry, doing hard work—getting only her room and board. That's exactly what she got in the cribs, only the work wasn't quite so drudging as washing and ironing. She—"

"She hated it, I'm telling you!" Honor said shrilly. "Can you imagine being twelve years old and having five or six men a day—every day—crawling over you! Yes, she was a whore, she's known men—but I'm telling you she would never go back there willingly." Honor stopped, her expression thunderstruck. "She would never go back there willingly," she repeated slowly. Her eyes went to Babs and the fear in them was easily apparent. "My God! Hoy Tai! Why didn't I think of it before? That Chinese boy—I knew there was something . . ." She started out of the room.

"Honor, where are you going? You can't possibly think you're going to go into Little China and bring Pia back if Tai has anything to do with it! You'd never find her!"

"Somehow he's been watching me all this time. He's seen . . . he knows how I got away from the miner, how you've given me a job—Walter Gordon—everything! He's taken Pia away because he knows that will hurt me! He wants to punish me because things didn't work out as he'd planned. I'm telling you, Babs, he's kidnapped her . . ."

Babs had run around the table and was clutching her arm as though afraid she would try to run away. "Wait, Honor. Wait until Brice gets back, for God's sake! You aren't going to go to Tai by yourself. He'll either kill you—or you'd disappear into one of his cribs and we'd never see you again!"

"I know he's taken Pia, Babs. She would never have gone anywhere by her own volition! Oh, God!" She rubbed her temples with her hands as she thought of what Pia must be going through. "We've got to bring her back!"

"We will bring her back, Honor," Babs said desperately. "Just give me time to think of a plan—and Brice will be back by then. Don't worry!"

"You don't know Tai like I do," Honor said, shivering at the memory. "He's evil and cruel. He won't think anything of sacrificing a young girl to boost his own ego!"

"I know, I know. Calm down a little and have some coffee. You'll feel better and it'll help you think."

Honor finally sat down and accepted the cup of coffee that Babs pushed over to her. "I blame myself for this," she said morosely. "If only I hadn't gone out with Walter, and then not checked on Pia to see if she was in her room. But I didn't think—I didn't know—he could be this cruel, this tenacious. Why won't he leave me alone!"

"I don't know," Babs replied, sipping her coffee and keeping a wary eye on her friend. "What did you do to him, Honor?"

Honor looked at the other girl and her eyes narrowed, catlike. "I wounded his pride, Babs. Isn't that the worst thing you can do to a man?" She was thinking of Brice, too, at that moment.

"He's a bad enemy to have, Honor. I don't know what to say, except we should be thinking of some plan—some way to get her out. Brice can't go in there by himself and expect to come back alive, much less with Pia too."

"You're right. Perhaps we can set up a trap of some sort." Honor wrinkled her brow and put her chin in her hand. "Something he might wish in exchange for Pia's release. Money, perhaps?"

"Money," Bab groaned. "Honey, you know everything I have is tied up in this gambling saloon. We'd need to set it up as collateral to get some kind of loan and these bankers around here—half of them are swindlers and loan sharks. If something went wrong, they would call default and take the saloon away from me."

Honor gazed steadily at the other girl. "You're right, Babs, I can't expect you—and Brice—to give up everything you've worked for because of someone's vendetta against me. I'll have to find the money some other way."

"What will you do—steal a shipment of gold? Rob a bank?" Babs shook her head. "Money, money all around and not a penny do we see," she said ironically.

"Walter Gordon!" Honor threw the name out like a challenge.

"Well, yes, he is loaded with the stuff," Babs admitted, "but—but what if he demands his own kind of collateral, Honor?"

The latter squared her jaw in determination. "All I've got is myself."

"Exactly."

Honor took a deep breath. "Then he can have me, Babs. It's that simple. I'd do anything to save Pia from that awful Tai. She saved my life once—it's the least I can do!"

She got up from the table, prepared to fly upstairs to get her shawl and bonnet in order to go to Walter Gordon. Babs followed her up, a look of distraction on her face. At the door to Honor's room, she stood nervously twisting her hands.

"Brice won't like what you're doing, Honor," she said finally.

Honor whirled around, her shawl clutched in her fist. "I'm not his property, Babs. He doesn't own me!"

"But he—"

"Don't tell me about Brice!" Honor went on heatedly. "He doesn't give a damn about me or Pia!"

"He went to the courthouse," Babs reminded her softly.

"I don't care—I can't wait for him to return. Every minute counts, I'm sure of it! When I think of Pia—" She uttered an exclamation and hurried past Babs out the door.

"You'll need Gordon's address!" Babs called after her, running to catch up with her.

The hansom cab had dropped her off in front of an imposing mansion, one of the first few to begin to dot the area around Nob Hill. Honor did not let the sheer size of the edifice intimidate her, but walked straight up the inlaid-marble steps between two of the imported Italian marble columns and picked up the solid brass knocker to pound hurriedly at the oak door.

A somber, bulky-looking butler answered the door and inquired her name and business, and then had left her standing in the tiled hallway while he disappeared through a door to find his employer.

"Honor O'Brien!" Walter Gordon was hurrying out from one of the maze of doors, his hands outstretched to take hers. "What are you doing here? What luck to see you here when all I've done all morning is think about you!"

His words heartened her and Honor allowed him her hand to kiss, a demure smile on her face. But she realized she had little time for such playacting and must get right to the point.

300

"Walter, I had to come to you! You're the only one who can help me!" she began dramatically.

His brow furrowed as he ushered her into the front parlor, decorated in soft tones of gold and brown. He gestured for her to take a chair and then took one immediately opposite her, leaning forward.

"What is it, Honor? How can I help you?"

"Oh, Walter, I need a small loan in a hurry!"

"You want money—from me?" Walter hid his hurt behind a smooth mask that fell easily into place through long years of practice working with unscrupulous businessmen. He had really thought this one was different, but perhaps she had fooled him completely with her standoffish air. Perhaps she was just like the other women he had come to know. Their type was all over the city, he thought contemptuously. He waited for her to bring in some hard-luck story about the ailing sister, the mother waiting back home to make the journey west. He knew from experience that if he gave her any money at all, he would never see her again.

"Yes, Walter. I'm ashamed to have to come to you like this. I—I know what you must be thinking, but I can't worry about your opinion of me now. A girl's life is in danger. And I—I don't know how to rescue her."

Ah, he thought, it is going as planned. How could I have ever thought she was different from those others? He felt a sadness welling up within him and had the desire to leave her now, walk away before the damning words fell from her lips.

"How much do you need—to rescue this—er—girl?"

Honor raised eyes huge with concern mixed with utter embarrassment. "I don't know how much it will cost, Walter. Hoy Tai is greedy, I know, but—"

"Hoy Tai?" This was a switch in the conversation. "What has Hoy Tai got to do with your need for money?"

"Do you know him?" she asked eagerly. "If you do, you must know what type of man he is—cruel and cunning. I hate him!" she cried out.

"Here, here, Honor, don't fly to pieces now." He soothed her awkwardly, reaching for his handkerchief. He thought that this wasn't going according to the usual plan and felt a small hope stir in his breast. Could she be telling the truth?

Honor took a deep breath and began to tell him how she had come to San Francisco to look for—her brother. (She could never have told him the truth there.) She told him that she had wandered unknowingly into the section of the city known as Little China, omitting the fact that someone had driven her there through her efforts at escape. She certainly did not wish to go into the sordid details of her flight from Don Esteban Sevillas. She explained how she had been taken to a crib run by Ling Chow and had been sold to Hoy Tai as a prostitute. She told him of Pia and how they had come to be friends.

"And when I—when I refused to—to—" She colored in humiliation.

"Go on," he said gently, feeling a smoldering hatred against the man who would abuse this lovely, innocent creature in front of him.

"He sold me for one hundred and fifty dollars to a crude miner who had come into town to spend his gold before returning to the fields. Tai sold Pia along with me. The miner took us to his hotel and—when he tried to rape me, Pia shot him. We escaped and found ourselves at Babs' Den, where I realized that Babs was a friend I had known from the wagon train that brought us west."

"My God!" he whistled sharply. He looked at her strangely. "And so, when you found out that Pia had disappeared, you assumed that Tai had kidnapped her?"

"Yes! He wants to get back at me, because he thought that miner would probably kill me before the year was out, but now he sees that I'm safe with friends, and he wants to hurt me!"

"Tai does carry a grudge," Walter said thoughtfully, rubbing his chin. "I didn't think the bastard would ever try to kidnap and rape a white girl, though."

"He assumed I had no friends or relatives in the city. It would be easy for me to disappear and no one would have cared. But white or yellow, Walter, he's an evil man and I can't—I can't stand to think of Pia in his clutches taking the abuse of his battered pride!"

"I'm only glad he didn't kidnap you, Honor," Walter said softly, reaching out for her hands. "Tell me, though, what makes you think Tai will take an offer of money in exchange for Pia's life?"

She blinked. "Why—what else could he possibly want? He loves money! I've been in his house and he has paintings, statues, so many beautiful things of value in all the rooms!"

"Perhaps you're right then. Maybe he would accept an amount of money in return for Pia's release." He rubbed his chin again. "But how can you be sure that he will stop now?

This could easily turn into a kind of blackmail, Honor. Maybe it's you he really wants to humiliate! Maybe you'll have to make payments to him for the rest of your time in the city—like those Sydney Town loan sharks who set their cronies on anyone who can't pay. It can be terrifying, Honor."

"Then, after Pia is released, I'll—I'll leave San Francisco," she declared solemnly. "Pia and I will go back east—somewhere . . ."

"You don't sound very confident, Honor," he said gently. There was a long silence before he spoke again. "Honor, I want to help you," he began after a long moment. "But I don't want to see you get hurt. I do—care—what happens to you."

She blushed. "Thank you, Walter." She passed her tongue over her dry lips. "I realize that you would be getting nothing in return for your money. All I have to offer is—myself." Her green eyes looked directly into his.

He had the grace to redden. "You would hate me if I accepted such an offer, Honor—wouldn't you?"

She took a deep breath. "If you're willing to risk the loss of your investment, Walter, I'm willing to do anything you wish. I would consider it an account paid."

He hated her businesslike attitude. He wanted something more from her than just a cheap whore's settlement. He found himself studying the young woman before him intently. God, she was achingly lovely, and wellbred . . . No, he was crazy even to think it! he chided himself. But the thought somehow wriggled into his brain and took root—remained there and flowered and the possibility hit him like a blow.

"Honor, I want you to marry me!"

Honor thought she hadn't heard him right for a moment, but when she looked at him, she could see the earnest sincerity on his face. His blue eyes met her gaze without deception and his hands were held out in front of him almost as though in supplication.

"Walter, I—you can't mean such a thing!" she countered in surprise.

"I do mean it. Honor, I know I love you," he said in a low, deep voice. "I've loved you ever since I first saw you at the gambling saloon. I knew, even then, that you didn't belong there. I was lonely and you seemed so bright and sincere and trusting. How could I help falling in love with you?"

"But, Walter, I don't love you," she said helplessly.

"It doesn't matter. I know everyone will say you're young

enough to be my daughter—that you are, in fact, the same age—but it doesn't matter. Let me take care of you, Honor!"

She sighed. It would be so nice to say yes, to put aside any doubts she might have, to let this strong man protect her from people like Hoy Tai and the miner and—and Brice . . .

"If I said no, Walter, would you refuse me the money to help Pia?"

He shook his head. "I couldn't do that to you, Honor. I wouldn't make it a 'Marry me or else . . .' proposition. I love you too much for that."

"I must think about it," she said desperately. "But I haven't got time to think about Pia. Will you help me now, Walter? We can—think about marriage after Pia is safe."

"All right," he said, clearly disappointed. "I know you're right. We must act quickly, for if I know Hoy Tai, he's quite capable of sending the girl back to China as a slave."

"Oh, thank you," she breathed and her impetuosity carried her over to his waiting arms. His mouth came down to find hers and she was surprised and vaguely stirred by the power of his kiss. God, and his arms were strongs—so strong!

He released her with regret and left her to wait in the parlor while he went upstairs to change and make arrangements to send a messenger on to Hoy Tai so that they could meet in his business offices. He had no intention of putting Honor in any danger by going directly to Tai's residence in Little China.

When the messenger had been sent, he ordered a carriage and he and Honor drove swiftly to his office on Montgomery Street next to the offices of Wells, Fargo. He commented with a touch of humor that it had been luck that he had been able to rent office space next to the famed guardians of gold shipments.

They were forced to wait nearly two hours before a carriage pulled up in the street and Hoy Tai, dressed impeccably in business suit and the absurd little derby, descended to the curb. He paused to brush an imaginary speck of lint from his sleeve and then entered the downstairs office, which housed Gordon's secretary and others in his firm.

In no time at all, a discreet knock on the door was followed by Hoy Tai, grinning disarmingly as he entered, swinging his walking stick jauntily ahead of him.

"Good afternoon, Mr. Gordon," he said, ignoring Honor's presence.

"Please sit down, Tai," Walter said perfunctorily. He

turned to Honor. "Perhaps it would be best if you would wait outside, my dear."

She nodded, her eyes flashing her hatred at the Chinaman, who returned the look with rude disdain.

Outside in the small waiting room, she strode back and forth nervously, her fingers itching to claw at the round, yellow face inside Gordon's office. It seemed forever before the door opened and Hoy Tai, looking debonair as always, left the office, an enigmatic smile on his face. The black, slanted eyes touched her for a moment and their malevolence was almost tangible. Honor stepped back instinctively.

"You have won—for now, green eyes," he said in a low voice. "But Hoy Tai will have the last round."

He left abruptly, leaving Honor weaving with the force of his hatred. Walter, seeing her pale face and closed eyes, hurried to her immediately and caught her as she was about to slump forward.

"Are you all right, Honor? What did he say to you?"

"Nothing, Walter," she whispered faintly. "I'm—I'm just relieved that it's over. He said—he said we'd won. Does that mean Pia is free to come back to me?"

He nodded. The look in his eyes told her that the girl had not come back cheaply. She felt terrible, knowing how the Chinaman must have been able to name his price. A sick feeling of nausea rose in her throat.

"When—how?"

"Tonight. Two of his men will drive her here to the office. I didn't want to take a chance of them hurting you at Babs' Den."

"Oh, thank God! Then you'll be here to bring her back?"

He nodded. "I'm going to order a carriage, Honor. I want you to take it back to my house and wait for me there."

She shook her head. "I must go back to Babs," she said. "She will be worried and I have to tell her what has happened. Please, please bring Pia back as soon as you can."

He nodded helplessly. "You're sure you don't want to go back to Nob Hill. I would feel better, Honor, knowing you were safe back there—"

"No, I can't go there—yet. Please, Walter."

The lovely green eyes looked so distressed, so unwilling to hurt, but so desperate that he had to give in.

"All right, then, but I forbid you to be at the roulette wheel tonight."

She nodded in acquiescence and he breathed a sigh of relief.

Honor was at the roulette wheel that night, for the simple reason that she couldn't stand the waiting alone in her room. She went through the motions of the play mechanically, looking up sharply when anyone entered the saloon. She knew Brice was watching her and remembered their earlier argument with a shudder.

He had been angry when she returned to Babs' Den, accusing her of going immediately where the money was to flaunt herself in order to get back her friend.

"What kind of deal have you made this time?" he asked sarcastically. "Don't tell me!" His look could have killed. "You couldn't wait for me to get back so we could sit down and think this thing out. You had to go flying off to Gordon and barter your body for his money!"

"I couldn't wait, Brice! I was too scared and worried about Pia! I knew the authorities weren't going to help us look for a lost Chinese girl! Please, don't be angry with me. I only did what I thought was best!"

"Best for whom?" he asked cuttingly.

She had stiffened at his implied accusation. "I don't give a damn what you think, Brice Devlin!" she had yelled at him then. "You don't care about me so stay out of my life!"

"Most happy to oblige!" he snickered. "Just make sure you're at the roulette wheel tonight or you're fired!"

"Fired!"

"I'm sure you won't have far to look for aid," he cut in contemptuously.

Then he was gone, leaving her quivering with anger and hurt so that she vowed she wouldn't play the roulette wheel whether he fired her or not. But eventually the worry and the waiting had gotten to her and she had changed and gone downstairs, only fifteen minutes late. She hated the smile of sleek satisfaction on Brice's face, but chose to ignore him for the rest of the evening, putting all her attention on the door.

It was nearly midnight, and she was gnawing distractedly at her lower lip when she glanced up to see Walter Gordon in the doorway, beckoning to her. His face was grim, paler than usual, and icy fear slithered up the back of her neck. She whispered to one of the other dealers to watch the wheel and hurried to Gordon, her mouth too dry to utter any questions.

He indicated the carriage. "She's in there, Honor, but—" He held her back. "She's dying," he said flatly.

"Dying!" Honor clutched at his jacket, her eyes round with dread.

"Let me carry her upstairs around back. I'll bring her up to your room," he said gently.

Honor nodded, her body numb as she saw Walter reach into the carriage and bring out the slight body of the young girl. She followed him anxiously, hearing the ragged breathing coming from the girl's chest as she watched it rise and fall with little continuity.

When they arrived in her room, she indicated the bed and Walter set Pia down on it carefully.

"When they brought her to us—"

"Please," Honor whispered, going to the bed, her eyes brimming with tears. "Please leave me alone with her for a few moments."

He bowed his head and closed the door. Honor took the girl's hand in her own and was struck at its coldness. Desperately she tried to warm it between her two palms.

"Pia, it's Honor," she got out with difficulty, leaning over the girl's closed eyes. "Pia, please come back to me," she choked.

The bluish eyelids opened, fluttered and opened again. The black eyes were cloudy as they looked at the face above her.

"M-missy Honor," she sighed and tried to smile.

"Pia, I tried to get help to you as soon as I could," Honor whispered desperately. "I'm sorry, I'm so sorry that I didn't come sooner."

"No blame s-self," the girl whispered with difficulty. "Hoy Tai w-wants your d-death!"

"Pia, I swear I will see you avenged," Honor said with an intense hatred in her voice. "How did he do this to you?"

"The d-drug—so many bright c-colors, and then m-much darkness."

"Opium! He gave you opium!" Honor ground her teeth and pressed the thin hand against her cheek. "Oh, Pia—he shall see hell for this, I promise you!"

Pia looked gravely at the face above hers, wishing she could speak, could tell her that she was glad it had been her and not Honor who had known the force of Tai's hatred. She knew he hated Honor with a poison in his blood that could not be rinsed away without her death. Yes, she was glad that he had not caught Honor, but—it was hard—this dying.

"I—shall—l-look down on y-you f-from the h-heavens," she gasped, and with the smallest of sighs, she was gone.

Honor held the limp, cold hand in her own, staring down at the face, the eyes closed forever in death. So young, so young! She wept despairingly, hating Tai, but pushing the hatred aside to hold the utter grief that consumed her at this child's death. Needless death—wasteful death. Why had this happened?

"I was too late, Pia," she whispered, wetting the hand she held with her tears. "Too late to save you, little one," she grieved, remembering anew how the girl had saved her from death at the hands of the miner.

Sobbing, uncontrolled, shook her body as she pressed her face into the bedclothes. Poor little child of destiny, she thought. She had never had control over her own life—had been the slave of others from childhood—had never really had a childhood. I promise, she thought, looking up into the still face, I promise that you will be avenged, Pia. You will look down from the heavens and watch Tai suffer for your death.

She didn't even hear the door open and close, nor the footsteps of the man who reached down to bring her up against his chest. She only cried the harder into his shirtfront, wetting the material.

"She's gone," she gasped. "He killed her!"

"Honor, I'm sorry." Incredibly, it was Brice holding her, stroking her hair and murmuring soothing words to her.

Honor looked up, tears shiny wet in her green eyes. "Oh, Brice, I—I couldn't save her," she whispered.

He held her close, his hands strong and tense against her back and shoulders. "Tai will be punished for this," he said softly. "Tomorrow I'll go to the courthouse and—"

"The courthouse!" She pushed herself out of his arms. "The law won't do anything about this! You know yourself that they could care less how many like Pia are killed!"

He looked at her carefully. "What would you want me to do, Honor? It would be suicide to walk into Little China and try to kill him! He's got men, bodyguards who watch for such attempts on his life. Don't you think others have tried! He's got many enemies all over the city—but he still lives, Honor."

"So you think the authorities are going to do anything about him?" she demanded.

"With enough money in the right pockets—"

"You're lying! You went up on your high horse about having to pay money out from your precious saloon for Pia's rescue! You certainly won't be able to grease enough palms sufficiently to bring Hoy Tai to justice!"

"Then what do you suggest?" he asked impatiently.

"A trap! Set a trap for him and kill him without benefit of any so-called trial!" Her eyes were blazing fiercely in her pale face.

"Honor, don't be a fool. Tai won't fall for any trap you or I could think up! He'd smell a rat quicker than we could set the bait!"

She shook her head vehemently. "I promised Pia that he would see hell, Brice. I'm not going back on my word. I don't care what it takes! I'll go in there myself!"

He caught her by the arms and shook her, hard. "You'll go in to your death! Honor, for God's sake, this is what he wants you to do! He knows just what effect Pia's death will have on you and what your reaction will be! Believe me, if you let yourself fall into his hands a second time, he'll make you suffer a hell of a lot more than Pia did! You won't come out alive either!"

"I don't care!" She looked up into his face, her eyes brilliant and determined. "I don't care, Brice! I'll find some way to kill him—even if it means my death would follow his!"

"Honor, you can't throw your life away!" he said just as fiercely.

"Why not! For whom should I save it, Brice?" she asked him steadily.

He glared down at her, wishing he could shake some sense into that stubborn head of hers. His silence seemed to Honor to be his answer.

"No one," she returned, fighting back the tears now. "Please ask Babs to come up," she said tiredly. "I'll have to make some arrangements for Pia's burial."

"Honor, I won't let you do something foolish," he warned her, heading for the door.

She smiled wanly, but said nothing.

Thirty-nine

"Goddammit, Devlin! You drove her to this!" Walter Gordon stamped up and down in his office, his hands behind his back, glaring at his unexpected visitor.

"It doesn't matter who drove her to it, Gordon. She's gone, disappeared—and I have a good idea where she went." Brice was leaning against the back of an armchair, his studied air of nonchalance belying the churning fear in his guts. The little fool had gone, had gone to Tai, he was sure of it! When he got his hands on her—if he got his hands on her—he'd bring that stubborn little mule to heel if he had to lock her in her room.

"She's gone to Tai, of course. To bargain with him?" Gordon shrugged. "I don't know what she's trying to do—I wish I did!"

"Well, we can't stand around here trying to divine what goes on in that stubborn little mind of hers," Brice put in impatiently. "We've got to go in there and find her!"

"We've got to figure out a way to go in without alerting Tai what we're up to." Gordon thought a moment, running his hands through his hair. "Tai knows me—and he knows of my acquaintace with Honor, so there's no way I can surprise him on that score. But you, on the other hand, have had no dealings with Tai directly."

"I'm not following you, Gordon," Brice put in pointedly.

"It might be a good idea, in order to allay any suspicions, to present you as a 'businessman,' an 'importer' who's interested in obtaining some Chinese tarts for a certain enterprise of yours. Tai can't object to that."

"But he'd want to meet in his business office—not his home."

"True. And we can't even be sure that Honor is there. She could still be in hiding somewhere in Little China, awaiting her chance. Or he could have already found her and put her in one of his cribs, assuming there would be a rescue attempt."

"So far, you've painted it all rather black," Brice said slowly. "I think your idea is good. I could pose as an interested purchaser of goods and suggest a meeting at our leisure in his place of residence. Do you think he'd be suspicious? At least, if I obtained access inside, I might be able to find out just where Honor is."

"You could be putting yourself in danger, Devlin."

The latter shrugged. "I've been putting myself in danger for that little termagant ever since I met her," he said thoughtfully.

Gordon would have liked to question the other man on just exactly what he meant, but realized that jealousy had no place in their present situation. If they succeeded in getting Honor out, there would be plenty of time for her to think about his marriage proposal. He knew instinctively that Devlin was not the man to offer marriage and Honor would have to see the wisdom of the more honorable proposal. But first things first . . . they had to get her away from Tai.

"I guess it's the best way to start out," he agreed to Devlin's idea.

"Good, I'll contact one of his agents first thing and hope for a meeting tonight."

"Tai works slowly," Gordon warned. "We might have to cool our heels for a while while he sniffs out the lay of the land."

Devlin shrugged. "I'll send the messenger as soon as I return to Babs' Den."

"Why don't you set up residence at one of the hotels? Tai might check on your cover and it would make more sense for you to be, say, at the International. Agreed?"

Brice nodded. "I'll move a few things over there this afternoon."

"Good, if you're low on cash, I'll be glad—"

"I've got enough," Brice returned stiffly and hurried out of his office.

Honor bit her lip and crouched low against one of the walls in the little alleyway where she had taken refuge from the man who had been following her since she had left Babs' Den and made for Little China. She hadn't gotten a good look at him, but she knew he was trailing her, for he was exceptionally tall and she had seen him several times a few yards behind her.

She wondered if he was one of Tai's men. It was a good possibility. She'd have to be careful to keep a good distance ahead of him, for she didn't want to be taken to Tai just yet. If it were possible, she had hopes of getting to his house and

311

somehow sneaking in. She remembered the little door in the fence around the back of his house. Perhaps there would be a way to get in. She patted the knife she had strapped to her ankle and felt the cool bulk of the derringer at the arch of her foot inside the boots. The gun impeded her from running too fast, but it might prove her only means of taking out her revenge on Hoy Tai, and she wasn't about to put it where he might easily find it.

She looked back and spotted the tall man lounging negligently against the wall. A group of small children, a rare sight in Little China, ran by, shouting and playing with sticks, drawing the man's attention for a moment to enable Honor to slip out of her hiding place and resume her dogged path toward Tai's house.

She wasn't sure she remembered exactly where it was. After all, she had been blindfolded most of the way out and had been driven to it the first time in a closed carriage. But she vowed to search every street until she found it.

Hours seemed to drag by while she passed raunchy cribs with small, round faces pressed curiously against the prison-like bars of the windows. Parlor houses, a step up from the cribs, were more gay, with music floating out of some. There was much squalor and refuse lined most of the alleys. Honor felt her heart go out to the people who were forced to live in such a way. And then there were those, like Hoy Tai, who thrived in such squalor, who used its power to threaten those men from whom he obtained tribute for his protection.

She hurried along, avoiding the open streets as much as possible, looking back constantly for the tall man following her. At last, when the hour was growing late and she despaired of finding the house in the encroaching darkness, she spied the place she sought. Her heart lifted at the thought of her revenge and she made her way toward the house, creeping softly around toward the short alley that was bordered on one side by the fence.

She found the gate, but it was locked fast and wouldn't budge an inch at her questing hand. Disappointed, she thought of climbing the wall, but judged it too smooth to gain a foothold. She looked around in dejection, for boxes or crates of some kind that would enable her to make a ladder to climb over, but the alley was clean.

"Why don't you knock on the front door, green eyes? I just might let you in."

She whirled around to see Hoy Tai, smiling cunningly at

her, dressed in his tailored business suit, which somehow made him seem more threatening than ever. She recovered from her shock at discovery and made herself smile back at him.

"Did you wish to see me, green eyes?" he asked when she remained silent.

"See you dead!" she hissed, still smiling at him, but her eyes had already picked out the bulge of a pistol beneath his chest.

"I see the sting of the viper in your eyes, little one. You dare to threaten Hoy Tai on his own ground?" He seemed amused by her defiance. "It does you little good to try to avenge yourself on me, green eyes."

"You killed Pia!" she accused, her voice low and vibrant with emotion.

He shrugged. "She refused to return to the cribs for me."

"You had no right to kidnap her!" she shouted. "She was paid for in gold. You no longer owned her!"

"I never give up anything of mine," he warned her steadily. "Just as you are still mine. The miner is dead, you belong to me again."

"I belong to no one!"

He laughed. "Stubborn little devil, I could crush you beneath my feet. I could raise my pistol and shoot you between those lovely eyes without a moment's hesitation."

"Or drug me as you did Pia? Overdose me so that I do not know what is happening?" she threw at him contemptuously. "Are you so little of a man, Hoy Tai, that you must first drug your women before they can bring themselves to serve you?"

He bristled at her insults. "You shall pay for that!" he warned her. "Hoy Tai has no need to listen to your dribble! You will serve me tonight, green eyes, without benefit of drugs to lessen your threshold of pain!" he said with a hint of promise in his black eyes.

Honor stood proudly, her defiance making her green eyes sparkle. She was lovely, Hoy Tai thought objectively. It would be too bad to have to kill her. He raised his hand and immediately two men appeared out of nowhere. The tall man was Cudow, the one Honor remembered from her earlier experience with Tai. Both men seized her arms and dragged her inside the house, taking her upstairs to the room she remembered.

"Strip her!" Tai ordered, leaving her with the two body-guards while he retired to change into his robe.

When he had returned, Honor was naked, flung on the pillows that lay in disarray about the floor. In Cudow's hands were the knife and the derringer. Tai smiled unpleasantly.

"How interesting to see just what your intentions were!" he hissed. "So, you planned to kill me, foolish girl! You could no more kill me than Pia could have!" He clapped his hands and the two men left the room.

"Now, since you did not wish the bliss of the opium, you will feel the lash of the whip, green eyes!"

Honor looked about the room, noting that her weapons had been placed on a small side table close to the outer door of the room. She made a move toward them and felt a scalding pain glance across her thigh. She looked down in surprise to see a red welt rising on her bare skin.

Behind her, Tai stood smiling, drawing the silky leather through his hands as he watched her reaction like a hunting master watching the hounds when they had failed to take advantage of the cornered hare.

"Yes, why don't you try to reach them?" he laughed, nodding toward the weapons. "Please do try, green eyes. For every step you take there will be another welt on your smooth flesh. Such a pity to mar its perfection." He shook his head in mock sorrow.

"But I will still keep going until I reach them," she returned defiantly, taking another step. She felt the sting of the whip against her buttocks.

With determination, she broke into a run, her hand stretched out to snatch the derringer, but on fleet foot behind her, Hoy Tai snaked the whip out to knock the weapons to the floor. He caught her leg with the whip and she fell to her knees.

"Get up, green eyes, get up!" he cried out, laughing at her attempts to rise.

She could hear the note of excitement creeping into his voice. He was dominating her, bringing her to heel, and it excited him beyond all reason. His breath was coming faster and his black eyes glistened as they roved over her nudity. She inched toward the weapons. If only she could reach one of them . . .

Hoy Tai's body knocked her to the side; she could feel his weight pressing in on top of her. He had pulled off his robe and knelt above her, reaching down to pull her onto her back. She could see the proof of his whetted desire and cringed away from the reality of how he meant to subjugate her woman's flesh.

"Green eyes," he whispered, smothering his face in her neck when he had rolled her over. "I must—have—you," he said brokenly, biting painfully into the skin of her shoulder.

"You'll not be having her where you're going, yellow bastard!"

Honor looked over Tai's shoulder and saw Brice Devlin's face, dark with rage and hatred as he leveled the gun in front of him. Tai had turned too, in a reflex action, his mouth open in astonishment, but before he could cry out, Brice shot him cleanly between the eyes, causing his body to jump back and fall away from Honor, who was shaking with reaction.

"Oh, Brice!" she cried out, beginning to weep at the enormity of what had happened.

She scrambled to her feet and ran to place her arms around him. "Oh, Brice! Thank God you came!"

He was so still, she thought he might have been wounded in getting upstairs. She looked up, her cheeks wet with tears, and saw him staring soberly at the man he had just shot.

"That's three men—dead because of you, Honor," he said slowly. "Three men I've killed because of you."

"But—but he would have killed me, Brice, if you hadn't—"

"If you hadn't gone off by yourself like some mule-headed fool, if you had listened to me and let me handle it, this wouldn't have happened!"

She looked up at him unbelievingly. "What do you mean! He deserved to die! He killed Pia—and—and how many others! He would have killed me without a moment's hesitation and yet you stand here as though I had condemned you for what you did!"

She stepped away from him and looked around distractedly for her clothing. "What of the others? There were two of them," she said, straining to keep her voice from cracking.

"Knocked out cold." His voice was flat.

She glanced up quickly. "We've got to get out of here, Brice, before anyone else comes along. How did you—how did you find me?"

"I followed Tai here after he refused to swallow the story Gordon and I made up. It was easy enough. He must have known you'd be here and I think the excitement of that made

315

him careless. It was easy to follow him. I surprised the other two with the butt of my pistol."

She shuddered. "Come along then, we must hurry," she urged after she had put on her clothes haphazardly. "You have a horse?"

He nodded, then shook himself. His gaze was as cold as winter. "That's the last time I'll kill for you, Honor," he said quietly.

She didn't answer him, but followed him silently as he led her downstairs and back to his horse, which led them out of Little China. Their work there was finished.

Forty

"Honor, you must realize how ridiculous this is!" Walter Gordon protested, as he paced around the chair in which Honor sat, her hands folded demurely in her lap.

"What is so ridiculous, Walter?" she asked innocently. "I told you already that I can't marry you. It wouldn't be fair to you."

"But it is fair to put yourself up to public scrutiny by offering to be my housekeeper?" He groaned aloud. "Honor, why are you doing this? Why don't you just marry me?"

She shook her head. "I can't, Walter. Please don't ask me again. Perhaps, someday when I can forget about—"

"Brice Devlin! That's it, isn't it!" He rubbed his forehead in irritation. "Honor, why throw your life away on that man when he has no intention of marrying you—ever!"

"I wouldn't marry him if he asked me," she put in quickly. "It's not just him, anyway. It's a lot of things, Walter. I can't honestly say that I love you or that I want to spend the rest of my life with you."

"Is it my age?"

"No, if I loved you, that wouldn't matter. Please, Walter, why can't you accept me as your employee for a little while? It would mean a lot to me."

"So you could get away from Babs' Den—and him?" Walter took several turns about the room before he stood in front of the girl, his legs braced apart.

"Yes, I admit it," she put in, chin up defiantly.

316

"Did he throw you out?" He looked like a bear, poised to attack.

"No." She looked away from his gaze. "The last few weeks have been—well—most uncomfortable, to say the least. I really don't think I could go on living here after everything that has happened. When Brice looks at me, sometimes I think he hates me! I—I can't explain it, Walter."

"But to offer to be my housekeeper, for God's sake! I've never had one in all my married years and I'm not sure I want to take one on now. Why don't you just come up and live here with me . . ."

She raised her brows teasingly. "Now who's talking about public scrutiny, Walter?" she chided softly. "Everyone would label me your mistress then."

"They will anyway," he assured her, then he leaned closer and looked into her eyes. "Maybe that's not such a bad idea, Honor."

She blushed. "If that's what you expect, Walter, then perhaps I had best try for employment somewhere else."

He pulled at his hair distractedly. "Dammit all, woman! Why must you be so damn stubborn! You'd be working flat on your back from midnight till four at most of those gambling saloons." He sighed heavily. "I still say it's ridiculous, and I don't know why I'm agreeing, but—all right, you can stay on as my housekeeper!"

"Oh, Walter, thank you!" She got up from her chair to throw her arms around him, hugging him with relief.

At the display, Walter Gordon felt his arms coming up around her slender back, pressing her closer to him while his head bent automatically to kiss her. Quickly she slipped out of his arms. He groaned aloud.

"It'll never work," he warned her direly. Then as she looked up at him with a puzzled look, "I'll have to make sure you've got a lock on your bedroom door." He started to leave the room, then turned back to her. "You can sleep in the room off the library. I had it built for the use of out-of-town business clients, but it will be yours from now on."

"And where is your bedroom, Walter?" she asked, eyes widening.

"On the second floor!" he threw back at her and left her with instructions to gather her things and he would be waiting downstairs in the hansom cab to take her to his home.

Honor watched him go, feeling guilty that she had extracted such a hard bargain from him, but also feeling relieved that he hadn't pressed her on marriage. She knew she couldn't marry him while she still loved Brice. Brice might never come to love her, nor would he ever ask her to marry him, but she couldn't ruin Walter's life by bringing secrets into their marriage. She just hoped that she could run Walter's house smoothly and somehow save enough money to go back east someday. Perhaps she could find work as a governess or secretary in one of the big cities. She hated to be vague about her own future, but she really didn't know what she was going to do at this point. She would just let things take their course, and hopefully they would turn out for the best.

She would have to inform Babs of her decision to leave and hoped that Babs would save her the formality of telling Brice.

After she had gotten her things together and had instructed one of the houseboys to take them downstairs to the waiting hansom, Honor went looking for Babs. She entered the kitchens, where Lolly was sampling a new concoction that she wanted to try out on the clients that night.

Unfortunately Brice had just returned from some business errand and had come through the kitchens to get a bite to eat. He looked up as Honor entered, then hooded his eyes as he studiously ignored her.

"Do you know where I might find Babs?" Honor asked tightly.

He shrugged. "I've been out all morning, Honor. I don't know where she is."

"I have to talk to her. I—I have decided to take another position," she got out with difficulty. It was hard to talk to the back of someone's head.

He turned curiously. "With another saloon?"

She shook her head. "Walter Gordon has—asked me to be his housekeeper in order to—"

"His *what?*" Brice laughed out loud, a contemptuous laughter that seemed to slice through the air.

Lolly had already discreetly disappeared into the pantry.

"His housekeeper," Honor replied defiantly, her green eyes challenging him to make anything else of it.

"Honor, you amaze me!" he said mockingly. "Do you expect me—or anyone else—to believe that you are actually going to be employed by Walter Gordon to keep house! Don't be ridiculous!"

"I don't care what you think, Brice Devlin. It's the truth and if you're too dirty-minded to believe me, that's your problem! You can't possibly think that I would remain here—perhaps as one of the fixtures on the wall?"

His silver-blue eyes narrowed and lit up with amusement. "Is that what's riling you, Honor? I'm not paying enough attention to you?"

He moved toward her like a stalking panther, and Honor backed up uncertainly, not sure what he intended. He came closer until they stood within arm's length.

"You know," he said silkily, "it *has* been a long time, hasn't it, Honor?"

"Not long enough!" she retorted quickly, beginning to back through the door that led into the outer corridor. "If you think—"

"Honor, you must forgive me for ignoring the needs of a young woman of such highly sexed parts as yourself," he continued, coming closer still. "If only you had told me, intimated that you were longing for—"

"Get away from me, Brice Devlin! Walter Gordon is waiting for me!"

"I don't give a damn, he can wait all day and all night! You've reminded me of my neglect and I mean to rectify it. Besides, you owe me, Honor, and I mean to lay claim to the debt."

"I don't owe you anything!" she cried out, beginning to panic.

With a quick flurry of skirts, she turned and made a dash for the saloon door, but he was too quick for her and in another moment, he had scooped her up in his arms and was carrying her upstairs. Mortified and angry, she tried to beat at him with her fists, but he lifted the skirt of of her gown and wrapped it tightly about her arms.

"God, I can't think why I've waited so long," he said to her with a victorious laugh. "It really is so damn simple."

"Brice, you can't do this to me. I don't want—"

"You want it, Honor, dammit, admit you want me!"

She colored fiercely and pressed her lips together. They had arrived upstairs and he kicked the door of his room open to allow them entrance. When he had set her down, he turned, closed the door and locked it. In a moment, she was flying at him, ready to scratch and claw.

"You always were a feisty bitch, Honor," he chuckled delightedly, catching her arms. "But I'm just the man who can tame you," he added arrogantly.

With an ease which infuriated her, he picked her up again

and flung her on his bed, holding her down with his body while he proceeded to rip at the buttons of her bodice. When he had succeeded in peeling her gown off her, he pulled her petticoats over her face to disorient her long enough to take off her shoes and stockings.

Impeded by the material of her petticoats, half-choking with his weight on top of her, Honor tried to break free of the muslin and lace, but realized it was futile until he pulled her petticoats down. She heard him laughing with amused mockery and stiffened. She would show him just how much she wanted him, she vowed angrily.

He pulled her petticoats over her head, giving her no chance to impede him, but she realized her arms were free as he threw the petticoats to the side and slid his hands to the waist tabs of her chemise to rip it away. Immediately she reached up and punched him in the chin with her fist.

He recoiled instinctively so that the blow was only glancing, but he looked down at her with increased amusement.

"Damn, if she doesn't fight like a street-bred whore!" he said to himself. And with one swipe he had ripped her chemise in two and had pulled the two halves apart. Before she could get her second wind, Honor realized she was naked beneath him.

Fearfully she looked up into the silvery-blue eyes and saw the lust in them. Lust and desire and something else mixed up and darkening his eyes to a smoky blue as he raked her flesh with his glance. She hadn't felt so vulnerable since Hoy Tai had drugged her and tried to force himself on her. My God! Panic welled up in her throat and her eyes widened into green pools of fear.

She hadn't truly had a man since Brice himself had made such tender love to her in the little valley on Sevillas' ranch. All the men since then—Esteban, who had tried to subjugate her; Hoy Tai, who had tried to drug her; Jaime, who had tried to understand her—they had all passed so quickly through her life without really touching her. She had been able to keep those men away from the core of her heart, around which she had built up a protective shell. But not this man—not Brice, she thought with despair. Brice would use her and then throw her away and her heart would break.

She turned her face away from the brightness of his gaze. She couldn't bear for him to see the turmoil, the fear, the love in her own eyes.

Brice was beginning to caress her, softly and expertly, as
320

she remembered from that time so long ago in the meadow on Don Esteban's ranch. Despite herself, she felt her body opening to him, responding as only he could make it respond.

His long-fingered, lean brown hands seemed to glide smoothly over her pale flesh, feeling the texture, the softness with intrinsic patience. Her breasts tightened and the points lifted to catch his palm as it glided over them. Her mouth was open as if gasping for air.

With complete authority, Brice was mastering her will to fight him. She admitted, if only to herself, that she *had* wanted this from him, that she didn't want to fight.

He was kneeling above her, unbuttoning his own shirt, his knees on either side of her hips as he stared down at her with lazy desire, knowing he had her completely at his mercy. God knew how many men she'd lain with, he thought, but right now, he didn't give a damn! She was the only woman he had ever known with whom he wanted only to be gentle and soft, but ended up being cruel and demanding. But now, she was acquiescing, her body responding exquisitely to his touch.

He had removed his shirt and was about to unbutton his trousers when a loud pounding on the door made them both jerk their heads up.

"Honor! Honor, I know you're in there, dammit! Is he hurting you?"

"Walter!" Honor whispered, her eyes flying to meet Brice's.

"Of course," he replied calmly, his mouth narrowing. "The forgotten cuckold, I presume."

Honor looked up quickly at the venom in his tone. She blushed. "Oh, Brice, it's not like that between Walter and me. I—"

But he was already sliding off her, flinging his shirt back on, leaving it unbuttoned as he went to the door, giving Honor only a moment to fling the heap of petticoats over the more strategic parts of her body.

Outside in the hall, Gordon was red-faced with rage. "You! I should have known you wouldn't let her leave you without first humiliating her like this!" he accused.

"Humiliating her!" Brice laughed with mocking contempt. "Gordon, you surprise me. Do you mean you didn't know how hot this young lady has always been for me? Why, I recall—"

"That's enough!" Gordon roared, bringing up his fists.

Brice sidestepped him swiftly, an infuriating grin still on his face. "Please, Gordon, I really don't think she's worth fisticuffs between two—gentlemen—like ourselves! As you can see, she is over on the bed, ready and willing to pleasure whichever one of us gets to stay. Shall we toss a coin?"

"You bastard!" Gordon got out. "I should kill you for that!"

Honor thought she was going to die at the cruelty in Brice's words. How could he talk about her like that! She took avantage of the two men's inattention to grab her dress and slip it over her arms, tugging it around her hips.

Walter looked up to see her bending to gather her underthings after slipping her shoes on. He held out a hand to her. "Come on, Honor. There's no need for you to remain here and listen to this man's insults."

"Oh, Walter, do you mean you would still have me?" she asked him quietly.

His eyes were understanding and she felt ashamed of herself for asking him the question. Between them stood Brice Devlin, his eyes wintery, hard as he noted the silent communication between the two of them. For a moment, he turned toward Honor as though to speak to her, to convey something of his mixed-up emotions—his anger that she had another man who wanted to protect her and his hungering need for her that made him want to kill the man who offered her another love. But he rejected the idea of love, telling himself that he would not commit himself to this one woman whom he felt he couldn't really trust. And so, he stepped back and the twisting in his gut made him hard.

"Go to your 'employer' then, Honor," he said savagely. "Tell him how much you love him and perhaps this time your ploy will work."

Honor gazed into his face, her green eyes wet with tears. It was as though he were tearing her heart out with his cruel barbs. "I did love you, Brice," she said tearfully, "but you have chosen to throw my love away. I will not allow you to hurt me again."

Then, regally, as though she were not naked beneath her gown, she walked out of his room, her hand lightly on the arm of Walter Gordon, leaving Brice to watch her with a wealth of jealousy, of bitterness and of something else that he refused to admit—even to himself.

Forty-one

August was bitterly hot that year of 1858. Even built as it was on a hill, Walter Gordon's house helped little to cool the sticky days and nights.

Honor's room, being on a corner, did get a slight cross-draft from the two windows on the two walls of her room, but it was still uncomfortable sleeping at night. She looked forward to the coming of autumn and the cooling rains.

The title of housekeeper had never really seemed to fit and so, by mutual agreement, she was known as Gordon's secretary. In fact, she did do quite a bit of paperwork for him as she wrote a clear, legible hand and he was often too busy to see to some of the minor details. She enjoyed replying to the mothers of marriageable daughters that Mr. Gordon would be delighted to join them for afternoon tea, but he had other engagements. Soberly she realized that she should be hoping for just the opposite—that Walter would go and find a woman who was more than willing to marry him.

Some of Walter's correspondence was private and she was not allowed to read it, but these were mostly having to do with different business schemes and she had an idea that he didn't especially want her finding out about some of his more unorthodox business methods. Walter Gordon, after all, did not make his fortune by being the kind of man that people walked over. She would read with the greatest enthusiasm the months-old papers that arrived from St. Louis or New York, surprised to see that the threat of war, which she remembered only vaguely even as far back as when her father had been alive, was now very real—at least back on the eastern coast. Here in California, war seemed very remote. There were very few Negro slaves as the Indians provided better labor and were more used to the conditions.

It was another hot, sweltering day in mid-August when Honor walked into Walter's office to see to the mail, when she was surprised to see Walter himself already seated at his desk, frowning over a letter in his hands. He looked up distractedly at her entrance.

"You're up early today," she remarked, pulling back the thick velvet drapes to allow more light into the room.

He shrugged. "Shouldn't sleep so late, it makes me feel older."

She noticed the continued frown and risked a question. "Is it some bad news, Walter?"

He looked up and she could see the indecision in his eyes. "Honor," he said finally, "have I ever told you about my daughter?"

She nodded. "A little—that she was married . . ."

"She's married to a bastard," he commented matter-of-factly.

"Walter, I don't think I—"

"It's all right, my dear. You'll be meeting him soon enough. My daughter and her husband will be arriving, according to this letter, this afternoon. Damned mail must have been delayed somewhere!"

He was truly agitated, but Honor was silent, knowing that whatever was bothering him had something to do with his daughter's marriage and that it was really none of her business. She only hoped his daughter was understanding enough to realize that her situation as her father's secretary was an honorable one.

"I suppose I'd better change the menu for tonight then," she said lightly. "And I'll have an extra bedroom made up—"

"Two bedrooms," he said sharply.

She veiled her expression and nodded. "Of course, Walter."

She hurried out of the room, wondering why he was so upset. She couldn't believe Walter was so prudish as to wish separate bedrooms for his daughter and her husband, unless his daughter had expressed the wish that it be so. Honor sighed aloud. Their visit might prove very interesting.

Honor smoothed the full skirts of her pink-sprigged afternoon dress, which had arrived only yesterday from the seamstress. As part of her "salary," Walter had insisted that he provide her with a suitable wardrobe and though she wasn't sure such an extravagant dress would be considered suitable, she had ordered it made up anyway. She was glad that she had now, because she wanted something special to wear at her first meeting with Walter's daughter.

She had done her hair in smooth coils at the back of her head, sticking a fresh pink blossom in her hair with a sudden flare of spirit. The honey-colored tresses shimmered and made her green eyes sparkle becomingly. The dress was short-sleeved, due to the weather, and although it really

324

wasn't proper to appear bare-armed for such an occasion, Honor decided to forget convention and be comfortable.

She could see by the look in Walter's eyes that he approved.

"Bewitching," he said, his eyes gleaming. "Perhaps I was foolish to have that lock put on your door."

She laughed. "The show is only to impress your daughter, Walter," she rebuked him.

"Hah! She'll never believe you're my secretary," he whispered. "Do you want her to think you're a lady of low virtue?"

"Walter! At such a question, I think I'd better leave you for a moment and check with Cook." She bustled off to the kitchens, sniffing the air appreciatively.

Marta, the cook, was savoring a spoonful of the steaming vegetables when Honor walked in. "Marta, it smells delicious!"

"*Gracias*, señorita. I hope Señora Marianne will enjoy it also."

"*Sí*, the señor's daughter, of course."

Honor frowned. She had heard the name before and vaguely recalled having done so, but couldn't place when and where. She shrugged. It probably wasn't important anyway. She would check on the rest of the dishes and then hurry back to the entrance foyer to be on hand to meet the arriving guests.

As she sailed gracefully down the corridor, she could hear voices in the hall already and hoped she hadn't kept them waiting too long. She hurried her step, her anxious anticipation causing her cheeks to bloom in order to match the blossom in her hair.

Walter was already turned, looking for her, and she could see the tiny frown between his eyes. At her entrance, he relaxed and held out his hand to draw her closer.

"Ah, Marianne, here is Honor O'Brien, who is acting as my secretary now," he proclaimed steadily.

Honor turned with a smile to meet his daughter and suddenly her face froze into a mask of shock. The light-haired young woman who had also frozen in surprise seemed suddenly so familiar that it was on the tip of her tongue to ask her where they had met before. And then, Walter was introducing his son-in-law and Honor thought the world must be caving in around her.

Wicked black eyes danced between the two women and

then smiled recklessly into Honor's green ones. "Señorita O'Brien, a pleasure." And Don Esteban Sevillas was bowing over her icy hand, pressing a kiss to it.

Time stood still and she felt nausea in her throat and fought to repress it. She recalled the last time they had faced each other with a vivid memory—him coming toward her like some lethal animal intent on its prey, and then the knife in her hand as she tried to murder him. Honor fought against the faintness, determined not to succumb in front of him. Suddenly she was recalling that time in Appina's tent in the village of the Comanche when Magda had given her that noxious brew to drink to determine whether or not she was a witch. Then, as now, she was determined to master the sickness within her—and then, as now, she had done it.

Marianne was staring at Honor, trying to recall when it was exactly that she had seen her before. It was obvious to her that the other girl had the same feeling of *déjà vu*, but she couldn't place the face and finally had to give up as her father was ushering all of them into the front parlor.

"I'm so pleased to meet you—may I call you Honor?" Marianne said timidly.

"Of course," Honor replied, warming to this unfortunate creature who was chained, by law, to that odious snake. "I do hope you approve of the few changes I have made in your father's household?"

Marianne smiled. "I'm sure I don't need to approve them, Honor. If my father is pleased, then so am I."

"Ladies, please sit down," Walter was saying gruffly, secretly pleased at the instant camaraderie which seemed to have sprung up between the two dearest living people in his life. "Marianne, I'm sure you must be tired from the journey. Would you like something to drink?"

She shook her head. "But perhaps Esteban?"

Honor noted that the poor girl seemed painfully aware of the tension between the two men. She was relieved that she hadn't remembered her from their brief introduction at Seal Rock House when she had been with Jaime.

"I would like a brandy, Walter," Esteban said grandly, relaxing confidently in his chair. He let his eyes roam freely over Honor's lovely face, dipping into the cleavage of her neckline and skimming over the delectable form.

Walter, muttering something to himself, got up to pour drinks for himself and Esteban. "Was the journey too draining, Marianne?" he asked once more. "If you wish, Honor

326

could take you up to your room and you might like to rest before dinner is served."

Marianne sighed. "I would like to freshen up a bit, Father. If you and Esteban will excuse us?" She turned to her husband dubiously.

Esteban smiled magnanimously. "By all means, my dear. You do look a little washed out from the ride. I'm sure the señorita can look after you very well."

Honor excused herself also and took Marianne to her room. The girl seemed greatly overshadowed by her dominating husband and Honor felt sorry for her. To think her parents had actually promised her at one time to that monster! She shuddered to think she could have been the one married to him!

"Oh, fresh flowers! How thoughtful of you, Honor!" Marianne sniffed at the blossoms with delight. "You look like a flower yourself—what a lovely gown!"

"Thank you. I only just had it made up. The seamstress still has the pattern if you would like to have something sewn up like it."

"That's awfully sweet of you, Honor." She paced nervously for a moment around the room, touching objects here and there, finally coming to a stop in front of the dressing table and almost collapsing on the chair.

Honor went to her, alarmed. "Are you all right, Marianne? You're as white as a sheet!"

The latter smiled weakly. "Just fatigued from the journey. I'm afraid my constitution is rather delicate right now. I—I lost the child I was carrying only a few weeks ago!"

"Good Lord!" Honor said, concerned. "Does your father know? I'm sure he would never have allowed you to make the trip if he had known that you—"

"He doesn't know about the baby, Honor, and I would rather he didn't. I wasn't that far along, only a couple of months and—it doesn't matter now. I wouldn't want him to think that Esteban—" She hesitated and looked away.

Honor bit her lip. "Well, it was silly of you to journey so far, really. I'm surprised that Esteban suggested the trip."

Marianne looked up in surprise and Honor realized that she had spoken Esteban's name familiarly. Well, it was too late to cover her mistake now; she would just have to be more careful.

"Here, why don't you lie down on your bed and I'll go downstairs and have Marta mix you up one of her special tisanes—the one that strengthens the blood!" She laughed fondly.

Marianne laughed too. "So, you've already been introduced to Marta's bag of medicines. Well, I suppose it can't do any harm. Yes, I think I'd like that."

Honor helped her to the bed and took off her shoes, then drew a light shawl over her. "I'll only be a minute," she promised.

She hurried downstairs, her mind flying as fast as her feet. She couldn't believe that Walter had allowed his only daughter to marry Esteban Sevillas. Had he been so greedy that all he could see was the Sevillas estate? As she passed by the parlor door, she could hear the men's voices raised in heated argument, and she wondered if Esteban had told Walter about the miscarried child.

After obtaining the tisane from Marta, she hurried back upstairs and gave the cooling liquid to Marianne. "You should feel better directly. I've taken them myself and always feel marvelous afterward."

"Thank you, Honor." Marianne drank, then leaned back on the pillows, closing her eyes drowsily. "I think I will take a short nap. Tell my father to have me awakened when he wishes to eat."

Honor nodded. She had just closed Marianne's door and was turning around to walk down the upper hall to the stairs when she nearly bumped into Esteban directly behind her.

"Oh!"

"You look, señorita, as though you've seen a ghost," he said, smiling evilly beneath the black mustache.

"Or a devil," she said beneath her breath.

She tried to push past him, but his arm had already snaked out to imprison her. "Why in such a hurry, señorita?" he asked softly.

She looked up into his black eyes, her hatred apparent in her gaze. "Get out of my way, Esteban, unless you wish for me to call Walter."

"Ah, yes! I had almost forgotten the enviable position you hold in his household. The mistress of such a man—"

"I am not his mistress!" she seethed. "Take your arm away before I call out!"

Obligingly he removed himself from blocking her path. "But we still have a score to settle, señorita," he hissed. "The scar in my shoulder is an appropriate reminder of my revenge," he promised.

328

She hurried away, telling herself that he could do nothing in this house with Walter to protect her. Still, she was uneasy and wished there was some way she could convey her misgivings to Walter without having to tell him the whole sordid past.

She was careful to seat herself next to Walter at dinner, putting Marianne on his other side and Esteban opposite Walter. The meal was silent, broken intermittently by small talk between the two women. There was tangible tension in the air and Honor hoped that Walter had not noticed it between herself and his son-in-law.

After dinner, Marianne expressed a wish to retire early and she and Honor left the men to their port and cigars although Honor privately thought both men would also be retiring soon. They heartily disliked each other. It was apparent.

After she had said good night to Marianne, she went back downstairs to her own room off the library, glad that Walter had installed the lock now. She had never really worried about him entering her room uninvited, but Esteban was another matter. He was perfectly capable of raping her cold-bloodedly because of some abusive idea of vengeance. She undressed quickly and got into bed, opening her windows a little to allow what little breeze there was to cool her bedroom.

She lay awake for along time, her mind in a turmoil over this new and unexpected development. She was fervently glad she was not Walter's wife. Otherwise the situation would be intolerable. At least now, she had the option of leaving his employment—and with Esteban as a son-in-law, she would consider the idea at length.

A sudden scratching at her door made her sit bolt upright, her heart pounding with fear. The scratching grew louder and then turned into a soft knocking. Honor swallowed convulsively. She knew it was Esteban and glanced for reassurance to the locked door.

After a few minutes, the sounds ceased and Honor relaxed once more in her bed. A fine sweat had broken out on her skin, owing nothing to the sultry heat. She felt a sudden surge of pity for Marianne, who could not lock her own husband out.

Forty-two

Walter had grudgingly taken Esteban down to his warehouses in the city. Esteban had expressed an interest at breakfast in seeing them, and Walter, whether he was pleased that his lazy son-in-law would show such interest or just hoping to allow his daughter some relaxation, consented to take him down.

Honor and Marianne were sitting companionably in the upstairs parlor. Marianne had been telling the other girl about Esteban's estate, a conversation distinctly unappealing to Honor, but she had listened, realizing that Marianne was very proud of her home.

"Tell me about yourself," Marianne urged when she was finished speaking. "How did you come to be my father's secretary?"

Honor laughed. "You may have already guessed, Marianne," she began frankly, "that if it was up to your father, I would be more than just his secretary."

Marianne colored delicately. "I certainly didn't wish to presume—"

"Please, allow me to be honest," Honor went on briskly. "I have never, nor do I intend to, sleep with your father, unless I am his wife. He just happened to come along at a very low point in my life and rescued me from a life I couldn't have borne." She paused thoughtfully. "I owe Walter a lot, but I told him I would never marry him until I felt I could truly give him happiness. He accepts my wishes and abides by them."

"I'm surprised," Marianne put in. "I know that my father has always liked women," she began hesitantly. "Even when Mother was still alive, but very ill, he would go down to the square to the gambling saloons and play cards just to be around the type of woman who was—easily accessible."

"I was a dealer at Babs' Den," Honor put in defensively.

Marianne reddened to the roots of her hair. "Forgive me, I hope I didn't offend you," she interjected quickly. "You certainly don't fit my image of the typical saloon dealer."

Honor relaxed. Why make it harder on the girl? "Please, don't worry about it. I probably would have thought the same

330

thing if I hadn't been one myself. Unfortunately, the image you have is pretty widespread, fostered simply because the women dealers are really like that for the most part."

"So my father did meet you at a gambling den?"

Honor nodded. "He used to play at my table often and was very kind. Always the gentleman too. He was the only one in this whole city I could trust. I will always be grateful for that."

"I can see why he likes you, Honor. Your name seems truly to fit you," Marianne said earnestly.

Honor blushed this time, thinking of all the deception that was going on behind both father's and daughter's back. She was almost ready to admit everything, when the butler walked in to announce the arrival of Babs Hampton.

"Well, of all the timing!" Honor trilled happily as Babs walked in. "We were only just talking about you, my friend."

Babs laughed. She was dressed handsomely and there was a bloom to her cheeks and a sparkle in her eye that puzzled Honor.

"May I present Walter Gordon's daughter, Marianne," she said. "Marianne, my friend and previous employer, Babs Hampton of Babs' Den."

The two exchanged greetings and then Babs pulled Honor down beside her on the settee. "Honor, I've got to tell you the news! I'm engaged!"

Honor felt as though her heart would stop beating. Babs engaged!

"Who—who is the lucky man?" she asked faintly.

"Honey, I'm afraid you don't know him," Babs babbled on happily. "He's only been in town a month."

Honor felt as though a constricting band had been removed from her breast. She took Babs' hand in genuine relief. The other woman was quick to note the look and smiled to herself.

"Did you think I was talking of Brice?" she asked her softly.

Honor colored and glanced over to Marianne, who was looking on with polite interest. "Well, I suppose I did fly to conclusions," she affirmed.

"Don't be a ninny, Honor! If Brice isn't going to marry you—he's certainly not going to marry anyone else!"

"What do you mean?"

"Why, my dear Honor, any fool can see that you're both besotted with each other and too damned—excuse me, Marianne—too darned stubborn to admit it! Honey, if Brice doesn't love you, I'm the stupidest woman who ever lived. You should see him, moping about like a shepherd who has lost the prized lamb."

"Now, Babs," Honor put in seriously. "I know you're lying. Brice wouldn't look like that if the gambling saloon burned down—and that saloon is more precious to him than I am!"

"Hah, and he's about to become sole owner of it, too! So, if that's your way of thinking, you may as well kiss him goodbye."

"You mean you're selling him your share!"

Babs nodded. "Charlie and I are off to the Fraser River. There's still plenty of gold up there, we've heard."

"Oh, Babs!" Honor groaned. "Not another miner!"

"Now don't go dampening my spirits, Honor. Charlie Morgan is as good as they come. He's not exactly down on his luck and with the money I'll get from Babs' Den—"

"Babs, are you sure you're doing the right thing?" Honor asked worriedly.

"Honor, I'm not about to sit around and wonder about right and wrong," Babs put in sharply. "You don't think I want to end up like you, afraid to do the *wrong* thing for fear you'll get hurt! Honey, I'm sorry to be so blunt, but there was one thing that my father did teach me and that was to take your chances when they come!"

"Speaking of your father," Honor put in dryly, still smarting from the criticism, "didn't he want you to be an independent woman?"

Babs shrugged good-naturedly. "I'm still independent in a lot of ways, Honor, but I really want to marry Charlie—and I'm going to. Now, that's about as independent as you can get!"

"Well, then I'm happy for you," Honor got out.

"I was beginning to think I'd never hear it," Babs returned heartily. "Now, to help us celebrate, I insist that you come with us to the International. Charlie and I will do it up right. We're going to be married tomorrow afternoon and—"

"Tomorrow! But why so soon?" Honor suddenly realized how much she would miss her friend.

"Our ship sails up the coast tomorrow night. Can you think of a more romantic honeymoon? We sail at ten in the evening, but we want to celebrate before we go. Will you come?"

"Of course," Honor said without hesitation. "What time?"

Babs outlined the arrangements and Honor promised to be there.

"Nice to meet you, Marianne. Honor, I'll see you tomorrow night. Don't be late!" And Babs was out the door in a swoosh leaving Marianne and Honor looking at each other in suppressed mirth.

"What an extraordinary lady!" Marianne laughed.

"I agree," Honor laughed. "I hope you don't mind my going."

"Of course not. Father and I will play some chess. Maybe I can persuade him not to let me win so easily."

Honor smiled, but noticed that Marianne did not mention what her husband would be doing.

Honor dressed with special care in an evening gown of emerald green watered silk, trimmed at the low neckline with Chantilly lace, which lent a pearly sheen to her breasts. She wore the emerald earbobs that Walter had given her and had dressed her hair high at the back of her head to show the jewels off to best advantage. Her green eyes sparkled as brightly as the jewels and she wondered at the excited anticipation that coursed through her. Could she be hoping that Brice would be there too? She shook her head as though to clear it of such thoughts and added a final touch of cologne to the vale between her breasts.

Marianne clapped her hands in delight at the picture Honor made as she whirled around on light feet for her benefit.

"You do look lovely, Honor," she sighed.

Honor glanced at the face which held a prematurely pinched look around the mouth and hurried over to hug her spontaneously. "It will be your turn to go out tomorrow night," she promised, "and I will be happy to lend you the gown."

Marianne blushed, but when she would have said no, Honor insisted.

"I'm not sure I should let you out alone looking like that," Walter said dryly, coming into the room to stare at the lovely vision the young girl made. "Are you sure you don't want me to come along—as an escort?"

Honor shook her head. "I'll be all right," she said. "I'm to meet Babs and her fiancé at the Virginia City International Hotel. There will be lots of people around," she assured him.

"Well, just be careful," he implored her. "After your experience with the inhabitants of Little China—" He trailed off at his daughter's look of puzzlement.

"I promise I will be careful," Honor said again, laughing a little at the serious look on his face. Then, glancing about the parlor, she asked casually, "Where is your son-in-law, Walter? Has he decided not to play chess?"

"Esteban hates chess!" Marianne grimaced.

"He had to go into town to take care of some business, he said, although what it could be, I have no idea." Walter frowned. "I do know he has shown considerable interest in exporting beef from his cattle herds through illegal channels. Marianne, do you know anything about that?"

Marianne, paling considerably, shook her head. "Father, you know Esteban does not confide in me," she put in softly.

"Well, I just hope he doesn't think he can twist those dock men from Sydney Town around his fingers like he does you," Walter said thoughtfully. "Although I wouldn't mind seeing the scoundrel roughed up a little by some of those ducks."

"Father!"

"Dammit, Marianne, he treats you more like a servant than a wife! You know I protested about this marriage from the beginning. If it hadn't been for your mother . . . and she was too ill to see that charming bastard for what he really is!"

Honor realized it was a good time to excuse herself, and she did so tactfully, draping a lace shawl about her shoulders to protect her dress from the mists. She bade father and daughter good night and hurried out to the waiting carriage which Walter had ordered for her.

In no time, she was in front of the International and she stepped out quickly, asking the driver to return a little before ten, as she knew that was the departure time for Babs' ship up the coast. She entered the two-story hotel, requesting the room number from the clerk at the desk. Glancing at the clock in the hotel lobby, she noticed she was running late and hurried up the ornate staircase and down the corridor to the room number.

At her light knock, the door was opened swiftly.

"Good evening, Honor."

It was Brice, smiling at her, the silvery-blue eyes alight with a wicked amusement that disconcerted her even as it drew her inside the room. He tapped the door shut with his foot and took hold of her by the wrists.

"What?" he asked lazily. "Not a word, not a question

334

about why I'm here?" He smiled again, looking into her eyes. "Could it be that this is what you were hoping for?"

Honor, whose surprise had temporarily restricted her tongue, shook loose of him furiously and stepped back, her green eyes flashing dangerously. "Hoping to see you, Brice Devlin? How very ludicrous! Why should I want anything to do with the man who has insulted me, debased me . . ."

"Honor, I'm sorry."

She was stopped abruptly, her lips still trembling from the unspoken words of anger. "What—what . . ."

"I'm sorry for everything," he said again, recapturing her wrists and caressing them slowly with the tips of his fingers. "Can you forgive me for what I've done to you?"

Honor was at a loss as she gazed into the mocking silver-blue eyes that were somehow no longer mocking, but looking at her with a tenderness that made her want to melt completely into his arms. But how could she be sure that he wasn't playing with her again? She stepped back cautiously and he released her.

"What—what has brought about such a—change, Brice?" she wondered, tensed, as though ready to flee should she see the need.

He shrugged. "I realized that you had been telling the truth about—everything."

"Was it Babs?" she asked with a glimmer of suspicion.

He laughed. "We had a long talk," he confirmed, "and she practically had to hit me over the head with a club before I'd listen." His voice lowered in that intimate caressing way that had always thrilled her. "I am sorry for all the pain I've caused you, Honor. You've told me from the very first that you loved me and I . . ."

She turned away, pinkening with embarrassment. What was this? An apology to make her feel better—a cleaning up of old problems so that he could start life anew? She didn't want to hear any more.

"I should be going. I really should. Babs . . ."

"Babs knows you're with me, Honor. Would you have it any other way?"

She hated the arrogance that still crept into his voice, even as she wished she could scream at him that—yes! dammit!—she did love him!

"Well," she began nervously, twining the fringe of her reticule around her fingers, "I accept your—apology, Brice—and now I would like to go . . ."

"Christ, Honor, I'm not just apologizing!" he exploded, his eyes turning to blue ice. "I'm trying to tell you how much of a fool I've been all along—and you act as though I had offered you a piece of cake, which—I take it—you're politely refusing!"

"Oh!" She stamped her foot, her anger rising to meet his. "What am I supposed to do! Fall into your arms and tell you, yes! yes!, I crave your forgiveness, just let me back into your life!"

"God Almighty!" he swore savagely. "I should have known polite conversation wouldn't work with you, Honor! Dammit, there's only one thing . . ."

"Oh, no, you don't!" she cried out as he came closer. "You keep away from me, Brice Devlin, or I swear I'll call out for help. I'll—I'll cause a commotion and that'll look awfully bad for the new owner of Babs' Den!" She backed away realizing that there was little room in which to keep any distance between them.

"I don't give a damn about the commotion!" he yelled back, succeeding in closing the gap between them. "Come here, damn you, I want to kiss you!"

He grabbed her arms and brought her abruptly against him, causing her to drop the reticule as he crushed her against his chest. His mouth came down to cover hers, pressing harder and harder until she thought he would snap her neck. He would not let her go until she returned the kiss, opening her mouth reluctantly, feeling a sudden shock wave run through her as their kiss deepened.

He had her imprisoned between his arms, her own arms pressed ineffectually against his body between them. He would not let her go, would not release her lips, but continued to kiss her until she responded, feeling a slow, insidious warmth creeping through her. For a moment, she fought it, and he held her even tighter, crushing the breath from her body until she felt as weak as a kitten.

When he lifted his mouth from hers, she gasped for breath and opened her eyes to look into his, which were blazing with passion and need.

"It's been too long, Honor," he whispered. "I want you now, my love."

And he pressed her backward onto the long couch, resting his weight on his elbows as he came over her. His kisses were shorter now, fired with desire, teasing, rousing her own passion so that she returned them eagerly, panting for more.

"Have you missed me, sweetheart?" he murmured, sending a thrill down her spine as he punctuated the sentence with a caressing tongue in her ear.

"Brice, I don't think . . ."

"Darling, I don't want you to think," he laughed wickedly. "Let me love you, Honor," he whispered vibrantly.

Honor felt shaken to the depths of her soul. Did he really mean that he loved her! Could he be lying to her, even now, as their kisses fired new life into their bodies? His mouth was warm, caressing on her neck and shoulders, lowering teasingly to the top slopes of her exposed bosom while his fingers worked urgently to pull the neckline lower in order to capture the burning tips of her breasts.

Impatiently, he would have torn the material, but with a laugh of sheer wantoness, Honor twisted out of his grasp and sat up so that he could unbutton the back of her gown. He did so with hurried fingers and pulled the material down with a quick swipe until it was impeded by her petticoats.

"Goddamn!" he swore emphatically.

"Darling," she reproached him, her eyes sparkling now as though she had had too much champagne. "Only a moment."

She wriggled out of the constricting undergarments and unveiled her charms with the shyness of an untried virgin. She felt the blush heating her entire body as those silvery-blue eyes devoured her with a passionate look that took her breath away. With hurried impatience, he divested himself of his own garments and took her back to the couch, settling his lean brown body over hers.

Honor closed her eyes and let him have his way with her. It had been so long, she thought, as his hands roamed over her aching flesh. She had been such a fool to try to deny the fact that she wanted him, she loved him still. He was the only man who could make her want to die from the sheer ecstasy of loving him.

His hands were wanton on her body, marking it forever with swift possession. She moaned with delight when his mouth followed his hands, arching her body convulsively, offering it to him with a passion borne of long unappeased hunger. He accepted her offering with a secret amazement at the wealth of her passion. Could any other woman ever give of herself as thoroughly as this one? It could have made him jealous, but he sensed that he was the only man who could awaken her spirit like this. His pleasure was her pleasure and he redoubled his attentions to the marvelous little body that seemed to attune itself to the touch of his fingers.

Honor's breath came rapidly, even her toes were tensing as she pressed her body against that of the man above her—the man whom she loved above everything else, despite of everything he had done. She loved him.

"Brice!" she groaned.

He smiled, perspiration dotting his forehead as he rose up to kneel for a moment above her. His hands slipped intimately between her legs, skimming the flesh with a master's touch so that the skin quivered and trembled as it responded to the commands of his fingers. She opened slowly, like a flower, offering the well of her womanhood to his heavy-lidded eyes.

He possessed her just as slowly, moving with a sureness that made her clench her teeth in desperation. When they were joined as one, she moved impatiently beneath him so that he laughed in amusement.

"Hold back just a little longer, sweetheart, and I promise you it will be better," he whispered to soften the fact of his laughter.

She arched against him, pressing her stiffened breasts to his furred chest, moving her hands against his back, as the nails dug deeper into his flesh. As his movements created more and more heat inside of her, she slipped her hands down lower to the strong muscles of his buttocks. She could feel a tidal wave of pleasure sweeping over her, so that she wanted to tear her mouth from his and laugh out loud with sheer happiness. His hands were tangled in her hair, which had somehow become unpinned and fell haphazardly over the couch, spilling down over the side. They rolled languourously over each other, until she could feel him swelling within her—and then bursting inside, sending the tidal wave crashing over her. She cried out as a single tear dripped into her hair.

She was crying and laughing at the same time, hugging him to her with a kind of amazed delight.

"Oh, Brice, we've both been such fools!" she said, looking up into his eyes, her own tear-bright.

He kissed the corner of her mouth with suppressed passion. "I admit to it," he said with humble gratitude that life had given this woman back to him before it was too late.

They lay together for long minutes, whispering endearments to each other until a discreet knock interrupted their idyll.

338

"It's only me."

"Babs!" Honor cried out, struggling to sit up, her face crimsoning.

Brice laughed at her reaction, kissed her nose and held her even tighter. "Come on in!" he called out, his silver-blue eyes teasing her.

"No!" Honor countered, horrified, struggling even harder.

Brice held her still tighter. "We've got to wish them well on their honeymoon," he said wickedly, his eyes sparkling. "Let them in!"

"Brice! Oooh, I'll kill you if you don't let me up!" she half-fumed, pummeling at him playfully.

"Listen, my friends!" Babs was calling, her voice filled with delighted laughter as she guessed at what was going on. "Charlie and I will meet you as soon as you're ready in the room two doors down. Don't take too long!"

"Now let me up!" Honor commanded. "If we don't hurry, Babs is perfectly capable of . . ."

"Be quiet!" he said lazily, looking down at her tenderly. "I'm not through with you yet."

She squealed as he bit softly into her shoulder. But as he began to caress her again, she sighed and stretched beneath him.

At the knock, Babs opened the door, looking first to the flushed face of Honor O'Brien, and then to the devilish smile on Brice Devlin's mouth.

"Well, damned if I was beginning to give up on you two," she said fondly.

"Oh, Babs," Honor began, hugging her swiftly, "you knew all the time, didn't you!"

Babs shrugged philosophically. "I'd have to be dumber than a backward mule not to see what was plain in front of me," she agreed, laughing. "I was beginning to think, though, that both of *you* were the backward mules!"

"How thoughtfully put," Brice returned insolently, smiling down at Honor.

"Well, are we all ready?"

Honor looked at Babs with a puzzled glance, then smiled shyly at the somber-looking man who stood next to her. "This is your Charlie?"

Babs nodded, and it was her turn to flush. "I almost forgot to introduce you two. Charlie Morgan, this is the other happy couple, Honor O'Brien and Brice Devlin."

Greetings were exchanged and Honor spied a parson, seated quietly in a chair, watching the proceedings with bemused interest. "Good Lord, Babs, I thought you had already had the ceremony—you'll be late for your boat!"

"Don't worry about that, honey. After Brice and I had a long talk today, we decided to change our bookings. Charlie and I won't be leaving until the morning." She eyed her betrothed devotedly.

Charlie Morgan seemed a serious-minded, attractive young man, and despite his reserved air, Honor warmed to him immediately. She would have warmed to anything on this glorious night.

"All right, Reverend Michaels, I believe we're all ready," he said, nodding to the parson.

The reverend cleared his throat, picked up his Bible and motioned to the company assembled. "Please stand over here." He looked at both men. "Now, who is it that is getting married?"

Honor blushed and gazed at Babs, who was watching her with a secret amusement that puzzled her.

"Both of us, Reverend," she heard Brice saying—and her heart seemed to leap up into her throat.

"Brice!" She turned to him, surprised shock on her features.

For once, the jaunty air about him was veiled by a sincere humbleness. "Honor, if you want me, I'm asking you to be my wife."

"Well, you sure give a girl a hell of a lot of time to think about it!" Babs put in, the suspicion of a tear in her warm brown eyes as she glanced over to Charlie.

Honor was speechless, but she finally found her tongue. "Yes, Brice! Oh, yes!" She threw her arms about him, laughing and crying at the same time. "I see—you're bound and determined to make an—honest woman out of me," she choked happily.

Brice grinned at her impudently. "I won't let you get away from me again," he said, "and besides, I'll be needing a new partner now that Babs is leaving me," he added wickedly.

The reverend cleared his throat to draw their attention. "Shall we go on with it, my friends?"

The ceremony was brief and simple, but to Honor it surpassed any huge church gathering her parents might have wished for her. Her life had changed so much since that innocent day that she had left Charleston, bound for the new,

340

wild land of California. She had changed, had adapted—and had found a man that she was willing to spend the rest of her life with. It didn't matter how they were joined. She loved him and he loved her. She was deeply touched when he slid the gold band on her finger.

Afterward the jubilant wedding party proceeded to order dinner and wine, the best champagne in the house and musicians to serenade them while they ate. Honor kept stealing loving glances at her new husband, telling herself that this wasn't a dream, that they were really married, that nothing would change that now. She was his forever.

It was well after midnight when the foursome descended the staircase. Honor was tired but happy, her arm pressed tightly to her husband's waist.

Oustide, she saw the carriage from Walter Gordon's house and her hand flew to her mouth. "Oh, my God, I completely forgot! I should have sent word to Walter!"

Brice, who had been seeing Charlie and Babs into their hansom cab, was walking back and heard her. His brows drew up in sardonic black wings. "You remind me of an unpleasant duty," he admitted.

She turned to him earnestly. "I really should tell him, Brice," she pleaded. "Can't we both go—now?"

He hesitated, then shrugged, his hands in his pockets. "I guess we may as well get it over with," he agreed. "I can refuse you nothing tonight, my love."

She smiled at him and they both entered the carriage.

"But we'll be returning to Babs' Den tonight," he said firmly. "I don't wish to spend my wedding night under the roof of the man who covets my wife."

She giggled sleepily. "Walter is a gentleman, Brice. I know he'll understand."

She leaned back in the seat, her head on his shoulder. Brice ordered the carriage back to Babs' Den first so that he could make arrangements to have his suite ready for his and his new bride's arrival. As they neared Portsmouth Square, he could see an orange-red glow over the buildings and urged the driver to hurry.

In the square, Brice leaned out the window and Honor heard him whistle sharply. "The Den's on fire," he yelled, his voice edgy.

They pulled up in front of the building, the back of which was already engulfed in flames while volunteer fire fighters sloshed it with water halfheartedly. The owners of the build-

341

ings on either side of Babs' Den, fortunately, were concerned enough for the safety of their own buildings to help out. Brice sprang from the carriage, tearing off his coat and flinging it back at Honor, who could only look out at the burning chaos with a kind of shock.

"Brice, let me help!" she called out, starting to descend from the carriage, but he turned on her quickly.

"For God's sake, Honor, what can you do! Go back to Gordon's house and stay put until this is over and I can come for you." He gave her a brief smile. "You'll have to explain to him yourself, my dear."

And then he was gone, sprinting over to the makeshift water line, rolling up his shirt sleeves as he cursed under his breath. Honor sat in the carriage a moment longer, her fear for Brice making her hesitate to leave him, but after watching the swift orders he barked carried out, she realized that he could organize things more easily with the worry of her presence out of his mind. She instructed the carriage driver to return to the Gordon mansion. Walter might be asleep, she thought hopefully, and it would save her from explaining to him right away that she was already a married woman. She could slip quietly to her room, get some much needed sleep, and in the morning, Brice would come for her and they could face Walter together. She chided herself on her cowardice, and then argued that it would really be better to confront Walter with Brice there to help explain.

With that comforting thought, she arrived at Walter's house and took the key from her reticule to slip inside. As she had thought, the candles were nearly all out and the butler, who had been instructed to await her return, was yawning sleepily on the hall bench.

"Go to sleep, Manchester. I'll see my own way back to my room. No sense in disturbing Mr. Gordon or his daughter."

The butler nodded and made his way gratefully to his own room, leaving Honor to hurry through the library and into her own room, lighting the candle swiftly. She told herself it would be best to pack now, but the excitement and the champagne were taking their toll and all she really wanted to do was go to bed.

She undressed, put on her nightgown and bolted her door out of habit. Then, stretching with a silly smile of well-being on her sleepy face, she got into bed and blew out the candle.

Forty-three

Honor had been asleep only an hour when a tall, slender shadow put out its hands to pull up the half-open window leading to her ground-floor room. The light of the moon was obscured by low-lying clouds as the shadow climbed in the window to stand inside the sleeping girl's bedroom.

"A pretty picture," Esteban Sevillas said to himself as he noted the girl's face turned toward him, her arm lying curved around the pillow. He could feel desire flooding him—desire for her body and desire for revenge as the old wound in his shoulder seemed to ache throbbingly. No other woman had ever given him so much trouble, left him helpless with rage, and yet continued to elude him. She was a maddening thorn in his side and now he was determined to pluck her out.

He reached into his pocket to draw out the handkerchief he had put there so he could gag her. He crept closer to the helpless figure and bent down to pull back the bedclothes.

Honor moved in her sleep, turning on her stomach, impeding him from stuffing the cloth into her mouth. He cursed silently and reached to pull her over onto her back. His hands trembled on her shoulders and suddenly she was coming awake, her voice reaching out groggily to penetrate the darkness.

"Brice?" she mumbled sleepily, turning over and balancing on one elbow.

"I'm afraid not, *querida*," came a silken voice in the dark.

Honor stiffened, her eyes opened wider as she tried to penetrate the last dregs of sleep. "Esteban! You!" She started to scream, but he shoved the cloth between her jaws and forced her down on the bed, while he knelt over her, tying another handkerchief tightly in back of her head.

Honor struggled in real fear. She knew, from experience, that Esteban was capable of anything. Was he going to kill her?

Above her struggling form, Esteban watched her with a merciless smile. God, but she was lovely—a pity to give her over to those crude ruffians on the docks. They'd turn her into a wasted, pathetic creature like the other whores he had noticed in doorways and leaning against the sides of build-

343

ings—shacks really—waiting dutifully for the next customer so that they could pay their brutal macks and keep their skins from being striped. He hesitated, his eyes growing accustomed to the darkness so that he could look into the frightened eyes beneath him.

Her struggling had caused the bedclothes to slip down as her arms came up to try to punch him with her fists. He caught them, flipped her over onto her stomach, and tied them tightly with a cord. Then he turned her onto her back again and pushed the covers down with a brutal movement.

Honor had never been so terrified, even with Hoy Tai. She felt helpless, totally vulnerable, as Esteban looked down at her silently. She cringed when his hands reached for the buttons at the top of her nightdress. It was ludicrously easy for Esteban to rip away the buttons, his knee prodding painfully in her stomach to keep her struggles at a minimum. As more of her flesh was revealed to him, he tore carelessly at the material, his breathing coming faster, until she was naked.

Honor whimpered deep in her throat. She knew he was going to rape her—and then what he would do with her, she could only guess. She worked desperately at the cords that bound her wrists, but there was no way to free them in time. She could discern through the darkness Esteban pulling at his own clothing to free himself for the rape. She shuddered and closed her eyes when he removed his trousers and smiled down at her triumphantly.

"Now, *querida*, let us see you get away from me this time," he taunted her, moving his hands lasciviously over her body.

Honor flinched at the contact from his skin. His fingers caressed the taut flesh of her breasts, the tips stiffened not with desire, but with fear. He moved his weight on top of hers, making the pain in her hands nearly intolerable as they were jammed back against the mattress. Tears of pain dripped down the sides of her face and she felt an awful sense of suffocation as she tried to catch her breath with the cloth clogging her throat. She coughed to clear it and thought for a dizzy moment that she was not going to be able to take another breath. She was so afraid of the suffocation that she hardly realized what Esteban was doing to her body.

She knew she was going to faint or die, or both, and she closed her eyes, trying not to think of Brice, of what could have been theirs together. She was slipping softly away, only

344

vaguely aware that Esteban's hands were sliding along her thighs in order to open them for his vengeful lust.

"Esteban! Let her go!" The voice was almost querulous, a soft, feminine voice that was sick with disgust.

Honor fought back the nausea, the darkness, and opened her eyes to focus slowly on the face of Marianne Gordon Sevillas. She could have wept, but there were no more tears left.

"Marianne! What are you doing here, for God's sake?" Esteban's voice was hard with impatience, biting with contempt for his cowardly little wife. "Get out and go back to your room—I'll deal with you later!"

"No, Esteban!" Marianne said, with more strength. "Get off her, I'm warning you!"

For the first time, Esteban really looked at his wife—and what he saw made him laugh disdainfully. She had pulled up a pistol, one of his own, he thought, and was pointing it with both hands at him. He noted that she was trembling visibly and that the gun wavered dangerously from side to side.

"Marianne, you'll do as I say, or you'll be extremely sorry," he said levelly. Cautiously he got up from the bed, standing next to it with a deceptive ease. "Give me the pistol now and go back to bed."

She shook her head once more. "Untie her," she ordered swiftly, nodding toward Honor.

He laughed. "Untie her! You've got to be loco, Marianne! This bitch is going to pay for everything she's done to me."

"What has she done to you, Esteban!"

He shrugged, keeping an eye on the gun. "She came to my hacienda, claimed to be my betrothed, when in truth everything she said was a lie only to get her greedy hands on my money. I admit I succumbed at first to her loveliness, but I soon realized that she was no good. She ran off to live with my brother." He eyed her speculatively. "I assume you must have remembered our meeting at the Seal Rock House when she was in the company of my outlaw brother?"

Marianne nodded hesitantly, her face becoming more and more uncertain. Honor strained at her bonds uselessly. Don't let her leave me, she prayed.

Esteban had taken a step toward her, then stopped as she backed away, the gun steadying once more. "*Querida*, listen to me," he said, switching to a cajoling tone. "This greedy bitch has her eye on your father now. She has no love for him—all she wants is his money, just as it was with me. She

345

won't rest until she's his wife and then—you and I will be written out of his will, believe me!"

"I don't care about Papa's money," Marianne said slowly. "We have enough, Esteban."

He shrugged again. "Of course, the money may not be important to you, *querida*, but your father is, isn't he? Would you really want him married to this stone-hearted adventuress? Where do you think she was tonight, eh?"

"She was with—her friend. She—she told me . . ."

He laughed cuttingly. "She and her friend are two of the same kind," he assured her. "I tell you, she was with a lover—the man who really holds her scheming little heart. She will marry your father and break him as she flaunts her lover in his face!"

No! Don't believe him, Marianne! Honor pleaded with her eyes, hoping the girl would look at her.

"But—but when I discovered you were gone from our bed, Esteban," Marianne was saying painfully, "and to find you here with her."

"I am sorry for that, *querida*. You see what a witch she is! I cannot keep away from her. It is better that you let me dispose of her where she cannot hurt your father, or anyone of us again."

Marianne was biting her lip, wishing desperately that she could believe her husband, the man she loved painfully with a part of her heart, even while she knew he held no love for her. She had suspected where his true feelings lay, and tonight, when she had awakened after his usual perfunctory lovemaking to find him gone, she had hurried to his own room to see his bed unslept in. Then, she had known where he would be and had followed in his footsteps through the open window. She hardly remembered picking up the gun— how could she actually be threatening Esteban's life!

"Now, won't you put the gun away, my sweet?" Esteban said, moving once again toward his wife. "Let me take her where she won't harm anyone."

"You—you wouldn't hurt her . . ."

He smiled, already sure of victory. "Go back to bed, Marianne," he said again. "She will never bother us again and her lover . . ." he laughed contemptuously. "He will be hard put to find her after he is finished with the smoking remains of his saloon."

Honor's eyes widened. So! It had been Esteban—it must have been—who had set fire to Babs' Den. Oh, surely, Mari-

346

anne could not be so gullible as to believe him—surely she knew what an evil, cruel dictator he was!

Marianne sighed. "I'm sorry, Esteban, but I can't think. I'm—I don't know if I can believe you or not. I know my father loves her and I—"

"Hush now, *querida*. Give me the gun."

"Esteban—"

"Give me the gun!" he said impatiently. "Damn you, Marianne. . . !"

He stepped toward her with a sudden lurch, surprising her. Involuntarily her finger, which had been poised on the trigger of the pistol, pressed downward, firing the gun point-blank.

A look of surprised shock appeared briefly on Esteban's face, and then, without a word, he slipped to the floor at her feet. Marianne dropped the gun in a reflex action and bent down over her husband, her face as white as a sheet. She swayed and dropped to the floor in a dead faint.

Minutes passed before footsteps outside Honor's bedroom door turned into a loud knocking. Honor, who was barely conscious herself from restricted air flow, heard Walter's voice only dimly.

"Honor! Honor, for God's sake, what's going on! Open the door!" The knocking continued until Walter realized it was fruitless and instructed the wide-eyed butler to get something to batter down the door.

Soon a loud pounding was replaced by the sound of the door splintering, the heavy wooden bolt cracking under the pressure. Honor's last conscious memory was of Walter's face, framed in the glow of a candelabra as he gazed in horror at the scene before him.

Forty-four

"How could I have known? She didn't tell me and even, even after Marianne suspected—" Walter Gordon pushed nervous hands through his hair.

He was sitting in a chair in the library opposite Brice Devlin, who hadn't even had time to wash the soot from his face. He had come straight from the charred remains of his saloon to tell Honor the disheartening news that everything—everything he had worked for was gone. He was slumped now in an armchair, his brow lined with worry as they both waited for the physician to appear from Honor's bedroom.

"Why didn't she tell me that she had known Esteban before?" Walter asked himself. "If only I had known!"

Brice shrugged tiredly. "If you had known, what could you have done? She knew it would have only made an embarrassing situation between everyone concerned."

"But my own daughter didn't even tell me . . ."

"For reasons of her own." Brice looked up at the older man and his silver-blue eyes were kind. "I'm sorry about what happened, Walter. You say the authorities have already begun on the assumption that she acted in self-defense—that it was an accident?"

Walter nodded heavily. "They've allowed Marianne to remain here, under my custody. The poor thing was still in shock and I suppose we won't know the full story until she recovers."

"At least the bastard is dead!" Brice growled to himself, letting his anger surface for a moment.

It had been easy for Walter to discern from Honor's nude body and the cords that bound her that Esteban had been intent on rape and that Marianne had surprised him before he had been able to fulfill the deed. He had only been glad that neither of the young women had been physically hurt. When Brice had told him the news that he and Honor had been married last night, Walter Gordon had thought that he was lying, had even accused him of it. But he remembered the gold band on Honor's finger, a small detail he had passed over in the initial shock of the scene, and he had had to accept the truth—that she could never be his now.

The two men sat silently, each wrapped in his own thoughts until the physician came out of Honor's room, closing the door softly behind him. Walter and Brice both stood, but the former slumped back in his chair when the doctor called for her husband.

Brice stepped forward. "Is she all right?"

The doctor nodded. "You may go in to see her now, but please try to keep your visit short this time. I gave her a little laudanum to help her sleep and she might be a bit groggy. There are a few minor abrasions in her throat and on her wrists, but otherwise she'll be fine."

"Thank you, Doctor."

Brice hurried to go inside, then closed the door behind

him. He walked silently over to his wife—Honor, his wife. Her eyes were closed, the long, golden lashes lying innocently against the smooth roundness of her cheeks. Her mouth was relaxed, the delicate nostrils of her nose flaring with her even breathing. Brice leaned down softly and kissed that soft, pink mouth, wondering how he could have borne it had she not been here.

Green eyes, cloudy with sleep, gazed up at him tenderly. "Brice . . . it really is you?"

He smiled. "Yes, Honor, I'm here now."

She sighed. "Marianne? The—the doctor wouldn't tell me anything."

Brice put a finger on her lips. "Don't talk now—just relax. You need to get some sleep."

"But—"

"I'll tell you everything in the morning."

She smiled softly and started to close her eyes, then they flew open as she gazed up with a look of horror. "Brice! The saloon—Esteban was the one who set the fire. He—"

"It doesn't matter, Honor."

"But the saloon must be all burned down and you—you have nothing left!"

He grinned rakishly, setting her fears at rest. "Did I never tell you a little about myself, wife? It so happens, Honor Devlin, that you are married to what is known as—an eligible heir, among the matronly set."

"An heir? You! Brice, you were always so secretive about your past," she accused him, struggling to hide the yawn she felt overtaking her.

He laughed. "Now, I didn't want you to marry me for my money, darling," he retorted, taking her hand to fold it between his own.

"Oh, Brice!" She was smiling, but there were tears in her eyes and Brice felt a suspicion of moisture himself as he returned her smile. "I would have married you if you were the poorest man on earth! I love *you*," she said firmly.

"And I love you, Honor."

"If only you had found that out a long time ago," she said to herself.

"I'll admit to being stubborn and stupid," he put in. "I just don't think I could quite believe that you were laying your love at my feet all those months ago. I was a man who hadn't been used to such trust," he admitted, gazing at her reflectively.

"And now, you do believe me—and we will trust one another?" she asked with a tiny bit of fear in her voice. This man was so very volatile, so masculine and virile she still could hardly believe he had married her—that she was his wife.

"I believe you with all my heart, darling," he affirmed, pressing her hand tightly. "You and I were made for each other, Honor, bound together for the rest of our lives."

She returned the squeeze and smiled sweetly up at him, but her eyes felt suddenly very heavy. "What did that old doctor give me?" she wanted to know.

He laughed. "Something to help you sleep."

"Sleep!" she groaned. "I was just thinking how nice it would be to begin our honeymoon right now."

He kissed her mouth and laughed to himself as her eyes closed, despite her stubborn desire to keep them open. There would certainly be time enough for the honeymoon later, he thought contentedly. After all—they did have the rest of their lives together.

Great Adventures in Reading

THE GREEN RIPPER   14345 $2.50
by John D. MacDonald

Gretel, the one girl the hard-boiled Travis McGee had actually fallen for—dead of a "mysterous illness." McGee calls it murder. This time he's out for blood.

SCANDAL OF FALCONHURST   14334 $2.50
by Ashley Carter

Ellen, the lovely mustee, through a trick of fate marries into the wealthiest family in New Orleans. But she must somehow free the man she really loves, the son of a white plantation owner, sold to die as a slave. In the exciting tradition of MANDINGO.

WINGED PRIESTESS   14329 $2.50
by Joyce Verrette

The slave: Ilbaya, of noble birth, in love with his master's concubine. He risks death with each encounter. The Queen: beautiful Nefrytatanen. To keep the love of her husband she must undergo the dangerous ritual that will make her the "winged" priestess—or destroy her! An epic of ancient Egypt.

FAWCETT GOLD MEDAL BOOKS

Great Adventures in Reading

EAST OF JAMAICA   14309 $2.50
by Kaye Wilson Klem
    She was a titian-haired New Englander who had fled to
the lush, volcanic island of Martinique. She never dreamed
she would be forced to become a pleasure toy for the island's
women-hungry planters.

THE EMERALD EMBRACE   14316 $2.50
by Diane du Pont
    Beautiful Liberty Moore sought refuge at sea in the arms
of a handsome stranger, unaware that he was the naval hero
Stephen Delaplane, unaware that she would be taken from
him and forced to become the bride of the most powerful ruler
in the East.

KINGSLEY'S EMPIRE   14324 $2.50
by Michael Jahn
    Here is the story of a great shipping dynasty built on the
ashes of a shore pirate's wiles and with the fire of an heiress's
beauty.

FAWCETT GOLD MEDAL BOOKS